Deep *Drop*

A
Shagball and Tangles
Adventure
By

A. C. Brooks

Other Shagball and Tangles Adventures Include:

Foul Hooked- 2011
Dead on the Dock- 2012
Weed Line- 2013

For more information go to: www.acbrooks.net

ISBN: 1500208884
ISBN 13: 9781500208882

Acknowledgements

Once again I would like to thank my beautiful and talented wife Penny for serving as my running editor and keeping me in check (or at least trying to). Without her encouragement I never would have written *Foul Hooked* and without her hard work and unwavering support there would be no Shagball & Tangles Adventure Series. *NOOOOOOOOOOOOOOOO!*

And, as always, a special thanks to the management and staff at the Old Key Lime House, who are big supporters of veteran's, local authors, and artists of all types. Personally, I find the OKLH a great source of inspiration, often facilitated by marination— and what a place to marinate it is.

Thanks also to the impeccably published and highly anticipated monthly magazine, *The Coastal Star,* for including me in articles featuring works by local authors ever since my first book, *Foul Hooked,* came out. It is very much appreciated. On the flip side, to the swale trash like *The Lake Worth Herald, The Coastal Observer,* and *The Palm Beach Post,* you suck.

Finally, I'd like to pay my respects to Captain Michael G. Malinowski, who passed away last year. Captain Mike was a good friend and the basis for the character Tooda in *Foul Hooked*. I'll never bring another banana on a boat for as long as I live. I swear. Tight lines, Captain Mike…tight lines.

WHAT THEY ARE SAYING ABOUT *Deep Drop*:

"It's the rare book like *Deep Drop* that fills your tummy like a fiery bowl of delicious jambalaya. There may be some intestinal discomfort but you'll definitely want a second helping."

- *Southern Fried Cooking Light Magazine*

"*Deep Drop* is like an aquatic *DaVinci Code* without all the religious references, directed by Harold Ramis—can't wait for the *DICK Files*."

- *The Midwestern Collegiate Book Review Club*

"Shagball & Tangles are the Crockett and Tubbs of the 21st Century… if Crockett was a perpetually primed fishing show host and Tubbs a surly white midget. Let the good times troll!

- *The Southern Florida Times*

"If you've never laughed out loud while reading a book, you may not this time either. It's funny though, *very* funny, in a stand-up serial killer kind of way."

- *Higher Times Magazine*

"Most of *Deep Drop* is filled with outrageous humor, excessive violence and scathing political dialogue… the rest of it I hated. Keep up the good work, Mr. Brooks."

- Soldier of Misfortune Magazine

"*Deep Drop* is a little like the movie *Taken,* if Liam Neeson's role was alternately played by Herve Villechaize and a rum-swilling Ricardo Montalban. Loved it!"

- damngoodreads.com

Prologue

(Two years earlier)

The electronic lock on the reinforced steel door of the tiny cell that held the most feared inmate at East Jersey State Prison in Rahway, New Jersey, snapped open. In handcuffs and leg-irons, the prisoner was escorted by four heavily armed guards through the oppressive corridor of cells that housed some of New Jersey's most violent and dangerous criminals. Unlike the treatment most prisoners received when paraded past the general population, the corridor was eerily silent. Gone were the customary taunts and threats that usually accompanied such a proceeding. Nor did any inmates dare fling bodily fluids or excrement toward the passing guards. Not this time. This time it was as peaceful and quiet as a country meadow on Sunday morning...except for the arrhythmic clanking of leg-irons. As the inmate passed each cell, hushed tones of reverence crisscrossed the corridor behind him.

Most of the inmates only knew him by his nickname, the Devil's Nephew—or *Nipote del Diavolo,* in Italian. No matter which name was spoken, it was always in fearful tones. He stood six feet four inches tall and carried 250 pounds of angry muscle on his overdeveloped upper torso. His biceps were bursting, thanks to three thousand push-ups a day. Bodywise he could have been a model; facewise, not so much. A bad case of acne as a teen was made exponentially worse by the compulsive scratching habit he developed in solitary. He looked like a cross between a pockmarked Mickey Rourke and a pit bull who stuck his face in a hornet's nest; his face was butt-ugly, dirt road bumpy, and swollen like the Red River in April.

One of the younger guards poked him in the back with a baton. "C'mon, let's move it." He turned and gave him an icy stare, sending a shiver down the guard's spine. The guard, like most Rahway residents, thought he looked like the meanest motherfucker on the planet, which he was rumored to be. The chief prison officer or CPO (also referred to as the chief), said, "It's okay, I got this." Then he turned to the prisoner. "There's a van waiting, we're on a schedule." The prisoner nodded and the procession resumed.

The prison van was escorted in the front and rear by two unmarked security vehicles as it made the hour-long trip from Rahway, New Jersey, to St. John Cemetery in Queens, New York. The threat of some type of ambush unfolding to free the prisoner was low, because he had less than a year and a half left on his twenty-year second-degree murder rap. Officially, the reason a prisoner so dangerous was granted permission to go to the graveyard was the minimal time left to serve on his sentence. Unofficially, the prisoner had arranged for a large campaign contribution to the brother-in-law of the warden. In other words, it was just politics: tit for tat. He wasn't allowed to attend the actual funeral per se; that was out of the question. There were far too many people in attendance who wanted him dead and vice versa. Nobody, including the immediate family, knew that he was being allowed to pay his respects while the funeral service was taking place.

An hour before the two-hundred-car procession left Holy Family Roman Catholic Church, the prison van pulled through the gates of the sprawling, 169-acre cemetery. The driver whistled as he approached a beautiful white stone building flanked by Grecian columns. Turning to the chief riding shotgun, he commented, "Wow, this is a pretty fancy place. That's some kinda front office."

The chief looked at him and shook his head. "That's no office, kid. This is a cemetery, and that's a mausoleum. Somebody's buried in there—somebody important."

"No shit. Like who? The pope?"

"No," replied the shackled prisoner in the backseat. "Like Salvatore Lucania, otherwise known as 'Lucky' Luciano. Please stop for a second, so I can pay my respects."

The driver glanced at the chief, who glanced at the two armed guards sitting behind the prisoner, and they both shrugged.

"Go ahead, kid, stop for a second, and let him do his thing."

The van slowed to a stop, and the prisoner bowed his head in silent prayer. Then he raised two fingers to his lips, kissed them, and pressed them to the glass. He looked at the chief and said, "Thanks."

The chief nodded to the driver. "Okay, kid, follow the road to the right...take it slow."

As the van worked its way through the cemetery, the prisoner thought of all the notorious gangsters that called it their final resting place. Besides "Lucky" Luciano, there was Vito Genovese, Carmine Galante, and Joseph Colombo, just to name a few. At the direction of the chief, they finally rolled to a stop behind another large and impressive building named the Cloister. It had a handful of private rooms inside, one of which held the body of one of the most respected and feared mobsters of all time: Carlo Gambino. The same Gambino who took control of the crime family in 1957 that still bears his name today.

The chief looked at the two guards in the rear with shotguns on their laps. "You guys sit tight while I go check out the sitch. We gotta get you-know-who in and out before the church service ends." The guards nodded, and he looked at the driver before exiting the van. "Keep your eyes peeled, kid, just in case. You see anything funny, call me on the radio."

"You got it, Chief."

The chief walked up the steps to the back door of the massive stone mausoleum and pounded his fist against the metal door a few times. Impatiently, he pulled out his baton and rapped on the door a half dozen more times before stopping. He was about to resume when the door suddenly swung open, and an elderly man in a black suit admonished him. "Please, sir, this is no place to practice a raid. This is a place of rest!"

"It's a place of *final* rest if I'm not mistaken, which is why I wasn't too concerned about waking anybody."

"That's beside the—oh, never mind, c'mon in, you're late!"

"Too fuckin' bad, Barnabus. Traffic was heavier than a Paula Deen biscuit."

The chief stepped through the door and followed the caretaker down a short dark hallway that led to a circular room about forty feet in diameter. There were several doors on the perimeter that led to private rooms and a longer hallway, opposite the one they entered, that led to the front of the building. In the center of the room, on a raised platform, was an elegant looking cherry wood casket with gold handles. The caretaker swept his arm toward the casket and then looked at his watch. "This is the viewing room. In about a half hour the family of the deceased and attendees of the church service will be coming in to pay their final respects. Obviously, your party needs to be gone well before then. I'll be in big trouble if you're not."

"Trust me, if we're not outta here in ten minutes, something's gone wrong, and big trouble doesn't *begin* to describe it."

The old man gulped and ran a hand through his thinning gray hair. "Okay then, let's get on with it. I'll prepare the deceased for viewing while you bring in the visitor."

The chief warily looked around the room and pointed at one of the doors. It had a brass plaque mounted on it that read, "Gambino."

"Any other visitors in the building?"

"No, all the doors to the private rooms are locked; same with the front door. Now please, let's hurry."

After personally checking to see that all the interior doors were locked, the chief turned and headed back down the hall. A few minutes later the clanking sound of the prisoner's leg-irons echoed through the chamber as he shuffled down the darkened hallway at gunpoint. Upon emerging in the circular viewing room, he stopped to look around. As he did so, the chief directed the shotgun-toting guards to either side of the room. A single overhead light shone down directly on the open casket. The elderly caretaker stood by the head of the casket with an open hand and announced, "The dearly departed awaits." He then took a single step to the side and watched as the prisoner shuffled up to the casket. The chief held his arm as he awkwardly stepped onto the platform.

"I got it from here," said the prisoner. The chief nodded and stepped back in the shadows. The prisoner knelt down and bowed his head in prayer.

Although stunned by the prisoner's massive torso and bulging biceps, the caretaker was transfixed by his grotesque face. It was swollen, splotchy, and oozing drops of blood from some open-scabbed pockmarks. It wasn't just hideous, but menacing, too. The prisoner glanced at him when he stepped up on the platform, and it was enough to send a chill down his curved spine. He couldn't believe someone in shackles and under heavily armed guard could give him the willies, yet he had. Suddenly, the prisoner's head snapped up, and he looked him straight in the eye. "What are *you* looking at?"

Incredibly, he couldn't stop staring and began stuttering. "Nu-nuthin', I, uh, I was just, uh, just, just leaving." Startled, he stepped backward and stumbled off the platform, nearly sprawling on the polished marble floor. After he gathered himself, he looked at the chief.

"I'll be, uh...I'll be up front."

"Good idea. We won't be long." The chief nodded and smiled. It wasn't the first time he had seen the prisoner cause people to shit their pants. In fact, it wasn't even the first time that day.

With the caretaker gone, the prisoner looked down on the pasty face in the casket that sported more jowls than a Richard Simmons video.

"I give you my word," he whispered. "I will find who did this to you, and I will make them pay. I will make them pay dearly. I shall avenge your death as I will my father's, and I shall destroy those who seek to prevent me from claiming my rightful place at the head of the family. Until I join you here, alongside my father, this is my word." He bent over the body and kissed his uncle on the forehead. Then he stood up and nodded.

The chief came out of the shadows and stepped up on the platform. When he grabbed the prisoner's massive arm to escort him away, he didn't budge. "C'mon, let's go."

"There's one small favor I ask."

Ever leery of the prisoner, the chief squinted. "What's that?"

"Reach in my jumpsuit. I have something for my uncle."

"You *what?*"

"In my jumpsuit, by my heart, please."

The chief signaled for the armed guards with the shotguns to approach.

"Okay, but if you pull any tricks, you'll be joining your uncle quicker than Donald Driver's two-step."

"No tricks, I give you my word."

The chief shrugged and unbuttoned the top two buttons of the orange jumpsuit. Then he reached in and pulled out a single long-stemmed red rose. "How the *hell* did you get this?"

"You don't wanna know. May I have it, please?" The guards were completely dumbfounded as to how a maximum-security inmate who came straight from solitary managed to get a rose in his jumpsuit. The chief shook his head in amazement and handed him the rose. The prisoner reached out with his cuffed hands, took the rose, and gently placed it on the chest of the enormous body in the casket. Then he bent over and kissed his forehead again, before delivering his final words. "*Dire ciao a mio padre, riposa a pace.*" Say hello to my father, rest in peace. He made the sign of the cross. Then he stood up and nodded to the chief, who escorted him down from the viewing platform.

As the prisoner shuffled down the short hallway leading to the back door, he counted the steps and smiled; twenty. It was the same number of years he had been sentenced. Things were going to change, though. Soon he would be back on the street, ready to fight for control of the crime family whose leader lay in the casket behind him. For the family members who turned their backs on him during his incarceration, scores needed to be settled, and debts repaid. His uncle had been a great leader, but the family name had been tarnished when it was discovered his death resulted in part because he hired outside help for what was supposed to be a simple job down in Florida. He vowed again to not only avenge his uncle's death, but to bring fear and honor back to the family name. The Devil's Nephew—aka Nipote del Diavolo, aka Marzio Giancarlo DeNutzio—would have it no other way.

Chapter 1

Ker-plunk! I watched the five-pound sinker with the baited hook above it disappear into the brilliant blue Bahamian waters for the umpteenth time and shook my head.

"What are you shaking your head for?" asked my producer, Jamie.

"Because this ain't fishing, that's why. This is fucking ridiculous."

And it *was* ridiculous. We had spent all morning deep dropping, which is somehow legal and considered fishing by guys who mostly don't know how to fish. It involves using an oversize electric reel that's usually mounted on a short stubby rod. The reel may contain upward of a thousand feet (or more) of line, and by using a large weight you can bottom-fish in extreme depths. The thing is, it doesn't require the user to do anything other than press buttons. You press one button to send the bait down, and then you watch the rod tip...and you watch the rod tip... and you watch the rod tip. If you see it twitch, you press another button, and the electric high-torque

1

reel retracts the line and whatever's on it. Unlike traditional bottom-fishing, or virtually any other type of fishing where the angler holds the rod and fights the fish, there is little skill required. The only thing truly required is a wallet fat enough to pay for the electric reel and gear, which can be a couple grand or more.

Jamie looked miffed as he peered out from behind his shoulder-held, high-def camera. "What the hell are you talking about? Of course this is fishing. We're fishing and filming, just like always. Suck it up. We have a show to do, or did you forget?"

"Some show it's gonna be. Make sure you get another close-up of me pressing buttons—you know, the ones that say 'up' and 'down.' I'm sure our viewers will be impressed." I looked over at Tangles and added, "Hey, Tangles, you sure you can handle removing another two-pound yellow-eye from the line?"

"He's right," answered my brother from a shorter mother. "This is like watching reruns of C-SPAN. Why aren't we trolling for big game? This is prime marlin—"

"Can it, Tangles," said Jamie, as he set the camera down. "You, too, Shag. If you hadn't blown up your boat, we probably *would* be fishing for marlin right now. But as it is, we're lucky to have a fishing show at all. Christ, do you have *any idea* what Dina had to do to land Lectra-Reel as a sponsor?" Jamie closed his eyes and shook his head in frustration.

I bit my tongue about what *really* happened to the *Lucky Dog*, and of course I knew exactly how Dina landed Lectra-Reel as a sponsor. It involved antianxiety meds, a bottle of chardonnay, a joint, and a pair of kneepads. Dina was Jamie's wife, and she was in charge of finding sponsors for the show. They had what was called an "open" marriage—at least that's what Dina told me when she tried to jump my bones after I landed the fishing-show gig. I looked at Tangles and pressed my tongue against the inside of my mouth while pumping a clenched fist—the universal sign for blow job.

Tangles started laughing, and Jamie said, "What are *you* laughing at? I shoulda left your scrawny ass back in Lantana."

"Take it easy, man. I know she worked, uh, you know…hard for the money."

"You're damn right she did."

"Dude," I added. "We both appreciate the…great lengths she went to, but c'mon, you know as well as I do this segment's got lame written all over it."

"That's because you two clowns aren't taking it seriously. You're not being professional."

"Please, I'm the only professional here."

"*You?* Since when?"

"Since I got a jeans jacket full of fishing-gear patches from our sponsors. That makes me at least *semi*pro."

"Bullshit! If you had a jacket like that, you'd never take it off. How come I've never seen it?"

"It's too fuckin' hot to wear down here."

"It's true," said Tangles. "He wore it one night to the Old Key Lime House. He was sweating so bad, I thought he was gonna have a heart attack. It looked pretty sweet until his pits started soaking through."

"Yeah? Well, a pimped-out jacket is about all he's got going right now, as evidenced by his weak performance today."

"Oh, so now it's *my fault* I can't make an interesting show out of flicking a switch? Gimme a goddamn break. Just because you got a camera on your shoulder, it doesn't make you Steven Spielberg. You're six foot nine with size fifteen feet. What the hell. If you had a top hat and some floppy shoes, you could work for Barnum and fucking Bailey."

"They're fourteen and a half, asshole."

"Same difference. If you woulda told me beforehand we were coming to the Bahamas to deep drop, we wouldn't be sitting here wasting *my* time and *your* money. And by definition, it also means we're wasting *my* money and *your* time, not that I care about your time. Do I make myself clear? It's quicker and cheaper to make a shitty show off Palm Beach."

"I don't make shitty shows! *You* make shitty shows! I get in the editing room and turn them into fucking *Masterpiece Theatre*, you—"

"FISH ON!" the old Bahamian captain hollered out. He was pointing at the stubby rod that normally jutted out from the side at a forty-five-degree angle and was now bent over.

I turned around and stepped over to the Lectra-Reel as Jamie picked up the camera and started directing. "Don't press the button yet! Give me some good background while the line comes up."

"I'll give you some background, all right," I muttered.

He held three fingers up and started the countdown. "We're rolling in three, two, one, go!"

I smiled at the camera and started my spiel. "Welcome back to *Fishing on the Edge* with Shagball and Tangles. As you can see, the rod is bent, and this is the critical moment—the moment when I press the button." I held up my index finger and zeroed in on the "up" button. "It's critical you press the correct button, because pressing the down button would create slack in the line, and whatever's hooked would likely get off. Okay, then, here we go." I slowly pressed the up button and knew Jamie was zooming in on the almighty Lectra-Reel. As the motor whirred, and the line slowly retracted, I recited our location and depth. "We are about fifteen miles northeast of Walker's Cay, bottom-fishing in area known as 'the drop-off.' We're in eight hundred feet of water, smack dab in the middle of the Bermuda Triangle. How can you bottom-fish in eight hundred feet of water, you say? Tangles? Care to answer that one?"

Tangles stepped into view and put his little hand on the bright red oversize reel. "There's only one good way I know of, Shag. That's with Lectra-Reel, the world's finest electric reel—don't leave shore without it!" He emphasized his pseudosincerity by pointing and winking at the camera.

"That's right, little buddy," I continued as I put my hand on his shoulder. "The only reel I trust when I'm fishing deep, and I mean *really deep*, is Lectra-Reel!"

Jamie said, "Tell 'em what you think is on the line, Shag. What do you think it is?"

I looked at the rod tip and noticed there was no tug of war going on. "As you can see, the rod tip appears to be steady on the retrieve. Hopefully it's not another large piece of coral like we pulled up earlier, but you never know. That's what makes deep dropping so exciting! Maybe it's a big grouper whose eyes are about to pop out, and whose bladder is about to explode, thanks to the rapid pressure change as it ascends to the surface. You know what they say, when you deep drop, everything goes pop!"

Tangles started laughing, and Jamie stopped filming, as he stuck his head out from behind the camera. "What the fuck are you doing, man? You're gonna get the fish-hugging groups all fired up!"

"People hug trees, not fish. You hug a fish, you might lose a lip. Plus, they're slimy."

"You know what I mean! C'mon, man, we got a show to do, don't make it sound so gruesome."

"All right, all right," I more than reluctantly agreed.

He signaled that we were recording, and after another minute of spewing mindless drivel, I saw the marker on the line indicating the leader was about to break the surface. "As you can see, the two-hundred-pound wire stranded leader has come into view, and we're about to find out what we hooked. Here it comes, ladies and gentlemen, and it's a…" I caught a glimpse of silver about twenty feet down and actually got excited for a second. "I see silver! Get the gaff ready, Tangles!"

"Gaff ready!" he answered at my side.

As it came more clearly into view, I said, "What the fuck?"

"What? What is it?" asked Jamie from behind the camera. The Lectra-Reel slowed and then stopped as a piece of barnacle-encrusted metal broke the surface. It was about three feet long and two feet wide, with a tapered end. The leader and weight were wrapped around it in a proper clusterfuck.

"You gotta be shitting me," commented Tangles.

Jamie set the camera down and cussed. "I can't fucking believe we just pulled up an old chunk of metal. How am I supposed to get a show out of this?"

Never one to pass up an opportunity, I replied, "I thought you said you could turn a shitty show into *Masterpiece Theatre*?"

"Shut up."

Tangles used the gaff to pull the snarled mess over to the side of the old thirty-one-foot Bertram, and I helped him lift it onto the deck. It weighed about fifty or sixty pounds and was pretty well barnacle encrusted. As Tangles quickly unsnarled the leader, the captain came down from the bridge to inspect it.

"What do you think it is?" I asked him. "A piece of shipwreck?"

"I'm not sure, mon, let's knock some stuff off and have a look." He stepped inside the cabin and came out with a hammer and chisel. He knocked off a large barnacle from the middle section of the piece and then scraped away some algae. "I thought it looked familiar."

"Yeah, me, too. Probably part of a ship's hull, right?"

"I don't think so. I seen somethin' like this before. I be thinking it from a plane."

Tangles tugged my elbow and pointed down at our mystery catch. "Look, boss! Da plane! Da plane!"

I started laughing along with the captain, but Jamie was not amused.

"Shut up, you little freak. We need some fish, or this charter's a bust."

"You really think it's part of a plane?" I questioned.

"Yeah, mon. Planes be crashed all around these islands—mostly from running drugs. This looks like a piece of tail section. There's a number written on it, see?" He scraped some more barnacles and algae away, and sure enough, we could see what appeared to be a number taking shape.

"That's a…that's a seven. Isn't that a seven?" Jamie said.

"Looks like a seven to me," I concurred. It was black and about eighteen inches high.

"There's another number next to it. Lemme see if I can scrape the rest of this growth away." The captain hammered and chiseled, and another chunk of barnacle flew off. "Somebody hand me the washdown hose." Tangles grabbed the hose in the corner of the cockpit, and the captain washed away some debris, exposing part of another number. He kept scraping with the chisel and used the hose again as the number came into view. To the left of the seven, was a one.

"Seventeen?" I asked.

"So far," the captain replied. "Looks like there's another number." He was hunched over and started chiseling again. After a minute he sprayed the metal with the washdown hose, and another number started taking shape. The captain scraped away the rest of the barnacles and mumbled, "One seventeen? Why do I know that number?"

I stooped down to get a better look and stated the obvious. "It's another one, right? One seventeen."

"Wait a second, this can't be," the captain said. He jumped to his feet and scrambled up the short ladder to the bridge. Sensing something dramatic was happening, Jamie grabbed the camera and started filming him.

"What are you doing?" he asked. "What's going on?" Jamie had the camera trained on the captain as he started pressing buttons on his GPS chart plotter.

"I'm, uh...I'm marking our location, just in case."

"Just in case what?" Jamie asked as he filmed the captain dialing on his cell phone.

The captain shushed him and spoke into the phone. "You in the bar? Good...over by the bathrooms, on the wall, that framed newspaper article... yes, the one with the planes on it, read me the tail numbers...uh-huh...uh-huh...what?...say that last one again. One seventeen? You sure? I can't believe it. Why? I'll tell you why, because I think we just pulled up a piece of it, *dat's why*. Where? Nice try. At the bottom of the ocean, where else?" He smiled and added, "We're heading back to the dock now; you can see it for yourself." He ended the call.

Tangles said, "So it says one seventeen. What's the big deal?" It was exactly what I was thinking. Jamie swung the camera down and filmed the exposed numbers on the piece of metal—a pair of ones and a seven. *So what.*

"What's the big deal? Are you kidding me?" Jamie swung the camera up at Captain Hiram, who could hardly contain himself. "The big deal is, we may have solved one of the greatest maritime mysteries of the twentieth century. That's what!"

"What the hell are you talking about, Cap?" I asked.

Tangles stood up and shook his head. "I don't get it."

"Flight nineteen. *Dat's* what I'm talking about. Don't you guys know nuthin'? I think we pulled up a piece of flight nineteen!"

"Flight nineteen?" I repeated in disbelief. "C'mon! What makes you think—?"

"Rosie's bar has a framed newspaper article about flight nineteen, which gives the individual tail numbers of the five navy Avengers that disappeared on a training run back in 1945. I've read it dozens of times. When I saw the number one seventeen, it jogged my memory. I just called a friend at the bar to read me the tail numbers, and it turns out my memory was right. One seventeen was the tail number of one of the planes that was part of flight nineteen!"

"But what makes you so sure our piece is from a navy Avenger?"

"Last year my cousin showed me a couple Avenger pieces he has at his junkyard in Nassau. He's got *everything*, and I'm telling you this tailpiece is from an Avenger, too. Same bolt pattern, same everything." He was pointing down at the tailpiece in question.

Jamie continued to film as he peered out from behind the camera and queried, "You sure about that, Captain?"

"You're damn right, I'm sure. People been looking for those five Avengers that disappeared over these parts for the last seventy years, and hotdamn if we didn't pull up a piece of one! I gotta radio this in. By the time we get to shore, we gonna be famous! And I ain't talking 'bout no fishing show on ESPN 10 famous. I'm talking *world* famous!" He fired up the engine and added, "Hang on, boys; we're headed for history!"

Chapter 2

Dr. Josef Himmler smiled at his young assistant as he zipped up his fly. It never ceased to amaze him what some young Mexican girls would do for a twenty-dollar bill, or in his case, the offer of a few days off with pay. He could afford to be generous, thanks to his newest patient, a large man who sought out his services for facial reconstructive surgery. He hadn't batted an eye at his $50,000 fee, which was naturally paid in cash. For five days the patient recovered in a special room in a dilapidated building on the outskirts of Guadalajara, Mexico, housing Dr. Himmler's so-called medical practice.

It was a "so-called" medical practice because in reality, he had lost his medical license years ago. In Mexico, however, there was virtually nothing you couldn't obtain for a price. So after purchasing a medical license, he bought a run-down building in Guadalajara and opened up shop.

Business was slow in Guadalajara, except for treating venereal diseases, until the day a drug lord walked in. He was on the run from both Mexican and US authorities and wanted to drastically change his appearance. He looked like an aging Roberto Duran after a losing fight and wanted to look like Ricky Martin. Himmler initially balked, knowing his mediocre track record as a surgeon, but he was persuaded by a duffel bag full of cash and the threat of great bodily harm if he refused. He did his best, and the drug lord was happy with the result, even if he ended up looking like George Lopez with sunburn. Word circulated through criminal channels that he specialized in facial reconstruction and keeping his mouth shut. Almost overnight, it seemed, he was the go-to guy for people on the wrong side of the law.

His young assistant turned at the door and smiled. "*Te veo el lunes?*"

"*Si, si,* I vill see you Monday. Bring zee last patient in before you leave."

"*Muchos gracias,* Señor Himmler."

He dismissed her with a wave of the hand, and a minute later the patient was led through the door. His face was completely covered in white gauze, except for the eyes, which followed the young girl as she closed the door behind her. Once the door shut, his eyes focused on the doctor.

"You kept me waiting."

"My apologies. I've been busy."

"Sure you have. You've been busy banging that little chimichanga. I'm here for a new face, not new ears. You think I'm fuckin' deaf? It sounded like Cujo humping the Taco Bell dog in here. You might wanna invest in some soundproofing."

The doctor cleared his throat and rose from behind his desk. "My job is very stressful."

"Stressful? You want stressful? Try getting your face rearranged with a scalpel. *That's* stressful…and painful, too, I might add."

"Yes, vell, I have some medications for—"

"Forget it. I know how to deal with pain *and* the people who cause me pain. So let's get to it. I'm anxious to see my new face."

"As you vish."

With great care the doctor removed the gauze from the patient's face. When the last section fell away, he turned the patient to face a mirror on the wall.

"Soooo…vhat do you tink?"

The patient blinked once, then twice, as if not believing what he was seeing. "What the *fuck*? What the fuck did you *do* to me?"

"I do not understand. You said you vanted to look like 'Average Joe.'"

"That's right; I wanna be able to blend in anywhere. Look at me; I look like a fuckin' cartoon character. Like that guy on the cover of *MAD Magazine*."

"Who?"

"You gotta be kiddin' me."

"You said you vanted to look like 'Average Joe,' so I make you look like most 'Average Joe' out there—Joe Kernin, from CNBC."

"CNB *what?*"

"CNBC, zee cable business channel. It's vun of zee few channels zee satellite gets. Joe Kernin hosts show on CNBC called *Sqvak Box*. Ven I saw you had gap in front teeth like him, I use his face as model. Believe me, it is *very* average."

"I been in and out of solitary for the last ten years, asshole, so excuse me if I don't know who the *fuck* Joe

Kernin is. Alls I know is I paid you fifty grand to make me look like an ordinary guy, and you made me look like Alfred E. Neuman."

"Who?"

"The guy on the fucking magazine cover!"

"Vell, I don't know about zat, but I can tell you zat except for zee hair, you are dead ringer for Joe Kernin. Zis is maybe my finest verk."

"Yeah? Well, guess what…it's also your last."

"Excuse—"

The patient pivoted and slammed his large fist into the doctor's gut. The doctor went to one knee, and the patient kicked him square in the mouth, sending a couple of teeth flying.

"Where's my file?"

The doctor was bleeding profusely from the mouth but managed to stand up and point at a file cabinet. "Please, please," he said as he spit out some blood. "I can fix it!"

The patient opened the file cabinet, and there were hundreds of folders in it.

"Which one? Which one's mine?"

"Zee vun in front that says, 'Average Joe.'"

As the patient was pulling the file out, he saw movement in the reflection on the adjacent cabinet. The doctor had gone behind his desk and opened a drawer. The patient spun and lunged for the doctor's arm, clamping his hand over the doctor's wrist as he pulled out a gun. With his other hand, he grabbed the doctor by the elbow and jammed it back in the opposite direction. The doctor screamed as his arm snapped like a twig, and the gun clattered to the desk.

"First you fuck up my face, and then you try to shoot me? What are you auditioning for, an Obamacare death panel? *Shit*. I got better medical treatment in prison, you fuckin' quack." The patient then slammed his elbow into the side of the doctor's head, knocking him out cold.

Noticing a set of scalpels in the open drawer, he had an idea. With one arm he swept the doctor's desk clean and then hoisted him on top of it so that he was lying on his back. He pulled a scalpel out of its case and pressed the point into the flesh just below the doctor's hairline. The doctor's eyes flew open, and the patient squeezed his throat with his other hand until he felt the larynx crush. Then he squeezed harder until the doctor's eyes filled with blood, and his legs stopped kicking. Satisfied the doctor was dead, he started with the scalpel.

He had made prior arrangements to obtain new identification, and less than an hour after leaving the doctor's office, he was studying his freshly printed passport. It displayed his new goofball face and the name he settled on after seeing it...Roger Kent. It was a play on the name Roger Kint, which was the role Kevin Spacey played in *The Usual Suspects*. He smiled at how clever he was, naming himself after a movie character who played a harmless con artist with cerebral palsy, when in fact he was a ruthless mastermind and diabolical killer. Fifteen minutes later he was in a considerably better mood as he headed to the airport in the backseat of a taxi. The more he thought about it, the more he thought his goofy-looking new face might actually benefit him, sorta like a wolf in sheep's clothing. People would be inclined to look at him as big and harmless, like the guy who wore the Jughead hat on *The Andy Griffith Show*. By the time they realized he wasn't harmless, it would be too late. *Maybe I overreacted with the good doctor*, he thought. *Too fuckin' bad.*

He started whistling a tune in the backseat of the taxi and then softly sang some lyrics. "I'm on a bus on a psychedelic trip, reading murder books and tryin' to stay hip, thinkin' of you, you're out there so...Say your prayers, say your prayers, say your prayers..."

"Ees a very nice song, señor," said the taxi driver. "A church song?"

"Not exactly, it's a Billy Idol song."

"What ees de name? I like very much."

"Me, too. It's a beautiful concept. The song's called 'Eyes Without a Face.'"

The taxi driver was watching him in the rearview mirror and got a sudden shiver down his spine. The gringo had a face that looked like he might have gone to school on a short bus, but his eyes didn't match. Something was wrong with him...*very* wrong. The passenger noticed the taxi driver staring at him.

"You looking at something?"

The driver quickly averted his gaze and adjusted the rearview mirror so the passenger wasn't in view. "Si, señor. I check traffic. We almost there." *Gracias a dios*, thought the driver. The gringo was creepin' him out.

The rest of the way to the airport not a word was spoken. The only sound besides the traffic came from the strange passenger who kept whistling the haunting melody to "Eyes Without A Face."

16

Chapter 3

In a seedy Jersey City bar located on the edge of a blighted warehouse district, Jimmy "the Mouse" Velotta pressed his back against an unforgiving booth and eyed the front door. The usual cast of rough-and-tumble characters milled about, and the decibel level remained fairly constant, something that was sure to change once the Devil's Nephew strode in. During his eight-year stint at Rahway, the Mouse had witnessed firsthand his unfailing ability to make people stop and stare. It wasn't just his imposing size that caught people's attention, it was his grotesque face. There was no other way to put it. He was the biggest, ugliest, meanest son of a bitch around. End of story. The Mouse picked up a glass of whiskey and swirled it before taking a measured sip. As he dabbed his lips with his ever-present scarf, he considered the unlikely friendship he managed to forge with the most feared gangster on the East Coast.

When he arrived at Rahway to serve his time, word quickly spread he was in for bludgeoning an associate with a laptop and then jamming the mouse down his throat. Somehow this translated into his being "computer savvy," which he happened to be, and he was dubbed "the Mouse." Soon after, he got word the Devil's Nephew wanted to see him in the exercise yard. Like everyone else, he was scared shitless of him, and warily approached as the large man finished a set of five hundred push-ups.

The Mouse signaled to a passing barmaid that he wanted another whiskey and glanced at the front door again as he recalled their first conversation in the yard nearly ten years earlier.

"I hear you're good with computers," stated the Devil's Nephew.

"Pretty good."

"That's not what I heard. I heard you were running numbers for Trivisonno. I heard you were better with computers than his dickhead brother who went to MIT."

"You heard right, but that ain't no big deal."

"I also hear there's some moolies on the block that plan on making the Mouse squeal, *Deliverance* style…if you know what I mean."

It had been true, he hadn't been there a week, and rumors were flying that some inmates were setting him up for an ass raping, something he was rather eager to avoid.

"You, uh, you know which ones?"

"'Course I do. I run this fuckin' place."

"So I hear…What are you saying?"

"I can get you in the prison library. You get me the information I need, and your ass won't bleed."

"What good does getting me in the library do? They won't let me *near* a computer."

"No shit. I got one of them smart phones stashed in a hollowed out book. That's how you get access. So, what's it gonna be? The information highway or the Hershey highway?"

For the rest of his stay at Rahway, the Mouse had protected status. Even after he was sprung, he continued to feed the Devil's Nephew information about his underworld rivals. Saying no to the man just didn't seem like a prudent call, and now that he was out on the street, it seemed like the smartest call in the world.

Suddenly, the front door swung open, and a large shadow was cast across the floor as a streetlight backlit the subject. As if on cue, the noise level dropped, and heads turned as the large man walked in. Then, strangely, everyone turned away, and conversations resumed as he walked toward the back of the bar. At first, the Mouse thought it was the Devil's Nephew, based on his size but knew by the bar patrons' reactions it couldn't be him. The barmaid set a whiskey down and walked away just as the big man approached the booth and sat down across from him. The Mouse stared at him for a second, just to confirm he didn't know who the fuck he was. "Sorry, big guy, that seat's taken. I'm expecting someone."

The goofy-looking guy smiled, exposing a familiar gap in his two front teeth.

"Not any more, Mouse, that 'someone' is here. Let's talk." Then he picked up the glass of whiskey and tossed it back in one motion. The Mouse leaned forward and stared with a perplexed look on his face. He recognized the voice and the gapped front teeth, but not the face. "What the…what the *fuck?*"

"That's what I said when I saw it for the first time, too. I know, it's a little…different."

"*Different?* Holy shit, I'll say. What the hell happened? You look like David Letterman with Down syndrome."

The big man glanced around and warned, "Keep it down, Mouse. Nobody's givin' me a second look, and I wanna keep it that way."

"Sure, sure thing, it's just I, uh—"

"I had an operation. It's not exactly the look I was goin' for, but it works like a charm. When people think you're a little retarded, they tend to underestimate you."

"I can see how that would work. I don't know if I should buy you a drink or a lollipop."

"See what I mean?" Suddenly, the eyes behind the friendly, off-kilter face took on a steely glare.

A shiver ran down the Mouse's spine. "I'm, uh, I'm just kidding. Let me get us a round." He flashed two fingers at the barmaid and nervously looked back at the big man. He didn't want to piss him off—no how, no way.

"So, you have any problem gettin' what I wanted?"

"No, your aunt let me in your uncle's office, just like you said she would. While I was downloading some files, I poked around and found some handwritten notes on a scribble pad. One note had the word GOLD underlined and in capital letters. The other had the words 'Lucky Dog' circled and the word 'midget,' with a question mark after it."

"That tells me a fuckin' lot. What does it mean?"

"Well, I don't know what the gold thing is all about, but I did a Google search and *Lucky Dog* is the name of a boat used in a fishing show based out of Palm Beach."

"A *fishing* show? You gotta be shittin' me."

"Nope, a fishing show with a midget sidekick and a host named Shagball. And get this, their boat used to be docked next to your uncle's at the Water's Edge Marina in Boynton Beach. That was the last place it was seen until the Coast Guard found it bullet riddled and half-sunk off North Carolina. But that was *all* they found. As you know, the two guys that worked for your uncle are still missing and presumed dead."

"Yeah, Gino and Marco, I know 'em from way back. I can't believe some fishing-show schmucks got the drop on 'em. Gino was a real pro. It's gotta be them, though; a midget would explain why they had their guard down. So, what else did you find?"

"It looks like they might have been involved in the shootout that left your uncle dead, too."

"Son of a bitch!" He slammed his fist down on the table just as the barmaid returned with two glasses of whiskey and set them down.

"Here you go, boys, there's not gonna be any trouble here, is there?" She shot the Devil's Nephew a look, and he glared back at her. "Not if you get me a beer to wash this rotgut down, there won't."

She looked at the Mouse, who said, "Make it two beers. What is this shit, anyways?" He took a sip of the whiskey and winced.

"It's the house whiskey, just like you ordered; you want Crown, you gotta pay the piper."

"Just get us a couple beers, will you?"

"Fine, two beers for the happy-go-lucky twins, coming up." The barmaid spun on her heel and huffed away.

"What a bitch," commented the Mouse.

"Don't worry. If the beers aren't cold, I'll kill her. Now, tell me about the shootout. I figured that DEA story about a drug deal gone bad was bullshit."

"It was. I was able to access the police report online and did some digging into who rented the storage units where the shootout occurred. Turns out the one your uncle was found in front of *was*—and still *is*— rented to the C-Love Marina. The same marina where your uncle's boat and the *Lucky Dog* were docked, which is the marina your uncle was trying to buy."

"Fuckin' A."

"I'm not finished. Get this—the C-Love Marina also happens to be owned by none other than this guy Shagball's girlfriend."

The barmaid set two glasses of beer down in front of them and left without a word.

"That's some kinda coincidence. You did good, Mouse, as usual." The Devil's Nephew nodded at the Mouse and raised his glass of beer. They clinked glasses together and shared a long pull of the amber liquid. The Devil's Nephew burped and wiped his lips. "Thirty-eight degrees, that's one lucky cunt." They both laughed before the Mouse acknowledged the compliment regarding his research. "Thanks, Marz. It's good to see—"

"Whoa, whoa, whoa. Not so loud."

"Huh? What is it?"

The big man glanced around before lowering his voice. "In private you can call me Marz, but not in a place like this. I got a new name to go with my new face."

"Oh, okay…so what is it?"

"Kent. Roger Kent."

"Better than Clark Kent."

He chuckled. "Yeah, a lot better. It's a typical douche-bag name. Totally forgettable, just the way I want." He smiled his new goofy smile and added, "Plus, ain't no kryptonite gonna turn my dick into dill weed."

The Mouse laughed, but the big man's smile evaporated as he cut him off with a simple hand gesture and leaned forward. The Mouse went silent and squirmed, nervously wondering what he did wrong. "I was just—"

"Shut up, Mouse. I may have a new face and a new name, but you best remember that's *all* that's changed."

"Sure, Marz—I mean…Rodge…er. I won't forget. No fucking way I'm gonna forget."

"Good, that's good." He leaned back and smiled again before adding, "I just wanted to make sure we're on the same page, you know?"

The Mouse relaxed a little and felt his asshole unpucker. "Absolutely. Same page, same chapter, same book, same library, same—"

"Okay, I get it. I was just making sure."

The Mouse let out a deep breath. "There is one thing, though."

"What's that?"

"Nobody knows me as 'Mouse' on the street. I hate the fucking name, too, makes me sound like a weasel."

"Don't worry, I know you're not a weasel. If you was, you'd a been popped like one."

"Thanks, but can't you start calling me Jimmy, like everyone else?"

"I dunno, Mouse. You got a memorable name like 'Mouse,' it's hard to shake. I gotta think about it." He took another sip of beer and studied the Mouse closely. His skin color was off, and his black hair was having its own recession. He was on the smallish side and looked a little like the actor Andy Garcia with malaria. And as Andy Garcia was prone to do, the Mouse was wearing a scarf.

"What's with the scarf?" he asked.

"What do you mean? It's a little chilly out, that's all."

"C'mon, Mouse, don't bullshit me, word is, ever since you got sprung, you started wearing a scarf. Why? What gives?"

The Mouse subconsciously started pushing the scarf inside his shirt so it wouldn't be so...out there. "All right, all right...When I got sprung, my mother brought me some new clothes to leave the joint in. The scarf was part of the ensemble, that's all."

"*Ensemble?*"

"Yeah, she said it makes me look sophisticated... you know, classier. And I gotta tell ya, the ladies love it."

"I know some guys who do, too."

"C'mon, man, I'm just trying to improve my image."

"Okay, how 'bout this? From now on I'm calling you...the Scarf."

"*The Scarf?*"

"Yeah, think about it...Jimmy "the Scarf" Velotta. It's mysterious and a little menacing. Is he hiding something under the scarf? Does he scarf things? Is he a professional thief? Or maybe...yeah, maybe he wears the scarf so he has something handy to strangle people with. Who knows? The Scarf knows, that's who."

They both shared another laugh, and Mouse started fluffing his scarf out from under his shirt as he warmed to the idea. "It's better than 'Mouse,' I suppose."

"It's a lot better. From now on you're the Scarf—end of discussion."

"If you say so."

"I just did. So now it's on to more important things."

"Like what?"

"Like me gettin' down to F-L-A to settle the score with these fishing-show clowns."

"No need to rush; they're not there right now."

"How do you know?"

"It's what I do. That's how I kept my cherry intact at Rahway, remember?"

"Good point, I almost forgot. The Scarf knows everything."

More laughter ensued, and the Scarf deflected the compliment as best he could. "I can't take *too* much credit for knowing where they are. It's posted on their friggin' website."

"What website?"

"Their fishing show has a website. These guys Shagball and Tangles are in the Bahamas doing some filming. They should be back in Palm Beach in a few days."

"Shagball and who?"

"Tangles. He's the midget."

"Talk about a couple guys in need of a nickname overhaul. No matter, they'll be called Dead and Deader when I get through with 'em."

"You got a plan?"

"Maybe. You said this guy Shagball's got a girl-friend, right?"

"Yeah, and from the pics I seen on the website, she's quite a piece."

"Good. I think I'll bang the shit out of her in front of her asshole boyfriend and then pick up the midget by his heels and use him to bash everybody's fucking brains in. I seen a show one time where these guys had a dwarf-throwing contest, and it was fuckin' hilarious. This is gonna be way better than that. I dunno, I gotta put some more thought into it. You don't get opportunities like this every day. You know, with the midget and all. Am I right, or am I right?"

The Scarf didn't answer right away, because he was thinking about how nobody in the bar would suspect the big goofy-looking guy was explaining how he was gonna rape and murder three people. They probably thought from the smile on his face they were talking sports or something, but they would be wrong. Dead wrong. The Scarf knew better, though. He had seen the look in his eye before, many times before, and he knew he meant every word.

"Hey…Scarf."

"Huh? Oh yeah, sure. 'Course you're right. Wish I could join you," he lied. The one time he killed a guy, it was a spur of the moment thing, unplanned, and he did eight long years for it. But he knew if it weren't for his symbiotic relationship with Marzio Giancarlo DeNutzio, aka the Devil's Nephew, aka Roger Kent, he might not have survived Rahway—a place he never wanted to see again.

"Not this time, Scarf, this time it's personal. But you did good, real good. Just remember, you don't tell nobody—but nobody—about my new face. When I get back, I'm gonna pay some people a visit, and I want it to be a surprise."

"Got it. I love surprises. Shit, I almost forgot."

"Forgot *what*."

"The fuckin' lawyer that clipped the four one for nearly three million gabonies is getting sprung in a couple days. I thought they were supposed to have brains, but stealing from the International Longshoremen's Association of New Jersey don't seem too brainy to me."

"How in the *fuck* did he get his hands in the till?"

"His college roommate was on the pension board."

"*Was?*"

"He disappeared."

"Skipped?"

"Not exactly. From what I heard, you gotta better chance of finding Hoffa before him."

"Good, so that leaves the lawyer. Like I even need a reason to break every *fuckin'* bone in his body. Where is he?"

"The federal pen in Atlanta."

"You thinkin' what I'm thinkin?"

"It's on the way to Florida?"

"No doubt about it. I'd say it's unavoidable."

"Well, before you express the totality of your displeasure with him, keep in mind he might have some dough squirreled away."

"He better fuckin' hope so, 'cause I want it *all* back...and then some."

"There's a good chance of that. Besides the longshoremen, he also clipped a teachers' fund in North Carolina and the endowment fund for the University of Georgia…almost ten million altogether. At trial he said what he didn't blow on strippers, gambling, and coke, he lost on bad investments, but I dunno. He wouldn't be the first guy to leave the can with a nest egg waiting…know what I mean?"

"I certainly do," responded the gap-toothed smile. "This guy gotta name?"

"And address. Here's both." The Scarf reached in his shirt pocket and slid a piece of paper across the table along with an eight-by-ten glossy photograph of the subject. The big man glanced at the photo and read the address for the US penitentiary in Atlanta, the time and date of release, and the lawyer's name. He looked at his watch and noted the lawyer was to be released in less than thirty-six hours. He nodded and looked across the table. *Time to get movin'.*

"You done good, Scarf." He reached inside his jacket and slid an envelope across the table. "Here, this is for you."

The Scarf opened it and let out a low whistle. "There's a lotta scratch here. You sure?"

"Sure I'm sure. You got a lotta work to do. Besides, as of now you're officially my right-hand man."

"I am?"

"Damn right."

"You really mean it? Like I'm gonna be a…what do they call 'em? A lieutenant?"

"This ain't the fuckin' army, Scarf. Don't get hung up on titles. The important thing to remember is as long as you work for me, I got your back. But if you cross me…well, we both know you don't wanna cross me, right?"

The Scarf swallowed hard as the big man rose from the table and then winced as he squeezed his shoulder with one of his large hands.

The Scarf forced out a laugh. "*Me* cross *you?* Hah. Not in a million years. I don't even like to cross the street."

The big man chuckled, but his eyes told a different story. "That's what I like to hear. Maybe you should head down to Old Navy and pick up another scarf or two. I hear black is the new blue. I'll be in touch."

On his way out, the Scarf watched him say something to a couple guys at the bar. They turned and looked his way before quickly averting their eyes. As he finished his drink, he caught them staring again from the mirror behind the bar. Emboldened by his new nickname and reestablished protected status, he yelled, "You guys looking at something, or what?!"

When they looked away, he straightened his scarf and muttered, "That's right, assholes, you best not fuck with the Scarf."

Chapter 4

As we headed back to Grand Cay, me, Jamie, and Tangles shared what little we knew about the infamous flight 19.

"Didn't they leave from Miami and get lost over the keys? How could they end up here?" asked Jamie.

"I think it was Fort Lauderdale," answered Tangles.

I decided to put my two cents in. "I saw a show on it recently, and you're right, Tangles, they left out of Lauderdale. There were five navy Avengers that went on a training run that was supposed to take them out over the Bahamas and then back. The leader got confused, thinking he was over the keys for some reason, and from there he made one bad decision after another."

"I do the same thing when I drink tequila. Last time, I jumped off a cruise ship."

"What are you talking about? That may be the *best* decision you ever made. Now you're a fishing-show sidekick basking in the effervescent glow of my charming personality."

"*Charming personality*? Like Aretha would sing, 'Who's zoomin' who?' You're about as charming as a snakebite. Seriously, dude, you've been acting a little surlier than normal, especially on camera."

"Sure I have."

"He's right, Shag," added Jamie. "Ever since you got back from St. Croix, it's getting more and more noticeable."

"You know what else is getting more and more noticeable? The fact that we spent all morning on a beautiful blue sea, and I didn't have a fucking rod in my hand once. All I did was press the goddamn buttons on that stupid-ass reel!"

"That stupid-ass reel paid for this trip! What's the matter with you? This is showbiz, pal; you gotta do what you gotta do. Get over it."

"This blows. This is blowbiz, not showbiz."

"Yeah? Well, it is what it is. Fortunately, we weren't on live TV when you were talking about exploding fish. That shit's never gonna see the light of day. So look at the bright side, you have the chance of a lifetime to redeem yourself when we hit the dock. If the captain's right and we—"

"Oh, c'mon! Do you have any idea what the odds are that we found a piece of flight nineteen? A million to one? Not even. More like a trillion to one."

"See what I mean, Jamie?" commented Tangles. "See how negative he's being? Very surly if you ask—"

"Nobody asked you!" I glared at Tangles. "So keep your little pie` hole shut, or you'll find yourself bobbing in the gulfstream again...where you belong."

"I survived it once, I can survive it again, asshole."

Tangles huffed past me toward the cabin, and as he slammed the door behind him, I yelled, "Not without me you can't!" I turned back to face Jamie, and he was shaking his head.

"What's the matter with *you?*" I asked.

"What's the matter with *me?* What the fuck's the matter with *you?*"

"Nothing. Never felt better. In fact, I think I'll have a beer." I reached into the cooler and popped the top on a coldie, not bothering to offer him one. I really hated to waste what should have been a great day fishing. *Really* hated it.

"Jesus, Shag, weren't you a little rough on him?"

Actually, I was feeling a mite petty for going after Tangles when it was Jamie I was really pissed at, and I wasn't through by a long shot.

I shrugged. "Hey, like you said, that's showbiz. Get over it."

"Wow. Okay, you wanna talk showbiz? Let's talk showbiz. You're missing the whole point about whether we found flight nineteen or not."

"How so?"

"'Cause it doesn't fucking matter. All that matters is the captain *thinks* we found it. You know why? 'Cause he's already radioed everybody and their brother, and we're gonna be swamped with inquiries when we get back to the dock. If there's a news affiliate on Grand Cay, you can bet your ass somebody's gonna be there with a camera. It's probably gonna take some time to figure out if this piece of crap we pulled up is from flight nineteen or not, but in the meantime, we might make national news, Shaggy. Shit, we might even make *international* news. Think about it. Some guy in Hong Kong gets home from a hard day working in the, uh…

rice fields, and he's having some sake, and boom, there's your face plastered on the six o'clock news and your voice is overdubbed in, uh, Japanese or Siamese or whatever they speak there, explaining how we pulled up a piece of flight nineteen."

"Sake's what they drink in Japan. I don't know what they drink in Hong Kong...probably hake." I reached in the cooler and grabbed another beer.

"Whatever. It doesn't matter if they drink carp piss. They're gonna be watching Shagball and Tangles holding up a piece of flight nineteen. I'm telling you, this could be huge."

"I think carp are called koi in Japan, and Hong Kong is under Chinese rule. They probably speak Chinese there. You're confusing the two." I stepped over to the cabin door and slid it open. Tangles was napping, and when his eyes popped open, I tossed him the beer. I slid the door closed without a word and turned back to Jamie, who had fished his own beer out and was glaring at me.

"*What?*" I said.

"What do you mean, *what?* Did you not hear a word I just said? Who cares what they're drinking and whether they speak Chinese or Japanese. I was just using Hong Kong as an example."

"Mandarin," said Tangles as he slid open the cabin door.

Jamie and I both looked at him, and Jamie said, "*Mandarin?* What *about* Mandarin? What the hell are you talking about?"

"In Hong Kong. I think that's what they speak there. Mandarin's some kinda Chinese hybrid, just like the orange it was named after. In fact, the Chinese ate so many little oranges it stunted their growth and gave them that unripened orange tint. That's why the Chinese are sometimes referred to as yellow bellies. True story."

I laughed so hard, beer came out my nose. It reminded me why I liked to keep the little guy around. He was unbelievable sometimes. After wiping my face on my T-shirt, I clinked beer cans with him and commented, "Dude, that was great. And I thought I was full of shit."

"What do you mean? I'm being serious."

"Oh, c'mon, man. Mandarin, my ass. I was giving you a compliment."

"Nice try," said Jamie. "But even *I* know a mandarin isn't a language, it's one of those little guitars, like a ukulele."

Tangles and I both started laughing, but inwardly I cringed. Deep dropping was bad enough, but when compounded with Jamie's desire to demonstrate just how stupid he really was, well, the writing was on the wall as to how successful our fishing show would ever be with him at the helm.

"What are you two laughing at?" he asked.

"Forget it," I replied. "It's been a long day."

"You're right, and it's about to get longer."

The captain slowed the boat, and we were passing the channel markers leading to Grand Cay and the docks at Rosie's marina. Jamie pointed toward the docks and continued his spiel. "After we get this hunk of metal up on the dock, I want you guys to lift it up and smile for the camera. And act excited, too. Think you can do that? After all, it just might be flight nineteen. Who knows? Either way, this is a big story. Scratch that—gigantic. It'll probably be the biggest one of your life, so don't blow it."

"Yeah, Tangles," I said. "Just imagine, some guy in Denmark gets home after a hard day in the clog factory, pops open a Grolsch, and boom! There we are on the six o'clock news holding up a piece of flight nineteen!"

"Shagball?"

"What's that, Jamie?" I smiled.

"See if you can translate some of your surly snarkiness into a pleasantly memorable news byte. Think you can do that? After all, the future of the show probably depends on it. It's not like we're the only fishing show out there, you know? We've been getting lots of e-mails asking when you're getting a new boat since you blew up your last one."

Jamie, like everyone else, didn't know the *real* story about what happened to my beloved *Lucky Dog*, and I was half past tired listening to him needle me about it. Check that—I was *way* past tired, and I felt the surliness wash over me like a hot shower on a cold morning. We pulled up to the dock, and there was a throng of people waiting for us, including a guy standing in front of a Range Rover that had a small satellite dish mounted to the roll bar. He had a shoulder-mounted camera, with a TV news sticker on it, and he pushed his way through the crowd as Tangles tied us off.

"Hey, Shagball!" yelled Jamie behind me.

I turned to look at him, and he was fiddling with the controls on his camera. "What."

"I *said*, do you think you can do that? Do you think you can give me a pleasantly memorable news byte?"

I forced a smile and answered, "I don't know about pleasant, but I'll make sure it's memorable. You wanna make international news? Consider it done."

As I jumped up on the dock and greeted the hoard of onlookers, I heard Jamie say, "Oh, shit."

Chapter 5

"Ladies and gentlemen, everybody step back, please,"
I announced. The crowd was a mishmash of humanity.
There were Bahamian dock rats, restaurant workers,
wealthy fisherman from stateside, old ladies, young
kids, customs agents, and of course, the local news
guy. Somebody identifying himself as the captain's
brother hopped on the boat as Tangles and Jamie
climbed off, and he helped the captain hoist the piece
of wreckage onto the dock. Naturally, everybody
ignored my instructions and pushed closer to look at
the rusted and barnacle-laden relic.

A little kid ducked past my legs and pointed at it.
"Look!" he cried, "it says a hundred and seventeen on
it!"

"That's right, son," I responded. "And if everybody
will just step back a bit, my associate Tangles here will
help me lift it up for all to see."

I looked over at Jamie, and he nodded to let me
know he was taping. As Jamie filmed Tangles stepping
through the crowd, I pulled out my cell phone and
activated an app called Phone Me. It would make my
phone ring in five minutes and then every few minutes afterward until I deactivated it. I was ready to have

some fun. With Tangles on one side of me and the captain on the other, I stuck my hands out and asked everybody to step back again. This time, the crowd, I estimated it to be sixty or seventy people, obliged.

After thanking them, I began laying out the story. "As many of you are undoubtedly aware, my name is Shagball. Me and my crew are here in the Bahamas filming our fishing show called *Fishing on the Edge with Shagball and Tangles.* Some of you, I'm sure, have seen it." I was expecting to hear some shouts of acknowledgment or maybe even applause, but the crowd was silent. After a few uncomfortable moments, I asked, "Has, uh, *anybody* seen the show?"

One guy, who appeared to be from the States, raised his hand. "A while back I saw the episode where the midget in an Elvis costume got hooked off the pallet, and you reeled him in. That was good stuff."

I held up Tangles's hand like a prizefighter and declared, "That would be this man here, and he may be short, but he's not a midget. There's a difference— Google it. Give it up for my man, Tangles!" After a smattering of applause, I said, "That's it, huh? Nobody else has seen the show?" When no one responded, I added, "Well, guess what, my fish-loving friends? 'Cause of what we pulled up today, that shit's gonna change!"

A native Bahamian lady in the front of the crowd stomped her foot and said, "Tell it like it is, Shagball!"

I winked at her and kept going. "While fishing in approximately eight hundred feet of water this morning, at a location known only to me, my crew, and Captain Hiram, we pulled up what at first appeared to be an ordinary chunk of metal. After removing some barnacles, Captain Hiram recognized it as part of a tail section from an airplane, something he has seen before in these waters." A few of the locals murmured in agreement that it was definitely a piece of tail section. "But not just any tail section. Captain Hiram identified it as being from the tail section of a navy Avenger, a tail section he's somewhat familiar with, isn't that right, Captain?"

The captain glanced at me and nodded. "That's right, I seen one in my brother-in-law's junkyard. It looked just like this."

The local news guy pushed closer, and I asked him if he was getting it.

"Yeah, mon, we be rolling."

"After removing some barnacles," I continued, "Captain Hiram exposed the numbers one, one, and seven, numbers he had seen many times while reading a framed article about flight nineteen that hangs right here inside Rosie's bar. After calling to verify his memory was correct, he realized we had a piece of legendary flight nineteen. C'mon, Tangles, help me lift it up, so everybody can get a good look."

We crouched down and slowly lifted the awkward chunk of metal. Everybody had their cell phones out and were snapping pictures and taking video.

"Lift it higher!" shouted someone in the crowd. I told Tangles to hand it off to Captain Hiram so we could hold it higher. As he did so, the captain inadvertently grabbed a piece of barnacle, slicing his finger. He yelled out as the wreckage slipped from his hand and crashed to the ground at our feet. Part of the tail section broke off, as did another large chunk of barnacle.

"Look, the number changed!" a young kid shouted. Sure enough, where the barnacle broke off, the top of what we thought was a one became a T. It was T17. *Shit*. While the captain disappeared to tend to his sliced finger, I picked up the main section with the numbers on it and Tangles picked up the broken-off part.

"That's not one seventeen anymore," someone from the crowd said. "It's T17!"

"That means it's not from flight nineteen, right?" said another.

I figured I only had another minute or so until my phone rang, and I wasn't about to go bad on my international news threat.

"This is incredible!" I declared with feigned excitement. "This is the proof we were looking for! We really found it!"

Tangles looked at me funny, and the local news guy said, "What are you talking about, mon?"

"Don't you realize what I'm holding here?" I pointed at the tail number with my finger. "In the naval aeronautical glossary of terms, T is interchangeable with the number one. T17…117…it's the same either way."

"It is?" Tangles said.

"I never heard that before," countered the newsman as the crowd began murmuring their collective doubts.

"I'm not surprised, seeing as how it's one of those little known historical facts. But the truth is the T1 interchange and the term T1 became so popular that it was adopted as the name for the modern high-speed, fiber-optic transmission line—the T1 line. I'm sure somebody here has heard of the T1 line, right? Ring any bells?"

A middle-aged man wearing an expensive fishing shirt and a Tilley hat answered hesitantly.

"My, uh…office building in Boca has a T1 line. It's fast as hell."

"Just like a navy Avenger," I added with a nod.

The ring tone on my phone started playing a guitar riff from Billy Squire's "Lonely is the Night." I handed the tailpiece to Tangles and pulled the phone out of my pocket. I held my other hand up and said, "Excuse me," as I pretended to try and quiet the crowd. The newsman stepped closer, and I could sense him zooming in on me while I talked to the nonexistent caller. I nodded my head a few times and said, "That's right, it's gotta be flight nineteen… uh-huh…yep, T17…that's what I think, too, the old T1 trick…I know, it's amazing…we were about fifteen miles—" I looked up at the newsman and turned my back to him, acting like I didn't want him to hear. Unwittingly, I wound up facing Jamie's camera. I said, "I'll e-mail you the coordinates in a few minutes…yes, thank you, thank you very much. It'll be an honor to work with you." I ended the call and turned back to face the newsman and the crowd.

"What was that all about?" asked the newsman.

I looked past him with a big smile on my face. "Ladies and gentlemen, all the good people of Grand Cay, I just received a call from Bob Ballerd of the Woods Hole Oceanographic Institute. He's the guy who found the *Titanic*. He thinks we hit the jackpot, and he's sending over a submersible from Florida to inspect the site." I pumped my fist, and the crowd applauded. Jamie leaned in and peered out from behind the camera.

"Dude, was all that flight number bullshit for real?" he whispered. "That was really Bob Ballerd you just talked to?"

I kept smiling and whispered back, "Would I lie to you?"

Tangles started chuckling, and Jamie glanced at him before looking at me and moaning, "Oh, no...no, no, no."

"Shut up and keep filming. This is showbiz." I gently pushed him back and addressed the growing crowd, which was now buzzing with excitement. Tangles placed the aircraft pieces at his feet, and they had him all but surrounded.

"I know this is a lot to take in, but I have another exciting announcement to make. Based on today's incredible discovery, we have decided to change the name and format of our show. Our new plan is to travel the globe and solve legendary mysteries, while simultaneously doing what we do best; catching the biggest and baddest fish around."

One of the dock rats yelled out, "I heard the biggest fish you caught today was a two-pound yellow-eye!"

"Shut up, wise ass. Who says I'm done fishing?" The crowd laughed. "Finding flight nineteen was just a warm-up. After lunch we're gonna look for the lost city of Atlantis." Another ripple of laughter swept through the crowd.

Somebody had the sense to ask, "Are you serious?"

"About lunch? Damn straight I am. Mystery solving is hungry work…thirsty work, too."

"No, I mean about Atlantis. How do you plan on doing that?"

"While trolling."

As the crowd continued to laugh, I signaled Tangles to get me a beer. I really *was* thirsty, probably from all the bullshit I was spewing. But when you're on a roll, you're on a roll. Like when Tom Arnold was on top of Roseanne Barr. One of the local dock rats with a Bob Marley T-shirt and a Guy Harvey cap looked up at me from the five-gallon bucket he was sitting on. I could tell he was baked like a clam. "This is some crazy shit, mon," he commented. "What be the name?"

"What name?"

"The name of the show. You said you be changing the name of the show."

"Oh, right. Thanks for reminding me," I lied.

Not that I'm a serial bullshitter or anything, but I've found that people fall into one of three camps when they're being conned. The kid with the Marley T-shirt, as well as a number of others, were firmly in camp one; they believed everything I said. I could have sold them sand at the beach. From the snippets of conversation I was picking up, I could also tell quite a few people were in camp two; camp two was on the fence, like the local news guy. He believed the wreckage *might* be from flight 19 but wasn't sure about my tail number story or the phone call. The people in camp three were the die-hard skeptics who weren't gonna believe a word I said no matter what. They were likely to be the ones silently lurking at the perimeter of the crowd. I couldn't worry about them, but to finish reeling in camp one, and firmly set the hook on camp two, I needed more bullshit. That's the problem with bullshitting. Once you start you only have two options: pile it on or throw in the towel. But like I said, I was on a roll, and the towel was not an option.

My mind raced trying to come up with a plausible name for my implausible fishing show as the crowd buzzed with excitement. I raised my hand and announced, "May I have your attention please?" As the crowd settled down, I stalled for time. "I almost forgot to give you the name of our new show. Don't ask me what channel we're gonna be on. With the magnitude of today's find, I'm guessing it'll be NatGeo, or Discovery, or the History Channel—something like that...something big."

"So what's the name?" asked a little Bahamian girl—a camp one'r.

I thought about everything I had said as I looked around the crowd, and it hit me—the perfect name. I *was* on a roll. "I'm thrilled to announce that from this day forward, the show will be called *Fishing for Answers with Shagball and Tangles*. Now that we're rewriting maritime history, we'll probably head up to Long Island Sound and fish the waters near a place called, uh, called...Pear Island, I think. Supposedly, Captain Kidd's treasure is buried around there. I figure we'll dig it up while snagging a few stripers."

The crowd laughed before a big guy in a loud Hawaiian shirt, a camp three'r, said, "You don't know what the hell you're talking about. I'm from Suffolk County, and there ain't no Pear Island in the sound.

There's a Plum Island, but no Pear Island. You got your fruits mixed up. Never heard of it before."

"Not many people have. That's probably why Kidd's treasure has never been found."

The lady who earlier told me to tell it like it is said, "Oh, snap!"

The crowd erupted in laughter as the guy slinked off toward the bar. I was feeling good and decided to keep piling it on.

"After that we might head to northwestern Mongolia to fish for man-eating catfish and search for the lost treasure of Kubla Khan. I'm pretty sure the lyrics to the 1980 Olivia Newton-John song *Xanadu* hold the clue to its location." My phone started going off again, and I repeated my earlier routine of trying to quiet the crowd. I put one finger in my ear and started talking. This time I let the news guy eavesdrop.

"Yes, yes this is Shagball. You're with who? Wow. Yes, sir, uh-huh, that's right...leave it to the navy to pull the old T1 trick...uh-huh, sure...as soon as he's done with it. You got it, sir, anything for my country... Thank you, yes, it's a bit overwhelming." I put the phone back in my pocket and shook my head in mock disbelief. "This is unbelievable," I muttered.

"What? Who was that?" asked the local news guy.

"You've been getting all this, right?"

"You kidding, mon? I be beaming straight to Nassau—the station told me CNN picked it up, and they be showing clips on *Headline News*. Anderson Cooper's on the way."

Tangles walked up shaking his head and handed me an ice-cold Kalik.

When I finished slurping half of it down, the news guy asked me again, "So who else called?"

"Better start filming," I told him as I wiped my mouth on my T-shirt. I saw the red light on his camera start blinking just like Jamie's did as he stood filming behind him. "That was the Smithsonian. As soon as Ballerd's done examining the tailpiece, they want me to send it to them. You got a Pak-N-Ship around here?"

Chapter 6

In a seaside tiki bar in a remote corner of the South Pacific, a customer strolled in and elicited a seat with the practiced perfection that can only be developed through years of experience. In other words, he sat down. The bartender glanced at him, held his index finger up, and returned to watching the knock-off brand TV precariously perched in the corner. The satellite picture was shitty, matching the homemade mounting bracket the TV was attached to, which looked like wreckage from a *Transformers* movie.

As he was prone to do, the customer sized up the bartender as he continued watching the TV. It took all of about two seconds. After noting the scar on his knee, he pegged him as an ex-football player of Hawaiian or Samoan descent. He was big, with the stereotypical flowery shirt and hair pulled back in a ponytail. The bartender finally turned and stuck a thumb over his shoulder as he reached under the bar to grab a rag. "You believe that shit?" he asked as he wiped the area in front of the lone man at the bar.

"Believe what?"

"Some fishing-show guy in the Bahamas claims he reeled in part of flight nineteen. What can I get you?"

"Got a local beer?"

The bartender seemed taken aback and gave the stranger the once-over. He was either a really tan white man or a really light dark man. It was hard to tell. What wasn't hard to tell was the sun-beaten look and leathery skin that could only be attained by spending years on the water...or half a day in a cranked-up tanning bed. It made his age and nationality hard to figure. He could be an old-looking forty or a young-looking ninety, or anywhere in between.

"Your first time here, huh?" he concluded.

"Yeah, just passing through. Why?"

"The local beer is iguana piss."

"Then I'll need a tequila chaser."

"You don't understand, the local beer literally *is* iguana piss—fermented iguana piss. Tastes even worse than it sounds...or so I've, uh, heard. Sure you don't want a Bud?"

"Good idea."

The bartender reached into a cooler on the floor and set an ice-cold bottle in front of him. "Run you a tab?"

"Thanks, but I'll pay as I go." He handed the bartender a twenty, and the bartender held it up to admire it.

"That's the way it should be. Just like this. Not like the government. They tax you for twenty and then spend two hundred."

The bartender made change, and after setting it down on the bar, he glanced up at the TV. Semicurious, the customer asked, "What government are you talking about?"

"All of 'em. They're all the same. It's the Big Kahuna keeping the Little Kahuna down. They're all crooks, too. They sink us in debt and—hey, look at that!"

He pointed at the TV. "There's one now."

CNN International was on the TV, and a breaking news ticker flashed across the bottom of the screen: *Virgin Islands senator pleads to corruption charges...drug trafficking charges dropped.* The screen showed a distinguished-looking man in a white linen suit smiling at the camera as he emerged from a courthouse. The caption read: *Virgin Islands Senator Chanceaux VanderGrift.*

The bartender glanced at the customer, who was leaning forward on his elbows and staring at the TV intently. "See what I mean?" he commented. "They're every—"

"Turn it up."

"What?"

"The TV. Turn it up, please."

The bartender pointed the remote and increased the volume as a reporter began doing a live shot.

"That was the scene earlier today when Senator VanderGrift strode out of a French courtroom after reaching a plea deal with US authorities. In a stunning turn of events, the senator was sentenced to just twenty-four months of house arrest after pleading guilty to a single corruption charge, while charges that he and his son ran a vast cocaine-trafficking operation out of their family-owned marina in St. Thomas—charges that carried a possible life sentence—were dropped."

The bartender noticed the customer's mouth was hanging open and commented on it. "Didn't you hear about that? Made big news last—"

"Quiet! Please." The stranger held his hand up to silence him. "I can't hear."

The bartender shrugged, and they both watched the reporter finish reporting.

"The events leading to today's startling developments began unfolding as tropical storm Tony lashed St. Maarten the week before Thanksgiving 2012. As the storm passed over the island, French authorities responded to reports that a sizable yacht had run aground in Tucker Bay, on the southwest shore. Onboard, the senator's son was found dead of a stab wound to the heart, and at their nearby family estate, both the senator and his ailing mother were found unconscious, the senator suffering from a gunshot wound to the shoulder. Less than thirty minutes later, a vehicle missing from the estate was involved in a spectacular chase and shootout at the Grand Case airport. The chase culminated with an undetermined number of suspects escaping in a stolen jet. The following morning, as authorities attempted to piece it all together, a mangled van was spotted on the side of a mountain less than two miles from the Vandergrift estate. A recovery team managed to rescue the lone occupant, who was identified as international fugitive Rico Cordero after it was discovered the stolen jet belonged to a corporation with ties to Cordero and his brother, Eduardo. The notorious Cordero brothers are the Colombian cocaine kingpins who the DEA charged were the suppliers to Vandergrift's extensive distribution network, believed to involve cruise ships.

It is widely speculated that trafficking charges against the senator were dropped in exchange for his cooperation in the case against Rico Cordero, who is also a suspect in the murder of the senator's son. Complicating matters is the senator's claim that he has no memory of the shooting or the day leading up to it, and his ailing eighty-seven-year-old mother has been unable to provide any meaningful information. What is known is that a giant anaconda believed to have been used for interrogations by the Cordero brothers has been terrorizing islanders ever since that fateful night. Authorities found corroborating evidence that a large snake had been in the van and likely escaped after the crash.

Since recovering from his injuries, Rico Cordero continues to be held at an undisclosed French prison here in the Caribbean while he fights extradition to the United States. Meanwhile, to the dismay of many, Senator Chanceaux "Lucky" VanderGrift once again lives up to his nickname. Just minutes ago he boarded a plane for St. Thomas, where he will begin serving his sentence at his family's luxurious mountaintop villa.

Live from the Caribbean island of St. Maarten, this is Coyote Kelly, reporting for CNN International!"

"I can't believe it," said the customer.

"I know. Who would name their kid Coyote, right?"

"No. Yeah. I mean, uh, what, uh...*when* did he say this happened?"

"A year ago, Thanksgiving. I can't believe you didn't hear about it. It was all over the news."

"I've been on the water."

"I figured."

The big bartender noticed an odd mark on the man's forearm, as he took a long pull from the bottle. The man shook his head and said, "I can't believe she's still alive."

"*She?*"

"The mother."

"Why? What, you *know* her?"

"Something like that."

"Well, let me tell you something, buddy. If she means anything to you, anything at all, you should let her know. I lost a close aunt unexpectedly last year. Never got to tell her what she really meant to me. I won't make the same mistake again. Not just with family, but with friends. Life is short, and death is forever."

"You don't believe in the afterlife?"

"No, but I believe in the after-party."

They shared a laugh, and the customer scratched the four-leaf clover on his forearm as he considered the bartender's philosophical musing. *Hmmm.* Maybe he was right.

Maybe it was time. Then again, maybe not. Maybe he should just let it go. As he rose, he plucked a few bills off the bar, and the bartender asked, "Sure I can't get you another beer?"

"Better not, I noticed the winds starting to pick up. I'm gonna get going."

"Where you headed?"

"Whichever way it blows."

Chapter 7

Mark Slayton was ecstatic to be out of federal prison after serving only three years of a ten-to-twelve-year sentence and let his attorney know it as they drove passed the prison gates. "You're the best, John. God, it's great to be out." He stuck his head out the window of the Mercedes and then playfully punched the attorney in the shoulder. "Where we headed? Club Platinum?"

The attorney shook his head in near disbelief. Near disbelief, because he knew there was no doubt his client meant it.

"Are you crazy? That's what's got you into trouble in the first place. Besides, you need to square up with the firm before you start blowing whatever money you have left. I'm dropping you off at the Holiday Inn."

"The *Holiday Inn?* I haven't been laid in three years, and you're taking me to a Holiday Inn?"

"At least they got a bar. It's either there or Motel 6. Take your pick."

"Shit."

"In the backseat is a duffel bag with a change of clothes and a bottle of scotch."

"What about money? All my credit cards are expired, and I have, like, eighty-seven dollars."

The lawyer reached into his suit pocket and handed him an envelope.

"Here's five hundred bucks. Expect to see it on your final bill along with three nights at the Holiday Inn, courtesy of the firm. The scotch is on me. After that, you're on your own."

Slayton fingered the money and changed his tone. "Thanks, John. I really mean it. I was kidding about going to the strip club, you know that. It's just...I can't believe I'm actually free."

"Well, you can thank Skilling for that. After that maneuver by his attorneys to challenge the sentencing guidelines, we just followed their lead. It was easy to argue that he bankrupted Enron to the tune of billions of dollars. If he was eligible for a reduced sentence, then those convicted of far lesser crimes certainly were, too."

"Not to mention I made restitution."

"*Partial* restitution. Paying back the University of Georgia endowment trust was what got you sprung. You still owe the Teachers' Fund of North Carolina and the International Longshoremen's Association of New Jersey."

"*Me* owe *them?*" He snorted. "I don't think so. I did my time. It was hard enough forking over nearly four million dollars to the Bulldogs. It left me with nothing!"

"If you didn't do it, you'd still be in jail. Seems to me you're forgetting it was their money in the first place."

"Not really. They were one of my early clients. I lost their money a *long* time ago. What I turned over came from the teachers and the longshoremen."

The lawyer turned off the interstate after eyeballing the Holiday Inn sign.

"Yeah, about that. You may not have to worry about the teachers, but you definitely might want to figure out some kind of repayment plan with the longshoremen."

"*Repayment plan?* Didn't you hear me? I did my time. I owe those dumb-ass dockworkers nothing. As far as I'm concerned I got a clean slate. Besides, I got disbarred. How am I supposed to make a living?"

"I don't know, but you don't seem overly concerned."

"Maybe I got a plan."

"That's good, 'cause there's something you should know."

"What's that?"

"That college buddy of yours on the longshoremen's pension board went missing."

"*Missing?* What do you mean...missing?"

"Just what I said. He went milk box. He disappeared. Left work one day and never made it home."

"Since when?"

"A couple of months ago. I just heard about it from a colleague in New York. His face is plastered on a billboard on the Jersey turnpike."

"Doesn't surprise me he decided to disappear. His wife's a bitch, and his kids are spoiled brats."

"You think he disappeared *on purpose?* You don't think it had anything to do with the fact that you stole three million bucks from the longshoremen, and he was the one who helped you do it?"

"First of all, I borrowed it, okay? I was gonna pay it back. Things just, uh, just went wrong. You know? Shit happens."

As they parked in the hotel parking lot, neither man noticed that the Cadillac trailing them since leaving the penitentiary had done so, too. A few minutes later, the lawyer returned to his car after getting his client checked in, and a man stepped out of a Cadillac parked directly behind them. A very *big* man. He pointed at the back window of the Mercedes sedan with its Police Benevolent Society sticker, next to one for the American Bar Association.

"You wouldn't happen to be a lawyer, would you?"

"Sure am. Why?" he leerily asked.

"I noticed the sticker when I parked. I'm looking for an attorney to represent my sister. She got rear-ended on I-75 by a Coke truck."

The attorney's interest was suddenly piqued. "How bad is she hurt?"

"Bad. Real bad. She's paralyzed from the eyebrows down."

"Jesus, I'm sorry to hear that." He wasn't really sorry to hear it. In fact, he was seeing dollar signs.

"Yeah, her patients will be sorry, too."

"Patients?"

"She's a brain surgeon. Does your firm handle cases like this?"

The lawyer practically creamed his pants trying to conceal his excitement. "Absolutely. It's right up our alley." He extended his hand and introduced himself as John Lytle as they shook. As he did so, he added, "You know, I could cancel my next appointment if you'd like to come down to the office and discuss your sister's case."

"You'd do that? Wow, that would be great."

"Excellent, you want to follow me downtown?"

"How about I meet you there? I have something to take care of first. Do you have a card?"

"A card? Sure." He pulled out his wallet and handed him one. "Okay." He nodded and looked at his watch, trying to hide his inner glee. "Why don't we meet at eleven then? Sound good?"

"Sounds great, John."

"You need directions?"

"I got GPS."

"Super. Okay, then, I'll see you there." As he pulled away in the Mercedes he noticed the big man walking toward the hotel entrance. He spun the car around and powered the driver's window down as he pulled up next to him.

"I forgot to ask your name. I need to leave your name, or you'll never get by security."

"Oh, sure. It's Roger Kent."

The attorney scribbled his name on a legal pad and looked up. "What about your sister?"

"What about her?" The eyes behind the off-kilter face flashed a different kind of look. The kind that made the lawyer wonder if he had misjudged the man as being a gentle giant.

"Her, uh, her name. I just, you know, wanted her name."

"Oh, sure...it's Lois."

"Lois Kent?"

"Yep."

"Great. I'll see you in an hour then." As he powered his window up, the big man pointed at him and winked. "Not if I see you first."

The lawyer feigned a laugh and muttered, "Got me there," as the window sealed shut. He looked in his rearview mirror as he drove away, and the big man with the gap-toothed smile was waving him good-bye. He wasn't sure, but he thought he might be retarded or something. It was almost too good to be true—a crippled brain surgeon with a retarded brother and the Coca-Cola Company to blame. The settlement could be worth tens of millions. *Yes!* He hit play on the in-dash CD player, and the whiny pleadings of the lead singer of Maroon Five filled the car. By the time he glanced in the rearview again, Roger Kent was gone.

Chapter 8

Tangles and I left Jamie and Captain Hiram in charge of securing the worthless airplane wreckage and headed to the room we were sharing at Rosie's. My jumbo-size platter of bullshit had runneth over, and I needed to clean up and regroup for the onslaught of questioning that would no doubt take place once we hit the bar. It was only a matter of time before someone checked into my tail number story and discovered it was a sham—not that I really cared. The only thing I cared about was we had wasted an entire day elevator fishing. We were in pelagic paradise and instead of hunting blue marlin and other game fish, we basically conducted a dredging operation. It was shameful.

As I came out of the bathroom toweling off my face, Tangles handed me another bottle of Kalik. "Dude," he said as we clinked bottles and drank. "That spiel you laid down back there was *awesome.* You even had *me* believing we found flight nineteen. Those people ate it up, especially the news guy. You should be one of those infomercial guys. That was frickin' amazing. You could sell slither to a snake."

"Slither to a snake?"

"You know what I mean. I don't know about Jamie, though, he seems a little flustered. He don't know *what* to think."

"Yeah? Well, fuck that beanpole. He wanted to make news, so we made news."

I plopped down on one of the twin beds, and Tangles plopped down on the other, facing me. He was sporting a week's worth of stubble, and I commented on it. "Have I told you you're starting to look like that guy on *Game of Thrones?*"

"Yeah? Which one?" He rubbed his scruffy chin, pondering it.

"Which one do you think? What do they call him… Halfman?"

"C'mon, man. That dude's a deformed dwarf."

"Like I said—"

"Yeah? Well, guess what? Halfman gets a whole lotta pussy."

"Maybe it was a bad comparison then."

"Now, wait just a goddamn—"

My cell phone started blaring Billy Squire, and it startled us. I looked at the display, which read "private caller." "Hello?"

"Mr. Jansen, I see your talent for self-promotion knows no bounds, especially in the factual arena."

This time I had the voice pegged right away. It was unmistakable. It was the voice of the car from the eighties David Hasselhoff TV series, *Knight Rider.* The caller could only be one person, the unknown head of the mysterious government agency we had become involved with who kept his identity hidden by speaking through some sort of voice-changing contraption. He was the man of a million voices, maybe more.

"I thought I asked you not to call me Mr. Jansen."

"And I thought I asked you to keep a low profile after having a Hollywood-style shootout with the French police and then fleeing St. Maarten in the Corderos' stolen jet."

I pointed to my near-empty bottle of Kalik on the nightstand and signaled Tangles to fetch a couple more.

"What can I say? My producer and I aren't exactly seeing eye to eye, and I got a little carried away back at the dock."

"A *little* carried away? You falsely profess to having found a piece of wreckage from flight nineteen and then claim to have both Bob Ballerd *and* the Smithsonian on the phone?"

"Hey, go big or go home, right?"

"Perhaps you should have taken your own advice and gone home."

"I would have...*if I had my own boat!*"

"Calm down, Mr. Jansen. Your new vessel is almost complete."

"*Almost?* Almost as in *when?*"

"We'll get to that in a minute. There was something you said in your most entertaining diatribe that I would like to discuss."

"If it's the part about the navy aeronautical glossary and that T1—"

"Mr. Jansen, please, if I may."

"I was just gonna say that was bullshit, too, in case you didn't know."

"No kidding."

"Right. So, what were you saying?"

"The part about changing the name of your show and traveling to far-flung places trying to unravel mysteries."

"You liked that, did you? *Fishing for Answers with Shagball and Tangles*...nice play on words, right? You gotta admit, that was a stroke of genius."

"A *very* short stroke. Clever, yes, genius, no."

"Tomato, tomahto. The crowd ate it up."

"Then they won't be surprised when it happens."

"When *what* happens?"

"When you change the name of the show and start doing it for real."

"Huh? But I was just bullshitting. There are no plans to—"

"There are now. The name you came up with suits our mission perfectly. Virtually every region of the world has an unsolved mystery that merits investigation. That gives us the perfect cover to be wherever we need to be."

"I told you it was genius."

"Genius isn't accidental."

"Tell that to the guy who invented Reese's Cups."

There was a loud exhale before he spoke again. "Mr. Jansen, please save the amusing quips for your show. What this organization engages in is intelligence gathering at the highest level. You can have all the fun you want on camera, like today for example, but when you're working for me, the fun ends. Lives depend on it—maybe even your own."

"I thought I just had to take some of your agents to wherever, so they could do their thing. What's the big danger in that?"

"Really? Let me ask you a question. Did you think you and your friends were in danger when you got tangled up with Donny Nutz?"

"We didn't know we were dealing with the mob when we queered the marina deal, but it definitely got squatchy."

"Squatchy?"

"It's short for Sasquatch. You know…hairy. Very hairy."

"Cute. How about more recently down in the Caribbean? Did you think it was dangerous crossing the Cordero brothers—the biggest cocaine distributors in the western hemisphere?"

"To tell you the truth, I thought we were goners when we were trapped in that sinking sub. But that was a fluke, snagging the sub with our downrigger."

"Exactly. Twice now you inadvertently got into situations that could have—check that, should have—easily caused your demise."

"What do you think? Third time's the harm?"

"That doesn't even deserve a response."

"Sorry, that was weak. What's your point?"

"My point is, you have managed to place yourself in extremely precarious situations purely by accident. When you work for me, you will be assisting in the gathering of information on terrorists and international criminals of the most the most cunning and devious sort…*on purpose.*"

"Terrorists and international criminals? You didn't mention that before."

"What did you think? We'd be snooping on Greenpeace activists?"

"I, uh, guess I—"

"If you're having second thoughts, it's been suggested I approach Bobby Martino about—"

"Wait a second! Did I say I was having second thoughts? I never have second thoughts."

"I'm willing to let that one go."

"Fuck Bobby Martino! That toothy, gold-chain-wearing bastard, left me stranded forty miles from Key West during the—"

"2008 KDW Offshore Classic?"

"You heard about that?"

"And your borderline psychopathic rivalry with him and his show? Yes. As I told you before, I know everything about you, Mr. Jansen."

"Then you know I hate that sleazy bastard, so why are you trying to get me all worked up?"

"Trying?"

"Whatever."

"Because I figured you wouldn't want him behind the helm of your new boat."

"Behind the helm? Are you kidding? The only place I want him is in my prop wash...in little pieces."

Tangles came waltzing in with a couple more beers and handed me one.

"So when *is* the boat going to be ready?" I added.

"It should be ready for sea trials in about forty-five days...if everything goes according to plans."

"I sure hope so, not having a boat just isn't working for me. If I had one I'd be on my way back to the mainland right now...minus one producer."

"Ah, yes. I hope those feelings are an accurate reflection of your desires."

"Like a Swiss mirror. Why?"

"You're going to have to part ways with Mr. Jamie Alderman. He can't be involved in the new show."

"After today, I say let the parting begin. So you like *Fishing for Answers with Shagball and Tangles?*"

"Yes. It'll be a new show, with a new producer—someone who works for me."

"What about sponsors? You know how hard it is to—"

"I have a company lined up that will be the so-called 'official sponsor,' as far as the public goes. But in reality, *I'm* your sponsor, don't forget that."

"As long as you keep paying the bills, I won't. So, who's the 'official sponsor'?"

"You'll know when you see the boat; it's a surprise until then."

"I hate surprises."

"You won't this time, I assure you. I'm glad to hear you have no problem cutting ties with Mr. Alderman."

"Hey, we had some good times and all, but I guess you could say our working relationship ran its course. I'm curious, though. You said Tangles and Holly were cleared to be part of the new team. Why not Jamie?"

"Well, for one thing, he had no direct involvement or knowledge of either the Donny Nutz affair or your more recent Caribbean adventure, thank God."

"Thank *God?* Why? What's the other thing?"

"He doesn't meet the minimum IQ requirement to be a member of our group."

"I shoulda known anybody as tall as a giraffe would have the brains to match."

"Actually, the giraffe is considered to be quite an intelligent creature."

"Really? If I had a two-foot tongue I wouldn't be using it to eat leaves, that's for sure."

Tangles laughed, and I thought I heard a laugh on the phone, but wasn't sure, because I didn't recall the *Knight Rider* ever laughing.

"Was that a laugh?" I asked.

"I was just clearing my throat."

"Now that I think of it, if you had a two-foot tongue, you could clear your own throat."

"Enough of the tongue talk."

"What's the matter? You getting all worked up?"

"No, just questioning my judgment at this point."

"Hey, once you get me in that new boat, I'll take your guys to places they never dreamed."

"Now you're starting to worry me. I take it that means you're on board with the new plans?"

"I'm on board, buckled up, and my seat's in the upright position."

"Good. Then from one Kitt to another, try and stay out of trouble…at least until the sea trials."

"One Kit to another?"

"You know, the car, the Knight Industries Two Thousand, otherwise known as KITT."

"Oh, right. I wasn't a big fan of the show. Hasselhoff was never my cup of tea."

"The Germans sure love him."

"What does that tell you? The Germans also love deep-dish Jew."

"Has anybody ever told you that you have a tendency to make sweeping characterizations that are borderline racist?"

"Since you know everything about me, you should know I don't care. Being politically correct is for politicians and pussies. I just call it like it is."

"How distastefully refreshing."

"Like a Fresca."

"I'll be in touch soon, Mr. Jansen."

"Can I hear a little Magnum or Mannix next time? Give me a voice I can relate to."

"So, no Chris Matthews or Rachel Maddow?"

"Funny guy—and to think I've been questioning your sense of humor. How 'bout if I say *please?*"

"We'll see."

When I pulled the phone away from my ear, Tangles asked, "What was that all about?"

"Great news, little buddy, the worm has turned."

"No kidding. Dennis Rodman finally had a sex change operation?"

"Funny. No. What I mean is our new boat is just about ready." I smiled and clinked my beer against his before taking a long pull.

"Sweet, I can't wait to check it out."

"Me either, but there's been a slight change in plans for the show."

"Such as?"

"Well, for one, we're changing the name."

"Why? *Fishing on the Edge* is a great name."

"I know, but our benefactor likes the new one better."

"What new one?"

"*Fishing for Answers.*"

"What? I thought you were just talking out your ass, like always."

"I was, but the man of a million voices thinks the new name and concept provide better cover. It gives us reason to be practically anywhere in the world."

"Wow. Be careful what you ask for, I guess. What else?"

"You seen Jamie?"

"Yeah, he's in the bar, and he's not too happy. CNN is now calling our find a well-staged hoax. Anderson Cooper canceled his travel plans."

"Well, boo-fuckin' hoo to that. You think he's unhappy now? Wait till he hears what I have to tell him."

"Which is?"

"We're getting a new boat, we're getting a new show, and we're also getting a new producer. For the record, it wasn't my decision, although I'm not complaining after today's deep-drop fiasco. So, there you have it." I stood up and finished my beer.

"Yowza. You're right about one thing. The old beanpole is gonna be one unhappy camper."

"Yup, like a grizzly pissed on his pork 'n' beans. Obviously, I can't tell him *everything*, so just follow my lead."

"As always. To the bar then?"

"To the bar."

Chapter 9

Franklin Post nestled into his command-center recliner at DICK headquarters on the Puget Sound and hit the speed dial for the forty-third president of the United States of America. Knowing his fondness for the cowboy lifestyle and values, he switched the Oralator to the voice of the late Lorne Greene. A couple thousand miles away at his ranch in Crawford, Texas, the president saw the name "Stargazer" light up on his cell display and answered accordingly.

"Stargazer! How the hell are you? Long time, no hear."

"I'm doing well, sir. Business is good."

"Business is good, huh? I guess that means you bagged another one of them no-good, goat-humping, rag-headed sons of bitches."

"Yes, sir. I wanted to give you a heads up before it hit the papers; I know how much it means to you."

"Damn right it does. Wait a second, that voice you're using, who is that? Hang on, don't tell me. Say something else."

"His name was Abu Khaled-al-Suri, a high ranking Al-Qaida—"

"Pa? Is that really you?"

"Yes, sir, I broke out the old Ben Cartwright in your honor."

"Forget the sir, Stargazer. Just call me 'Little Joe' for the rest of the call, aw' right? Just this once?"

"Yes, sir—I mean, sure, Little Joe, whatever you want."

"Oh, man, this is great! Okay, go ahead and give me the juicy details, and don't leave nothin' out."

"I had one of our overseas DICK agents feed some intel to a rival Islamic group of Al-Qaida based in Syria. They fitted up one of their own with a suicide bomb, and he blew up al-Suri along with a half dozen of his associates. I'm sure the current administration will take credit for it, but trust me when I say they had nothing to do with it."

"Shoot, you don't have to tell *me* twice. Obama's got nothin' to do with nothin' but trying to destroy this once-great country. Only thing he knows how to do is lie and spend, lie and spend. Student debt is over a trillion dollars, we got fifty million people on food stamps, the welfare state's turning into a nation, and now he wants to wave a magic wand and put another thirty million illegal immigrants on the payroll. I'm telling you, he's got no conscious."

"I think you mean conscience. He's got no conscience."

"I know what I mean, Stargazer. When I say he's got no conscious, he's got no conscious. It's like he's in some sort of a feud state."

"I think you mean fugue state, Little Joe."

"Damn, Pa, why you always trying to correct me? I know what the hell I'm talking about. He's in a feud state against the law-abiding, hardworking, tax-paying

American citizens. I guess I oughta throw the Constitution in there, too. He's been feuding with that since day one. Sumbitch had the nerve to accuse me of abusing my executive power and then goes on national TV and says he plans on circumspecting Congress. Even I know you're not supposed to circumspect Congress. You gotta keep 'em in the loop, even if it's the bottom of the loop—you know, the flat part."

"I guess I see your point. His actions have been the epitome of hypocrisy."

"Tell me about it. He also says one thing and does the other. I mean, he actually said he's got a pen and a phone, and he's gonna use 'em to go around Congress. What the hell. The only thing he uses a pen for is writing checks, and the only time he's on the phone is to order *more* checks! *Sheeeit.*"

Franklin Post laughed before conceding, "Go get 'em, Little Joe."

The president exhaled deeply before apologizing. "I'm sorry about that, Pa, but as you know, I've publicly refrained from criticizing Obama and his so-called 'administration' for the last six years. It's been tougher than watching Matt Lauer fill in for Bob Costas during the Olympics. Seriously now, I've done more tongue biting than Miley Cyrus during a hunger strike. You talk about tough!"

"Well, it's a good thing you've kept a low profile. If the current administration ever caught wind about the existence of DICK and how you created it, the repercussions would be unfathomable."

"I don't know about that, but it sure would be mind-bogglin'—like how Obama could keep delaying approval of the Keystone pipeline. I mean, who doesn't want cheap Canadian beer, right?"

"Please tell me you're joking, Little Joe."

"Heh. That was a good one. Everybody knows they make Keystone in Colorado—it's the poor man's Coors. Not that I touch the stuff anymore, no sir. Ol' Dubya's drier than Pelosi's...well, let's just say I think you know what I mean. Hey, did I mention I finally figured out where Obama keeps his jobs plan?"

"No, you didn't. Where? Millions of unemployed Americans would like to know."

"It's obvious. It's on Malaysian Flight 370. Heh. Seriously, he's like the Houdini of jobs. Forget about creating them, he makes them disappear! I'll tell you something else; if Benghazi woulda been on my watch, there'd be a new desert in Africa. I'd call it: Bushwanna. Heh. That's funny because bushes would wanna grow there, but they couldn't. Not for four or five million, billion years, or however long it takes for the atom rays to decompose."

Ever since his first conversation with the former president, Stargazer kept a laugh towel handy so he could gag himself when needed. It was needed. He bit down hard on it and managed to regain his composure as the president shifted subjects.

"So, what else is going on? Whatever happened with those fishing-show guys that broke up that big drug shipment down in the Caribbean?"

"Shagball and Tangles? Funny you should ask. I just got off the phone with Kit Jansen. I took your advice and offered to sponsor his fishing show in exchange for helping DICK do some intelligence gathering in far-flung places. Shagball's girlfriend, Holly, is excellent with computers, and she'll be part of the team, too. We're putting the finishing touches on their new boat right now; it's going to be an amazing vessel."

"You see, Pa? Sometimes it pays to listen to Little Joe and not just big ol' Hoss and your creepy son, Adam. I mean, hell, you even listened to that Kung Fu hand-me-down, Hop Sing, the cook, more than me. What's up with that? Same goes for the ranch fore-man, Candy Canady. Who ever listened to a cowboy named Candy? I swear it was like I didn't even exist sometimes. It hurt, Pa, it really hurt."

"You're just, uh, kidding...right?"

"Heh. Got you again, Stargazer. Damn, I loved that *Bonanza*! Never could figure out why they did a big screen remake of *Starsky and Hutch* and *Wild, Wild, West*, but not *Bonanza*—doesn't make sense."

"Could be that they were both box office flops, and the studios got gun-shy, no pun intended."

"That was a good one, Stargazer. *Of course* they were flops, you don't do a *Starsky and Hutch* movie without that slick cat, David Soul, and you don't give the role of James West to Will Smith. I mean, news-flash, he's James West, not, James West African, know what I mean?"

"I do indeed, sir, I do indeed."

"Oh, well, I can hear the wife hollerin' for me, guess I better get goin'. Sure was good hearing from you. Every time you knock off one of Bin Laden's bud-dies, it makes me happier than a hen in a fox house. When I was prez, the press painted me as someone who never got dick right. If they only knew. Heh. Till next time, Stargazer, keep making me proud."

"Till next time, sir." Click.

Chapter 10

Marzio DeNutzio (aka Roger Kent), circled back to his rental car and pulled out the manila envelope that had the picture of Mark Slayton in it, along with directions to the federal prison. *The Scarf did well,* he thought. Not only had he given him the directions and the picture of Slayton, but he had also arranged the rental car and for an "associate" to supply him with the three items he requested: a shotgun, an automatic pistol with a silencer, and a knife. With confidence he strode through the front doors of the Holiday Inn and up to the front desk. The young man behind the counter wearing a name tag that read "Brent" greeted him.

"Welcome to the Holiday Inn. How may I help you?"

Roger Kent flashed his gap-toothed smile as he held the business card of the attorney out in front of him, careful to keep his large thumb over the name.

"Hi there, I'm Mike Kubicki, of Lytle, Cotter, and Kubicki. My colleague, John Lytle, just checked in a client of ours?"

"Yes, of course, how can I help you?"

He held up the manila envelope and shrugged. "He forgot to get his signature on some paperwork and asked me to get it while he made a call. Can you point me to the elevators?"

"Sure"—he pointed—"Just around the corner to the left."

"Thanks."

"My pleasure."

He took a few steps toward the elevator and slapped his forehead before turning around.

"Oh, crap. What did John say that room number was again?"

The young man's fingers fluttered over the keyboard in front of him, and he quickly responded, "That would be four twenty-three."

He flashed his disarming smile again. "*That's* right. I must be getting old." He chuckled and added, "Thanks again, Brent."

"No problem."

Less than two minutes later he exited the elevator, and Mark Slayton rounded the corner holding an ice bucket. *Bingo.* Slayton paid him little attention while slipping a keycard into the door of his room and pushing it open.

Seizing the opportunity, he called out, "Mark? Mark Slayton?" and closed the distance between them with a few large strides.

Surprised, Slayton turned toward him with a questioning look on his face and quickly sized up the imposing figure in front of him. Slayton wasn't exactly little at six feet and 190, but he gauged the man to be a good four inches taller and fifty to sixty pounds heavier. None of it appeared to be fat. The man wore a pair of slacks and a black V-neck sweater that hugged the bulging muscles of his upper torso tightly. In his left hand he held out a large manila envelope that had "Mark Slayton" written across it. *Was he a courier?*

"What, uh, what do you have there?" he asked.

The man smiled, exposing a gap in his front teeth. He thought his face looked kinda goofy and didn't jibe with the overdeveloped biceps and thick neck.

"What a lucky break to catch you here," he said. "I came a long way to give you this."

"Ooookay." With his back to the door, Slayton reached out apprehensively. Just before his fingers grasped the envelope, the man pulled it back, and the smile vanished when he spoke. "Not that—this."

With stunning speed the man smashed a large fist into his sternum, sending him flying through the doorway. He ended up at the foot of his bed. Ice cubes scattered everywhere as he struggled to catch his breath. The door slammed shut, and the next thing he knew, he was lifted up like a rag doll and thrown across the room. He crashed into a floor lamp and struck his head on the air conditioner. Dazed and bleeding from a cut on his head, he started pleading.

"Stop! Please! Take what you want."

"Oh, I intend to," came the reply. "And then some."

Slayton rolled over and leaned up against the air conditioner. Curiously, his attacker made no move to grab his wallet, which was sitting on top of the TV in plain sight.

"Go ahead, take my wallet there on the TV, just take it and leave...please just leave me alone.

Here"—He removed his wristwatch and tossed it on the bed—"You can have my watch, too. It's a Bulova. You can get a couple hundred for it."

The man casually picked the watch off the bed and inspected it. "Wow…A *Bulova?* Are you kidding me? Fuckin' watch doesn't even have numbers on it. Lot a good that does—might be good for Stevie Wonder. Do I look like Stevie Wonder to you?" Slayton watched in disbelief as he dropped it on the floor and stomped it with the heel of his shoe, crushing it along with a couple of ice cubes.

"What do you—what do you want from me then? Who are you? What are you doing here?"

"That's a lot of questions, Mark. Hey, that's pretty funny—questions Mark. Get it?"

Even though the big man laughed, it did little to quell the uneasy feeling in Mark Slayton's stomach. Despite the situation he was in, his lawyerly instincts took over, and he did what he did best: he started talking. "Do I know you? I would have remembered if you were a client of mine. Let's talk this out. I'm sure we can resolve whatever the problem is here without any more violence." He eyed the chair in the corner next to him and added, "Mind if I have a seat?"

"Not at all. Here, take this one." The man snatched up a chair on the other side of the bed and threw it at him.

He put his hands up to deflect it and yelled, "No!" But it was too late. The chair somersaulted through the air, and one of the legs nailed him right in the balls. As the chair clattered to the floor, he curled up and massaged his throbbing 'nads. "Jesus, stop! Please! Will you? What did I do to you?"

"It's not so much what you did to *me*, it's what you did to my brothers in the four-one."

"The four-one? What the hell's that?"

"Maybe you remember them better as part of the International Longshoremen's Association of New Jersey. Ring any bells now? You know, like *three million bells*?"

Mark Slayton knew he was in deep shit, but the realization of who the big man represented struck a new chord of fear in him. "Oh, fuck me," he muttered.

"You don't take me to where you got the loot stashed, I just might."

"I, I just got out. I got nothing. Please. I'll pay it back with interest, I swear, I just need some time."

"That's the wrong answer, Mark. The time for pay-back is *now*. If you don't got the money, you gotta pay the piper. Care to guess who's leading the band?" He put his foot up on the credenza and pulled out a glistening double-edged knife from an ankle sheath. Slayton actually felt his asshole quiver and realized it was high time to play his hole card.

"Wait! I can get it. I can get you the money."

"You just said you didn't have any."

"I don't, but I can get it."

"Explain."

"My wife has some money."

"*What* wife? You're still married?"

"Yes, and half of whatever she has is mine."

"You said she has some money. How much? I expect three million, plus a little something for the effort."

"She can swing it."

Slayton watched as the big man rubbed his chin before shaking his head.

"You're a fuckin' liar. If you were still married, she woulda picked you up from the joint, and you wouldn't be here." He raised the knife and took a step forward. Slayton raised his hands again and rapidly pleaded his case.

"No! It's true! She didn't pick me up because she doesn't live here anymore. She moved away, but we're still married. Like I said, half of what she has is mine… and it's a lot. I can repay you, I swear."

The big man hovered over him and switched the knife from hand to hand. "If you're lying to me I—"

"I'm not! It's true!"

"So where *is* this rich bitch of a wife?"

"She moved to Florida."

"*Florida?* You don't say. Well, guess what, I happen to be headed that way. Looks like you and me's takin' a little road trip." He reached down and snatched up the cowering lawyer by his throat, eliciting a few gasps in the process. In a shocking display of strength, he continued to lift him until he was four inches off the ground.

"I…I can't breathe."

The big man looked him square in the eye and smiled. With his gapped front teeth, he thought he looked like the *Leave It to Beaver* kid under demonic possession. He would never mistake him for being goofy again. *Ever.*

"Get used to it," the big man whispered. "You try to run or scream for help, and I'll carve you up like it's Thanksgiving at OJ's…unnerstand?"

The most he could manage was a petrified nod, and when the big man set him down, his knees buckled like a Bolivian bridge in a mudslide.

Chapter 11

We passed the docks on the way to the bar, and I noticed a familiar face in the cockpit of a thirty-six foot Tiara. It was one of my old buddies—a charter captain who worked out of Sailfish Marina in Palm Beach. He was dumping some ice into a fish box, and I surprised him when I called out his name.

"Hollywood!" I nicknamed him Hollywood because he was a dead ringer for the actor Christian Bale, with a little more meat on his bones. Needless to say, he was a big hit with the ladies, and most of the other charter captains secretly hated him for it. The thing was, you couldn't help but like him, and you *had* to respect his ability to raise fish. He was relentless on the water, and he was good—real good. He looked up and tilted his sunglasses down before recognizing me.

"Shaggy! What's up? Still living the dream?"

"Oh, you know, dream, nightmare, whatever…I am living."

Tangles stepped out from behind me, and Hollywood said, "You got the little guy with you? It's about time I met him." He held up a Budweiser and added, "How 'bout a beer? C'mon down."

We hopped aboard, and I introduced him to Tangles. I said, "Tangles, this is Hollywood, a good buddy of mine from back in the day." As they shook hands, I continued. "Hollywood, this is Tangles, my pint-size protégé and first mate extraordinaire."

Hollywood eyeballed Tangles and said, "Love the show. I can't believe it, you're not a midget at all, you're like, uh, a real person, only, uh…only not."

"*What?*"

"I mean, you know, what I meant to say was, you're not, uh, like the size of a real—I mean, normal, er, *average* person."

Tangles looked at me with a blank expression on his face. "Why am I not surprised he's a friend of yours?"

"Dude, I didn't mean anything by that—sorry," responded Hollywood before adding, "How 'bout that beer?" He handed us both a beer and looked at Tangles. "We good?"

"Good as in done with the awkward dissertation in regards to my statutory nature?"

"Yeah. Like I said, sorry about that. I've seen the show, dude. You can mate for me anytime."

I raised my beer and said, "Now that that's settled, good seeing you, bro."

He raised his beer, and as we clinked cans, he said, "You, too. And it's good to finally meet you, Tangles."

He clinked cans with Tangles, and after we all took a pull, I asked, "What's in the fish box?"

Hollywood bent down and opened it up to display a pair of forty pound wahoo and a big yellowfin tuna.

"Nice," commented Tangles. "That's what we should have been doing this morning."

"That's for sure," I agreed. "I take it you're working a charter?"

"I was," answered Hollywood. "They flew out of Spanish Cay on a private plane this morning. I'm taking the boat back myself. As soon as I get fueled up, I'm out of here."

I thought about my pending confrontation with Jamie and saw an opportunity for a clean break. "How would you like some company?"

"Are you kidding? That'd be great, but what happened to filming?"

"You didn't hear about what we pulled up today?"

"No, I just got here."

"It was a fiasco. I'll tell you about it on the ride. Bottom line is my producer's in the bar, and I'm headed in there to tell him me and Tangles are quitting the show."

"Are you serious? You sure you wanna do that?"

"Don't worry. We have a bigger and better show lined up with somebody else."

"Good, it's the only fishing show I watch. I'd hate to see it end."

"No worries, we'll be back on the boob tube soon." I looked at Tangles.

"How 'bout loading our gear on board, while I drop the bomb on Jamie."

"Works for me," he nodded, and then hopped up on the gunwale and onto the dock. I did the same and then turned back to Hollywood.

"This shouldn't take long."

He pointed at me and smiled. "That's what she said."

One thing about Jamie, he isn't hard to spot. All six foot nine of him was engaged in animated conversation with the bartender and a customer who was pointing at the TV behind the bar. Jamie had his back to me and his hands up in the air in a defensive position.

"I was there," he pleaded. "It wasn't a hoax! I thought we found flight nineteen, too, everybody did!"

I slapped him on the back and said, "Not everybody."

"I knew it!" said the customer. I recognized him as being one of the skeptics during my impromptu press conference.

"What can I say? Sometimes I get a little carried away on camera."

"A little—a *little* carried away?" stammered Jamie. "You mean, you knew all long it was—it was just, just—"

"Bullshit? Yeah, pretty much. I mean, once Captain Hiram dropped the tailpiece, and another number was exposed, I figured, so much for that. That's when I really let it fly, no pun intended."

"How the fuck was I supposed to know? Jesus, Shag! You mean all that T1 interchange stuff—"

"Total bullshit, I made it all up. You don't need to be Emilio Earhart to know that—especially you, of all people."

"You fuckhead. I guess I don't have to ask about the calls from the Smithsonian and Bob Ballerd."

"You're a quick study, Jamie. Don't ever forget that, no matter *what* the IQ test says."

"*What?*"

The bartender started laughing, and I hit him up for a beer. When he handed it to me, I nodded at Jamie, and told the bartender to put it on his tab. "In fact," I added, "My producer wants to buy everybody in the bar a drink, isn't that right, Jamie?"

Jamie didn't like to spring for spit. It was written all over his face as he did a quick headcount and hissed at me. "There's gotta be fifty people in here, asshole. *You* buy the drinks."

"What's that?" asked the bartender.

I pointed at a bikini-clad patron and told Jamie to check out her rack. When he turned his head, I stepped forward and leaned over the bar. Under my breath, I replied, "He said he'll buy drinks for fifty people. Start pouring."

The bartender smiled and started working his way down the bar. As Jamie turned to face me, he was commenting on the girl's lovely assets.

"I'd like to take those sweater puppies to the bark park in my pants. Wow! What a pair of—" Suddenly his smile was gone, and he looked worried. "What did you tell him, Shag?"

"Tell who?"

"The bartender! Who do you think? He just gave me a thumbs-up. I better not be buying drinks."

"Relax, will you? I told him we're gonna find flight nineteen, come hell or high water."

"Really? You said that? You think we can find it?"

"Absolutely, you know why?"

"Why?"

"'Cause we got a *Lectra-Reel!*" I clinked my bottle of Kalik against his and took a big swig.

He eyed me skeptically. "I thought you didn't like using it."

"That was before I realized its dredging potential. We attach the proper getup to that baby, and the sky's the—or should I say, the ocean floor—is the limit. Power down, drag and dredge, power up...and boom! Another mystery solved. You never know. Maybe flight nineteen crashed on top of Atlantis, and we'll get a twofer."

A sea of red-faced fury washed the skepticism off his face in record time. He really *was* a quick study.

"You fuckin' asshole!" He was fuming. "Why do you keep bashing Lectra-Reel? They're *paying* for this trip!"

I pointed at the bartender who was at the other end of the bar and was pouring drinks like he was auditioning for *Cocktail II*. "The drinks, too?"

"*What?*"

"I'm thinking as long as Lectra-Reel is paying, you should have you're favorite drink. You know, the one with the umbrella in it, the peniscolada."

"I swear to God, if those drinks are on—"

"Be sure to ask for a Meyer's floater, the more rum the better. Hides the penis taste."

"I don't want a peniscolada!"

Conversations stopped, and nearly everybody turned to look at the tall red-faced man who was clearly flustered.

I put my hand up sideways to my mouth and addressed the curious onlookers. "You should see what he does with the cherries."

The bartender worked his way back, and when I ordered another beer, Jamie tried to wave him off.

"No more beers, Shag, we're going back out. Captain Hiram wants to work the area where we found the wreckage. He still thinks flight nineteen could be nearby."

I held up my empty beer for the bartender to see.

"Don't listen to him, he's delusional. Just bring me a beer, thanks."

As the bartender handed me another, Jamie shook his head. "Goddammit, Shag! I'm serious. We're gonna film this afternoon, and I want you acting professional for a change."

"What's with all this 'professional' talk, all of a sudden? You expect me to be serious while I'm pushing buttons on that goddamned contraption they have the nerve to call a reel? Like *that's* fishing? Are you kidding me?"

"It's called the Lectra-Reel, asshole. Power fishing—it's the wave of the future."

"You know what else is the wave of the future?"

"What?"

I waved my hand in front of his face and answered, "This one. It's called waving good-bye. I quit."

"Yeah, right."

"And I'm taking my midget, too." I drained the rest of my beer.

Jamie looked down at me in an accusatory manner. "Are you *serious?*" Suddenly he didn't sound so confident.

"Yup."

"Fuckin' Tangles is in on it, too?"

"No, the *other* midget I have in my carry-on, what do you think? Jesus, I don't know how I put up with you this long. See ya!"

I brushed past him, and he started blabbering as he followed.

"You can't quit! You're under contract! We have a contract! What do—?"

One of the bar managers appeared out of nowhere and stepped in front of Jamie to prevent him from leaving. "Excuse me, sir," I heard him say as I strode into the welcoming sunlight. "I need you to settle your rather extensive bar tab before leaving. It'll only take a minute."

Chapter 12

Senator Chanceaux "Lucky" VanderGrift cursed his ankle monitor for the umpteenth time since being sentenced to house arrest. Even though he knew he got a sweet deal for agreeing to testify against the Cordero brothers, the confinement was cramping his style. To make matters worse, his ailing eighty-seven-year-old mother had put his beloved Tiara Bay Marina and the hilltop villa in St. Thomas where he was serving his sentence up for sale. Unthinkably, even the staff was let go. While drinking a glass of orange juice, he contemplated how he was going to rebuild his fortune after the impending trial, finally admitting to himself that his reputation was beyond repair. He would no doubt go down in the annals of political history as being one of the most corrupt politicians ever, anywhere at any time. Without a single bulb of inspiration to lighten his gloomy mood, he turned on the TV. Images of police cars and chaos in the streets filled the screen before cutting away to a young reporter for CNN International who excitedly broke the story.

"That was the scene on the streets of Guadeloupe last night after dozens of dangerous criminals escaped from the notorious Basse-Terre prison during the island's annual

Bastille Day festival. The prisoners escaped when a front-end loader being used in an expansion project for the famously overcrowded prison was instead used to knock down prison walls. After a significant section of the three-hundred-and-fifty-year-old prison came crumbling down, the front-end loader was then used to drive through two sets of barbed-wire fence."

The senator shook his head in amazement at the video of the crumbled prison walls and destroyed fencing as the reporter continued.

"Already undermanned and hampered in pursuit of the escapees due to streets filled with parading residents, French authorities contacted their US counterparts when reports surfaced that a helicopter landed during the mayhem and whisked away infamous Colombian drug lord Rico Cordero."

The senator nervously glanced at the open doors leading to the veranda and quickly crossed the room to shut them as the news report continued.

"A short time later, residents of the small neighboring island of Terre-de-Haut reported an explosion at an airstrip followed by a window-rattling takeoff of a darkened jet. When DEA agents arrived, they found the charred skeletal frame of the helicopter thought to have been used in the escape along with the body of a tower guard from the Basse-Terre prison who was believed to have been an accomplice. The fleeing jet was intercepted approximately seventy miles northeast of Aruba by a pair of US fighter jets dispatched from an aircraft carrier conducting exercises in the central Caribbean. The tail numbers identified the jet as belonging to hip-hop star Akorn who reported it stolen the day before while performing at a music festival on Montserrat. After repeated attempts to establish contact with the pilot failed, and after ignoring instructions to change course, the jet was shot down just

twenty-five miles off the coast of the Colombia/Venezuela border."

"Yes!" The senator pumped his fist in the air before turning up the volume with the remote. He muttered, "This is fantastic," before once again focusing on the news report.

"*Although a perfunctory search by the US Coast Guard is underway at this time, experts agree the chance of finding any survivors is nearly nonexistent and that the bodies of those on board may never be recovered. It would seem to be a fitting end for Rico "The Freako" Cordero, a ruthless and savage drug lord who grew up idolizing Pablo Escobar and is rumored to have taken his love for exotic animals to a level that is both illegal and immoral in virtually every country in the free world. The timing of the escape, which is believed to have been masterminded by Rico's brother Eduardo, should come as no surprise to prison officials. Cordero was scheduled to appear in federal court in Miami next week for the start of his racketeering and international drug-trafficking trial. Cordero's suspected death seems to be another fortuitous break for disgraced US Virgin Islands Senator Chanceaux "Lucky" VanderGrift, who agreed to testify against Cordero in exchange for a sentence of two-year's house arrest—a plea deal that has widely been described as being a complete miscarriage of justice. VanderGrift, as you may recall, was charged with using his family-owned marina on St. Thomas to move cocaine supplied by the Cordero brothers onto cruise ships, where it was distributed throughout the Caribbean basin and beyond. Reporting for CNN International, this is Coyote—*"

The senator turned off the TV and ran his fingers through his salt-and-pepper hair. *This is unbelievable,* he thought. He had been dreading the trial in Miami and was more than slightly concerned about his personal well-being, given the Cordero brothers' fearsome reputation. Now, well, everything had changed. *No more Rico, no more court...right?* He chuckled out loud just as the buzzer for the front gate sounded. It startled him for a moment, but as he looked out the window past the For Sale sign in the front yard, he remembered there was a showing scheduled for eleven. He looked at his watch, and it was ten thirty. *Fucking realtors.* He pressed the intercom and voiced his displeasure to the occupant of the Mercedes parked at the gate.

"It's only ten thirty; you're not supposed to be here until eleven."

There was a slight pause, and the speaker sounded confused. "Eleven?"

"Yes, eleven. It's halfway between ten and twelve. You're a half hour early to show the house. You guys are never on time."

"Oh, sorry."

"I bet. Lucky for you I'm in a good mood." He pressed the button to open the gate and added, "The front door will be open, and I'll be in the library if you need me."

"Thanks."

A few minutes later he looked up from his desk as a beefy Latino-looking man nonchalantly opened the library door and walked in.

Strange...he doesn't look like a realtor. "What, you forgot how to knock?" he asked, rising to his feet.

"No."

"So what are you smiling about? Your client make a decent offer? Good for you. My mother will be happy, the old bitch."

A second man carrying a briefcase entered the room. Every hair on the senator's body stood up a split second before he soiled his Bermuda shorts. The senator had trouble facing the fact that he was looking at Rico Cordero in all his hideous glory. He wore a guerilla-style beret pulled over his gnarled head in an attempt to hide the disfiguring scars that a pissed-off mama tiger inflicted on him while he was assaulting one of her cubs. Rico nudged the other man and pointed at the senator's crotch.

"Manny, look. He's so excited to see me, he wet himself." They both laughed as the senator sat back down in his chair, scared and embarrassed at the same time. If he hadn't been so stunned, the senator would have immediately gone for the gun he had in a desk drawer. Instead, before he had a chance to react, the smile disappeared from Rico's face, and he said, "Tie him up."

Rico stepped forward and opened the briefcase on the desk so that the senator couldn't see what was inside. The senator's eyes glanced at the drawer that held the .38 special, but when he looked up at Rico, Rico warned, "Don't even *think* about it."

The senator slumped in his chair as Manny pulled some zip ties and a roll of duct tape out of the briefcase.

As Manny started tying him up, the senator tried to make sense of the situation. "But I...I just saw the news. You're—they said you were dead."

"Then you have nothing to worry about...if you believe everything you see on TV." Rico smiled, and the senator winced. *Jesus was he ugly.*

"But what about...what about the plane?"

"A decoy. Eduardo correctly anticipated the stupid Americanos would chase after the plane like a hungry dog after a garbage truck. While they did so, I came here by speedboat. One stop in St. Kitts to refuel, and here we are. It was nice of you to let us in. Extremely stupid, but nice. I love it when a plan comes together. Don't you?"

Manny finished tying and taping the senator and looked at Rico.

"You want me to tape his mouth?"

"Not yet." Rico pulled one of those ultrathin, transparent painter's jumpsuits, out of the briefcase, and started putting it on.

The senator instinctively struggled against the restraints and stammered, "What're you doing? What are you planning to do to me?"

Rico stopped zipping up the jumpsuit long enough to lower his menacing gaze at the frightened senator.

"As you are well aware, the price for crossing the Cordero brothers is death. The only question is how long and painful it will be. Under normal circumstances, you would already be dead by now, but these are not normal circumstances. Not only have you crossed us, you made a deal to testify against us. While I was made to suffer in a godforsaken Guadeloupian prison, facing a life sentence, you have been living in the lap of luxury counting down the days until your freedom. By now, you know that day will never come."

"But I—"

"Shut up!" Rico backhanded the senator so hard, he dislodged a tooth and sent his reading glasses flying. "You have a lot of 'splaining to do, and I've had much time to dream up new ways to motivate you to tell the truth. Since you are a politician, I know how hard that must be. That is why Eduardo and I feel you will be more forthcoming in different surroundings, like...oh, I don't know...maybe in our private zoo."

"*Zoo?* What are you talking about—*zoo?*"

"You're coming back to Colombia with us, but don't worry, you don't need a passport." Manny and Rico both laughed.

It took a moment for the senator to realize he was serious, and the fear factor rose exponentially.

"No, no, you can't be serious. *Please!* I have a medical condition! I need my medications! Wait! You can't take me. I'm on house arrest. I have an ankle monitor. If I leave the premises, the police will find us before we even get off the island."

Rico smiled and rubbed his hands together. "I think you mean 'if the ankle monitor leaves the premises.' No?"

He cocked his head at Manny and added, "*Now* tape his mouth shut."

As Manny tore off a piece of tape, the senator, momentarily confused, said, "What's the diff—?"

Manny slapped the tape over his mouth, and the senator's eyes bugged out when Rico extracted a hacksaw and mini-blowtorch from the briefcase. In full panic mode now, his muffled screams went ignored.

Rico held up the hacksaw and grinned. "What's the diff? You're about to find out the hard way. We're not *taking* the ankle monitor. I tell you, my brother Eduardo is a fucking genius. He thinks of *everything.*"

Chapter 13

As we rounded West End Bahamas and began our crossing to Palm Beach, we were all struck by the utter lack of wind and the amazingly flat ocean surface, which appeared mirrorlike. Hollywood was driving the Tiara from the half tower, and he shouted down to me and Tangles in the cockpit, "It's like a lake out here!"

We nodded in agreement, and I shot him a thumbs-up. Hollywood throttled back so we could hear him better, and he turned to face us. "If it's this flat when we get to the gulfstream, why don't we fish for a little while? I picked up a new lure at Tuppen's I'd like to test out. You two aren't in any particular hurry, are you?"

I answered for both of us, as I was prone to do. "Hell no, let's drag it around and see what we can scare up. It'll be just like the old days."

"Excellent. I have some rigged ballyhoo, too. Hang on, my brothers, I'm gonna double-time it out to the fishing grounds."

Hollywood hammered the throttles, and we skimmed across the ocean like we were on a greased sled. Every so often, some flying fish took to the air and veered off to either side of the boat in an effort to not meet a premature fiberglass-induced death. After forty minutes, he throttled down again, and we coasted forward in near silence. Hollywood had his hands up under his visor to block the sun as he peered intently to port.

"What is it?" I asked. "You see a nice weed line or some birds or something?"

"I thought I saw a reflection or—there!" He pointed as he spoke. "Ten o'clock. There it is again. Something's flashing. Shaggy, there's a pair of binoculars hanging on a hook inside the cabin door. Can you toss 'em up?"

"Sure." I slid open the cabin door, and as I grabbed the binoculars, I noted Tangles snoozing on the couch. I quickly tossed them up to Hollywood, and he lowered his sunglasses before peering out the 'nocs.

"Shit," he muttered.

"What is it?"

"There's a boat with a tattered sail that's dead in the water, and it looks like someone's signaling us with a mirror or something. Fishing's gonna have to wait. Crap."

Hollywood tossed the 'nocs down to me and altered course as he throttled up again. When I hung the 'nocs on the hook inside the cabin door, Tangles rolled over and asked what was going on.

"There's a boat dead in the water, and we're going to check it out."

"Great. I'm gonna take a dump."

"Thanks for sharing that with me." I slid the door shut and shook my head.

A few minutes later, we slowly approached the sailboat, which appeared to be virtually motionless in the water. You didn't have to be a subscriber to *Yachting* magazine to realize it was a pricy sloop. Everything about it oozed luxury; from the teak decking, to the gleaming railing, to the impeccably lustrous paint job. Everything but the sail and rigging, that is, which was a mess. I looked around, and there was no land to be seen in any direction. With the oppressive heat, a haze hung over the water, and the whole setting took on an eerie feeling. I didn't see anyone on the sailboat and voiced my concern to Hollywood.

"I thought you said someone was sending you a signal."

"I thought I saw—wait a second, there's a small mirror taped to the railing. Hello! Hello! Anybody there?!"

I yelled, too, but nobody answered. "What do you think?" I asked.

"I'm gonna pull alongside. Why don't you hop aboard and check out the cabin."

"Really?" I wasn't too keen on the idea of jumping on someone else's boat in the middle of the ocean without permission.

"Yeah, somebody might be inside, maybe injured or something. You never know."

Hollywood navigated us next to the sailboat, which was about the same size as the Tiara, and I hollered out one more time before jumping aboard. As soon as I hit the deck, the cabin door popped open, and I was looking down the barrel of a shotgun. *Fuck me.* From the angle he was at on the tower, Hollywood couldn't see what I was looking at. I backpedaled a step, and my eyes never left what appeared to be a twelve-gauge barrel. I couldn't see the face of whoever was holding the shotgun, as it stayed shrouded in the darkness of the cabin, but the voice sounded oddly familiar.

"Jump in the water, asshole," the voice hissed.

"What?"

"Jump in the fucking water, or your head's gonna beat you to it."

"What's going on?" asked Hollywood. "Is somebody there?"

I didn't dare chance an answer and dove into the ocean as ordered. I held my prescription Ray-Bans tight to my face before letting them dangle on their safety straps as I swam under water. I held my breath about as long as I could, until I thought I was out of lethal range, maybe fifty feet from the stern. When I surfaced, the guy was pointing the shotgun at Hollywood and yelling for him to cut the engines. I couldn't place where I had heard his voice before and slipped my sunglasses back on to see if I recognized him. Hollywood cut the engines, and the guy jumped from the sailboat into the cockpit of the Tiara. I swam a little closer to get a better look as he kept the gun pointed at Hollywood on the tower.

"Jump in the water with your buddy, asshole. Jump, or I'll blow your fucking dick off."

Hollywood put his hands up and tried to reason with him. "Dude, what the fuck are you—?"

"I said JUMP!" The guy chambered a round with the pump action on the shotgun, but before he could resteady his aim, Hollywood snatched his sunglasses off his face and dove off the tower. The guy pointed the shotgun at Hollywood's wake as he swam underwater toward me.

When I got a good look at the guy's face, I couldn't believe my eyes. *It was McGirt!* McGirt turned toward the cabin door just as Hollywood broke the surface next to me. I didn't know if Tangles was still taking a dump but decided it would be prudent to buy him some more time. I shouted, "Hey, McGirt! I guess you sail about as well as you run a sub!" He spun around and stepped to the stern.

"Who the fuck are *you?*" he asked, as he pointed the shotgun at me and squinted.

"I'm the one who foul-hooked your sub last year, down in the Caribbean. You know, the one with the special cargo?"

As we both treaded water, Hollywood whispered in my ear, "You *know* this guy?"

"Unfortunately," I whispered back.

McGirt sounded as incredulous to see me as I was to see him.

"*You?* It's *you* again? I shoulda blown your fucking head off, all the trouble you caused me. What's that stupid name of yours…Scumball?"

"It's Shagball."

"Right. Well, guess what, Scumball. I ain't got time to reminisce right now on account of being thirsty. Haven't had a thing to drink in nearly three days. I need water, lots of—Wait a second! Where's that little monkey that was running around with you? What was his name? Shingles?" The cabin door slid open, and McGirt must have heard it because he spun around. He was a tad too late, though, and Tangles fired a flare gun into the side McGirt's chest. The force sent him over the stern, onto the swim platform, and into the water. He let out a scream before the ocean swallowed it up along with the shotgun. Hollywood and I swam toward McGirt. Just as we reached him, Tangles jumped up on the gunwale and pointed the smoking flare gun down at McGirt.

"The name's Tangles, dickhead...best not forget it."

McGirt was struggling to stay afloat, because he had one hand probing the singed hole in his side. Hollywood grabbed one arm, and I grabbed the other, and we managed to get him back to the swim platform. Tangles hopped down and lowered the ladder, and in between gasps of pain, McGirt sounded shocked as he looked up at him. "You, you, shot me... aaagh!"

"Well la-di-fuckin'-da to that. You hijacked and blew up our boat then left us for dead. Now you're trying to do it again, like you're making a career out of it." Tangles looked at me and added, "Can I drop the anchor on his head? Please?"

"No way, not until I show him how much I miss the *Lucky Dog.*"

"I didn't—aaagh! I didn't blow up the boat, it... aaagh! It blew *me* up."

"Oh, that's okay then. I feel so much better. Not." I gave him a vicious elbow to the nose, and it broke like Octomom's water. Blood started gushing like it was coming out a spigot. I climbed onto the swim platform, and Tangles helped me pull up McGirt while Hollywood shoved on his skinny ass. Once we had him in the cockpit, Hollywood climbed aboard and said,

"Put him in the corner by the scuppers. I don't want him bleeding all over the place."

We propped him up in the corner, and then I ripped open his shirt to survey the damage from the flare gun. "Huh, it doesn't look too bad. Probably a good thing you doused it so quick."

"Fuck you. You broke my nose." He used his grimy T-shirt to try and stanch the flow of blood. "C'mon, man, give me some water. *Please.* I'm dying here." I tossed him a rag, and he shoved it up his nose.

I told Tangles to get him some water, and he began to protest, but I cut him off. Reluctantly, he disappeared into the cabin and came back with a bottle of water for everyone. McGirt chugged his down in record time and let out a big sigh of relief as he winced in pain.

"God, I love water. I wasn't sure anybody would ever spot us. A first-aid kit. I need—"

Hollywood beat me to it. "*Us?* What do you mean, *us?*"

"Oh, yeah, there's a lovey-dovey couple tied up below deck. I sorta borrowed their boat."

The three of us said it at the same time. *"What?!"*

Everybody but McGirt turned to look at the sailboat, which had drifted a couple hundred yards away. Hollywood scrambled up to the tower and fired up the engines.

"Hey, I got a hole in my side, and I'm bleeding like a stuck pig. How 'bout that first-aid kit and another bottle of water."

"Let me tell you something, McDirt. If those people are hurt you're a dead man. You understand what I'm saying?"

"Yeah, sure…right."

I told Tangles to get some more water and the first-aid kit, and he protested again, as I knew he would.

"But—"

"Not for him, for whoever's on the sailboat."

"Got it."

Tangles set some water and the first-aid kit on one of the lower helm seats and then helped me tie off to the sailboat. Hollywood jumped aboard and disappeared into the cabin. Less than a minute later, he popped his head out. "I just cut them loose. They're shook up and dehydrated but otherwise look okay. Toss me some water." Tangles tossed him a couple of bottles, and he disappeared into the cabin again.

McGirt said, "Hey, Shingles, save one for me."

I reached down and grabbed him by the throat. As he clawed to try to dislodge my hand, I punched him right in the kisser, a half inch right of the center of his chin. His head snapped down and then up, and his eyes started to roll back in his head.

"That's for messing up our fishing plans, asshole." He shook his head, and as his eyes started to regain their focus, I grabbed him by the throat again. "And this is for sinking my boat." I punched him in the same spot, and this time it knocked him out cold. As I stepped back to admire my handiwork, Tangles started blasting McGirt with the saltwater washdown hose.

"Good idea." I nodded. "Wash the blood down the scuppers." Tangles sprayed him in the face, and McGirt came to and began rubbing his chin.

"Fuck," he moaned. "I think my jaw's—"

Without warning, Tangles flashed by like Adam Vinateri attempting a fifty-yard field goal and kicked McGirt solidly in the ribs. McGirt gasped for air as he curled up in the corner of the cockpit, and after a few moments he said, "Enough, already! Aaagh...what— what was that for?"

"That was for interrupting me on the crapper when I got the conch chowder blues. So, can you tell I've been watching World Cup soccer? Pretty good corner kick, right?"

Chapter 14

Hollywood came out of the cabin of the sailboat followed by a shirtless, tattooed guy in surfer's trunks. He was wearing a headband that unsuccessfully tried to rein in a scraggly mop of black hair. Call it demographic profiling, but he didn't fit the image of who I pictured might be the owner of that boat. He followed Hollywood by hopping onto the gunwale of the Tiara and into the cockpit. Hollywood looked at Tangles and said, "Why don't you help the girl when she comes out of the bathroom, she was pretty shaken up."

"Will do, skipper." As Tangles jumped onto the sailboat, Hollywood turned to me as he slid open the cabin door.

"Be right back, just gotta hit the head."

I pointed at the name written across the stern of the gleaming sloop, which read, *Downtime*/Bahamas. "Is the boat yours?" I asked.

He brushed the hair out of his face, and I could see he was sporting a small goatee and mustache. *Why did he look familiar?*

"Yeah, man. I can't thank you guys enough for coming along when you did." He pointed at the beaten and bloody McGirt in the corner. "I think that dude was gonna kill us or leave us to die."

"You're right, that's his MO." When he pointed, I noticed he had a tattoo of a sparrow over water on his forearm with the word "Jack," and on his bicep, he had inked "Wino Forever"...*Strange.*

"You know the bloody scoundrel?" he asked.

"Unfortunately, yes, we had a run-in with him last year, too."

"He's a snake, that one. Slithered onto me boat when me and my...uh...my friend were snorkeling."

"He's a real weasel." I nodded in agreement.

"Aye, which makes him the dreaded sneasel, lowest of the low. I say we make him walk the plank. What say ye?"

"What say ye? Why are you going all piratey on me? Wait a second..."

McGirt pointed at him and said something, but the words came out garbled. His nose was lying sideways on his face, clogged with blood, and his jaw was swollen and possibly broken. I crouched down in front of him and said, "Didn't your mother teach you it's rude to interrupt?" Then I punched him in the chin again, knocking him out for the second time.

Hollywood came out of the cabin and set a couple bottles of water down before wiping his sunglasses off with a paper towel.

"Hollywood, doesn't he look familiar?" I shot a thumb sideways at the tattooed oddball and took the paper towel from Hollywood as he slid his sunglasses back on. I began cleaning the salty crust that had formed on my own glasses as tattoo-boy turned to

Hollywood and said, "Think movies." He framed his face with his hands and gave Hollywood a goofy, raised-eyebrow look.

"Movies?" Hollywood asked.

"Yeah, you know, the cinema? Motion pictures? Picture a rakish hat on me head and a sword on me swashbuckling belt." Missing the prompt answer he expected, he threw his hands down in disbelief and glanced at me as I put my shades back on. "Are you serious? You guys never been to the movies or what?" My sunglasses were prescription, and I was finally able to focus clearly on his face.

As the realization of who he was suddenly dawned on me, Hollywood said, "Oh...my...God! You were in *The Three Musketeers*, right? You're Robert Downy Jr.!"

"No! No, I'm not Robert Downy Jr. Good God, man! I'm—"

"Johnnie Depp! Holy shit! Are you really Johnnie Depp?" I answered. He turned to me and grinned as he did some sort of curtsy with a hand flourish. "At your service, kind sir."

Now that I could see clearly, there was no question in my mind it was Johnnie Depp. I should have picked up on it earlier, but between my nearsightedness and crusty glasses, I didn't put it together.

Hollywood still didn't seem convinced, though. "Hold on now," he said. "Johnnie Depp wasn't in *The Three Musketeers*."

Johnnie turned to Hollywood with his hands on his hips. "And neither was Robert Downy Jr. Although I *was* offered a tidy sum to play the flaming Duke of Buckingham. Turned it down, though; been there, done that. Fortunately, I'm lucky enough to be in a position where I don't have to take every role I'm offered. Far from it, in fact."

I knew better than to say what I was about to say, but rarely does that stop me. So I cleared my throat and let it fly. "Dude, I saw *The Lone Ranger* on DVD."

His head swiveled like it was on a pivot, and he thrust his right arm up at my face. "You see that tattoo?"

"Wino Forever?"

"No! The Indian." Below WINO FOREVER was a tattoo of the profile of a Cherokee chief in full headgear.

"Yeah, what about it?"

"Well, for one thing, I felt compelled to play the role of Tonto due to my native American heritage."

"You're part Indian? *Really?* What's the other thing?"

"Twenty-five million dollars."

"*Twenty-five million?*" Hollywood let out a whistle.

"Wow," I added. "I *totally* get that."

"I mean, somebody offers you that much dough to dress up like a gender-confused Tonto and smoke peyote all day, you're just not gonna turn it down, right?" He held his fist out, and I bumped it.

"Amen to that, bro," I nodded with newfound respect.

He turned to Hollywood and said, "I mean, am I right, or am I right?"

Hollywood fist-bumped him, too. "That's serious money, dude...cash money."

"That's what I'm saying. I got bills to pay, you know?"

Suddenly, Tangles exited the cabin of the sailboat in near hysterics. "Guys! Guys!" He had his hand up beside his mouth and glanced quickly down into the cabin before talking in a loud whisper. "You're not gonna believe who she is! Oh my God! Oh my God!" Then he reached his hand down for whoever it was and helped a blond-haired girl up the cabin steps.

Johnnie Depp shuffled from one foot to the other and whispered, "Uh, guys, I'd really like to keep this on the down low, if you know what I mean."

Hollywood and I shared uncertain glances, and I whispered back, "Yeah, sure."

Hollywood added, "Sure, whatever."

Tangles was fawning over the blonde and made sure to use both hands as he helped her step onto the gunwale of the Tiara.

I was trying to get a good look at her face when Tangles said, "Careful, Debby, it's slippery."

She said thanks, and Johnnie helped her into the cockpit. She also had a familiar face, but once again I couldn't quite place it. Hollywood lowered his shades and stared at her intently. Tangles hopped aboard and looked back and forth between me and Hollywood, apparently oblivious to Johnnie Depp.

"Don't you realize who this is?" He seemed incredulous that we didn't immediately recognize her. Although I didn't know off the top of my head who she was, I had just heard him call her "Debby."

"Sure," I answered. "It's Debby."

She smiled and held out her hand for me to shake. "Hi, thanks for saving us."

As we shook hands, I replied, "No problem, we're glad to help. My name's Kit." I nodded at Hollywood and added, "And that's Hollywood. I take it Tangles already introduced himself."

"Wait a second!" cried Tangles. "She's not just *Debby*. She's Debby Gibson! The great Debby Gibson! You know, the eighties pop star, movie star—"

"I thought you were great in *Sharknado*," commented Hollywood, as he shook her hand. "Nice to meet you. This is awesome."

"C'mon now! *Really?*" said Johnnie Depp. "For someone named Hollywood, you sure don't know shit about movies."

"I wasn't in *Sharknado*, unfortunately," conceded Miss Gibson.

"You should have been," cut in Tangles. "Those idiots at the SyFy channel put that train wreck of an actress, Tara Reid, in it, when you would have been perfect in the role of—"

"Tangles!"

"What?" He looked at me and held his hands open like he didn't understand why I wanted to shut him down.

"I think it's fair to say we're all fans of Miss Gibson here...clearly." I smiled while acknowledging her presence with a hand gesture, and she smiled back. *Damn, she had a nice smile—nice bod, too.*

"You got that right," said Hollywood. "I was thinking of *Megapython vs. Gatoroid*. That was awesome, you and, uh, who was the other girl? Sheena Easton?"

"Wrong again," said Johnnie. "What a surprise."

"It was Tiffany," corrected Tangles.

"That was hot." Tangles looked up at Debby all gooey-eyed and added, "not to say that you weren't totally hot in *Mega Shark vs. Giant Octo*—"

"Dude!"

"Why do you keep interrupting me?"

"Not to take anything anyway from Miss Gibson's extraordinary talents but—"

"Please, just call me Debby." She smiled.

"Right. As I was saying, not to take anything away from Debby's many talents, but don't you realize who *this* is?" I grabbed one of Johnnie's arms and held it up like a prizefighter. "We are in the company of possibly the greatest and most successful actor of our generation, certainly one of the top—"

"No, you had it right the first time," interrupted Johnnie with a sheepish grin on his face. "Just saying..." He shrugged, and I let his arm drop before putting Tangles on the spot.

"Don't you recognize him?" All eyes were on Tangles as he lowered his shades and peeked up over the frames at Johnnie Depp.

"Holy shit! I can't believe it!"

"Believe it." Johnnie beamed. "Small world, huh?"

"I'll say. Never thought I'd meet Debby Gibson and Robert Downy Jr. on the same—"

"I am *not* Robert Downy Jr!"

I said, "It's Johnnie Depp, you idiot."

"Oh, shit." To Tangles's credit, he looked properly embarrassed. "Sorry about that." He reached his tiny hand out to shake Johnnie's, but Johnnie hesitated, still fuming. Then Tangles added, "Loved your work as the gypsy, Roux, in *Chocolat*. You should have won an Oscar for that." Johnnie slowly reached his hand out and leerily shook it.

"You saw *Chocolat*?"

"Absolutely *loved* it...The range of emotions, the story line, the cinematography—you were brilliant.

Didn't it win the Screen Actors Guild award for best picture?"

"It did indeed." Johnnie looked at Hollywood and added, "Now *there's* a man who knows a little something about movies."

"I think you mean a *little* man who knows something about movies." Everybody laughed but Tangles, and me and Johnnie both fist-bumped Hollywood.

"You guys suck," complained Tangles. "But since we're in the presence of greatness, I'm going to let that one go."

I looked at Hollywood and asked, "Did you radio the Coast Guard when you were down below?"

"No, I better do that now." He stepped up to the lower helm and grabbed the ship-to-shore radio transmitter off the hook.

"Hold on a second," Johnnie said.

Hollywood looked at him, and said, "What?"

"Do we really have to involve the Coast Guard? The Coast Guard means the press, and the press means the paparazzi. Aside from the fact that we both abhor the media hounds, we're not ready to be linked together romantically. It would be bad for our careers."

"Speak for yourself, Johnnie. It couldn't hurt mine. My next film is *Pirhannaconda vs. Zombie Turtleoid.*"

"And you're great in those flicks, baby, it's just gonna take a little more time before we can go public." He brushed the bangs from her face and gave her a gentle kiss on the lips before adding, "Patience, love, that's all I'm asking."

"A year, Johnnie. It's been almost—"

He put a finger to her lips and pleaded, "Please, my little Giblet?"

That did it for Debby, and she went all Velveeta on him as they kissed passionately. Hollywood looked at me with his hands held open and a what-the-fuck expression on his face; Tangles licked his lips. *Yuck.*

I let out a fake cough loud enough to stop the tongue-hockey match that had broken out and said, "Uh, excuse me, guys." They separated and looked at me as I pointed down at the unconscious McGirt. "You see that guy in the corner there? He's an international drug trafficker, boat hijacker, thief—"

"Is he dead?" asked Debby. "He looks dead."

"Unfortunately, no, which I'm sure the DEA will appreciate."

"I don't know, he looks pretty dead. Can't we just toss him over?" said Johnnie.

"Not that I would mind it, but he's not dead...I don't think. Tangles, you better hit him with the hose."

Tangles picked up the saltwater washdown hose and blasted McGirt in the face. He put his hands up with a cry, and I signaled for Tangles to stop. "See what I mean? We have to turn him over to the authorities. I can't see anyway around it. Sorry, guys. Right, Hollywood?" I deferred to Hollywood, as he was the captain and responsible for his client's boat.

He glanced at his watch and said, "Yeah, we can't wait any longer. It's going on two o'clock, and we still have to make the crossing." Hollywood raised the radio mic to his lips.

Johnnie quietly said, "I'll give you fifty thousand dollars to take us back to the island."

Hollywood set the mic back on the hook and lowered his shades. "*Fifty thousand dollars?*" It was a lot of money, and when I looked at Tangles his eyes were bugging out of his Pez-head.

"Like you said before...cash money. I have a safe at the house."

"Where is it?"

"In the floor."

"No, I mean, you said, 'Take us back to the island.' Which island?"

"It's in the Exumas, about eighty-five miles southeast of Nassau. Where are we, anyways?"

"The Exumas?" Hollywood glanced at the GPS. "Dude, we're twenty-eight miles southwest of Freeport, which is a good hundred and twenty miles from Nassau. Eighty-five miles southeast of there is the Bahamian boondocks."

"That's what he was looking for when he bought it—seclusion," said Debby.

"You have your own island?" I asked.

"Guilty as charged."

"Sweet," commented Tangles.

"He bought it after filming the first pirate movie and named it Fuck Off Island," said Debby, with a giggle. "But I told him he should drop the 'Off.'"

Johnnie stepped next to Hollywood, who was sitting in the captain's seat, and put his hand on his shoulder. "Take us to Freeport, then, before you call the Coast Guard. I can charter a flight from there. I'll give you twenty grand." Hollywood looked at me and said, "What do you think, Shag? Twenty grand for twenty-eight miles. You and Tangles can have five each."

"I dunno, let me think for a second."

"What would we do about the sailboat?" asked Tangles. "What about McGirt? What about customs in Freeport?"

"I'm not concerned about the boat, and all the customs people know me," answered Johnnie. "They won't be a problem."

"Yeah, but what about McGirt?" Hollywood pointed at the beaten and bloody lump in the corner and then looked at me. "Shag, you got any ideas?"

I tried to convince myself that I was looking out for Hollywood and Tangles, but I was never averse to making some easy money myself, especially if we weren't really breaking any laws, just bending them a little. Then I considered the secret romance between Johnnie and Debby and tried to convince myself I was doing it for love. *Right.*

"Shag?" Hollywood asked again.

I shook my head with resignation and replied, "I'm probably going to regret this, but yeah, I got an idea or two. Let's get out of the sun and discuss it below deck. Tangles, you better get McGirt a wet towel and another bottle of water."

"You got it, boss."

We went down into the luxurious cabin of the Tiara, and Debby kept saying how nice it was. Hollywood pulled some sandwiches and beers out of the fridge. When Tangles went back outside with a towel and a bottle of water, Johnnie turned to me and said, "He works for you?"

"Yeah, sort of."

"I could use one of those."

"Johnnie!" Debby pushed him in the shoulder.

"I was kidding, love."

"He's a sweetheart. You be nice to him."

Almost on cue, Tangles slid open the cabin door and came down the steps.

"How is he?" I asked.

"He'll live…unfortunately. Can I have a sandwich?" Debby and Johnnie were on the couch eating like they hadn't eaten in two days, which they hadn't.

As soon as Tangles got a sandwich, Hollywood got down to business. "So, what's the plan?"

I washed down some salami and cheese sandwich with a frosty Kalik and laid out my plan. "How about we put McGirt back on the *Downtime* and have Johnnie call it in stolen? Halfway to Freeport we radio the Coast Guard and say we came to the aid of a sailboat in distress but were fired upon when we approached. They'll want us to stick around, but we'll say we don't want to be involved and have already left the scene. They probably get that all the time. We'll give them the last-known coordinates of the *Downtime* and hang up."

"Works for me," said Tangles.

"I like it. Let's get moving then," responded Hollywood.

For once, one of my plans went off without a hitch. After disabling the life raft on the sailboat, Tangles disabled McGirt by smashing a fish tamer (billy club) into his knee. He declared it payback of sorts for Ferby, who had a permanent limp thanks to our previous encounter with him. Johnnie managed to get a hold of his island manager, who was in a state of near-panic and minutes from reporting him missing. After calming him down, Johnnie had him report the sailboat stolen and then arrange for a charter to pick him up in Freeport and fly him to Fuck Off Island. We were barely in sight of Freeport, maybe twelve miles from shore, when Hollywood radioed the Coast Guard. Debby was lying down in one of the forward cabins, but Johnnie was next to me and Tangles, listening to Hollywood's spiel. After describing the *Downtime* and claiming to have been fired upon, he gave them the coordinates and abruptly hung up. He looked nervous and asked, "What do you think?"

Tangles and I both looked at Johnnie. He was squinting at Hollywood and nodded his head slowly as he spoke. "Has anyone ever said you look like Christian Bale?"

I gave him a light smack in the shoulder and pointed at myself. "That would be me. That's why I nicknamed him Hollywood. He's a dead ringer, right?"

Johnnie rubbed his goatee and nodded some more. "The resemblance *is* rather striking."

Hollywood perked up. "So, what do you think? You think maybe I got a chance in show biz?" Hollywood sounded skeptically excited, like a fat kid being told he might get McDonald's for dinner.

That was until Johnnie put his hand on his shoulder and broke the news. "No, but I could probably get Tangles some work as a stunt double for Tom Cruise." Everybody but Hollywood laughed.

"I'm serious, man. I thought I did pretty good."

"Sorry, mate, you look like Bale, but you act like Pitt. Pretty good doesn't cut it unless your last name's Paltrow or you're a reality show host. You're a helluva captain, though. What say we get moving?"

With his bubble thoroughly burst, Hollywood fired up the engines and floored the throttles enough to send Johnnie staggering back into the cockpit. Tangles and I were still laughing as we followed Johnnie into the cabin. We all settled down with a fresh coldie. I pointed at Johnnie's bicep and asked, "So, what's with the 'Wino Forever' tattoo?"

He glanced at it and let out a wry chuckle as he shook his head. "It used to say Winona, but I had it changed after we broke up."

"You used to bang Wynonna Judd?" asked Tangles.

"*What?* No! Ryder. Winona Ryder."

"Winona Ryder? You mean the actress turned klepto turned wannabe actress again?"

"She's no klepto, though the little minx did steal my heart for a while."

"Wow."

"Don't get me wrong, she's got nothing on the Giblet. That girl is pure hellcat."

"I was kinda wondering about that," I said.

"Wondering about what?"

"I thought Debby Gibson liked girls."

"Who doesn't? Besides, I love a challenge," he said with a wink.

"Touche," agreed Tangles, who clinked bottles with Johnnie. I did the same, and we all shared a laugh before a voice came from the forward cabin.

"Johnnie? Why don't you come lie down for a few minutes?"

Johnnie set his beer down and rose from the couch. "Gentlemen, I shall see you in Freeport. Until then, the glorious Giblet will have my full and undivided attention." He saluted us and called out, "Coming, love!"

Once he disappeared into the forward berth, Tangles and I looked at each other and busted out laughing again—just another day on the high seas. *Unbelievable.*

Chapter 15

Some two thousand miles away, in the heart of Colombia's Atriz Valley, Rico Cordero staggered from his bedroom to the bathroom. Underneath the sink he found his homemade ointment and applied it liberally to his overworked private parts. *Ahhhhhh.* As he pulled his boxer shorts up, he gave the bottle another shake and was alarmed to realize how little was left. *That's odd.* Hadn't he whipped up a new batch just before being captured on St. Maarten? With a shrug he gingerly trod into the kitchen, trying to keep the genital friction to a minimum.

His brother, Eduardo, was sitting on a stool at the large island counter and looked up from his laptop to greet him. "I haven't seen you walk like that since you got kicked in the cojones by Papa's favorite mule."

Rico helped himself to some sweet tea and poured a half gallon of milk into an oversized bowl on the floor.

"What can I say about my sweet Elvira? Her—"

"Okay, okay, I get the picture. You're a sick man, Rico, but I think I may have topped you this time."

"What do you mean?"

"I have devised a plan to get the truth out of the senator, as improbable as it may seem, a method we haven't used before."

"I'm pretty sure I got him thinking about it since I chopped his foot off."

"True, but I think you will agree he deserves to suffer far worse for betraying us."

"You are right, of course. I can't wait to see what you have planned. I assume it has something to do with having me tell him that if he urinates without permission I will cut his dick off."

"It does indeed."

Eduardo's phone rang, and he answered, "Yes, Paco... I bet he does. Good. You have the bucket ready? Excellent. We'll be right there. C'mon," he said to Rico. He stood and started walking to the door.

"Where are we going?"

"It's time to talk to the senator."

"I need to get dressed. I'll be right there." He yelled to his brother who was halfway out the door, "Don't start without me!"

After throwing on a pair of jeans and a T-shirt, Rico paused outside the bedroom door and looked for Elvira. Not seeing her, he started calling her name and whistling for her as he headed to the front door. He expected to see four hundred pounds of white fur and sleek muscle coming around one of the hallways of the large villa, but as he looked back from the front door, there was no Elvira. He called for her again, and when no response came, he muttered, "Where the fuck?"

As he made his way through the villa compound toward the holding cell where they had the senator held, he was puzzled by Elvira's behavior. Normally, she rarely left his side. He chalked it up to the fact that he had been gone quite a while and she probably developed some other routine.

He opened the door to their private prison, and his nose twitched. It was the unmistakable scent of Elvira. *Elvira was there?* He turned the corner and stopped dead in his tracks. There at the end of the hall, Paco was talking to his brother. Elvira was at his side, and he was absentmindedly stroking the nape of her neck. *What the fuck?* Eduardo *never* petted Elvira. He always kept his distance, and Elvira usually did the same. Now she followed him around, and he was petting her?

"Eduardo, what are you doing?" he asked as he approached.

"I was just thanking Paco for the candiru." He dismissed Paco, and as Paco walked away, he pointed at the five-gallon bucket on the floor, which was two-thirds full of murky river water.

"No, I mean, what are you doing with Elvira?"

"Huh? Nothing. She followed me down here. Why?"

"I never saw you pet her before." Rico wasn't smiling.

"You've been gone a long time, little brother. I've been taking care of her for you."

"I see."

"Why are you acting this way? You should be doing cartwheels. Forty-eight hours ago you were locked up and facing life in prison."

"Of course, you're right. I can't thank you enough for getting me out of that Guadeloupian hellhole.

And I appreciate you taking care of Elvira in my absence. Thank you, my brother." Rico stepped forward to give him a hug and stopped when Elvira let out a low growl. "What's the matter, girl?" He slowly reached his hand down to pet her, and she reluctantly dropped her head in submission. "So, what's with the candiru?"

"I had Paco net some after you said you had the senator. That's why we've been withholding his bathroom privileges. When he urinates in the bucket, we shall see for ourselves if the candiru is deserving of its vampire-catfish moniker. They haven't been fed in a couple days."

"You're right, you *have* outdone yourself. This is truly diabolical."

"Only if it works, my brother, only if it works…and the time to find out is now."

Eduardo picked up the bucket, and Elvira and Rico followed him down the hall. They rounded a corner and stopped at a door that had a small window in it. Eduardo set the bucket down and peered in through the one-way glass to see the senator sitting on a bench in the small cell. He turned to Rico and whispered, "Best to stay back from the door. If he sees you, he might have a heart attack. I will give him false hope, and then we will watch when he uses the bucket."

Rico grabbed Elvira by her diamond-studded collar and stepped to the side, out of sight.

When Eduardo threw back the deadbolt and swung the steel door open the senator's head slowly lifted from his chest. He did not look well. He did not look well at all. He looked like somebody chopped off his foot, cauterized the stump with a blowtorch, and then zip-tied it off with a dirty dishtowel—because somebody had. Rico.

"Please," he said weakly. "I need a doctor. It's infected...my leg, it's infected...and I need to use the bathroom. Please, please let me use a bathroom"

"You can use this, and then we'll talk." Eduardo picked up the bucket and placed it on the floor in front of the senator, before adding, "If you are truthful, I will summon the doctor. If you lie, I will summon the coroner."

"I already told that maniac brother of yours the truth. I had nothing to do with what happened. It was those fishermen with the TV show. They must work for the DEA. They're the ones—"

"If you keep repeating the same old lies, I'm afraid things are not going to end well for you. Think about that while you relieve yourself. I'll be back when you're done."

As soon as Eduardo shut the door behind him, the formerly proud politician slid the bucket next to the bench. Unable to stand because of his missing foot, he straddled the bucket by kneeling with his stumpy leg on the bench and his good leg on the floor for support. He had to piss like a racehorse and was way past the point of caring who might be watching through the window. After unzipping his fly, he dangled his fat little penis mere inches above the dirty water and let loose. Overcome with relief, he looked up at the ceiling and started praying to God for somebody to rescue him. After twenty seconds he detected a break in the steady flow of urine and looked down at the bucket. He saw an unusual swirl where his urine stream entered the water. He figured he was pissing so hard that he was creating a whirlpool effect. Under normal circumstances, it would be something he would be proud of. He hadn't pissed in two days, and his bladder was in full drain mode. He tilted back his head and relished the relief of a good piss.

Suddenly, the urine stream began to sputter as he felt a pinch at the tip of his penis. "Ow! What the hell?" He felt like he was still pissing hard, but only a trickle was coming out. The next thing he knew, he felt like he had been stuck with a thousand red-hot needles. He screamed. In a panic, he tried to stand up, and his good leg kicked the bucket over. Dirty water spilled over the floor and about a dozen little minnow like fish began thrashing around. He screamed again as searing pain engulfed his now throbbing member.

The door flung open, and Eduardo Cordero stepped in. The maniacal brother who sawed his foot off stood in the doorway with a white tiger at his side. He let out another scream as Eduardo reached down and picked up one of the tiny little fish. It was maybe an inch long and slender from a lack of food. The tiny fish was translucent except for the little black head, and it wiggled around in his palm.

"I am pleased to introduce you to one of the Amazon Basin's worst nightmares. It is known as the toothpick fish, or vampire fish, but locally it is called the candiru."

"AGGGGH!" The senator was writhing in pain and barely heard the words coming out of Eduardo's mouth as he continued.

"The candiru are bloodsuckers who swim inside the gills of larger fish and feed from the inside. We are taught from a young age to never urinate in the river or even from the bank because of what can happen. Good advice, no?"

"Oh my God! Oh my God, agggh!" The senator had both hands on his burning unit and was desperately squeezing it like a tube of toothpaste—not a good plan.

"It has been determined the candiru commonly mistake a urine stream for water passing over the gills another fish. Like a salmon, they swim up the stream into the urethra until they get stuck."

"Aghhh! Aghhh! Dear God in heaven, help me!"

"When they try to turn around, the rear-facing spines on their gill covers dig into the wall of the urethra, causing what has been widely described as mind-numbingly excruciating pain. From what I gather, it would seem to be an accurate description, no?"

The senator started weeping and pleading for help.

"Not until you tell the truth about what happened to the last shipment," replied Rico from the doorway.

"I *have* been telling the truth. Aghhh! Oh my God, the pain!"

"After the candiru get stuck and realize they aren't going anywhere, they do what they do best. Their little vampire teeth start chewing on the urethra to get at the blood. You may be feeling that now."

"Aghhh! Aghhh!"

"They will gorge themselves until their stomachs explode and they die, which may take a few days. If the dead candiru is not removed you will develop what will almost certainly be a devastatingly painful and fatal infection. Unfortunately, the only way to extract it is by incision."

"No! No! Aghhh!"

"So I will ask you one more time. You were working with the American fishermen to steal the shipment, no?"

"No! I swear! They even killed my son, Remy! Oh Jesus! Please help me!"

"There is no God here. There is only pain and misery for fork-tongued liars like you. Try not to think about that squirmy little devilfish devouring your puny prick." Eduardo turned, and Rico stepped aside as he went into the hall, ignoring the senator's desperate pleas by slamming the cell door shut.

"So, what do you think?" Rico asked.

"I think he might be telling the truth for once."

"Probably the first time. The candiru don't lie. So what are we going to do?"

Rico and Elvira followed Eduardo as he headed down the hall and laid out his plan. "The American fishermen with the TV show that he claims are responsible for our troubles have a website. They're scheduled to do some fishing in Panama in a few months. We'll deal with them then."

When they got to the main door, Eduardo headed out, but Rico didn't follow.

Eduardo turned back and asked, "You're not coming? I have the help preparing a big breakfast in honor of your return."

Rico pulled a straight razor out of his back pocket and held it up to see. "Sounds good, but first I thought I'd try a little surgery, no pun intended. It might be good to know how to cut one of those things out. You never know. Besides, if he was telling the truth, I almost feel bad for him."

Eduardo laughed. "You going soft on me, little brother?"

"Why don't you ask the senator that in about ten minutes?"

Eduardo shook his head. "That's more like it. I'll see you back at the house, we have much business to discuss."

As Rico walked down the hall toward the senator, he slapped the razor in his open palm, considering how he was going to proceed. Halfway down the corridor he reached his hand down to pet Elvira, but she wasn't there. *What?*

Thinking he must have closed the door on her and she was probably waiting outside, he hurried back down the hall. When he opened the door, he saw Elvira trailing Eduardo around the corner of the house. As he headed back toward the senator, he thought about Elvira's new fondness for Eduardo and remembered the near empty bottle of lotion. Being the jealous hothead that he was, his blood started to boil. *How could he?* With seething anger in his eyes, he opened the door to the senator's cell and announced, "Good news. The doctor has arrived."

Chapter 16

Franklin Post, aka Stargazer, rubbed his chin thought-fully as he read the data on the screen in front of him. As head of the über-top-secret Department of International Criminal Knowledge (DICK), his main job was to disseminate the vast amount of data gathered by various US intelligence agencies. He had access to everything and was charged with making sure any information on terrorist or international criminal activity was fed to the appropriate channels. After hanging up with the head of the FBI, Post called his field agent in South Florida.

DICK agent Thomas Cushing was having a scotch and water in his Pineapple Grove townhouse in trendy Delray Beach, wrapping up some computer work of his own, when he got the call. He answered his DICK phone on the second ring when he saw it was the boss and wondered whose voice he would hear. He wondered because his boss had invented a device he called the Oralator that could alter his voice to sound like anyone he chose. Although Post had a fondness for TV and movie characters, politicians and international celebrities of all ilks were fair game. The voices were so convincing that he rarely had a problem identifying them.

"Hey, boss, what's going on?" he answered, curious as to whom he might hear.

"A couple things."

Surprisingly, Cushing couldn't put his finger on the voice, so to speak. *Some kind of southern accent?*

"Okay, shoot."

"That's one of 'em."

"One of what?"

"You need to teach them boys how to shoot, 'fore they hurt somebody. Right now they couldn't plink a sleepin' squirrel from a sickly sapling."

"*What?* What boys? Wait a second, what voice is that? You sound like Daniel Boone crossed with Larry the Cable Guy."

"I'll take that as a compliment."

"So who is it?"

"You must be one of the rare few who haven't seen the reality show phenomena heretofore known as *Duck Dynasty.*"

"Heretofore? Now you're sounding like Matlock. No, I haven't seen *Duck Dynasty.*"

"That would explain your failure to recognize the voice of the patriarch of the Robertson clan, Phil Robertson."

"Yep, that would explain it. Now I have another reason not to watch."

"Your loss."

"I can afford it. So what boys are you talking about that I need to teach how to shoot?"

"That would be the fishing-show guys that saved your butt when that feller got the drop on you during that storage center shootout a couple years back."

"That's not exactly the way I—"

"Doesn't matter. We're using them and their fishing show as cover on an upcoming assignment as soon as their boat's ready. I can't have my newest DICK agents not knowin' how to handle a firearm, as remote as the likelihood of armed conflict may be."

"Famous last words."

"Remember the Alamo."

"What are you talking about?"

"Those are famous last words. You don't want something, don't ask for it."

"Sir, I love the Oralator as much as the next agent, but you're doing it again."

"What's that?"

"You're not just assuming someone's voice, you're role playing."

"Nuthin' wrong with that. Miss Kay likes role playing."

"Who the hell's Miss Kay?"

"Watch it now. You disparage my woman, and I'll tan your hide faster than a jackrabbit in a wildfire."

"Okay, I give up. You're the boss."

"Agreed. So like I said, take Shagball and Tangles to the firing range, and go over the basics."

"What about the girl?"

"Holly? Yes, she needs some training, too."

"I'll personally escort her to the range after I get the A/C in the Porsche fixed. It's hot enough without *her* inside."

"Hey, now. Fraternizing between DICK agents is highly frowned upon by yours truly. Besides, she's Shagball's girlfriend, and I don't need you causin' problems right from the git-go."

"Are you sure it's a good idea making them DICK agents?"

"Course not. It's an experiment, is what it is."

"You mean like when they put Dennis Miller on *Monday Night Football?*"

"I said it was an experiment, not a train wreck."

"My point, exactly."

"Well, we'll see what happens. We need a way to get close to some remote targets, and the fishing show is an ideal cover. As you well know, they've already proven themselves extremely resourceful under very trying circumstances."

"All right, I'll arrange to take them to the range. What else?"

"It has something to do with the storage center shootout I previously mentioned—the one you and our newest DICK agents are intimately aware of."

"The Donny Nutz deal? What's going on?"

"A few weeks ago a so-called medical clinic in Guadalajara went up in flames. When fire fighters sifted through the ashes they found the charred remains of the doctor who owned the clinic inside... minus his face."

"What do you mean, like it burned off?"

140

"No, like he was skinned with a scalpel. The investigators are uncertain whether he was alive at the time."

"Wow. What's up with that?"

"The good doctor was known to be the surgeon of choice for those unfortunate enough to have their faces placed on the FBI's most wanted list. He practiced facial reconstructive surgery...and I stress the word 'practiced.'"

"I get that he's dead and not practicing anymore, but what's the connection to Nutz?"

"I was getting to that. You got about as much patience as a coyote in a chicken coop. I stressed 'practiced' because he literally practiced on his patients. He wasn't particularly skilled at his vocation, and rumor is that one of his recent patients, the head of the Zeta cartel, now looks like Cheech and Chong."

"Cheech and Chong are two people."

"That's what I'm saying. Half his face looks like Cheech, and the other half Chong."

"Ouch, that's a tough pill to swallow, but I see what you're getting at. Makes sense."

"*What* makes sense?"

"When the head of the Zeta cartel realized what a bad face job he got, he decided to get even with the doctor and then torch the place, right? I mean, look at the symbolism. You gotta admit, it's pretty clever."

"What are you talking about?"

"Up in smoke, get it? The clinic went up in smoke, and Cheech and Chong's biggest movie was *Up in Smoke.*"

"Hmmm, sometimes I wonder about you, son. I'm not sure the Mexican authorities tied the two together, but the fugitive cartel leader *was* the prime suspect."

"*Was?*"

"Yes, *was*...until the DNA came back."

"What DNA?"

"A piece of bloody gauze was found at the scene, and when the Mexicans couldn't tie the DNA to anybody, they gave some to the FBI to run through CODIS, and they got a hit. Care to take a guess whose DNA it is?"

"Mickey Rourke?"

"Good guess, but no. The hit came back to a notorious con that just got sprung after serving nearly twenty years for second-degree murder, the last ten mostly in solitary."

"Notorious *how?* Do I know him?"

"Depends, you ever heard of the Devil's Nephew?"

"Oh, shit. *That* guy? Sure, I heard of him. One of my roommates at the academy was from Jersey. He told me about this guy who had everybody quaking in their boots up there. Rahway, right?"

"That is correct."

"Yeah, I remember. He said he had an informant on the inside, but he was useless 'cause he was too scared what would happen if the Devil's Nephew found him out. He had another name for him, too, if I recall."

"Nipote del Diavolo. It means the same thing in Italian."

"That's it. He said he was one mean son of a bitch. Said he ran the prison with an iron fist, even from solitary."

"He did indeed, and now he's wanted for questioning in the good doctor's death as well as the strangulation of a pair of Mexican hookers. I'm going to send you his most recent prison photos, but they're probably of little use except for his body size, which is rather large. We can assume he has a new face, albeit a botched one, and a new identity."

"And you're sending me these pics because?"

"Oh, right. I'm sending you the pics because the Devil's Nephew is none other than Marzio Giancarlo DeNutzio, nephew of Donny Nutz."

"You gotta be kidding me."

"'Fraid not. I was as surprised as you when I found out, but there's no reason to believe he's headed to Florida or is seeking payback for what happened to his uncle."

"You think?"

"There's no way he knows about you, and as far as Shagball and company goes, their names never made the paper. I just wanted you to know. I'm being cautious, as usual. He could be anywhere."

"Donny Nutz was onto Shagball and Tangles. He arranged for their kidnapping, planned to have them killed, and knew they were responsible when his guys disappeared."

"So?"

"If he knew, who's to say his nephew doesn't know, too?"

"He was in prison the whole time—in solitary, in fact."

"If he ran the joint like he was claimed to, he could've found out. Or maybe somebody filled him in when he got sprung."

"There's no sense speculating, but I don't see any reason to tell Shagball and Tangles at the moment, especially when they're so close to their first assignment—wouldn't wanna spook 'em. Naturally, if we develop any information that indicates DeNutzio is headed your way, you'll be the first to know."

"Naturally."

After hanging up with his agent, Franklin Post leaned back in his command-center recliner and gazed up at the starry domed ceiling of his massive estate/data hub on the Puget Sound. He closed his eyes and tried to imagine where the Devil's Nephew was, what he was thinking, where he was going. *Nothing*. Then he tried to trick himself into feeling he was happy, happy, happy, like *Duck Dynasty* patriarch Phil Robertson would, but that wasn't working either. *Shit*. The Devil's Nephew was on the loose, and Franklin Post had a bad feeling there would be hell to pay.

Chapter 17

After nearly nine hours of nonstop driving, the Devil's Nephew glanced at his passenger and pulled in the driveway of the waterfront home. Upon observing the wide-channeled waterway that wrapped around the back of the ranch-style house, flanked with palm trees, he commented, "Nice place."

"I told you, the wife's loaded—park there, next to the Jeep." The disbarred attorney pointed to where he wanted him to park.

The Devil's Nephew pulled to the side of the turn-around and parked next to the spanking new Jeep Grand Cherokee as directed. After killing the engine, he said, "Okay, let's go put the squeeze on her."

As he opened the door, the attorney said, "Wait," and grabbed at his massive bicep. Instinctively, the Devil's Nephew clenched his fist and snapped it backward as he straightened his arm. The powerful blow caught the attorney just below the eye, and he winced in pain as his head banged against the passenger window. "Ow! God damn! What the hell did you do that for?" He gently rubbed the swelling knot below his eye as the Devil's Nephew turned to face him.

"Don't ever touch me again—*ever*. You touch me, you die. Got it?"

"Yeah, I got it. Christ. I just wanted you to wait here."

"Why would I do that?"

"Because I got a better chance of getting the money without you breathing down my neck. I mean, c'mon, man, I haven't seen my wife in over three years."

"She never visited you in the pen?"

"No, things got a little...strained, you know? She's gonna be surprised enough to see me as it is."

The Devil's Nephew glanced at the house before brandishing the silenced 9 mm automatic he had in the driver's door storage area. He glared at the way-ward attorney, who was massaging an eye socket that was destined to turn as purple as a Prince album, and spoke.

"You got ten minutes to lay out the sitch for wifey. I get three million bucks and you live; otherwise, you both die. It's that simple. It works the same way if I hear a siren, or get a whiff of cop—you're both dead. Got it?"

"Unfortunately, yes."

As he walked across the driveway to the front door, he smoothed out his slacks and straightened his button-down shirt. *Fuck, is she gonna freak when I tell her,* he thought. *I am soooo fucked.* When he got to the door he made like he was gonna knock, but reconsidered and checked the doorknob. It was open. He shook his head and muttered, "Figures." If he told her once, he told her a thousand times to keep the doors locked when he wasn't home. *Some things never change.* He licked his fingers and ran them through his hair before glancing back at the scary freak in the car, who gave him the, I've got my eyes on you, sign. He had no doubt that he was more than willing to fulfill the threats he made. *Oh, man, is this bad.* He noticed a FedEx envelope propped up against the side of the house and picked it up. With a deep breath he pushed open the front door and called out, "Honey, I'm home!"

As soon as the scumbag attorney disappeared inside the house, the Devil's Nephew pulled out his cell and dialed the Scarf. Two rings later, the Scarf picked up.

"Yo, Marz—I mean, uh, Rodge—how's it going with that scumbag lawyer in Atlanta?"

"It's going, but we ain't in Atlanta anymore, we're in Florida."

"*We're* in Florida? He's with you?"

"Yeah, he said he's broke but claims his wife came into a lot of money, and she lives down here. He says since they're still married, whatever's hers is his, but I dunno—Fucker's squirrellier than Alvin and the Chipmunks. I'll know soon enough, though; he's talking to her right now."

"Where exactly are you?"

"Not sure, but we passed signs for West Palm Beach before getting off at Lantana Road. We went over a brand-new bridge that dead-ends into a big hotel called the 'Eau de Palm Beach,' or something like that."

"The oh de *what?*"

"What am I, a fuckin' tour guide? It looked like a Ritz. I'm a few miles south of there—just past an inlet."

"South of the Palm Beach inlet?"

147

"What did I just tell you? I'm south of the hotel. Fuckin' A, Scarf."

"Sorry, hang on a sec." The Scarf's fingers fluttered over the keyboard of his laptop, and he read the search results from the screen. "There's a Ritz-Carlton in—scratch that. Good eye, Rodge. There *used* to be a Ritz-Carlton in Manalapan, but they changed the name to 'Eau de Palm Beach Resort.'"

"That's it."

"Huh, well ain't that a coincidence."

"What's that?"

"You're only a stone's throw from the C-Love Marina, in Boynton Beach."

"That's what I was thinking. I saw a sign for Boynton Beach Boulevard before we got off the freeway. As soon as I finish with this schmuck, I'm headed over there to straighten things out with, uh, what the fuck is her name again?"

"Holly. Holly Lutes. She's the one who inherited the marina and maybe some gold after your uncle's deal—"

"I know the backstory, Scarf. You find out anything new?"

"Yeah, and you're not gonna like it."

"I don't like a lot of things, like people. What is it?"

"I went online and did some more digging into the shootout that left your uncle and his crew dead. Not a single newspaper article mentioned any involvement by the girl, or her boyfriend, Shagball, or his sidekick, the midget, Tangles. Not a one. Nor was there any mention that the shootout occurred in front of a bay that was rented by the C-Love Marina. Apparently nobody bothered to look into that."

"You don't say."

"Yeah, and get this. Buried in one of the police reports it says a red Beemer convertible was seen leaving the storage center immediately after the shootings."

"So?"

"So it seems nobody bothered to follow up on the lead, or if they did, it was swept under the rug."

"*What* was swept under the rug?"

"I did a vehicle registration search. Connor 'Kit' Jansen, aka Shagball, drives a ninety-four red Beemer convertible."

"Son of a bitch! When I get done with that miserable fuck, the only thing he'll be driving is his dick in the dirt."

"Don't I know it. But one might take such obvious obfuscation to mean that Mr. Dirtdick and company are being protected."

"*Obfuscation?* Cut the library lingo. What do you mean, protected?"

"Think about it. Nobody even questioned these guys. On top of that, neither the police nor the paper reported which federal agency was involved in the shootout. A local news station said it was the DEA, but that was never corroborated. No matter who it was, though, they did a good job of keeping our friends out of police hands *and* out of the papers. It was *obfuscated*, covered up, if you will. That can only mean one thing."

"Yeah, you say *obfuscated* one more time, and I'm gonna rip your fuckin' tongue out next time I see you. Of course I know what it means. I spent nearly twenty years in the joint. I can sniff out a rat blindfolded. They're fuckin' snitches for the DEA."

"Your uncle Donny weren't no drug smuggler, so I doubt it's the DEA. But who knows? Maybe they're with the ATF. Either way, you gotta be on your toes. Those guys don't ride around in black-and-whites. They're sneaky bastards."

"Fuckin' snitches. They're dead. They're fuckin' dead."

"Such is life."

"Good work, Scarf." The Devil's Nephew processed the new information for a second as he watched the sun setting across the water then added, "You know, for a guinea, you been lookin' kinda pasty. It's time you work on your tan."

"Whatta you mean?"

"Between collecting the money from Mr. Asshole Lawyer and dealing with these fuckin' ATF snitches, I could probably use an extra hand. Book yourself on the next flight to Palm Beach."

Chapter 18

Holly had been filleting some snapper at the fish-cleaning table on the dock behind her Sabal Island home when she got the call from Kit that he was back from the Bahamas. She wasn't expecting him for a couple more days and was excited to see him. When he told her he had an unbelievable story to tell, she felt a twinge of jealousy because she missed out on the trip, but it was fleeting, unlike her feelings for him. It had been a crazy set of circumstances that had thrown them together after her divorce, and it got even crazier when they got tangled up with mobsters, drug lords, and a secret government agency. The net result of their mutual attraction to each other, combined with their shared adventures, left her in a place she wasn't ready to be: hopelessly in love. While she knew Kit would never admit to being hopelessly anything, she knew in her heart he loved her. She also knew they were both eagerly anticipating the new boat they had been promised and embarking on their first secret mission together.

After she dropped another snapper fillet into the cooler next to the table, she glanced at the back of the house to see if the hunky agent Kit referred to as Peter

Porsche had arrived. Right after Kit called, Peter Porsche called to say he needed to meet and had been unable to reach Kit. Since Kit and Tangles were coming over for dinner, and she had plenty of fish, she invited him over. She left the front door unlocked and told him to let himself in when he arrived. She was hoping he was going to tell them the new boat was ready and start briefing them on their first assignment. The mere thought of it gave her goose bumps. *What girl doesn't dream of being an Angelina Jolie-type, badass secret agent?* She laughed out loud at the preposterousness of the notion and reminded herself Kit was assured they would just be information gathering. Her role was to run the computer systems on the new boat and nothing more… supposedly. Regardless of the risks involved, she felt it was worth it to have a chance to find Millie's son, Patrick, her long-lost cousin. He was her last connection to Millie and she desperately wanted to find him. Knowing this, Kit made it the only condition in agreeing to work with an intelligence-gathering agency shrouded in secrecy, and she loved him even more for it.

The sun was rapidly sinking in the burnt August sky when she dropped the last fillet into the cooler. There was a good two hundred feet of lawn and palm trees between the dock and the sliders at the back of the house. When she glanced back she saw her expected guest's silhouette as he slid open the patio doors. She waved and yelled, "Make yourself at home! I'll be in as soon as I clean up!"

When he waved and stepped back in the house, Holly quickly hosed off the table and hung the fillet knife on a hook. Cooler in hand, she traipsed up the coquina path and across the patio to the sliding doors. She expected to see her guest sitting in the living room, but nobody was there. When she rounded the corner to the kitchen she saw why. The refrigerator door was open, and he was rummaging through it. On the few occasions she had met him, he'd exhibited impeccable manners, but now he had his head stuck in her fridge. *Odd.* She set the cooler on one of the kitchen counter bar stools and cleared her throat. "Looking for something special?" she asked.

He was holding a beer in the hand that held the door open, and when he popped his head out of the fridge, he replied, "Not anymore."

Stunned, she grabbed the stool for support and knocked the cooler over onto Mexican tile floor. *Impossible. It can't be.* There in front of her stood her ex-husband, Mark, sporting a fresh shiner. As ice and yellowtail fillets spilled across the floor, he added, "We're having fresh fish for dinner? Great. You don't have shit in the fridge, and I'm starved for a decent meal. Prison food is even worse than you think."

Holly took a couple deep breaths and tried to gather her thoughts. Her hands were shaking, and her head was spinning. "You're—you're supposed to be in prison."

"Got out on a technicality. Those Enron guys really set the bar high. Here, let me help you with the fish." He bent down and started scooping the fish back in the cooler.

Holly shook her head in disbelief. "Get out!" she yelled. "Get out of my house! Now!"

Mark put the last fillet in the cooler and threw a handful of ice over the top before standing up to face her.

"I think you meant to say *our* house. I'm not going anywhere."

"What the hell are you talking about? We're divorced! I inherited this from Millie. Get out of here before I call the cops, and don't *ever* come back!"

"Calm down, all right, babe?"

"Don't you 'babe' me! Are you crazy?!"

"No, and I'm not divorced either. Same goes for you."

"You're either crazy, or you got amnesia in prison. We got divorced before your trial was even over!"

"Really? Did you ever get a copy of the divorce decree? You know, the one with the judge's signature on it?"

"*What?*"

"It's a simple question. Did you ever see the final decree?"

A single seed of doubt began to sprout in the pit of her stomach as the wheels churned on the locking mechanism of her memory bank.

"I, uh…my, my lawyer said he got all the paperwork back, and it was final. He called to tell me when I was in Jupiter getting the condo ready for sale. I remember thinking it was all that was left of our marriage, you asshole!"

"That's what I thought. You never saw it, because it doesn't exist. Trust me on this."

"*Trust you?* You cheated on me with half a dozen strippers and went to jail for embezzling from your clients. Fuck you, Mark!"

Chapter 19

I missed my old Robalo, especially after the *Lucky Dog* got blown to smithereens in the Caribbean. It was the longest I had been without a boat since moving to Florida some twenty-five or so years prior, and it sucked. The only consolation was that I got to occasionally use it, because I had given it to Tangles when I acquired the *Lucky Dog*. Understandably, Tangles fell in love with it much as I had. What's not to love about a nineteen-and-a-half-foot T-topped center console with an eight-foot beam? It was built like a tank, and thirty-plus years on the ocean had yet to make it any less seaworthy than it was on its shakedown cruise. It had twin engines to boot, something you can't even find on a small boat anymore. Tangles had installed a molded step beneath the helm for him to stand on, and he captained us down the Intracoastal Waterway in the fading light. Within ten minutes, we left the left the main channel for the cut that led to Holly's house on the point, and he throttled back to idle.

"I'm gonna dock on the side," announced Tangles. It was his way of letting me know he was leaving as soon as dinner was over. He had plans with one of the Key Lime hostesses and wanted as quick and easy a departure as possible. If he had been spending the night, he would dock on the canal behind the house, where the boat was more protected from the wind and waves. He passed by the dock and then looped back, so he would be facing toward the main channel when he left. As he did so, I noticed a car parked behind Holly's new Jeep. I couldn't tell the make, but it definitely wasn't a Porsche 911. Holly had texted me that Peter Porsche was coming over because he needed to talk to us about something, and I was anxious to find out what. We tied up in short order, and as we crossed the deck to the kitchen door, I looked up the driveway again. There was a brief moment before foliage and the corner of the house blocked my unobstructed view, and I could see it was a Cadillac.

"Whose Caddy?" asked Tangles.

I looked through the glass French doors leading into the kitchen, and Holly was in animated conversation with someone who had his back to us.

"I don't know. Guess we're gonna find out," I answered. There was a time when I would have knocked or waved or something before entering, but that was when Millie owned the house. Now that it was Holly's, and I was more or less living with her, I opened the door just as Holly yelled, "Fuck you, Mark!"

Holly wasn't one to drop a lot of F bombs, and it caught me off guard.

"Whoa, what's going on? Who's Mark?" I was looking at Holly and had my finger pointed at the guy's back. When he turned, my finger was only inches from his face.

He swatted my finger away and replied, "*I'm* Mark, and *I'm* her husband. Who the fuck are you?"

156

"You're her *what?*" I looked at Holly, who looked like she just came down with something.

"Kit, he's my ex. He just showed up."

"We're still married, babe, like it or not."

"What's he talking about? You said you were divorced, and he was in prison."

"I'm, I'm ninety-nine percent sure we're divorced. And he *was* in prison. I can't believe this."

"Me either," said Tangles.

Holly and I both said, "Shut up."

"What?" He shrugged. Holly gave him her death-laser stare, and he said, "Okay, okay, I need to use the bathroom anyways." He wisely chose not to use the bathroom off the kitchen and instead crossed the great room to use the bathroom off the spare bedroom.

"Who the hell is *he?*" asked Mark. I took a step toward Holly and then turned to look him square in the eye.

"*He* is the only one besides Holly who's occasionally allowed to drink my Negra Modelo. Gimme that." I snatched the beer out of his hand and set it on the counter. "You touch my beer again, and you'll have another black eye to match." I turned to Holly and put my arm around her. She was looking ill.

"You all right?" I asked.

"Been better."

"What did you mean by 'ninety-nine percent sure'?"

"I don't know...I don't know what to think." Holly put her hand on my chest and added, "Why don't you and Tangles run over to Three Jacks for a beer. I'll call as soon as I sort this out. It won't take long. Please?"

I looked at Mark, and he said, "This is between man and wife. It doesn't concern you."

"I'm not your wife anymore!"

I wasn't going to wait for him to drink another one of my beers, I was gonna drill him right then and there. I stepped toward him and muttered, "You son of a—"

Holly grabbed my arm. "Kit, please, just give me a few minutes. I'll call…I promise."

"Are you sure? You sure you'll be all right?"

"Yes, please. I'm sorry about this."

Tangles came walking up and said, "Sorry about what?" For the second time, Holly and I gave him the double-barreled, "Shut up."

"Go to the boat," I added.

"But we just—"

"Wait in the boat!"

Exasperated, he threw his hands up. "All right, all right, I'm going to the boat." As he headed out the kitchen door he grabbed the half-full bottle of Negra Modelo off the counter. I turned back to Holly and gave her a kiss on the forehead.

"I won't be far," I promised and held up my cell. "Call me if you have any problems with Dickhead, and I mean *any* problems. Either way, I'll be back within the hour."

"Thanks, Kit. I—"

I put a finger to her lips and said, "Just do what you need to do and call, okay?"

"Okay." I gave her another kiss, and as I briskly walked past Mark, I leaned my shoulder into his. I had him pegged at about six foot, 190, so I had him by two inches and some thirty pounds. As planned, my unanticipated shoulder bump spun him around, and he smacked into the fridge.

He said, "Hey, watch it!"

"Watch this," I said, and flipped him the bird over my shoulder before shutting the door behind me.

Chapter 20

Mark Slayton looked at his watch as soon as the door shut. "Look, I don't have all day, so I'm gonna get right to it. My old firm has a new partner."

"So what."

"Care to guess his name?"

"I thought you didn't have all day, but here you are being a typical asshole lawyer. Get to the point, or I'm calling the cops." Holly picked up the cordless phone on the counter and held it up, daring him.

"It's Lytle, Cotter, Kubicki and...wait for it... Beasey. Ring any bells, dear?"

Holly slowly placed the cordless back in the charger when she heard the name Beasey. The seed of doubt in her stomach blossomed into a full-fledged shrub. She noticed a FedEx envelope sitting on the counter and tore it open, as she tried to quell her uneasiness.

"Ah, so it *does* ring a bell. Thought it might." He smirked.

"Beasey? As in my divorce attorney, John Beasey?"

"That's right, babe. Your attorney is a new partner in my old firm. You see, the firm was also named as a defendant in the civil suits brought against me. Naturally, they expect me to pay what I can, so they did some digging into all of my assets, including marital ones."

"No, you're—you're lying."

"They dug deep enough to know your aunt had a very valuable marina, and when they discovered you were the only full-blood relative, they decided their chances of squeezing any money out of me in the future were much better if we weren't divorced. They offered Beasey a partnership in exchange for making sure the divorce papers never got finalized."

"Oh my God." Holly dropped the FedEx envelope and sat on the bar stool because her legs were about to go out from under her. She could hardly think straight.

"I don't mean to be blunt, but how much did we inherit?"

"What?"

"How much money did Millie leave us?"

"She didn't leave *us* anything, and it's none of your damn business what she left me."

"I think I've established that we're technically still married, for richer or poorer, as they say. It's the richer part I'm more concerned with right now. Half of whatever you have is mine." He nervously glanced at his watch, walked past her into the great room, and looked out the front window. "So how much are we talking about?"

"We're talking about nothing, so dream on. I'm calling my lawyer first thing in the morning. You'll never get away with this." She followed him into the great room and pointed to the Cadillac parked next to the Jeep.

"Is there somebody sitting in that car?"

He grabbed her by the arm and marched her back into the kitchen as she struggled and protested, "Let me go!" Once in the kitchen, he did, and when he looked at her, he was running his fingers through his hair. She didn't need to be an ex, or an almost ex, to recognize he was nervous about something.

"Look," he explained. "We're in a serious pickle here."

"*We're* in a pickle? What the hell are you talking about?"

"That guy in the car?"

"Yeah? What about him?"

"If I don't pay him three million dollars ASAP, he's gonna kill us. *Both* of us."

"WHAT?!"

"Shhh. Keep it down. I don't want him coming in."

"Then why did you bring him here?! My God, what's the matter with you? I'm calling the police!" She picked up the phone, and he grabbed her wrist.

"Let go!"

"Wait! Listen to me…just listen. I didn't bring him here, he kidnapped me. He was waiting for me when I got out of jail this morning. We drove straight through from Atlanta." He pointed at his swollen eye socket and added, "He gave me this black eye."

"You deserve a lot more than that. Thanks for bringing him to my door."

"I didn't want to, but I have nowhere else to turn. After I paid back the University of Georgia, I have nothing—zip."

"Who is he?"

"He's with the longshoremen's union in New Jersey—probably connected with the mob."

"Did your brain go to mush? Why didn't you pay them back?"

"I didn't have a choice who I paid; it was by order of the court. They could care less about the longshoremen."

"I'm calling the cops. This is crazy, Mark. *You're* crazy!"

"No! You can't! Listen to me, please. You remember my college roommate, Scotty?"

"Of course I do. He was in our wedding party."

"Right. Scotty worked his way onto the pension board of the union. He was my in, the one who persuaded the board to invest through me."

"He was? What a surprise. You never told me that."

"I know, I know, I'm an asshole. Anyways, about six months ago, Scotty left work one day and never came home."

"What do you mean? Like he left his wife and kids?"

"No, more like somebody made him disappear. Somebody like the guy in the car. He's got a big gun and a sharp knife, and if I don't pay him three million bucks, he's gonna use them on us. He said if he so much as hears a siren, or sees any police, we're both dead. There's something wrong with him, Holly. There's no question in my mind he'll kill us."

"Oh my God, Peter Porsche is coming. I have to warn him."

"Who?"

Holly pulled her cell out of her shorts pocket and started dialing as she walked back in the great room.

Peter Porsche had just pulled in and was looking dapper as ever in a blue blazer as he walked up to the driver's door of the Cadillac. Holly's heart was pounding as she waited for the phone to start ringing. "Ring, ring already," she urged.

It finally started to ring, and she saw Peter Porsche pat his jacket pockets as he stood up after leaning toward the open driver's window of the Cadillac. Suddenly, the landscape lights in the back courtyard area went on, and a few seconds later the front circle lights flicked on as well. Mark had noticed earlier you could see right through the front of the house into the back yard and realized they were exposed. "Don't let him see you on the phone!" He warned, as he pushed Holly into the bedroom hallway. Only 150 feet away, Peter Porsche reached in the passenger window of his Turbo Carerra and picked his phone off the seat.

"Hi there," he answered, recognizing Holly's number on the caller ID. "I was just wondering who—"

"Watch out, he's got a gun!"

"What? Who?"

"The guy in the Cadillac!"

"The guy in the Cad—?" He stopped talking in midsentence, and Holly heard a clattering noise before the line went dead. As she started redialing, Mark asked, "What happened?"

"I don't know. The line went dead."

Mark followed her into the front bedroom, and they both peered out through a crack in the blinds. Between the darkness and the big banyan tree in the middle of the driveway circle obstructing their view, they couldn't make out a thing. This time the phone rang twice and went silent. No voice mail, no nothing. Holly looked at Mark and said, "Oh my God, he's not answering. Something's wrong!"

Chapter 21

The Devil's Nephew looked at his watch and said to himself, "Times up." He pulled the keys out of the ignition and was about to exit the Caddy when he noticed a small boat pull up to the dock on the side of the house. A kid jumped onto the dock and began tying off the lines that the other guy tossed him. He couldn't help but notice the speed and efficiency of movement the kid displayed. In a matter of seconds, the kid was following the other guy across the deck to the house. *Shit.* More people meant more complications. As they walked across the deck he slid low across the passenger seat and peeked over the dash. They were wearing typical fisherman garb, but for some reason the kid didn't look like a kid. He was too stocky, too well put together. He was short, too, *really short*, like a midget. *Wait a second—a midget?* As soon as they disappeared into the house, he sat up and looked out the back window at the mailbox. The name on the box was Lutes. *Why wasn't it the same name as the asshole attorney?* He quickly pulled out his cell and dialed the Scarf again. Like always, he answered on the second ring.

"Yo, you got the Scarf."

167

"I know, I was the one who dialed. What was the name of the girl who fucked over my uncle again?"

"Holly."

"Holly *what?*"

"Lutes. Holly Lutes."

He was looking out the back window of the Caddy at the mailbox and started shaking his head.

"That's what I thought you said. You're not gonna believe this, but I think I'm sitting in her fuckin' driveway."

"What?"

"You heard me, it says Lutes right on the mailbox."

"Really? Are you sure? I mean, what are the—?"

"Odds? Pretty fucking good, since I think I just seen her boyfriend and the midget."

"Are you stroking me?"

"I think I know what a fucking midget looks like. There he is again!" He slipped down in the seat and watched as Tangles walked past the big bay window in the front of the house.

"Where? Where is he?"

"I just saw him walk through the house. This is unbelievable."

"Holy shit! You know what this means? It means the attorney who fucked the longshoremen out of three mil is married to the bitch who fucked your uncle out of the marina. Small world, huh?"

"And when I'm through with them, it'll be even smaller. I hit the jackpot on the first pull, Scarf. I got all my ducks in a row, and it's time to start makin' 'em quack."

"Don't forget about the gold. Your uncle left a note implying there was some gold involved."

"Scarf, I plan on taking every fuckin' cent the bitch has, and after that, I'm gonna make her pay. Oh, am I gonna make her pay. Same goes for the attorney and the other two assholes, especially the midget. I can't wait to kill a midget. It's on my bucket list. There he goes again!"

"Don't forget what I said about being on your toes. They gotta be connected to the ATF, or the FBI, or somebody with some serious pull. Plus, it's Florida, I hear everybody down there carries. You gotta figure anybody could be packing."

"Good point."

"So what's the plan?"

"I'm working on it, but I didn't expect all my marks to be havin' a fuckin' get-together. If I was just whackin' 'em, no problem, but I got some finessing to do to get my hands on the loot. I shoulda brought you with me."

"I booked a flight leaving Newark in an hour. I'll be in Palm Beach just before midnight."

"Good, we're gonna have a busy day tomorrow. What's this?"

"What?"

"They're leaving on the boat already—isn't that nice. Douche bags just made my job a lot easier. We can deal with them later."

"I gotta head to the airport. You gonna pick me up?"

"Yeah, I'll rent a room. Call me when you land."

"Okay, see you later." The Devil's Nephew set his phone down and chambered a round in his 9 mm automatic as he prepared to head in the house. He happened to glance in his rearview mirror and was startled to see a Porsche pull in and park only ten feet behind him. *Who the fuck is this?* He tucked the gun into his waistband, underneath the big Hawaiian shirt he had changed into, and waited.

DICK agent Thomas Cushing, aka Peter Porsche, pulled in behind the Cadillac with Georgia plates and wondered who was sitting in the driver's seat and what they were doing. He told Holly he needed to talk privately and hadn't expected anyone except Shagball and Tangles. *Shit.* He got out of the two-seater, slipped on his jacket, and casually walked up to the driver's door of the Cadillac.

The Devil's Nephew was pretending to have a conversation on his cell in the hopes the guy in the sport coat wouldn't interrupt him and walk past. It didn't work. He powered the window down as the guy leaned toward him, and they both heard a cell phone ringing. When the guy briefly checked the inside pocket of his jacket, he saw a flash of leather from his shoulder holster and the butt of his piece. *The Scarf was right, everybody packs in Florida.* When the guy excused himself to retrieve his cell from the Porsche, the landscape lights flicked on in the backyard, and he could see the attorney and the girl standing in the front room of the house, plain as day. The girl had something held to her ear, and then they both disappeared to the left side of the house in a hurry. *She had a phone to her ear, and she was calling the fuckin' guy in the Porsche!*

He took a quick look in his side mirror and saw the guy reaching through the open passenger window of the Porsche with his back to him. He quietly opened the door and quickly crossed the space between them.

The guy said, "Cad—" a split second before a silenced, high-velocity 9 mm bullet smashed through the back of his head. The guy dropped his phone and fell forward into the open window of the Porsche.

He took another step and shot him through the ear at point-blank range—the money shot for mobsters. Then he slipped the gun back into his waistband and popped the trunk on the Caddy, which he had lined with a vinyl drop cloth. He dragged the body to the trunk, and just before he was going to toss him in, the guy's phone started ringing again. *Fuck.* He unceremoniously dumped him in the trunk and rushed back toward the Porsche. On his third giant stride, the heel of his foot came crashing down on the phone, which was lying on the edge of the asphalt drive. He stomped on it again for good measure and then kicked it into the nearby bushes.

Adrenaline coursed through his veins, and he felt good. Real good. Nearly twenty years in the joint had left him a little rusty, and it was nice to be working the kinks out. Other than slicing Dr. Himmler's face off, burning his medical office down, and killing a couple of Mexican hookers, he thought he'd been keeping a pretty low profile since being sprung. He rolled the dead guy over in the trunk and removed his weapon and wallet. He found an FBI badge in one jacket pocket with the name Dan D. Kramer on it and a Homeland Security badge with the same name in the other. *Whoa, the price of poker just went up.* He shut the trunk and put the IDs and weapon under the driver's seat of the Caddy. Keeping the big tree in the middle of the circular driveway between him and the house, he crouched and dashed behind it for cover. His adrenaline level spiked even higher as he paused to consider his next move. He had just killed an FBI agent, or maybe a Homeland schmuck, or both. The price of poker wasn't just going up; it was now an all-or-nothin' proposition. It seemed killing a federal law enforcement officer was more unpopular than ever. *Go figure.*

If he was just collecting a debt, even one as large as three-plus million, he would have probably headed for the hills. He had nine hundred grand stashed in a storage unit in South Jersey, and it was tempting to run. *Almost.* But it was more than that, much more. In the name of his beloved father and departed uncle, he felt it was his duty to uphold the DeNutzio name. Although it was payback time, he was no fool. He'd give himself until noon the next day to get his hands on the money. If he didn't have it by then, he'd kill everybody who had it coming and *then* disappear. He peeked around the big banyan tree and didn't see anybody. "Let's get this party started," he softly said and quietly slipped around the east side of the house into the darkness.

Chapter 22

"Please"—Mark followed Holly into the master bed-room at the back of the house—"I'll give you the divorce, just lend me three million to give to this guy. I'll pay you back, I swear. I didn't mean to drag you into this—what else could I do?"

She turned to face him and the fear in his eyes was becoming contagious. Still, she couldn't believe her ears. "What *else* could you *do*? How about falling on your sword for once, instead of burying it in my back like always? My God, what do you think happened out there?"

"The same thing that's gonna happen to us if you don't lend me the money." One of the bedroom win-dows was cracked open, and Holly heard the familiar rumblings of the Robalo. *Yes! Kit was nearby.* Mark noticed her cock her head to listen by the open window.

"What is it?"

She slid open the sliders to the courtyard in back and pulled out her phone. As she was about to press the speed dial for Kit, a large man stepped out from the side of the house and shoved her so hard she dropped the phone and went flying into a nightstand next to the bed. A lamp and framed picture fell to the carpet, and before she got to her knees, she heard a thud. Mark was lying on the floor next to her, rubbing his head. When she looked up, the big man was zip-tying Mark's hands behind his back. She started to get up.

"You move one fuckin' inch, and I'll break every bone in that pretty face of yours." He was big and powerful, but while his face seemed to belie his menacing attitude, his eyes let her know he was serious. *Dead serious.* Holly was scared, and when she thought about Dan D. Kramer, aka Peter Porsche, her fears heightened.

"Where's, uh, where's Dan? What did you do to Dan?"

"The guy in the Porsche? The same thing I'm gonna do to you if you don't shut the fuck up. Get up, asshole." He yanked Mark off the floor with one hand and looked at Holly. "You, too. Let's go."

She got up, and he pulled a semiautomatic handgun with a silencer on it out of his waistband. Holly raised her hands in the air in a panic. "Please don't shoot. I'll give you the money, I swear, please, I—"

"Oh, I know you're gonna give me the money—every fuckin' penny and then some. That was never in question. The only question is how much pain I'm gonna inflict on your sweet ass if you don't do what I say." He pointed the gun at a picture on the wall. It was a picture of Kit and Tangles holding up a big yellowfin tuna on the day that they first met. "Where did those clowns on the boat go?"

She was thinking about the millions in gold she had stashed in a wall safe and whether he would let them go if she gave it to him. It didn't seem likely, especially with Peter Porsche unaccounted for, and she worried that Kit and Tangles might come strolling in at any moment, with deadly consequences.

"They're, uh…they're—" She inadvertently glanced at the sliders, and he picked up on it.

"What, you're expecting them back already?" He stepped over to the sliding door and stuck his head out. He could faintly hear an outboard motor and could see running lights in the back basin through the palms. He briefly considered his options then said, "Let's move it. I can deal with those bozos later."

Holly's phone, which was lying on the floor, started to ring. The three of them looked at it, and they all saw Kit's picture pop up on the screen.

"Don't answer it," warned the man with gun.

"That's him—my boyfriend, Kit. If I don't answer, he'll come running. He's probably on his way right now; he didn't want to leave me here with Mark."

"Then we better move, let's go!" He shoved Mark toward the hall and waved at Holly with the gun. Holly had one of the latest smart phones on the market, and its capabilities were nearly endless. Even if she didn't have access to it, she knew just having it with them greatly increased her chances of escape or rescue. *I have to convince him to bring it*, she thought.

"You—you don't understand," pleaded Holly. "He knows I don't go anywhere without my phone. When he comes back and finds us gone, he's going to be worried enough. If he sees I left my phone behind, he'll call the police. That's not going to help you get your money."

He considered her words as the phone rang one last time before going silent. *She was right.* "Good point. That's not gonna help you two in the breathing department either. I would say you got brains to go with your beauty, but then again, you married *this* asshole." He pointed the gun at Mark.

She responded, "I divorced him, too."

"No, you didn't. That's what I've been telling you. We're still married in the eyes of the law."

"Don't you talk to me about the eyes of the law. You practically gouged them out! You're a scumbag, Mark. He's right. I can't believe I married you."

"You two lovebirds just gave me an idea." He pointed the gun down at the phone and looked at Holly. "Turn it off and give it to me." She did as she was told, and after checking to make sure it was off, he slipped it in his pocket.

"Okay, let's go!" He prodded Holly with the gun, and Mark led the way down the hall. When they got to the great room, he said, "You got a notepad somewhere?"

"In the kitchen," answered Holly.

He directed them to the kitchen and pointed at the notepad on the counter below the phone. "Leave him a note that says you and douche bag need some time to work things out—that you'll call him tomorrow. Make it short and sweet."

Holly picked up a pen and hesitated a moment to consider what to write. She was confident Kit knew her well enough to know she would never abruptly leave with her ex, but she wanted to leave him a clue that all was not well, just in case. The Devil's Nephew could sense the wheels churning and placed the silencer to Mark's temple.

"Get cute on me, and I'll grant you the world's quickest divorce."

Mark's eyes went wide, and he winced as the silencer touched the welt around his eye.

"Do what he tells you, please."

Holly shook her head. Part of her *wanted* him dead, but the other part felt a twinge of sympathy for her battered and broken ex. She looked at the Devil's Nephew and said, "That's not much of a deterrent. I thought we *were* divorced. I *want* a divorce."

"I can't blame you. I bet you'd like to forget all about him."

"You're right."

"So look at it this way, you do something stupid, and I'll splatter his brains all over your kitchen. You'll never get the image out of your head and have nightmares for the rest of your life. So make it short and sweet, like I said."

Holly realized he wasn't joking and nodded, "Okay." She wrote, *Dear Shag, I just need a little time with Mark to sort this mess out. I'll call you tomorrow. Love, Holly.* She added a little heart with a smiley face inside it and said, "There."

The Devil's Nephew looked at it and said, "*Shag?*"

"It's short for Shagball."

"Right, and the other one's name is Jingo, or Jango, or—"

"It's Tangles, but why do you care? Wait a second, how'd you—?"

"Move it! Let's go!" He shoved Mark toward the front door and prodded Holly with the gun.

When they got out to the Caddy, he pushed Mark in the backseat on the passenger side and pointed the gun at Holly. "Hold out your hands." She held them out, and he tucked the gun in his waistband before zip-tying her hands. He put her in the front passenger seat and fastened her seat belt. Once he got settled into the driver's seat and started the car, he turned toward his captives.

"You only get warned once. If you try and get somebody's attention or do something stupid, it'll be the last fuckin' thing you ever do. But if you do as I say, maybe you'll live. Got it?" They both nodded, and he drove out onto the quiet street.

After they turned north on A1A and crossed over the Boynton inlet, Holly asked, "Where are we going?"

"Don't worry about it. Just worry about comin' up with six million bucks."

"*Six* million? *What?!* That's insane!"

"Yeah," said Mark. "Where did six million come from?"

"Simple. The three million you stole from the longshoremen and another three million for what your wife and her fishing pals did."

"*Me?* What did I do? I don't even *know* you." The Devil's Nephew remembered what the Scarf told him and decided to put it out there.

"Did I mention I want the other three million in gold?"

Holly's mouth hung open, and she looked at Mark, who said, "*Gold?* What gold? What did you do?"

A really bad feeling started to form in Holly's stomach, as if she wasn't already scared half to death. "How do...what makes you think I have gold? Who *are* you?"

"My uncle told me," he lied.

"Your *uncle*? Who's your uncle?"

"You mean, who *was* my uncle."

"He's dead?"

"You should know, you were there when he was killed. Maybe you even pulled the trigger."

"Oh my God."

"Praying ain't gonna save your ass, honey, only paying will. That, and telling me exactly how it went down at the storage center shootout. And I want names."

Mark leaned forward between the driver's seat and passenger seat and said, "What's he talking about, Holly? What storage center—?"

The Devil's Nephew snapped his fist backward, squarely into his nose. Mark fell back in the seat and cried out in pain. "Aghhh! Crap, I'm bleeding again."

"Get used to it."

Holly heard what he said, but she was in denial. *It couldn't be, could it?*

The Devil's Nephew saw her stunned expression and said, "What's the matter? You think you and your friends were gonna get away with screwing Donatello DeNutzio on a marina deal? You think you were just gonna steal his boat, kill his crew, and then set him up to get whacked by the Feds without paying the piper? *Really?* Who the *fuck* do you think you are?"

"Your uncle was...he was—"

179

"Donny Nutz. That's right, you fuckin' cunt, Donny Nutz was my uncle. I spent the last few years of my sentence thinking of all the ways I'm gonna rectify things, and after getting a look at you, I think rectify is exactly what I'm gonna do if you don't fork over the loot and dish out the truth. And I got a big appetite for both."

"You fucked over his uncle? Are you *crazy?*" The words came out with a nasal ring to them because his nose was bleeding, but Mark felt better, because Holly had apparently fucked up as bad as he had. Maybe even worse.

Holly leaned her head against the window and looked out at the dark ocean. The moon was hidden behind some clouds, and the only light came from the white frothy wave tops as they rolled onto shore. Like her life since she moved back to Florida, the ocean appeared relatively calm on top, but turmoil and danger lurked below. You never knew when a triangular fin might break the surface, but *she* knew—one was driving the car she was in. She tried to be strong like Kit and quell her fears, but it wasn't working, and for the first time since Aunt Millie's funeral, she began to softly cry.

Chapter 23

Although Three Jacks was only a mile or so away by water, I wasn't about to amp up my drinking, given the sudden appearance of Holly's ex, or whatever he was. I had Tangles spin the boat around and head into the basin behind the house.

As we putt-putted toward a bridge about four or five hundred yards away that connected another small barrier island to A1A, Tangles asked, "So is Holly the first married woman you've had a relationship with?"

"Funny guy—what do *you* think?"

"Probably not, you definitely have man-whore tendencies."

"It's called being a bachelor, asswipe. Besides, it doesn't count if she thinks she's divorced, and you do, too—I mean me. I thought she *was* divorced. Everybody did. Who knows? Maybe she really *is* divorced, and he's trying to scam her. I sure *hope* she's divorced. Man, this is fucked up."

"I know what you mean, take away the shiner, and old Mark's pretty easy on the eyes. I can see why she fell for him."

"I know I've asked you before, but are you gay?"

He downed the rest of the Negra Modelo and held up the empty bottle. "I'm gay for this beer. I gotta tell you, this is really good shit."

"You probably like it because it's got Dickhead's spit slobbered all over the rim."

"Well, something tastes good. It just needs some lime."

"You're a sick little man."

I pulled a spinning rod out of one of the rod holders on the T-top. It was rigged with a Rapallo lure, and I cast toward a light hanging off somebody's dock. I wasn't really interested in fishing; I was just trying to take my mind off the possible ramifications if it turned out Holly really *was* still married to Dickhead.

After a few minutes of casting with no bites, Tangles said, "I wonder what they're doing."

"What do you mean? They're talking. That's why she asked us to leave. She's freaked out, thinking she might still be married to Dickhead."

"Or *is* she?"

"Is she *what?*"

"Forget it."

"Forget *what?* What the hell are you getting at?"

"I probably shouldn't even bring it up; your emotions are running hot."

"You're damn right they're running hot. Some dickhead just showed up and claimed my girlfriend is his wife."

"A very good-looking dickhead."

"You *are* gay. So what's your point?"

"Look, hubby's been in the clink for three years, and he's probably hornier than a Chicago record. You've been out of town for a while, and Holly's womanly needs haven't been met. You put the two of them together, and the old sparks could be flying by now."

"*What?* She's crazy about me. No way."

"If you say so." He pointed back at the house and added, "But it looks to me like her bedroom light is on."

I turned to look. It wasn't easy to see, but it did appear the bedroom light was on. *Huh.* "That doesn't mean anything."

"Maybe, maybe not."

"You know, you're the biggest little asshole I ever met. I'm gonna call her just to prove you're wrong." I called, and her phone rang several times before going to voice mail. As usual, I hung up without leaving a message. When she saw I called she would call me back. I wasn't thrilled.

"Hey, don't worry about it," commented Tangles. "She probably didn't wanna be disturbed. That's why she didn't answer."

"Shut up."

"Wanna check it out?"

"Definitely."

We motored toward the house, and a few minutes later, we were tied up at the back dock. I didn't know what to expect and decided a stealth approach would be in order versus letting our presence be known by docking on the side, in view of the kitchen. Although I had told Holly we'd be back within the hour whether she called or not, it had only been fifteen minutes or so. I figured we'd take a quick peek inside to confirm everything was copacetic and then slip back to the dock undetected and wait for her call. Tangles followed as I made my way toward the master bedroom, using the coconut palms in the yard as cover. There was a bedroom window facing the dock, and I decided it was as good a spot as any for a little look-see.

"You wait here," I whispered to Tangles. "I'm gonna take a quick peek."

"You sure you don't want me to look? You know… in case there's something you don't wanna see. I'll peek through the sliders."

"*Very* sure. Just shut up and stay down."

I hunched over and ran the last fifteen feet to the house. The window was open a few inches, so with my back pressed against the wall, I listened for any sounds. Not hearing any, I rose up on my tiptoes and peered over the sill. There was nobody there, like I suspected, but something was odd. The nightstand by the bed was askew and the lamp that normally sat on it was on the floor. *What's up with that?* I gave Tangles a hand signal and headed to the southeast corner of the house. There was a shrub-lined walkway that led to the driveway, and I waited for Tangles to catch up before proceeding.

"I saw a pair of headlights swing around the circle and head out the drive," he whispered. "You see anything?"

"I didn't see Holly and Dickhead, but there's a lamp lying on the floor."

"Huh?"

"That's what *I* thought. Let's go around the front."

As we crept down the path, I noticed the spare bedrooms were dark, and I stopped where the path morphed into the driveway to survey the scene.

"Peter Porsche is here," I quietly noted. "And the Caddy's gone. That means Dickhead's gone. Wonder why she didn't call?" I pulled out my phone to make sure I hadn't accidentally turned the ringer down or something, but the ringer was properly set. There were no text messages either. "Hmmm, let's go in and find out what the hell's going on."

I started walking toward the front door, but Tangles grabbed me by the arm. "Wait, Dickhead might not be gone."

"What do you mean? The Caddy's gone."

"Yeah, but maybe the other guy left, and Dickhead's still inside with Holly."

"*Other* guy? *What* other guy?"

"When I went to take a leak, I looked out the front window and thought I saw someone sitting in the Caddy."

"*What?* Why didn't you say something?"

"I would have, but every time I opened my mouth, you guys shut me up."

"Why would somebody be waiting in the car? Are you sure?"

"Yeah."

"What the hell? C'mon, let's go around to the kitchen."

As we walked across the drive, we could plainly see nobody was in the great room, so they had to be in the kitchen or the living room. Quietly, we crossed the deck and then hesitated to the side of the glass-paneled French doors. If anybody was in the kitchen we would have seen shadows cast out on the deck, but there were none.

"Wait here," I told Tangles and quickly stepped past the kitchen doors. With little hesitation and a general feeling of uneasiness settling in, I peeked in the living-room bay window—nobody was there. *Huh?*

Tangles followed me through the kitchen doors, and I called out, "Holly?" No answer came back. I took a quick look in the garage, but it was empty except for my Beemer.

Tangles said, "Look at this." He was holding up the notepad that Holly kept on the island counter by the phone. When I read the message on top, I couldn't believe my eyes. *She left with Dickhead?*

"This doesn't make sense," I commented as I pulled out my cell and speed-dialed her.

Tangles said, "Women. Just when you think—"

"Shut up."

Holly's phone went straight to voice mail, and I shook my head. "She's not answering. What the *fuck*." It wasn't a question, it was a statement. I quickly walked to the master bedroom with Tangles a step behind.

"Look," I pointed next to the bed at the crooked nightstand and the lamp on the floor. I noticed a picture on the floor, too, and picked it up. It was of me and Holly on the *Lucky Dog*. Millie took it when we got back to the house after our first date at the Sailfish Marina. I had my arm around her, and there was no denying the authenticity of the smiles on our faces. It had been a great day. The first of many. I looked up at Tangles and said, "Something's wrong, man. Holly would never leave her bedroom looking like this. Something happened."

"Dude, I don't know, maybe—wait a second, what's this?" Tangles knelt down and poked his finger at a small stain on the carpet. "It's wet." He held up his finger and showed me the dark-red smudge on his finger before sniffing it and dabbing it on his tongue. "It's blood," he added. "Fresh blood."

"Are you sure?"

He held his finger out and responded, "Positive. Care for a taste?"

"That's gross. What are you, part tick? Shit, I knew I shouldn't have left. What the hell happened here? Let me see that note again."

"It's still in the kitchen."

We hurried back to the kitchen, and I reread the note twice. Something was definitely wrong. I handed the notepad to Tangles and said, "She called me Shag."

"So?"

"She never calls me Shag—or Shagball, for that matter."

"I didn't know that."

"Well, now you do. She always calls me Kit. Plus, what's with the smiley face? I've never seen that before, either. I think she was leaving me a message. I can't believe this. The only reason I was okay with leaving her here with Dickhead is because she said Peter Porsche—wait a minute, where the hell's Peter Porsche?"

"Good point. His car's in the drive. Why would *he* leave with them?"

"I don't know. I don't know what the fuck's going on. C'mon!"

We went out to the driveway, and I clicked on the small but powerful Surefire flashlight I wore around my neck on a lanyard. Holly's Jeep was empty, and when I shone the light on the Porsche, we could see it was empty, too. The windows were down, and I shone the light on the driver's side—nothing. I didn't see anything in the small area behind the seat and shone the light on the passenger side. "Oh, shit, look at that."

There was a puddle of what appeared to be blood in the crease of the leather. Tangles reached in through the open window and started to stick his finger in it, but I stopped him.

"Don't touch it, tick-boy," I warned. I walked around to the passenger side and shone the light around the doorframe. It glistened. "Jesus, it looks like blood splatter going toward the rear."

"Holy crap, this is bad, Shag."

I swept the Surefire all around, and as I looked along the edge of the driveway, something glinted in the ground cover. I pushed some shrubbery back and picked up an oversize cell phone. It was crushed, and the screen was cracked.

My own phone started to ring, and it startled us. I pulled it out, and the caller ID read: Mannix. It was the man of a million voices (presumably) who ran the secret organization that recruited us to do some "light" intelligence-gathering work. At least it was supposed to be light. Nevertheless, I was glad to be hearing from him.

"I'm glad you called," I answered. "I was about to dial the emergency number."

"What's going on there? I received a signal from Agent Kramer's phone."

It was the rough and gruff voice of Joe Mannix reincarnate. *Amazing.*

"What kind of signal?"

"It's like the black box on an airplane. His phone had a catastrophic failure, and the GPS chip shows he's there at Miss Lute's house with you and Tangles. Is he there? Can I speak with him?"

"Wait a second, how did you know me and—"

"Your phones. I always know where you are by your phones, among other things. You can thank the NSA. Now let me talk to him."

"He's not here. I found his phone in the bushes, and it's all smashed up. I'm no crime scene investigator, but I gotta tell you, it doesn't look good. There's a puddle of blood on the passenger seat of the Porsche, and there's splatter on the door frame and the rear quarter panel."

"*What?!*"

"I'm afraid you heard me right. We also found a little blood on the floor of Holly's bedroom, but nothing like the Porsche. And guess what? She's gone, too. She's gone, her ex is gone, and so is Agent Kramer. Why was Kramer here in the first place?"

"I asked him to meet with you to arrange some firearms training. It was supposed to be a routine visit. But what do you mean, her ex is gone? He's in jail."

"Not anymore. The dickhead showed up out of the blue and claimed they were still married." Tangles tugged my shirt and whispered, "Don't forget about the guy in the Caddy."

"Tangles said he saw another guy, too, waiting in the car outside—a Cadillac."

"*What* other guy? This isn't making sense. Tell me everything that happened from the start."

"All right, but you said you can track us by our cell phones, right?"

"Yes."

"Then track Holly's. She's not answering, and I didn't see or hear it inside."

"Hang on a sec." He briefly put me on hold, and Tangles and I headed back into the house.

When he came back on, he said, "I'll have a fix on her cell in a minute. Now start from the top."

After I finished telling him exactly what happened, he said, "And you're sure she didn't leave of her own free will?"

"Positive. The note was a tipoff that something was wrong; she never calls me Shag, *ever*. And there was obviously some sort of scuffle in her bedroom. Jesus, she might be hurt, man. I need to find her. I need to find her *now*."

"I just got a fix on her cell, but it looks like she's still on the move. The GPS tracker has her heading north toward West Palm Beach. When she stops moving, I can pinpoint her location within a hundred feet or so. For now, just stay put, and I'll call when I come up with a plan. I need to look into the situation with her ex getting out of jail and who might be traveling with him. I don't know exactly what's going on, but it shouldn't take long to find out. I'm putting every available resource on it."

"Good."

"I take it none of the neighbors saw or heard anything?"

"No, if they did the police would be here."

"Best to keep them out of the picture then. In fact, I'd appreciate it if you would clean up the Porsche. If somebody sees blood, it could be a problem."

"Okay, we'll take care of it. I'd put the windows up and move it, too, but the keys are missing."

"You'll find a spare key in a magnetic container in front of the rear passenger-side wheel well."

"Got it. Anything else?"

"Just this; we may be behind the eight ball right now, Mr. Jansen, but the game is far from over. We'll get Holly back and find out what happened to Agent Kramer, I promise you." Click.

I put my cell in my pocket and looked at Tangles.

"What's the plan?" he said. I grabbed a couple dish towels from underneath the sink and handed them to him along with my Surefire flashlight.

"Will you do me a favor and clean up the Porsche? There's something I need to do."

Now normally, Tangles would balk a little or press me as to why I wasn't helping, but this time he didn't. This time he just said, "No problem. Be back in a few."

While he headed out the front door, I walked back into Holly's bedroom and picked up the picture of the two of us on the *Lucky Dog*. She was absolutely beautiful, both inside and out, and I was…well, I was just me. I probably didn't deserve her, but that didn't matter. I wasn't ready to lose her, and I wasn't about to let her go without a fight. All the women before her, they were just appetizers, but she was Sunday brunch and a trip to Dairy Queen all rolled into one. Although I was raised Catholic, I wasn't a very good one. I didn't go to church except for Christmas and Easter. I wasn't even sure I believed in God anymore, except in the ancient alien context, but with a lump in my throat, I dropped to my knees and did something I hadn't done in years. I prayed.

Chapter 24

It wasn't until I reread Holly's note for the fourth or fifth time that I paid the open FedEx envelope on the counter any notice. When I saw the return address was from St. Maarten, my curiosity was piqued. I wasn't normally one to snoop, but then again there was nothing normal about Holly's running off with her ex, either. Thinking whatever was inside might possibly have something to do with her sudden disappearance, I pushed protocol aside and pulled out a letter-size envelope that had Holly's name handwritten across it. Although the envelope was unsealed, the way the letter was folded tightly inside gave me the impression that maybe it had yet to be read by Holly. After all, it was still inside the FedEx envelope. Regardless, I had the letter in my hand and began to read. The letter was handwritten, and the writing appeared rickety, as if the author were frail. I quickly scanned to the end of the letter and saw that it was from Genevieve, the Frenchwoman who raised Aunt Millie's son as her own until helping him stow away on a ship as a teen. I went back to the top of the letter and began to read.

Dear Holly,

As you can see from my writing, I am an old woman with little time left on this earth. While my strength is all but gone, I fortunately still have my eyesight and was thankful to read about your thrilling escape from the French authorities. I can tell you the gendarmes were none too happy about it, nor were they with me when I claimed memory loss over what occurred at the villa that night. As my time grows near, I realize I must tell you there is one more secret I have been burdened with for all these years. If not for the shock of realizing my own son, Chanceaux, was a murderous snake and the startling appearance of the man who shot him, I might have told you that night, but admittedly, it has been difficult to come to terms with, even now. You see, Millie not only gave birth to a beautiful son on February 22, 1948, she gave birth to a beautiful baby girl as well. She had twins.

"What?!" I don't usually talk to myself, but this was another bombshell. *Millie had twins?* Holy crap. I quickly read the rest.

Millie barely had time to count Patrick's fingers and toes before the doctor gave her a shot of something to knock her out. He handed me the baby, and I carried him into the adjoining room. I heard the doctor start yelling to his assistant. "There's another one coming!" he screamed. "Get me some fresh towels!"

Needless to say, we were all in shock, especially the doctor, who had no idea she was carrying twins. Five minutes later, the doctor handed his assistant a beautiful baby girl. Kilroy showed up and was not pleased with the unexpected development. He lambasted the doctor for not knowing Millie was carrying twins and wondered aloud what to do with her. I suggested we keep the girl and give the boy back to Millie, because we knew she had a change of heart regarding the bogus adoption. Kilroy would have none of it though; he wanted a boy, and that was that. The doctor's assistant was cradling the infant and quickly offered to take her as her own. I started to object, but Kilroy shut me down. He made the assistant swear to never divulge what happened that day and agreed to let her have the baby girl. Being the cheapskate that he was, he later complained to me that the doctor demanded double payment for the twins, which he reluctantly paid.

I know how stunned you must be to discover you have not one, but two blood relatives, and God only knows what has become of them. As anxious as you are to find Patrick, I am sure you are now equally eager to find the little girl whom Millie never knew she had. To that end, I can offer you only the following tip in your search. Like Patrick's birthmark, the little girl also had a distinguishing characteristic; one of her eyes was blue and the other was green. And while Patrick's skin was lighter, like Millie's, the little girl's was darker, like Joseph's. There's one other detail that may also help. While the doctor has surely passed away by now, his assistant was an islander who was no older than I was, and she had an unusual name: Elnora.

As you may have heard by now, Chanceaux has been placed on house arrest and is living in the family villa on St. Thomas, which I have put up for sale along with the Tiara Bay Marina. While I have plenty of extended family here on St. Maarten and have included most in my will, a portion of my estate will be set aside in a trust for Patrick and his sister, should you ever find them. It is for this reason (aside from not trusting my own attorney), that I have decided to make you executor of my will. I hope you understand, and of course you will be fairly compensated for your efforts, regardless of

whether you find your cousins or not. I have prayed every
night since the day we met that you forgive me for what I've
done, and I wish you Godspeed in your search.

Sincerely,
Genevieve

I dropped the letter on the counter and muttered,
"Jesus H. Christ."

Tangles came walking around the corner holding
a wad of bloody paper towels and replied, "At your
service. What's going on?"

"You're not gonna believe this, but Millie had
twins."

"What?!"

"That's what I said. Five minutes after Patrick was
born, she gave birth to a little girl. They knocked
Millie out after Patrick was born, and she never knew
about the girl. It's all spelled out in this letter Holly
just got from Genevieve." I held the letter up for
Tangles to see and added, "I'm not sure if she's read it
or not, but if she did, she must be freaking out even
more."

"Wow, that's crazy, but so is this." He held up the
paper towels before throwing them in the trash.

"There was a lot of blood, huh?"

"Yeah, and it had some other stuff mixed in. I gotta
tell you, if it came from Peter Porsche, I don't think
his future's too bright. So what do we do now?"

"We go looking for Holly. What else?"

Chapter 25

As the Devil's Nephew drove the Caddy north on US 1, he suddenly remembered he had Holly's cell phone in his pocket. He pulled it out and briefly pondered what to do with it before coming to the conclusion it had to go. Although he had been in prison a long time, he knew that so-called smart phones, such as the one he was holding, had GPS tracking abilities. He wasn't sure if the GPS part still worked when the phone was turned off but decided it wasn't worth the risk. He looked to his left and noticed under the streetlights that the road was approaching a wide canal. He powered his window down and held the phone up for Holly to see. "You won't need this anymore," he said, and as the vehicle crossed over the canal, he lobbed the phone up and over the roof. Holly pressed her forehead against the passenger window and saw a glint of light reflect off the phone before it disappeared into what she recognized as the dark waters of the Lake Worth spillway. She knew her phone was her lifeline, and her hope sank faster than the phone did.

Less than a mile or so later, the Devil's Nephew noticed the commercial corridor on US 1 had more of a seedy feel to it, which was just what he was looking for. In between the fast-food restaurants, bars, convenience stores, and small Latino strip centers were an increasing number of run-down motels. Up ahead he saw a neon sign for the White Horse Motel. It had a half-lit picture of a white horse on it and a flashing light advertising a vacancy, with some of the letters unlit. *Perfect.* He shook his head at how ballsy it was to name a motel the White Horse, which he knew to be an old street term for heroin. As he pulled in, he could see it was a decrepit twelve-unit motel with eight or nine cars parked directly in front of the rooms. There was a small office at one end, so he pulled up next to it and cut the engine before addressing his captives.

"All right, I'm gonna go in and get us a room. I know I don't need to tell you, but I'm gonna tell you anyway." He reached down and pulled the large double-edged knife from its ankle sheath. "Anybody tries anything stupid, and I'll slice and dice you like a fuckin' Ginsu commercial. Just sit there and keep your trap shut, got it?" Holly could see the blade glisten in the motel sign light, and she shivered before nodding yes.

From the back seat, Mark said, "We're not going anywhere. Just put that thing away, will you?"

With surprising speed he reached over and grabbed the former lawyer by his neck, yanking him up against the front seat. "I said to keep your trap shut. If you don't, I will."

Mark could barely breathe as one large hand squeezed his larynx and the other pressed the point of the knife under his black eye. It took everything he had to force out a gargled reply. He wanted to say

"Okay," but he couldn't pronounce the O. "K-kay" was all he could manage. The big man pushed him back into the corner of the seat so hard he cracked his already aching head against the side panel. He was about to cry out in pain when the big man pointed the knife at him and warned, "Not a fuckin' word, shyster. Stick your hands out."

Mark held his zip-tied hands out, and he used another zip tie to secure them to the headrest. Then he zip-tied Holly's hands to the steering wheel and said, "The car alarm goes off, and you're both dead. I'll be right back." He put the knife away and then locked the doors and activated the alarm using the remote as he walked up to the office.

Less than five minutes later he had the keys to adjoining rooms that were supposedly the last two available. He was asked to fill out a guest register and write down the license plate number of the Caddy, but as he figured, for another twenty bucks cash he was good to go. Such was the modus operandi of the White Horse Motel and hundreds of others just like it that littered Florida's US 1 from Key West to Jacksonville. The names changed, but rarely the game. They're cash-driven businesses fueled mostly by drug-dealing and prostitution—always had been, always would be. Such motels were the lodging of choice for those who had just committed a crime, were in the process of committing one, or were about to commit one. On any given night you could bet that the majority of the occupants of such motels fell into one of those dubious categories. It's a numbers thing.

The Devil's Nephew felt right at home as he escorted his two frightened captives the fifteen feet from the darkened parking lot to room number twelve. Once inside, he duct-taped them together so they were back to back and pushed them onto the queen-size bed. After turning on the TV, he unlocked the door leading to the adjacent room and said, "I'll be right back, not a peep out of you two." He exited the room and opened up room number eleven and then unlocked the connecting door joining the rooms, pushing it open.

"I need to take a leak," said Mark.

"So take one." The Devil's Nephew turned on the TV in room number eleven for a little more background noise, but Mark kept complaining.

"I'm serious, I gotta go."

"I'm serious, too," he responded as he walked back in the room and stood by the bed, towering over him. "Be thankful you don't have to drop a load."

Looking to change the subject, Holly interjected, "Why did you have to tape us together? I told you I'll get you the money. We're not going anywhere."

The Devil's Nephew walked around to her side of the bed and looked down at her. "I taped you up because I'm going into the next room to catch a few winks." He put his foot up on the nightstand and pulled out the large double-edged knife again. Kneeling down, he looked her in the eyes and traced the tip of the knife under one of her breasts. She shuddered, and he laughed.

"Hate to have something happen to those nice jugs of yours, but that's exactly what's gonna happen if you start—"

Mark heard the menace in his voice, and when he felt Holly tremble, he pleaded, "Leave her alone!"

The Devil's Nephew hopped on the bed and straddled both of them before pummeling Mark with a succession of short but powerful jabs that left him unconscious. Holly yelled for him to stop and was immediately silenced by a powerful hand that clamped down over her mouth. The left side of her face was pressed into the filthy comforter on the bed, which creaked with the added weight of the animal hovering over her. Out of her peripheral vision she could see him bending down and both smelled and felt his breath on her ear. Neither was pleasant.

"It's just me and you babe—hubby's out cold. When I take my hand away, the only thing I wanna hear is a nod. Got it?"

Holly nodded as best she could, considering the rising panic she felt. He removed his hand from her mouth, and she took a big gulp of air as he got off the bed. With a disturbing chuckle he hesitated in the open doorway between the rooms and added, "You're lucky I need to get some rest, or I'd be drillin' that sweet ass of yours like a Nazi dentist. But don't worry, we got *all* night."

Holly pulled her face out of the musty pillow and stifled a cry.

Chapter 26

Franklin Post sat in his command center recliner at DICK headquarters on the Puget Sound and shook his head in disbelief at what he learned about Holly Lute's supposed ex-husband, Mark Slayton.

He looked up at the twenty-thousand-square-foot star-studded ceiling and thought, *What are the odds?* With a sigh he scrolled through the Oralator and selected the voice of actor John Forsythe of *Dynasty* and *Charlie's Angels* fame. It was his go-to voice when he needed to come across as strong but compassionate. Then he pressed the hyperspeed dial on the armrest and waited for DICK agent Joe Davis to pick up. Davis was a former roommate of Thomas Cushing (aka Dan Kramer, aka Peter Porsche), during their FBI training days at Quantico. Franklin knew they were close and suspected Davis would be upset by the news that Cushing appeared to be the victim of foul play.

At a vacation rental house on Fernandina Beach, on the Georgia-Florida border, Davis answered even more jovially than usual. "Hey, boss, what's going on?"

"I'm afraid it's not good news, Joe."

"I guess not, or you wouldn't be breaking out the old Forsythe on me when I'm on vacation. What is it? We're losing our insurance and have to go on Obamacare?"

"I wish."

"Holy crap, now you've *really* got me concerned."

"It's about Thomas."

"What about him?"

"He's…unfortunately, Joe, he's missing."

"Wouldn't be the first time. Remember when—"

"His phone was destroyed, and there's blood all over his Porsche."

"*What?* Who told you this?"

"One of the new recruits he was on his way to see."

'What new recruits?"

"He didn't tell you about the fishing-show guys?"

"Well, sure, but he didn't say anything about them being new recruits."

"That's probably because they haven't been on assignment yet. We're building a special boat for remote surveillance missions and they're going to run it. It's almost ready. Their fishing show will be cover. Thomas was supposed to meet them tonight to arrange some firearms training."

"So what happened?"

"I…don't know. That's what I need you to find out. I'm sorry to interrupt your—"

"Say no more. If Thomas is in trouble, I'm on the way."

"Great. How soon do you think you can get there?"

"Thomas has a Porsche, but I have a Viper. If you can clear it with the Florida Highway Patrol, I can probably make it in four and a half hours, give or take.

I'll use the flashers and whatever ID I need to if someone pulls me over."

"Consider it done, and you can tell that lovely wife of yours the company's picking up the tab for another week on the beach when you get back."

"Thanks, that'll help. I'm curious though; you hesitated when you said you didn't know what happened. I take it you know *something*, right?"

"Yes, if my suspicions are correct, Thomas may have unknowingly crossed paths with a convicted murderer by the name of Marzio Giancarlo DeNutzio."

"*DeNutzio?* You mean, as in—"

"Yes, as in the nephew of Donatello DeNutzio. He's otherwise known as the Devil's Nephew."

"Holy crap, *the Devil's Nephew?* I thought that bastard was locked up somewhere."

"He was—Rahway. But he got sprung a few months ago after serving out his sentence."

"Damn, I heard that guy is one big bad motherfucker. Maybe I better bring a wooden stake. So he's out for revenge? Is that what—?"

"There's more to it than that. There's a girl missing, too, one of the new recruits. I'll fill you in on the road. Now get moving and be careful."

"Got it, boss." Click.

Franklin Post exhaled deeply and pressed the hyperspeed dial for Kit Jansen.

***

After retrieving the keys to the Porsche, I unlocked the glove box and found an ATF badge along with a loaded .45-caliber semiautomatic—a Colt. I pocketed the badge and showed the Colt to Tangles, who said, "Looks like the gun Magnum used."

"It does...I got dibs."

"What about me?"

"I'll bet he's got another piece stashed somewhere. Check under the seats. Here." I handed him my Surefire. While he looked under the seats, I put the .45 back in the glove box.

"Nothing...there's nothing under the seats, or behind them," announced Tangles. I took my Surefire back to shine around the dash and finally found what I was looking for—the hood release button. I knew the 911 Porsche had the engine in the rear and a small storage area under the hood.

After popping the hood, we both walked around to the front, and I shone the flashlight underneath as I lifted it. On the side of the compartment was a small recessed area about two feet long by a foot wide that held a metal box. When I tried to remove it, I realized it was bolted in place. "Of course," I muttered.

The box had a recessed circular lock on top, and I shone the flashlight on the ring of keys in my hand. I knew the glove box key wouldn't work, and obviously neither would the key to the transmission. There was one key that looked a little like a cigar punch, and when I slipped it into the lock and turned it, the lid opened. Inside was a sawed-off shotgun, a .357 revolver, and a small concealable—a Glock 42 .380 automatic. They were all neatly strapped to a foam bed.

Tangles let out a low whistle and said, "I thought you said we were getting involved in some light intelligence gathering or something like that. What's with all the guns?"

"I don't know, but—" My phone started ringing, and the caller ID read, Charlie. *Charlie? Who the fuck is Charlie?* I answered the call and hesitantly asked, "Hello?"

"Mr. Jansen, I'm afraid I have some troubling news." The voice was instantly recognizable. It was Charlie of *Charlie's Angels*, aka John Forsythe.

"So trouble me." I shut the hood, and Tangles followed me into the house.

"Holly's ex was released from a federal prison near Atlanta this morning and taken to a Holiday Inn by one of his former law partners. Soon after, he was—"

"Hold on a sec. So he *is* her ex?"

"What do you mean?"

"He claimed he's still married to her, that the divorce was never finalized."

"Oh, I, uh…I don't know about *that*, but that's irrelevant."

"Maybe to you, but not to me. Some dickhead swindler shows up and claims my girlfriend is his wife, it's pretty fucking relevant. In fact, on a scale of—"

"Okay, okay, I'll check into it."

"And before I forget, you might as well check to see if the Coast Guard recovered a stolen yacht named the *Downtime* about thirty miles off Freeport this afternoon."

"*What?* Why?"

"Because the guy that we left tied up on board, the guy who hijacked it, is none other than McGirt."

"*McGirt?* You don't mean—"

"I'm afraid I do. The same slithery sub captain we got tangled up with in the Caribbean tried to kill us again this morning. Can you believe it? Every time we try to help him, he tries to kill us. What's up with that?"

"As they say, no good deed goes unpunished. I'm sure the DEA would like to talk to him about the Cordero brothers' operation. I'll give them a call."

"Fucker tried to hijack me again. I'm starting to get a complex."

"I take it there's more to the story."

"Are you kidding? I could write a book about it. But, as you say, it's irrelevant. So what's up with Dickhead?"

"Well, as I was saying, surveillance cameras in the lobby show an unsub escorting Mr. Slayton out of the hotel within minutes of his arrival."

"Unsub?"

"An unidentified subject."

"Oh, right, like a UWO."

"A *what?*"

"An unidentified walking object."

"I, uh, guess you could call it that. Anyways, another camera in the parking lot shows them getting into a Cadillac with Georgia plates. They must have driven all day to get to Holly's. The plates come back to a rental car agency and show the vehicle was rented by a Mr. Roger Kent."

"Roger Kent? Who the hell is Roger Kent?"

"That's the troubling part. The license he used to rent the car was bogus, and Roger Kent is undoubtedly an alias. One possible clue to his identity is that airline records show us the city he arrived from."

"Which is?"

"Newark."

"Newark? What the hell."

"We dug a little deeper and also found that a Roger Kent flew from Guadalajara to Newark on the same day a notorious facial reconstruction surgeon was murdered and his clinic burned down."

"So what...what's going on here?"

"As you may or may not know, Mark Slayton went to jail for pilfering some pension funds."

"Holly told me."

"Did she tell you *which* funds?"

"No...what difference does that make?"

"Because one of the funds he stole from was the International Longshoremen's Pension Fund in New Jersey. His cohort on the pension board went missing a few months back and hasn't been seen or heard from since."

"The longshoremen? Don't they have mob ties?"

"Very good. They most certainly do."

"Hey, I saw *Goodfellas,* or maybe it was *The Sopranos.* So, how much did Dickhead steal from them?"

"Three million dollars."

"Ouch, that'll sting ya."

My mind was racing with the implications of what I was being told. Holly's ex shows up on her doorstep claiming to still be married and has some mobster waiting in the car because...because...*because the fucker was hitting her up for three million bucks!*

"Mr. Jansen?"

"Quit calling me that! I was just thinking. Dickhead must be trying to shake Holly down for three million to pay off the mob. I mean, that's gotta be it, right? What else could it be?"

"You reached the obvious conclusion, as did I, but there's a little more to the story, and I'm afraid it's not good."

"It never is. Great. What."

"Several months ago, the facial reconstruction surgeon I mentioned was brutally murdered, and his office in Guadalajara burned to the ground. And when I say 'brutally murdered,' I mean his face was cut off. A bloody piece of gauze found at the scene was linked by DNA to a recently released inmate from the East Jersey State Prison, in Rahway, with known ties to the longshoremen's union. While it's clear he went to Mexico for a new face, what *isn't* known is why he killed the surgeon, or what his new face looks like. Did he kill him because of a botched face job, or was it something else? Due to the surgeon's shady background and shoddy track record, either is possible. Although we don't know what his face looks like, we do know his physical attributes. He stands six feet four inches tall, and when he left prison he weighed two-hundred and fifty pounds. He has an overdeveloped upper torso and comparatively skinny legs. He also has a small gap between his front teeth. Based on the surveillance video from the Holiday Inn, it's likely he's Roger Kent, the man who rented the Cadillac. I'll send some photos to your phone, but the video image isn't great. Like I said, the body appears to match, but without fingerprint or DNA confirmation, and not knowing what his new face looks like, we can't be certain."

"So, if Roger Kent is the guy who killed the surgeon, then you know who he is."

"Yes, I'm afraid so."

"That doesn't sound good. That's the second time you said you were afraid. Now *I'm* starting to get afraid. Who is it?"

"His name is—shit."

"Wow, that's not a name you hear every day."

"That's not what I meant. Holly's phone just went dark. It stopped transmitting…*shit!*"

"Where? Gimme a location."

"Hang on."

My heart pounded as I waited for him to come back on the line. Tangles was drinking another one of my Negra Modelos, so I snatched it and wiped the rim before taking a swig.

"You there, Mr. Jansen?"

"Yes—quit calling me that! Where did her phone go dead?"

After brief consideration, Franklin Post decided not to give the exact location. He was confident in his assessment of the situation and worried that Kit would go charging off and get himself killed, despite recent history which would suggest otherwise.

"Let's see. They're north on US 1—oh, crap, my link just went down."

"You gotta be kidding me. What are you linked through, Healthcare.gov?"

"I'll get it to you as soon as I can, but don't worry, he probably won't do anything to Holly until he gets the money."

"Probably?"

"She didn't have any large sums in the house, did she?"

"Not that I—oh, shit, the gold."

"What gold?"

"Gimme a minute, I need to check something out."

I dashed to the master bedroom and stopped in the doorway to survey the scene again.

Tangles was on my tail. "What's going on?"

I pointed to an oil painting on the wall by renowned Florida artist Geoffrey Bate that I had given to Holly for her birthday.

"Does that painting look like it's been moved? Does it look straight? It looks straight, right?"

Tangles looked at me funny. "Yeah, it looks fine, why?"

I crossed the room and lifted the painting off the wall, exposing the safe Holly had installed. The safe was locked, and there was no way to know if it had been cleaned out, because I didn't have the combo. I raised the phone and spoke. "I can't say for sure, but it doesn't look like anybody was in the wall safe. There's a painting that covers it, and if she had been forced to open it, I think she would have left it tilted or written something in her note to let me know."

"That's good. Maybe he doesn't know about the gold. He probably snatched her to keep her from going to the police and intends to take her to the bank in the morning. As I said, chances are he won't harm her until he gets what he's after."

"What do you mean, 'chances are?' I'm thinking if you give somebody three million dollars, they might let you go, right? I mean, why wouldn't he let her go if he got the money? He's got no axe to grind with Holly." When he didn't answer right away, a growing seed of dread started sprouting in my gut, because he knew who Roger Kent was. "Charlie? I said he's got no axe to grind...right?"

"There's no need to be alarmed."

"It's a little late for that. So who is he? Who the hell's this Roger Kent guy?"

"I have an agent on the way. He should be there between twelve thirty and one in the morning. I think it's best if you just stay put. The banks don't open till—"

"WHO THE FUCK IS IT?!"

I heard him let out a deep breath, and then he answered, "As I said, we can't be a hundred percent sure at this point, but if Roger Kent is the same guy who killed the Mexican surgeon, his name is Marzio Giancarlo DeNutzio."

"*DeNutzio?* You mean—?"

"Yes, DeNutzio as in Donny Nutz's nephew. He's also known in the prison system as Nipote del Diavolo, or the Devil's Nephew."

"Ho-lee fuck."

Chapter 27

"Did I just hear you say 'DeNutzio'?" asked Tangles.

I had slipped my cell in my pocket and was looking out the kitchen doors at the running lights of a small boat motoring down the channel. I managed to make out the silhouette of a lone captain, flanked by an arsenal of spinning rods protruding from the T-top and both gunwales. He was likely getting ready for a little night fishing/scouting expedition in preparation for the opening of snook season. I'd done the same thing countless times on my little Robalo. All you had to do was set up by any barnacle-laden dock with an overhanging light and let the games begin. And if the docks weren't producing, you always had the bridges to fall back on. While you had to throw back any snook until the season began, mangrove snapper, moonfish and sheepshead were both fair and tasty game. As it idled out of view, I pictured someone who could have been me: at his side a five-gallon bucket of live shrimp kept alive by a rim-mounted aerator that steadily hummed along. I pictured a small cooler full of cold ones sitting on the deck and a fish whistle tucked in the breast pocket of the guy's Guy

Harvey T-shirt—even a bag of Chili Cheese Fritos on the console. *Those were the days.*

"Shag?"

"Fuck," I repeated as my fishing fantasy went to shit.

"Fuck *what?* What did you say DeNutzio for?"

"Donny Nutz has a nephew who just got out of prison in Jersey. Care to guess where he is now?"

"Disneyland?"

"No, asshole, he's here. *Right here.*" I pointed my finger toward the driveway and added, "He was the guy in the Caddy."

"WHAT?!"

"Yeah, but it gets better."

"*Better?* It never gets better when somebody says, 'It gets better.' It's like when somebody says, 'But there's more to the story.' There's always more to the story, and it usually gets worse...*way* worse."

"Better, worse...same difference. We're on Fuck Street either way. It seems Donny Nutz's nephew is a chip off the old block, except he's bigger and badder. He's known throughout the prison system as Nipote del Diavolo. Know what that means?"

"Sure. It means something like spicy noodles. I think I had it at Olive Garden."

"Cute. It means 'the Devil's Nephew.'"

"That, uh, that doesn't sound good."

"It's not. The first thing he did when he got out of prison was go to Mexico for a new face. I'm guessing his first one wasn't anything to write home about."

"Maybe he just wanted to disguise his appearance."

216

"Or maybe both. One thing's for sure—his surgeon's not talking."

"Why's that?"

"Oh, I don't know, it might have something to do with having his face cut off."

"His face was—?"

"Yeah, you heard me right. DeNutzio was so pleased with his new face that he cut the surgeon's face off and then burned his clinic down. The Mexican cops got lucky and found some DNA linking him to the scene."

"Holy shit. See, I told you it always gets worse."

"But it gets better."

"You mean, worse."

"Right."

"So what's Holly's husband doing with DeNutzio?"

"You mean ex-husband."

"Husband, ex-husband, same difference."

"No, no it's not. It's the complete opposite, in fact."

"Whatever. So what's the connection?"

"Holly's ex got sprung from federal prison in Atlanta. He did a few years for scamming some pension funds out of a lot of money. One of them was the International Longshoremen's in New Jersey. Somebody from his old law firm picked him up from prison early this morning and dropped him off at a Holiday Inn. Soon after, he was seen being escorted into a black Caddy by someone who fits the physical description of our boy DeNutzio, who has known ties to the longshoremen's union. They ran the plates and found it was rented by a Mr. Roger Kent. Travel records show a Roger Kent flying from Newark to Atlanta the night before, and also from Mexico to Newark the same day the surgeon got murdered. Roger Kent and the Devil's Nephew are likely one and the same."

"You can never trust a guy with two first names… Roger Kent. What kind of parents would do that? It's confusing, like Chuck Todd or Matt Damon. Which is it—Matt or Damon? You shouldn't be able to have it both ways. It's just wrong. It's the Benedict Arnold syndrome. It's a curse."

"Worked out pretty good for Matt Damon."

"True, but how else could you explain Greg Norman never winning the Masters—Larry Mize? Wrong. Two first names. Don't even get me started on Neil Patrick Harris."

"That's great, but the only name I'm concerned about right now is Holly's, and finding her. And to find her, we need to find DeNutzio."

"Right. You said he was bigger than his uncle. How big?"

"Six four and two hundred and fifty pounds, with a big upper torso and skinny legs."

"That doesn't sound *too,* too big."

"Only if he plans on leg wrestling you. Did I mention Holly's ex had a partner on the longshoremen's board who went missing?"

"No, you didn't."

"He left work one day and never came home. The Feds think he's swimming with the fishes."

"He moved to Orlando and got a job at SeaWorld?"

"Glad to see you've kept your sense of humor, considering *you're* the one who shot Donny Nutz. You better hope old Marzio wasn't tight with Donny, but I wouldn't count on it."

Tangles started talking fast, like he was prone to do whenever he got nervous. "He can't know it's me, right? I mean, how could he know? There was nothing in the papers. He was in prison."

"Yeah, you're right. Maybe he doesn't know that Holly's aunt screwed his uncle out of the C-Love Marina and that we were involved in the shootout at the storage center. Maybe he's just here to collect the money Dickhead owes the union."

"Shit. You don't believe that, do you?"

"About as much as I believe Susan Rice on a Sunday morning."

"You see, I *told* you it always gets worse!"

"The only thing we have going for us is that DeNutzio probably won't touch Holly until after he gets what he wants. Maybe she figured that out and didn't tell him about the gold in the safe."

"Assuming it's still in there."

"It's gotta be, otherwise she would have left a sign or something."

"So what the hell are we supposed do?"

"Mission control wants us to stay put until Peter Porsche's replacement gets here. He's on the way, but he's not gonna be here until twelve thirty, maybe one o'clock in the morning."

"That's a long time."

"Too long. I can't sit on my hands knowing Holly's in DeNutzio's."

I opened the fridge and popped the tops on a couple more Negra Modelos before handing one to Tangles.

"We need a plan," I said. "C'mon." While exiting the kitchen door to the deck, I could see the little boat that passed by earlier was anchored a few hundred yards away next to a neighbor's dock. For a brief moment I saw the glow of soft red ember from the cockpit and sighed. Once again I found myself scrambling to put together a makeshift plan—this time to save Holly—when I should be fishing. *Damn.*

I sat down on one of the patio chairs, and Tangles took the couch.

"This is fucked up," he said. He pointed toward the small boat. "We should be out on the Robalo, fishing, like that guy. Hell, its calm enough to go out on the reef and do some yellowtailing."

I didn't think it appropriate to tell the little squirt I was thinking the same thing, and I didn't. Holly was too special to trivialize, and I felt embarrassed to be thinking about anything else but having her back in my arms. The reality of it hit me hard, like an Aqua Velva slap on a sunburned face.

"There's no time to be thinking about fishing, dude, this guy's a fuckin' maniac. Where would he go? Where would he take her?"

"I don't know, but he's got hubby to deal with, too, so he's got his hands full."

"Quit it with the 'hubby' shit, will you? Even if they're technically still married, they won't be for long."

"Especially if DeNutzio whacks him. Now that I think of it, he doesn't need hubby now that he's got Holly. She's the one with the money. Hell, he may *already* be dead."

"That'd be a shame, one less dickhead in the world, but it doesn't get us any closer to finding Holly. Before the GPS tracker on her phone went dead, it showed they were on US 1 north. They could be going anywhere."

"*Where* on US 1? That would be a good place to start."

"Don't you think I asked that? The computer went down, and I'm supposed to get a call back with the address."

"The computer went down? You gotta be kidding me. I thought this was some sort of high-tech group we're working with. What gives? They linked through the Obamacare website?"

"Get out of my head."

"*What?*"

"Forget it."

"You know who might be helpful?"

"Who?"

"Rudy."

"Rudy your *dad?*"

"No, that lawyer, Rudy, whose house you care-take for in Hypoluxo—*of course* I'm talking about my dad. He worked the casinos in Biloxi for years. If anyone knows how criminals think, it's him."

"I'm gonna tell him you said that."

"You already have. I bet he's rubbing elbows with some shady characters at the Hard Rock Casino right now."

"So call him already. This may be the first good idea you've had since you jumped off that cruise ship."

Tangles pulled his cell phone out of his pocket, muttered "asshole," and started dialing.

Chapter 28

About seventy-five miles south-southwest of Lantana, perched on the edge of the Everglades, Travis K. Rainbow, aka Rudy, shook a pair of dice in his hand. He was up over fifteen hundred bucks at the Miccosiouxkee Resort and Reservation and had over two thousand dollars' worth of chips on the line. Ten was his point number, so he needed to roll a ten before rolling a seven and crapping out. One flick of the die could end up making or breaking his night, and he urged their cooperation as he raised them to his lips.

"C'mon, my little porcelain puppies, ol' Rudy needs a ten like a rooster needs a hen. Don't even *think* about laying a six plus one on me. I won't even *say* that number, because it's evil. Ten is the number, the perfect number. Like Bo Derek. Think about Bo Derek, don't be thinking about no—"

The big guy next to him wearing a cowboy hat nudged his shoulder and said, "How 'bout you think about rollin' them dice, pardner?"

Rudy looked up at him in disbelief. "What the hell you doing, Bubba? In case you haven't noticed, I'm hot." He pointed at the pile of chips on the table and added, "See that pile? It's about to get a whole lot bigger." He pushed a hundred-dollar chip onto the double-five square, which paid eight to one if he rolled a pair of fives. "There, that oughta do it," he said, and slowly raised the die to his lips again. "Now, where were we, my—?"

"Hey! How about throwing the dice? You know... while we're young," said a man across the table wearing a hideous-looking designer shirt.

Rudy gave him a look like he accidentally swallowed some soy milk and countered, "Nice shirt. The gift shop have a clearance sale?"

"If you will, sir, please," said the croupier, who motioned for Rudy to throw the dice.

"All right, all right, better get your umbrellas out, 'cause it's about to start rainin' cash." He raised the dice to his lips for the third time and whispered, "C'mon, die, think about Bo Derek's toes. She got ten perfect little toes, five on each foot. Gimme a pair of fives." He kissed the dice and let them fly across the table with a final request. "Gimme Bo's toes!"

The table was full, and everybody bent forward to watch the dice careen off the wall. A loud cheer went up as they came to rest showing a pair of fives.

Rudy raised his arms in triumph like a referee signaling a touchdown and accidentally knocked the cowboy hat off the guy next to him. The croupier announced, "Ten's a winner! The shooter wins with double fins!" There was a lot of backslapping going on, and the man who got his hat knocked off lifted Rudy up in a bear hug as the croupier settled the bets. When the man set him down, Rudy tried to apologize for knocking off his hat, but the man would have none of it.

"Forget about it, I shouldn't have interrupted you," he said as he picked his hat off the floor. "In fact, you can talk to those dice as much as you want. Hell, the way you're getting along, you may need to get a room!" He gave Rudy a wink and let out a big guffaw.

Rudy felt his cell phone vibrate in his pocket. It took him a few moments to realize it, as he was focused on all the chips the croupier was stacking in front of him. When he saw it was his son, Tangles, calling, he stepped back from the table and answered. "Son, you would not believe the hot streak I'm on. I'm like a comet with hemorrhoids. I'm like a—"

"Holly's in trouble, Dad...big trouble."

Rudy had a finger stuck into his nonlistening ear as he tried to snuff out the considerable background noise.

"What did you say? You hate Barney Rubble?"

"No! Holly, Holly's in trouble. Big trouble."

"You said Holly's in trouble?"

"Yes, I thought you might be able to help. Where are you, the Hard Rock?"

"No, I'm—"

Suddenly the man with the cowboy hat spun Rudy around by the shoulder and pointed at the craps table.

"C'mon, pardner, put that dang phone down and git to tossing them bones. Don't wanna let that hot hand get cold now, you hear?"

Rudy swatted the big man's hand away and told Tangles he'd call him back after he found a quiet place to talk. He told the croupier he was passing the dice and handed them to a little old lady who was next in the rotation. After picking up over $3,000 worth of chips, he tossed the croupier a hundred-dollar chip and winked. "There's a little justice for ya, Bubba."

The croupier acknowledged him, and Rudy ignored the players who begged him to keep throwing with the hot hand. As he walked away he heard the little old lady scream, "Show me those Ho's toes!" There was a second or two of silence and then a collective groan before the croupier declared the inevitable, "Craps."

A few minutes later, Rudy found a semiquiet bar near the poker tables and called Tangles back. After listening to him tell the story of Holly's disappearance, Rudy said, "This Devil's Nephew guy sounds like a job for the FBI. He crossed state lines, right? That's my advice, call the FBI."

"We can't. There's things that might come out about the C-Love Marina deal that would be bad for everybody."

"What do you mean *everybody?*"

"Who else? Yours truly, Shagball, Holly, Hambone, Kodak...I'd tell you about it if I could, but I can't. At least not right now. We've been in touch with the, uh, the authorities, and they're sending help, but it's not the FBI."

"So who is it then?"

"We're not exactly sure at this point, but they've come through for us a couple times."

"You're not sure? What the hell have you got yourself into, son?"

"Forget it, I just thought—"

"Now hold on just a damn second! You pulled me away from a craps table on a streak so hot I coulda set a gator's ass on fire. The least you can do is tell me how you think I can help."

"I thought with your, uh, background, you know, you might be able to shed some light on where this guy might take Holly. We were told to stay put until help arrives, but Shagball can't wait, and I can't blame him."

Rudy knocked back his ginger ale and looked around the bar before answering. "You said he drove down from Atlanta?"

"Yeah."

"Well, if this Devil's Nephew is half the badass you say he is, he probably has some anger management issues. That's good, because guys like that don't always think things through, like, where's he gonna take her? It's not his home turf, so he probably didn't have it all planned out."

"And it's not just her, remember? He's got Holly's ex with him, too. We think he's trying to get her to repay the money he swindled."

"So he's got the both of them to deal with until the banks open tomorrow, is that about right?"

"That's the theory."

"Then he's probably tired of driving by now. It's getting late, and he's gonna need some shut-eye. After twenty years in the joint, sleeping habits are hard to break. My money says he finds a place to hole up in, but he won't go too far."

"A hotel? But there's a million of them."

"Did I say hotel? No. I'm talking about a *mo*tel. He'll go for one of those roadside dives you see on Military Trail or Dixie Highway. You know the ones

I'm talking about—those eight- to fifteen-unit deals with bad lighting, bad décor, bad owners, and bad tenants. They look scary, and they are. Most important to him is those kindsa places usually don't have cameras."

"There's a million of those, too."

"He'll be backed up to the room so he can get away fast if he needs to. Most people driving a Caddy would only stay in one of these joints as a last resort when nothing else is available. Since it's the off season, there should be some vacancies. A Cadillac should stick out like Miley Cyrus's ass on an awards show. It might not be as hard as you think to find it."

"What? Miley Cyrus's ass?"

"No, the Caddy with the Georgia plates. If you know he was traveling on US 1, just check…uh, actually, now that I think of it, maybe you *should* wait for help to arrive. If this guy is such a—"

"Thanks, Pops, gotta run."

"Tangles? Tangles don't—" He looked at the screen on his cell and confirmed the connection was gone. "Shit," he muttered. Knowing Tangles wouldn't answer if he called back, he didn't bother to. He headed back to the craps tables, but half way there he stopped in his tracks. He was still learning to be a dad after the shock of discovering Tangles was his son, and his long-dormant fatherly instinct kicked in. He headed to the cashier, and after cashing in his chips, he walked over to a pit boss he knew.

When the pit boss saw him approach with a fistful of money, he said, "I heard you tearing up the craps table all the way from here. Don't tell me you're calling it a night already."

"No, I'm afraid my night's just getting started."

"So what can I do for you?"

"Is the chief in?"

"The chief? What do you want with the chief?"

"I need a favor." Rudy stuffed a hundred-dollar bill in his shirt pocket and added, "What do you say, Bubba? Think you can help out a brother?"

The pit boss pulled a cell phone out of his pocket and smiled. "I say it sure is good to see you again, Brother Rainbow. Let me see if I can hail the chief."

Chapter 29

Less than five minutes later, Rudy was escorted into the chief's triple penthouse suite by a burly security guard. As the door closed behind him, he eyed the surroundings with wonder. The cypress walls were covered with animal mounts of all types. There were boar heads, otter heads, coon heads, fox heads, gator heads, bird heads, fish heads…pretty much any kind of head you could think of. Sprawled on the polished oak floor was a black bearskin rug whose head pointed at a giant mahogany desk. The desk was littered with flat screen monitors that showed the casino floor, cashier, lobby, parking garage, and various other points of interest. Behind the desk, a glass wall faced northwest across the vast Everglades and sitting at the desk facing out into the darkness sat Chief Willie in full headgear. Rudy cleared his throat as he walked across the bear's back before breaking the ice.

"Hey, Chief, thanks for—"

The chief raised his hand to cut him off, and without facing him, he pointed at the glass wall. "Tell me, brother, what do you see?"

Rudy squinted as he looked into the darkness and shook his head. "Is this a trick question? It's the

Everglades out there. It's pitch black, you can't see anything."

"Exactly. That's what we're telling them in Tallahassee. We should be seeing more casinos out there. I had a vision late one night of what this area could be, and the sign in front read; Welcome to Swamp Vegas."

"Smoking the peyote again, huh?"

The chief spun around with a frown on his face.

"I ate some mushrooms, but that's beside the point. Travis K. Rainbow should be one hundred and ten percent in favor of building another casino, even in the middle of Lake Okeechobee."

"Swamp Vegas, huh? It does have a nice ring to it."

They both laughed, and Rudy stepped up to the desk to shake the chief's hand. The chief slapped him on the back and said, "Good to see you, Rudy. What brings you by? I know you don't need me to extend your line of credit, you're up thirty-seven hundred tonight."

"Closer to thirty-three; I spread a little around."

"That's why the staff loves you, even if you've been spending more time at the Seminole Hard Rock than here."

"How did—?"

The chief put his hand up again. "Seems the Seminoles were skeptical that Travis K. Rainbow was a member of the Miccosiouxkee tribe and called me to verify—can't imagine why. How did you come up with that ridiculous name again?" The chief sat back and laughed.

"Laugh all you want. It works like a charm. It even gets me half price airboat rides. Speaking of ridiculous, what's with the headdress? You trying out for the new Village People tour?"

Rudy and the chief were going through their usual ritual of teasing each other; the chief would tease Rudy about pretending to be Indian for the perks, and Rudy would tease the chief about being...well, the chief.

Fifteen years earlier, the chief wasn't the chief; he was a rising political force in the tribe named Willie Leadfoot. Rudy and Willie became fast friends one night at the Palm Beach Kennel Club and met up at a nearby strip joint afterward. Willie overdid the Wild Turkey, and a dancer complained to the club owner that he got too frisky during a lap dance. The bouncers started bouncing, and before long there was a free-for-all involving Willie, his Indian entourage, the bouncers, and several customers. Willie and his buddies were cuffed and in squad cars, about to be transported to jail, when a commanding officer that Rudy knew showed up on the scene. After slipping him a couple Benjamins and agreeing to pay for the bar damage, Willie Leadfoot and company were freed. Willie realized that his fast rise up the Miccosiouxkee ranks could have been derailed and thanked Rudy profusely. They remained friends, and when he became chief he made Rudy a pseudo-official tribe member, which got him special perks in virtually any Indian casino in the country. Rudy loved it to no end and once again thanked the chief, who was strangely silent.

"I was just kidding about the Village People, Chief; you know I appreciate you vouching for my Native American heritage."

The chief laughed again. "You earned it, my friend. So, what I'm curious to know is, what could possibly make you walk away from a craps table in the middle of a hot streak?"

"My son has gotten himself into a situation."

"The son you told me about last year? The one you didn't know you had?"

"Yes. I haven't had any more since...that I know about. Don't plan to, either."

"Ah, I see. Isn't fatherhood wonderful?"

"Actually, he's a good kid, but it's complicated."

"It always is, brother. So what kind of situation are we talking about?"

"The kind that involves getting on the wrong side of the wrong people."

"What about the police? Are they involved?"

"No, like I said, it's complicated. Twenty years ago, I'd round up a couple guys from the other side of the tracks and deal with it myself, but these guys today play by different rules. Some of them play to kill. I need a specialist. You know, someone with special skills in dealing with violent individuals."

"Maybe someone like a magician? Someone who can make things disappear?"

"If necessary."

"Like maybe in the swamp?"

"Maybe...the swamp's good. It's good at keeping secrets. I need someone who can do the same."

"I happen to know such people, but silence is golden, which is why it costs so much."

"How much?"

"A lot more than you won tonight."

"What can I get for three grand?"

"Let me think a minute." The chief spun his chair around and gazed out into the foreboding darkness of the Everglades.

"I need someone with a car, too, someone who can leave as soon as possible."

"At least when you visit, you don't ask for much," the chief quipped.

"Sorry, Chief, I just found out and—"

The chief raised his hand. "Say no more. I thought of someone who can help you, a fellow brother. His methods are rather…primitive, but his price is right, and he's not much for talking."

"Works for me."

"Let me see if he's available." The chief pulled out his cell and was soon speaking in a Native American tongue. After a minute or so, he slipped the phone back in his pocket and turned to Rudy. "You're in luck. I talked to his brother and they just got back from python hunting. He'll be here in a few minutes. So what happened to your car?"

"My fiancée's got it. She dropped me off and went to visit a girlfriend in Key Largo. She's supposed to—"

"Did you just say *fiancée*? Travis K. Rainbow is taking a squaw?"

"Not just any squaw. Her name is Marie Dupree, and she's the mother of my son."

"Talk about making up for lost time. That's two more tribe members. This calls for a drink!" Rudy hadn't had a drink in ages but didn't want to offend the chief. Against his better judgment, he acquiesced. For ten minutes they chitchatted, and one drink led to two as Rudy told the chief about Marie and Tangles. A buzzer sounded, and the chief briefly glanced at one of the monitors on his desk before pressing a button that opened the door to the suite.

Rudy stood only five feet four inches tall and 140 pounds soaking wet, and he figured the young Indian who walked in wasn't a whole lot bigger. He had on moccasins and wore jeans with a black long-sleeved T-shirt. As he walked toward them, Rudy could see his jet-black hair was tied back in a ponytail and topped off with a camo bandanna. The young man stood next to Rudy and bowed to the chief, who then walked out from behind his desk. Rudy noticed a long black knapsack covered the young Indian's back. The chief stopped directly in front of the young man and placed both hands on his shoulders.

"Brother Flingblade, thank you for coming so quickly." They embraced, and the chief stepped back to introduce him. "Brother Rainbow, this is Brother Flingblade."

The young Indian smiled and nodded at Rudy who shook his hand and said, "Nice to meet you, uh… what's the name again?"

"Flingblade," said the chief. Flingblade nodded and crossed his hands at his waist like an altar boy. Rudy thought him oddly silent and not at all what he was looking for. He looked at the chief and expressed his doubts.

"Chief, I dunno, he's not exactly what I was thinking of. He's not much bigger than me. These guys—"

"Flingblade," said the chief, who pointed at the far wall. "The bobcat's balls." There was a full-body mount of a bobcat on the wall, sandwiched between an armadillo and a red fox. The young Indian reached over his shoulder and in one fluid motion snapped his arm forward in a blur. Rudy instinctively turned his head to the side and felt a rush of air on his face as something flew past. In a split second there was a loud, reverberating *thwack* as a hatchet buried itself in the wall, followed by the soft thump of the bobcat's balls as they hit the oak floor.

"Sweet Lady Marmalade!" cried Rudy. "You almost took my ear off!"

Flingblade shook his head no, and the chief responded, "Not even close; he's the best blade man in the business."

"Chief, I'm pretty sure these guys have guns."

"Of course." The chief pointed at the opposite wall, which was loaded with stuffed birds. "Flingblade... the owl's eye." Flingblade reached over his shoulder again, removed a small crossbow from the knapsack, and after barely hesitating to aim, squeezed the trigger. In a millisecond, an arrow only eighteen inches long pierced the owl's eye and with a *crack* pinned it to the wall.

As feathers silently fluttered to the floor, Rudy looked at Flingblade and said, "Damn, Bubba, remind me to stand behind you before you start putting the mustard on Custard." Flingblade nodded, and Rudy looked at the chief questioningly. "He the silent type?"

"You could say that. He's mute." Rudy looked at Flingblade, who made a gesture with his hand like he was locking his lips. Rudy pointed at him and looked at the chief. "But...but he understands what we're saying?"

"He's not as good with English as he is with our native language, but he gets it for the most part. He's just mute, not deaf and dumb. One shouldn't forget that."

"I'll say, or one's balls might end up as cat food."

As Flingblade retrieved his hatchet and arrow, Rudy tossed back the rest of his whiskey. The familiar burn of the liquor as it passed his larynx and settled in his stomach helped calm the nerves. He was upset with Tangles for getting in over his head, and here he was doing the same. *What the hell am I doing?* he thought. Rudy looked at the empty glass in his hand with horror. *Why am I drinking?* He abruptly set the glass on the chief's desk and pushed it away.

"Want a refill?" asked the chief.

"No...Lord no. I shouldn't have had any in the first place. I need all my wits and then some."

"Well, you've seen a little of what Flingblade can do. Anything that can be thrown as a weapon, he's more than proficient at. I once saw him take a grasshopper's head off with a beer bottle top. He's hell with a boomerang, too. That reminds me." He lowered his voice and added, "Whatever you do, don't let him drink. He's got a problem that way."

"*He's* got a problem?"

"A little one, but as far as I know, he hasn't been off the wagon in a good six months."

"Oh, boy."

"What?"

"Nothing."

Rudy heard a faint scraping sound, turned his head, and did a double take. Flingblade was standing right behind him sharpening the hatchet blade.

The chief laughed at the "where did *you* come from?" look on his face and said, "I forgot to mention he has a habit of appearing out of nowhere, like a ghost. I swear he could sneak up on his own shadow… if he had one."

"What?" The whiskey had Rudy a bit flushed, and he wasn't sure *what* to believe.

The chief busted out laughing and slapped him in the back. "I was just kidding. He's not a vampire. Right, Flingblade?"

Flingblade shook his head no, and the chief took him aside and started speaking in Indian again. Flingblade did a lot of nodding and then rubbed his index finger and thumb together—sign language for "show me the money."

The chief turned to Rudy and said, "Give me a thousand bucks." Rudy counted out a thousand and handed it over. Flingblade shoved it in a pocket and gave Rudy a big smile along with a thumbs-up.

"Okay," said the chief. "He's all yours." The chief held out an open palm toward the door, and the three of them proceeded to it. Rudy had a bad feeling in his gut and prayed it was the whiskey. Nevertheless, he thanked the chief at the door, and they hugged.

"Good luck, Brother Rainbow."

"Thanks, Chief."

They separated but the chief kept his hands on Rudy's shoulders. He sensed Rudy's apprehension and asked, "What is it?"

"I'm just wondering if this is a bad idea. What if Flingblade misunderstands me, and the wrong person gets the bobcat treatment?"

"Oftentimes a bad idea is just a good idea gone bad. Don't let it go bad."

"Right."

"And as far as Flingblade goes, just treat him like you treat our staff, and you'll be fine. He responds well to progress payments."

"Sure…okay."

The chief opened the door.

After Rudy followed Flingblade out, he turned to the chief and tried to sound positive. "Thanks again, Chief, I really appreciate this. I'll let you know how it goes."

"Please," answered the chief as he slowly shut the door. "Only if it doesn't go bad."

Chapter 30

I paced around Holly's house for what seemed like an eternity while waiting for a callback to let me know exactly where her phone went dead. I spent most of the time running through different scenarios in my mind as to what might have happened when whatever happened to Holly happened. Then I thought about what might be happening to her presently and got nauseated. As I glanced at my watch for the umpteenth time, I muttered, "This is fucked up. I can't do this anymore."

"Dude," said Tangles. "They shoulda called by now."

"I know. Are you thinking what I'm thinking?"

"What, that Miley Cyrus should have won *Time* magazine's Person of the Year?"

"No, you idiot. I'm thinking, let's go. Let's go looking for them! I can't wait around any longer. I'm going crazy." I opened the door to the garage and pressed the automatic garage-door opener. As the motor whirred, and the door trundled open, I pulled a small cooler out of the trunk of the Beemer and handed it to Tangles. "You take care of the cooler, and I'll get the guns from the Porsche. Make sure to pack some water."

"I'm telling you, bro, if she woulda twerked the pope, she woulda beat him."

"And I'm gonna beat you if you don't get that cooler packed, posthaste."

"No prob, but why don't we just take the Porsche?"

"Because DeNutzio has seen it, and unless he looked in the garage, he won't recognize the Beemer. Now move it!"

While Tangles went into the kitchen to start packing the cooler, I gathered up Peter Porsche's weapons. I put the .45 automatic in the glove box and everything else into the vintage Donnay tennis bag I had in the Beemer's trunk. With all but one racquet removed, the sawed-off shotgun and .357 fit nicely. The back seat of the Beemer was pretty useless as a back seat, but it had one key feature: between the rear seats was a removable cushion that provided a pass-through into the trunk. BMW designed it so that a pair of snow skis could be carried inside the vehicle, but as I well knew, it also worked perfectly for fishing rods. I placed the tennis bag in the trunk near the pass-through, so it could be reached from the backseat. I heard Tangles in the kitchen dumping ice in the cooler and yelled, "Hurry up!"

"I'm coming, dude. Relax."

A few moments later Tangles handed me the cooler, and I placed it in the back of the trunk next to the tennis bag. With as much time as I spent on and around the docks, I made it a habit to always have a cooler in the trunk. South Florida can be Africa hot at times, so it's always a good idea to have the essential life supporting elements on hand: water and beer. It's all about hydrating; it's a health issue.

"Dr. Shredlove?" Tangles asked. He was pointing at the custom lettering across one side of my tennis bag. "You gotta be kidding me."

"Advertising my exponential shred factor gives me a psychological edge."

"Oh my God—it's *yours*? That's even *more* ridiculous. Since when do you play tennis?"

"*Play?* That's what kids do. When there's so much felt flying you can't see across the net, Dr. Shredlove won't seem so ridiculous. You know what the net is, right? It's that thing you can't see over."

"Fuck you, man."

"Hey, you wanna get your shred on? Bring it—chicken say chicken. It'll have to wait, though."

Tangles gingerly placed something wrapped in a towel next to the cooler.

"Watcha got there?" I asked.

He folded the towel back, exposing a bottle of Padron tequila.

"Never know when you might need a little Mexican antiseptic—you know me, safety first."

I put the tequila in the tennis bag with the guns and added, "Okay, we got what we need. Now let's find Holly."

We headed north on A1A through Manalapan, and as we rounded Chillingsworth curve, my cell started playing more Billy Squire. I looked at the display, and it read, Charlie. He was still in John Forsythe mode. I answered, "What took you so long?"

"Mr. Jansen, I asked you to stay put until the other agent arrived."

"I stayed for as long as I could. Did you really think I was gonna be able to sit around with my thumb up my ass while Holly's in the hands of some face-slicing psycho? Sorry, no can do. We're gonna try to find her."

"Look, I know you two have survived some sticky situations, and I don't doubt your capabilities, but this is different. This guy—"

"Blah, blah, blah. I don't give a shit how badass this guy is. I'm not waiting around. Have your agent call me when he gets here. If we haven't already found her, we'll be glad for the help. And tell him to bring more ammo."

"*Ammo?*"

"Yeah, you know, the stuff that goes bang? I got the guns from the Porsche, but there's not much ammo. If we get into a shootout—"

"No! Please, no shootouts. You haven't even been through basic firearms training yet."

"Load the gun, point the gun, pull the trigger. Did I miss something? I don't think so."

"Mr.—"

"Mr. Schmister. Look, I'm sorry to say it, but you and I both know Peter Porsche is likely dead. So if you don't have anyone else to help until another agent gets here, then we're the best you got. Now you either tell me where Holly's phone went dead, or I'm throwing this one out the fuckin' window."

I heard an audible sigh, and then, "The C-51 canal."

"What about it?"

"That's where her phone went dead. The C-51 canal and Federal Highway."

"The C-51 and Federal? Are you sure? That's the Lake Worth spillway. It's a residential area."

"So?"

"We were thinking—forget it. It doesn't matter. We'll be there shortly. I'll let you know if we find anything."

"Okay, I'm sending you a better photo of DeNutzio. We obtained a still frame from the lobby of the Holiday Inn where he picked up Mark Slayton and enhanced the image. It should help you ID him. The picture doesn't show it, but his two upper front teeth may or may not be gapped."

"What do you mean?"

"There's a gap between them."

"I know *that*. What do you mean, 'may or may not'?"

"When he got his new face, maybe he got his teeth fixed, too, we don't know…yet."

"If he touches my girl he's gonna look like he went to a Mexican dentist whether he fixed them or not."

Tangles said, "Fuckin' A" and gave me a fist bump.

"Mr. Jan—I mean, Kit, please, if you think punching DeNutzio is—"

"Who said anything about punching?"

"Look, DeNutzio may not be the sharpest tool, but he's no dummy either. He made a name for himself by ruthlessly dispatching those who crossed him, yet despite his efficiency, he's been repeatedly underestimated. Don't do the same."

"We won't. We'll shoot first and dodge questions later."

"Please, if you manage to find him, call me before you do anything."

Tangles pulled the .45 out of the glove box and chambered a round. The metallic sliding action was picked up by the mic on my phone, and the voice of John Forsythe asked, "What was that?"

"That was the sound of anticipation. I'll keep you posted."

Chapter 31

When Flingblade began to ease his old F-150 pickup off the Sawgrass Expressway at 441 North, Rudy said, "It's faster if you take I-95."

Flingblade pointed at the gas gauge and shook his head. Rudy saw that it was registering near empty and understood. "Good call, Bubba. Ol' Rudy's a bit parched anyways. That whiskey left me with some fierce cottonmouth. I need a little water." A couple minutes later, Flingblade pulled up to a pump at a gas station/convenience store. After killing the engine, he looked at Rudy and rubbed his index finger and thumb together.

"Oh, right," said Rudy, as he dug into his pocket for some cash. "I know the drill." He handed Flingblade a hundred-dollar bill and made a hand gesture like he was drinking something. "Can you get me a big bottle of water and something to eat while you're in there? I have to make a call. Get yourself something, too."

As Flingblade walked to the store, Rudy pulled out his cell and called his fiancée, Marie—his *secret* fiancée, Marie. They had been engaged for three months, and Chief Willie was the first and only person he had told. Since they had planned to have a surprise wedding in less than two weeks, he was confident his secret was still safe. Much less confident was his feeling that he had done the right thing by hiring an Indian ninja for muscle.

"Hey, sweetheart," answered Marie on the third ring. "How you doing at the tables?"

"Not good, darlin'. I hit a streak so cold, it coulda made a polar vortex seem like a summer breeze."

"Oh, honey, that doesn't sound good."

"It doesn't feel good either. I went bust. I'm headed home."

"Headed home? What do you mean you're headed home? I have the car."

"I ran into an old friend, and he's giving me a lift."

"But you have a room. I thought we were going to South Beach for lunch tomorrow."

"I'm sorry, darlin'. I can't stay in the casino without any coin in my pocket. Besides, there are a few things I need to square away. I have to meet with Ty at Ragtops in West Palm. I need to choose which classic car I want picking us up at the Old Key Lime House when we get back from the tiki boat cruise. Ty's a friend of Layne's, and he's giving us a deal."

"Can we get a convertible? I always wanted to drive away from my wedding in a fancy convertible."

"A convertible it is, but don't be talking about a wedding, okay? Everybody thinks we're celebrating your sixtieth birthday."

Rudy noticed Flingblade come out of the store and walk up to the pump.

"You told them...you told them my *age?*"

"Well, yeah, darlin'. It had to be a special occasion to keep up the ruse. It's not like I'd charter the tiki boat for your fifty-ninth. It's a surprise, remember?" When no reply came, he said, "Marie?"

"I can't believe I'm turning sixty," she sniveled.

"Now hold on there, Sugarbum. Haven't you heard? Sixty is the new forty, and you're the poster child."

"I always wanted to be on a poster."

"Sally Struthers would be proud of you."

"What does *that* mean?"

"It means I miss you, darlin', and I can't wait to make you Mrs. Travis K. Rainbow."

"I miss you, too, but we'll have to talk about the name thing."

"No problem. You wanna hyphenate? That's okay with me. Mrs. Travis K. Marie Dupree-Rainbow. Has a nice ring to it. You might have a little trouble at the DMV, but I like it."

"Like I said, we'll talk about it. Right now I need to get back to the girls."

She made a kissing sound into the phone and added, "Love you, honey. See you tomorrow."

"Love you too, darlin'." Rudy let out a deep breath and looked on as Flingblade finished pumping the gas. Moments later he sat behind the wheel after slipping his knapsack off and placing it on the seat between them. As they pulled onto 441, Flingblade reached into the knapsack and pulled out a bag of Cajun-flavored pork rinds that he quickly tore into. Leery of reaching into a knapsack that he knew also contained arrows, a hatchet, and God knows what else, Rudy asked, "You got my water in there, Bubba?"

Flingblade reached in the bag and pulled out a tall can of something wrapped in a little brown bag. After he popped the top and took a long pull he set it between his legs and reached back in the knapsack. When he handed Rudy another similarly wrapped bottle, Rudy said, "What's this?" and slid it out of the bag. It was a pint of Mad Dog 20/20.

"What the hell, Bubba! I said get some water, not some fire water! Wait a second, what are *you* drinking?" Flingblade correctly anticipated Rudy would reach for his drink, and he switched it to his left hand and held it against the door. Rudy peered into the top of the open knapsack and pulled out another beverage shrouded in brown paper. He slid out a sixteen-ounce can of Schlitz Malt Liquor.

"I ask you for water and something to eat and you come back with Schlitz Malt Liquor, Mad Dog 20/20, and Cajun pork rinds? What kind of monster are you?"

Flingblade smiled and held the open bag of pork rinds out to Rudy, who looked at them with disdain. "Pork rinds? *Really?*" He shook his head in disgust, having never had the courage to eat a pork rind before. He was flat-out starving, though, so all bets were off. He took the bag from Flingblade, and as he reached in to grab a rind, Flingblade waved his hand in front of his mouth to warn him they were hot.

Rudy wasn't fazed in the least and let him know it. "Yeah, I see it says Cajun on the bag, but that don't necessarily mean it's hot. I spent over twenty years in the Big Easy eating *real* Cajun cuisine, Bubba, and I know hot. I mean there's hot, and then there's hot." He popped a bright-red pork rind into his mouth and quickly downed it. "See, that's not that hot." He popped another one in his mouth as he continued to tell Flingblade what constituted hot. "I remember I ate this gumbo dish one time that—"

He choked and coughed as he swallowed the second pork rind. "Shit! On second thought, that does have a little kick to it...wow." He peered into the top of the knapsack again and asked, "You really didn't get any water? Sweet Jesus, these things are hot!"

Flingblade took another swig of his Schlitz and then held it out for Rudy and smiled. Even though his mouth was on fire, Rudy hesitated when he put the Schlitz to his lips. "This mute thing you got going on, it's not contagious, is it?" Flingblade shrugged and reached in the bag for some more pork rinds.

"I'll take that as a no." Rudy finished off the Schlitz and found that his mouth was still burning. Shaking his head, he popped the top on the second one and took a long swig before Flingblade reached over and took it. Without thinking, Rudy reached into the bag and popped another pork rind in his mouth. As the burn permeated the lining of his mouth, he waved his hand in front of it in a futile effort to ease the pain. "Gimme that beer, Bubba, I'm burning up here." He reached out, but Flingblade placed the beer in a drink holder hanging from the driver side window. "What are you doing, man, I'm on fire!"

Flingblade pointed at the pint of Mad Dog on the seat.

"You think I'm drinking *that*?! Are you crazy? I haven't had a drink in ten years, and I've already had two whiskies and a Schlitz. You're not supposed to be drinking either! Sweet molten molasses, are those things hot!" He waved his hand again, but Flingblade remained unmoved as he reached across the seat and held the Mad Dog up, mere inches from Rudy's burning lips.

As he took the bottle, Rudy shook his head and lamented, "Keep your eyes on the road, Bubba. This is fixin' to be a rough ride."

Chapter 32

As soon as their captor went into the adjacent room to get some rest, Holly's technically-still-a-husband quietly resumed apologizing for the predicament they were in. For nearly an hour she listened to him go on and on about what an idiot he had been, how he wished he could turn back time, and yada, yada, yada. Finally, he got to the point of confessing his wrongdoings: Reconciliation. He wanted a second chance. He swore this time it would be different. Even though she expected it, it still made her blood boil. Only the fact that they were duct taped back to back prevented her from smacking him.

"Are you insane?" she whispered. "If we make it out of this, I don't ever want to see you again."

"Is it about the hookers? I don't know what else I can say other than I usually used condoms. I mean, it's not like I *totally* disrespected—"

"Will you shut up?" she hissed. Suddenly, both rooms were dead quiet for a couple seconds as the infomercial playing on the TV in both rooms finally ended. The brief lull was interrupted by a snore coming from the adjacent room. *Their captor was asleep!*

As a regular commercial began playing, she excitedly asked, "Did you hear that?"

"Yeah, those ShamWows really work."

"Not *that* for God's sake! The psycho in the next room—he's snoring. He's asleep."

"I guess he won't be ordering any ShamWows."

"Forget about that! This is our chance to escape. C'mon!" Holly started wriggling toward the foot of the bed, and Mark joined her, despite protesting.

"I don't know about this. If he catches us—"

"He's not gonna catch us."

When their legs were dangling over the end of the bed, Mark asked, "Now what? How do we stand up?"

"On three, let's start rocking. One, two, three…" They both strained to lift their torsos off the mattress. Mark got his feet on the floor but couldn't get enough momentum to bring them upright. They fell back on the bed.

After the rocking strategy failed for the second time, Mark said, "Wait a second. Even if we get to our feet, how are we going to get out the door? It's chained."

"Use your mouth. I'm sure you had worse things in it in prison."

"What's that supposed to mean?"

"C'mon! Third time's the charm. If you-know-who isn't enough motivation to get the hell out of here, just pretend you're trying to escape responsibility for your actions. That oughta do it."

"That was cold. You gotta believe I would—"

"*Believe?* You want me to *believe* you? Fat chance. We're not in an episode of *Glee*, and this isn't a Journey sing-a-long."

"I said I was sorry."

"You want forgiveness, Mark? Help get us out of here and then I'll forgive you."

"Promise?"

"Yes, I promise. Now c'mon! Let's try another way. We rock a little on one, a little more on two, more on three, and then we give it all we got. Ready?"

"I'm always ready to rock, you know that."

"Right." Holly rolled her eyes and started rocking as she said, "One…two…" They rocked a little higher, and she said, "Three." After they hit the mattress for the third time, she urged in a loud whisper, "Now!"

With all their might they flung themselves up toward the foot of the bed. Mark got his feet planted first and felt they finally had enough momentum to carry them upright. Unfortunately, they also had enough momentum to carry them *past* upright. Mark felt them passing the point of no return and muttered, "Shit."

Holly sensed it a split second later and tried to lean back toward the bed, but with the zip-tie constraints and duct tape hampering her motion, she lost her balance and fell backward on top of Mark, who face-planted into a cheap floor lamp.

In the next room, Marzio Giancarlo DeNutzio, aka Roger Kent, aka a lot of things, woke up with a start. Like many ex-cons after a long prison term, he was a light sleeper. His eyes popped open, and a few steps later he was standing over the pair of wannabe escapees. Seeing they weren't going anywhere, he tucked his gun back in his waistband and shook his head. "Nice try. You almost made it."

The floor lamp lay on its side, and Mark's face had a shard of glass sticking out of it. "I'm bleeding here," he cried.

"I told you not to try anything stupid."

"I didn't want to. She made me do it."

Holly was looking straight up at him, and he saw the anger flare in her eyes. "I had to go to the bathroom," she lied.

"Yeah? Then why were you headed toward the door? You was gonna squat in the parking lot?"

"I lost my balance."

"And I've lost my patience...with *both* of you lovebirds. Now it's gonna get a little uncomfortable."

"We're not lovebirds," said Holly. "We're more like birds of a different feather. His have scales."

"I can see that, how quick he was to throw you under the bus."

"I told her it was a bad idea, and I was right. I forgot that doesn't matter when you're married."

"We're not married!"

The Devil's Nephew rolled them so they were lying on their sides on the floor and then pulled out the duct tape from the carry bag on the nightstand.

"What are you doing?" Holly asked.

"There's something stuck in my face," Mark complained. "I'm bleeding here, man! C'mon, gimme a break."

Instead of pulling the shard out of his face, he turned the volume up on the TV, ripped off a piece of tape, and slapped it across his mouth.

"You wanna break? You got it. One break, coming up." He knelt by Mark's feet and with minimal effort twisted his right foot until the ankle snapped. Mark's eyes bulged, and Holly felt his body tense as a muted scream was swallowed by the duct tape.

"Oh my God! What did you do?" Cried Holly cried.

"I just made sure lover-boy doesn't get any ideas about running off again." He tore another piece of tape off and added, "And I've had enough of you, too."

He slapped the tape across Holly's mouth and then pulled out the knife from its ankle sheath. Holly tried to remain calm so she could breathe through her nose, but the sight of the big knife made it difficult. She closed her eyes as he used the knife to cut the tape binding her to Mark. Once they were separated, the Devil's Nephew picked her up and threw her on the bed. Fearing the worst, she closed her eyes and felt herself being hog-tied. Moments later he lifted her off the bed and positioned her against the bathroom door. To her dismay, he wrapped duct tape around her neck and then around the handle of the bathroom door. She watched as he focused his attention on Mark and dragged him across the floor to the other side of the bed. A trail of blood coming from the shard stuck in Mark's face marked the way. She couldn't see it, but he hog-tied him too, and then duct-taped him to the leg of the headboard.

Satisfied with his handiwork for the moment, Roger Kent stood and looked at her. "I told you not to try anything stupid, but you went ahead anyways." He walked over to her and crouched down so that his face was only a greasy whisker away. Softly he said, "I have to take care of something right now, but when I come back, you and I are gonna get better acquainted." He slipped a hand up inside her shorts and squeezed her ass so hard she gasped. He released his grip and laughed, but she gasped again when he reached under her shirt and pinched her breast until a tear formed in the corner of her eye. "You think that hurts?" he whispered. "I'm not even worked up yet."

He let go of her, and as he stood, Holly tried to steady her breathing again. She watched as he stepped into the adjacent room and shut the door behind him. Moments later she heard another door shut and then the engine of the Cadillac as it pulled away.

Roger Kent had two main reasons for slipping out. Number one, he wanted to dump the body of the dead federal agent in his trunk. Number two, he was hungry as shit. As he drove south on US 1, he slowed at the spot where he tossed Holly's cell phone. Looking east, he could see the large gates of the Lake Worth Spillway, which appeared to be open. Correctly figuring that the water flowed into the Intracoastal, he thought it would be as good a dump site as any. He headed farther south a couple blocks and turned on the first street that looked like it went somewhere: Columbia Drive. A couple of blocks later he turned North on Federal Highway and pulled to the east side of a second bridge that spanned the spillway. Although it was dark, he could see numerous boats lining either side of the canal that fed into a wide part of the Intracoastal. It was called Federal Highway, but in this particular section where the spillway separated the cities of West Palm Beach and Lake Worth, it was primarily a residential area. Traffic was light at eleven thirtyish on a week night in August, and he waited patiently for a lone car to pass before he popped the trunk latch and stepped out of the car. He glanced around, and after not seeing anybody, he went to the trunk and put his foot on the bumper to remove the knife from its ankle sheath. He wanted to make the body less buoyant and knew an old trick. Working by the light in the trunk he rolled the body over and stuck the knife deep through both eyes. Then he gutted the torso from the navel to the breastbone and wrapped the body in the heavy plastic lining. He glanced around once more and then unceremoniously dumped the body over the bridge. It hit the frothy white water below with a loud splash, and he saw it bob once before the current carried it away into the darkness. As soon as he shut the trunk, he heard, "Yo! Piss-boy! What the *fuck* did you just dump in my canal?"

Chapter 33

When we got to the spillway bridge on Federal Highway that separated Lake Worth from West Palm, I pulled a U-y and parked the Beemer facing south on the berm. We exited the car, and I looked over the railing facing west toward the spillway gates.

Tangles jumped up on the ledge so he could see better, and commented, "The current's nasty. Look at all that foam."

He was right, it *was* nasty. The western part of the county had received a bunch of rain, and the engineers had the gates wide open to direct the water to the Intracoastal. The elevation differential as the water flowed through the gate created a powerful cascade that churned the crap out of the downstream side and produced a thick, slimy foam that carried with the current. This was the spot where Holly's phone had gone dead.

"What do you think?" I wondered out loud. "You think the guy in the Caddy chucked her phone over right here?"

"That would be my guess. Looks like Rudy's theory about going down US 1 or Military Trail looking for a seedy motel is wrong."

"That's what it looks like, there's none of that in this area, it's all residential, it doesn't make..." I had been looking at a big glob of foam that broke off from a larger glob at the base of spillway gate and was impressed with how fast it came toward us on the bridge.

"Doesn't make what?" asked Tangles. "Doesn't make sense? Who knows? Maybe—"

"Wait a second!" I pointed west. "US 1 is on the other side of the spillway gate."

"So?"

"So look at the current. You said it yourself. It's nasty. Maybe DeNutzio chucked the phone from US 1, and it got sucked through the gate. By the time it got done tumbling and shorted out, it ended up here by this bridge."

"You don't think her phone would go dead as soon as it hit the water?"

"Holly had one of those waterproof covers on it, just like you and I do."

I held up my phone.

Tangles nodded. "I guess it's possible. It makes more sense than—"

"Yo! What the hell are *you* two doing here?" I recognized the voice immediately and turned to see my good buddy, Big Mike, walking his dog, Redgie. He lived a couple blocks away in the College Park neighborhood in Lake Worth.

"How's Redge doing?" I asked as I crouched down to scratch his beloved pooch. Old Redge was a mixed-breed rescue dog of unknown age somewhere north of sixteen years, and he had been having health issues of late.

"Monkey ass almost got him last week, but the vet came through."

"Monkey ass?"

"Yeah, he had this thing coming out his ass that looked like a chunk of bloody cauliflower. I thought he had doggy hemorrhoids or something."

"He probably does, the way you feed him."

"Nah, it was some kinda rectovirus or something. He's doing good now." I gave Redgie a last pat on the head and stood up to fist bump Big Mike. As I did so, Tangles kneeled down and started petting Redgie. He was just one of those dogs that people love to pet.

"I see you brought your mini-me with you," commented Big Mike. "I have a spare leash if you need one." Big Mike was a Long Island transplant who shared my twisted sense of humor—heavy on sarcasm, light on subtlety, and directly to the point. As long as it was funny, making fun of someone was usually okay, and it was always okay if that person was named Tangles.

Tangles thought otherwise. "Why you always busting on me, man? What did I ever do to you?"

Big Mike feigned like he didn't know where the voice came from and looked all around. "Who said that?" Then he looked down at Tangles and added, "Oh, there you are."

As we laughed, Tangles said, "Screw you. You don't even *deserve* a dog."

Big Mike wasn't really that big. He was a few inches shorter than me, but twenty years peddling granite and marble left him sneaky strong. By sneaky strong I mean he had big arms without the bulging biceps that weightlifters get. Even though running his highly successful business (Palm Beach Kitchen and Bath), required some finesse and diplomacy, he could turn on the cocky swagger and intimidate when needed.

He shrugged and put his hands on his hips as he stepped forward, towering over Tangles. "Hey, I don't deserve a lot of things, like having someone who looks like Frodo tell me I don't deserve a dog. Get over it. What are you guys doing here, anyways? Don't tell me you were dumping shit in the canal like the last guy."

"What do you mean, the last guy?" I asked. "*What* last guy?"

"About fifteen minutes ago, Redge was taking a dump at the foot of the bridge when I heard a loud splash. We come up on the bridge, and this big jabroni is closing his trunk."

"A *jabroni?*" Tangles said.

"Yeah, a *jabroni*—a gaboon, a big guinea. When I asked him what he dumped, he tells me to mind my own fuckin' business, jumps in his Caddy, and drives off. I ever see that motherfucker again, I'll straighten his shit out. Some people have no respect for the environment, know what I mean?"

"Did you notice anybody else in the car?" I probed.

"Huh? No, I think he was alone."

"What color was it?"

"What color was what?"

"The Caddy."

"I don't know, brown, black, blue, something dark. Why?"

"Just wondering."

Tangles and I shared a furtive glance, but Big Mike picked up on it.

"What's up? You know something about it?"

"Huh? No, not really," I answered.

"What do you mean, *not really*? Then what are you doing here?"

"Snook season opens September first; we were just scoping things out on the way back from Clematis Street."

"Really. Huh. Well, you can't fish from the bridge. You know that. You gotta go up by the gates."

"Yeah, I know, so what makes you so sure the guy in the Caddy was Italian?"

"It was obvious, the way he told me to fuck off. He sounded just like me."

"Any idea what he dumped?"

"Hell no, it's too dark. It was something big, though. It made a big splash. Could have been an old fridge or something. Who knows?"

"Did he dump it right here?"

"No." He pointed to the other side of the bridge. "Over there. Why?"

"Maybe we can see something."

"*Shit*, not with that tiny little flashlight around your neck."

"You had to bring it up," said Tangles.

I reached inside the door well on the driver's side of the Beemer.

"Had to bring *what* up?"

"Sir Shag-a-lot has developed an unhealthy flash-light fetish."

New flashlight in hand, I said, "C'mon," and they followed me to the other side of the bridge. I held the flashlight up by my ear and pressed the tail cap activation button. An amazingly brilliant beam of light cut a laserlike swath down the channel, and I slowly swept it from one side to the other.

"*Jesus*, is that bright," said Big Mike. "What the hell kind of flashlight *is* that?"

"A Surefire R1 Lawman. It puts out seven hundred and fifty lumens. It's rechargeable with three different output levels and a strobe. Holly got it for my birthday."

"Wow. Who needs candles when you got *that* fuckin' thing. Can I see it for a second?

"No." I shone the light under the bridge but didn't see anything except slimy foam and murky, fast moving water. *Crap.*

"You didn't happen to catch the license plate, did you?" asked Tangles.

"Hell no, it's practically pitch black out here unless you got one of those plutonic flashlights."

"You said he jumped in the Caddy and took off," I queried. "Which way did he go?"

"He went—wait a second. Why all the interest? It's not like you live on the canal. You don't even live in Lake Worth."

"We all live on the same planet, dude. As far as I'm concerned, anybody throwing shit in the water is public enemy number one. I got a fishing show, remember? It's bad for business. Just once I'd like to nail one of these idiots and sic the FWC on them."

Big Mike gave me a skeptical look and then glanced down at Tangles and asked, "How long's he been acting like a Greenpeace spokesman?"

"Quite a while. He's got whales on his underwear."

"You gotta be kidding me. Really?"

"Yep. Sperm whales. True story."

"I almost forgot what a smartass you are. Thanks for reminding me."

"Hey, I'm not the only one who hates polluters," I pointed out. "So which way did he go?"

"Lemme see that flashlight, and I'll show you."

"Okay, but be careful." I handed it to him and added, "Press the tail cap once, for the high beam."

He switched it on and directed the beam down the canal, like I had just done.

"Holy crap, this thing is awesome. What did you call it again?"

"The Lawman—the Surefire R1 Lawman."

"What's the 'R' stand for?"

"I don't know...probably retina, 'cause if you shine it in someone's eye, they're gonna need a new one. So where did the Caddy go?"

He swung the beam north, toward West Palm, and lit up a distant street sign. "He went that way and then turned left on the first or second street. Either one takes you to US 1."

"Well, we gotta get going, too." I took the flashlight from him, and he complained. "Damn, where can I get one of those things?"

"Just go to surefire.com. Tell 'em Shagball sent you."

"What are you, some kinda promoter for them?"

"Not yet...officially, but I'm working on it." I gave Redgie one last scratch, and Tangles and I got back in the Beemer. Big Mike rapped on the window, and I powered it down.

"What?" I asked.

"I'll give you twenty-five hundred for the Beemer... caashhhh."

I powered the window back up. "Keep dreaming." And I headed down the road. He knew I had briefly considered trading in the '94 Beemer on something newer, and I made the mistake of telling him what the ridiculously low trade-in value was. Now, every time I saw him, he offered to buy it...for caashhhh. I could afford a new car, but I couldn't bear to let the Beemer go for a song—not with the engine still humming.

I turned right on the street that Big Mike lived on, which connected to US 1. "What do you think?" I asked Tangles.

"If we didn't know Holly's phone went dead back there, I'd say the odds are slim that the guy in the Caddy is our man. But it's too much of a coincidence."

"What about the splash that Big Mike heard? You thinking what I'm thinking?"

"That it *really* doesn't look good for Peter Porsche?"

"No, it doesn't." I pulled to the side of the road before we hit US 1 and began laying out a possible scenario. "Let's assume Rudy was right. This guy is driving down US 1 with a dead body in his trunk and Holly and Dickhead in the car, probably handcuffed, or tied up, or something. As he's looking for a motel to hole up in, he notices the spillway and decides to chuck Holly's phone in the drink. A little bit later, Big Mike happens upon him dumping something big, presumably Peter Porsche, on the east side of the bridge. But—and this is key—Big Mike said he didn't notice anybody else in the car."

"Soooo, he must have found a motel and left Holly and Dickhead there while he went to dump Peter Porsche, right?"

"Right, and it's probably not too far away, either. Once he has Holly and Dickhead secured, he back-tracks to the spillway and dumps Peter Porsche where the current will carry him away."

"That means he probably turned down this street, or the next one, and when he got to the bridge on Federal, he pulled to the side and dumped the body. It fits." Tangles nodded.

"Like a sticky glove. And when he skedaddles, he heads west on one of the side streets that connects back to US 1. Why? 'Cause that's where his motel is, somewhere on US 1."

"Maybe my old man *was* right."

"I think we're about to find out, because I don't see this guy going too far from the motel to dump a body." I put the Beemer in drive, turned north on US 1, and as we crossed over the spillway, I added, "I'll look left, and you look right. We'll check every motel until we find the Caddy. Keep your beady little eyes peeled."

"They're not beady. I have perfect vision...unlike you."

"Well, keep 'em peeled anyways. We find the Caddy, we find Holly, and that's all that matters."

Chapter 34

After dumping the body in the spillway canal and speeding away from a local yokel out walking his dog, the Devil's Nephew noted the Caddy was low on gas and pulled into a station. While filling up, he focused on his stomach and the lack of contents therein. He spotted the golden arches up the road and minutes later was scarfing down a pair of Big Macs in the restaurant's parking lot. As he finished off his fries and had a last slurp of soda, his phone rang. He recognized the number and was a little surprised to be hearing from the Scarf so soon. "Scarf, you here already?"

"Almost. The pilot announced we're ahead of schedule, thanks to a tailwind. We should be on the ground in the next fifteen minutes or so. You're coming to get me, right?"

"No, I need you to take a cab, I got my hands full."

"Sounds like you got your mouth full, too."

"A man's gotta eat, Scarf. I'd come and get you, but I got the lawyer and his supposed wife tied up. I need to get back; they already tried to run once."

"You left them alone?"

"No, I hired a babysitter. What the fuck do you think? I had to take care of a couple things. They ain't going nowhere. Here's the address..." He started to read the address off the business card he got at the front desk.

The Scarf interrupted him. "I got nothing to write with. I'm in the friggin' bathroom 'cause I'm not supposed to be on the phone. Can you text it to me?"

"Sure, no prob."

"You said it's called the White Horse Motel?"

"Yeah, but the E is burned out on the sign, so it say, 'Hors.'"

"Sounds like a classy place. They leave mints on the pillows?"

"Not hardly. Maybe Crème de Mints, if you know what I mean."

"Super. I'll sleep in a chair."

"Quit whining, we'll be out of there as soon as the banks open."

"The girl keeps the gold there, too?"

"That's where her money is, so I'm guessing that's where the gold is, maybe in a safety deposit box."

"She said that?"

"We were in a rush to get out of the house. I didn't ask. I'll check when I get back to the room. Like I said, you better take a cab."

"I, uh, guess I can do that."

"You guess?"

"Okay, I'll take a cab."

"Fuckin' A right you will, that way I can get back and get busy."

"Busy doing what?"

"Plowin' the girl, what else? Like you said, she's a tasty piece, and I haven't had any since I got back from Mexico. Plus, I owe her for my uncle."

"If I know you, you'll overpay her. Shit, they just announced we're getting ready to land. I gotta get back to my seat. How far is the motel from the airport?"

"Not far. The guy in the office said ten to fifteen minutes, that's it."

"Okay, I'll see you in a bit. You shouldn't do anything to the girl until I get there."

"Hey, Scarf, since when did *you* start telling *me* what the fuck to do? Who the *fuck's* running things here? *I'm* paying *you*, capeesh?"

"Sure, of course, I didn't mean nothin' by it. It's just that I found out something that changes things. Something about your uncle."

"Yeah? Well, we'll see about that." Click.

The Scarf set his phone down on the tray in front of him before leaning his forehead against the window and closing his eyes. The shit was definitely gonna hit the fan, and in usual Scarf fashion he planned to be on the upwind side. The FBI agent next to him picked up his phone and unplugged the ear jacks he had been listening in on.

"*What* changes things?" He asked.

"Nothing…at least not as far as my end of the deal goes."

"If that was some sort of tip-off, and DeNutzio runs, the DA's gonna throw the book at you so hard—"

"It wasn't a tip-off! All right?"

"Then what was it? Why were you trying to protect the girl?"

"'Cause DeNutzio's an animal, that's why, and he's fueled by revenge. The thing is, it's misguided. At least as far as the girl and the fishing-show guys are concerned."

"How so?"

"Because, uh, because his, uh—"

"Spit it out, Mouse. Spit out the cheese, or it's back to Rahway."

"I guess it don't make any difference at this point." He shrugged. "I found out his uncle Donny was the one who ordered the hit on his dad."

"*What?*"

"You heard me right. Donny Nutz offed his own brother. So if the girl and her friends were responsible for killing him, they were doing the Devil's Nephew a favor, and maybe, *just maybe*, he won't feel the driving need to make them suffer and kill them."

"So why didn't you tell him?"

"On the *phone?* Are you *nuts?* He'd know something was up for sure."

A second FBI agent leaned forward in the seat behind him and said, "If you're lying, Jimmy, if he knows we're coming, or if—"

"He doesn't know nothing! You know how I know? 'Cause I'm still alive…and I wanna stay that way. If he had the slightest inkling I was talking to the Feds, I'd be a dead man. In fact, if anybody on the street even *thinks* I ratted him out, I'm dead, end of story. I can't believe I'm doing this."

"Sure you can. It was either this or going back to Rahway for…what? Ten years?"

"With my prior record, ten years minimum, that's what the DA said. Since when is lifting a little credit card information a federal offense?"

"A little? *Please.* You hacked your way into the database of one of the largest department stores in the country, stole the personal information of more than three million customers, and then started selling it on Craigslist."

"*I* didn't sell it on Craigslist, somebody I allegedly sold it to did…allegedly."

The agent next to him said, "Allegedly. Right. Not too smart for a computer whiz called Mouse."

"I just told you I didn't do it, and my name's not Mouse anymore, it's the Scarf. You heard the call."

"Scarf, my ass. You beat somebody with a keyboard and then shove a mouse down his throat until he chokes to death, the name sticks."

"It was self-defense; he came at me with a stapler."

"You pleaded to manslaughter."

"So? You know the game. I did what I had to do to make sure I didn't spend the rest of my life in the joint. I'm not an animal, not like DeNutzio; I got a few scruples left."

The agent had a laptop in front of him and was feverishly working the keyboard.

"That remains to be seen. How come you didn't let him give you the address? I can't seem to find anything on this White Horse Motel."

"'Cause I had to pretend I was in the bathroom where nobody could hear, or he might suspect something. I don't know about you, but I don't usually bring a pen and paper to the toilet."

"That was good thinking, unlike the Craigslist idea."

"I already told you. Ah, nuts. Look, fughedabout the address, all right? You heard him, he's gonna text me. What you should worry about is what he might do to those poor bastards he's got tied up. The dickhead lawyer deserves whatever he gets, but not the girl. I sure wouldn't wanna be in her shoes. DeNutzio's capable of anything—anything except having a conscience."

"So we heard, but we also heard he's no dummy. If he thinks he can squeeze the girl for a few million, that's what he'll do, he'll squeeze, but he won't squish. She should be all right until we get there."

"Easy for you to say."

"Relax, we'll be there in no time—Hey! Here it is." He pointed at his laptop and added, "It's on Dixie Highway, in West Palm, not too far from the airport, just like he said."

"Wait a second. What's this *we?* I'm not going anywhere *near* that place. I'm done. I thought I was done. What do you need *me* for? You know where he is. Go arrest him."

The agent sitting behind him leaned forward again and explained. "He's armed and extremely dangerous—psychotic, like you said. We go busting in all willy-nilly, and all hell could break loose. You need to be in the room to tell us when to come in. Even better, maybe you could lure him outside into the parking lot."

"You *are* nuts! He's got a sixth sense for snitches. He'll sniff me out in a second. No fucking way!"

"You go back to Rahway, Jimmy, you won't have any protection. Ten years is a long time." The FBI agent reached over and tugged his silk scarf. "Of course the upside is, in ten years, maybe your scarf will be back in style."

"Fuck you."

The pilot told them to prepare for landing, and the agent sitting next to him closed his laptop before reiterating the deal. "You cooperate fully, and all charges will be dropped. No probation, no house arrest, no nothing. You'll be free to scam again."

He fluffed up the silk scarf around his neck and muttered, "I shoulda listened to my mother and become a florist."

"What?"

"Nothing."

"Then you'll do it, right?"

"I'm telling you right now, if DeNutzio goes back to the slammer, I gotta go into the witness protection program. He'll know I ratted him out. That's the only way."

"He just made the ten most wanted list, so if it plays out that way, we'll put you in the program. You have my word."

"You're not yanking my chain, are you?"

"Not at all. He's number eight."

"I don't care what number he is! I'm talking about witness protection!"

"Oh, right. Like I said, if it plays out that way, no problem."

"It fuckin' better. You don't know this guy like I do. If anything, his new face makes him more dangerous. At least before, you feared him right off the bat. Now, with his goofy new look, you got no idea what's going on in that demented noggin of his. But believe me, it ain't nothin' good."

Another FBI agent, who was also the copilot, announced they were on final approach. The Scarf pressed his forehead against the window again. The unmarked government jet banked to one side, and he could see the lights flash by below. He briefly wondered if his life would soon be flashing by as well. He had betrayed the one man he thought he would never betray and he would have to bear the consequences. He contemplated a new life in the witness protection program, where nobody would know a thing about him. No more Jimmy Velotta, no more Mouse, no more Scarf. He finally got a nickname he liked, and just like that he would have to give it up. He took a corner of his scarf and blew his nose into it before discreetly wiping it on the armrest. *It ain't fair*, he thought. *It just ain't fuckin' fair.*

***

It didn't take much to piss the Devil's Nephew off, so having the Scarf tell him what to do had him talking to himself. As he slipped the small phone into the breast pocket of his shirt, he muttered, "Give a guy a decent street name, and he starts acting like he knows something. What the fuck." In all the years he had known him, the Scarf had never told him what to do... not once. He thought about their conversation, and a few things bothered him. If the Scarf was in a confined space like an airplane bathroom, wouldn't the sound of a PA announcement be heard over the phone? Even if he couldn't make out what was being said, wouldn't he have heard *something?* Then the Scarf told him not to do anything until he got there. *Why?* Why the fuck would *he* care if certain carnal liberties were taken with the girl? And what was that cryptic shit about his uncle? What the fuck was that all about? And then there was the fact that he managed to catch a flight on such short notice, and it was landing ahead of schedule. Was it just good timing and a fortuitous tailwind, like he claimed, or was it something else? Has a flight that originated in Newark *ever* landed ahead of schedule?

He pulled his phone out and dialed the airline the Scarf told him he was coming in on. Maybe he'd head over to the airport and surprise him, just to be safe. After a few minutes, he finally had a live person on the line.

"Thanking you for choosing JetBlue airlines, how may I help you?" the cheerful female attendant asked.

"You've got a flight from Newark to Palm Beach that's supposed to land about midnight. Can you tell me which gate they'll be arriving at?"

"One moment please..."

He waited patiently on the line and less than forty-five seconds later, the girl said, "That would be flight number fifteen forty-two?"

"You tell me. It's supposed to be your last direct flight into Palm Beach tonight."

"Yes, sir, that would be flight fifteen forty-two. It's been rescheduled to arrive tomorrow morning at ten thirty, we're sorry for any—"

"Whoa, whoa, whoa! What do you mean, *rescheduled?*"

"There was a mechanical problem with the plane, sir. We had to cancel the flight. Most of the passengers were put up in a hotel near—"

The Devil's Nephew disconnected the call and muttered, "That flip-floppin' motherfucker. Son of a bitch!"

Chapter 35

"I never realized there were so many of these shitty little motels," said Tangles. "They're all over the place."

"Believe it or not, it used to be worse before Walgreen's and CVS decided they needed a drugstore on every corner."

We had done a slow troll through the parking lots of four or five places and had yet to spot a single Cadillac. They had names like the Relax Inn, the Shangri-La, and even the Reindeer Inn. Seriously, the Reindeer. In South Florida—go figure. Tangles announced he had another prospect on his side of the road.

"Okay, Shag, here we go on the right. What does that sign say? The White Hors Motel? What about the black ones? Where are they supposed to stay?"

As I pulled the Beemer in the parking lot, I could see the E was burned out, and I corrected him, as I often did.

"The E is burned out, you moron. Besides, that's not how you spell 'whore.'"

"I guess you would know."

I abruptly hit the brakes in the middle of the parking lot and glared at him.

"What the hell's the matter with you, dude? Holly's life is in danger. We gotta find this Caddy el pronto. Quit fucking around."

Tangles had his hands up in a defensive position and actually sounded contrite for once. "You're right. I'm sorry. I'm like you. When I get worried, I resort to cracking jokes. It's a survival mechanism."

"It bodes well for your longevity."

"What?"

"Forget it. The joking's fine when it's you and me who are in trouble, but not Holly. If anything happens to her, I'm gonna be permanently sick to my stomach."

"Nothing's gonna happen to her, man, think positive. DeNutzio won't touch her until he gets paid."

"That's what everybody seems to think. I sure hope you're right." I looked around at the cars in the lot and shook my head. "Shit, there's no Caddy here either."

Tangles pointed at the sign and said, "The No Vacancy sign is on. I guess they're full." Actually, the sign said, No can, because the other letters in vacancy were burned out. It was clear Tangles took my warning to heart, because under any other circumstance another wisecrack would be in play. The lot was full except for a couple spots on the end, which seemed a little odd considering it was the end of August. Business was apparently good at the old White Hors. *Huh.* As I pulled out on to Dixie and continued north toward West Palm Beach, Tangles slowly turned and looked out the rear window for a second or two. Suddenly, he swiveled around and stared at his side mirror.

"What are you looking at?" I asked.

"Pull over!"

"What? Why?"

"Pull over and turn around! Didn't you see that Caddy that just pulled out of the convenience store?"

I pulled into a vacant gas station lot and started turning around.

"What Caddy? I was looking ahead for the next motel."

"I'm pretty sure it was a Caddy, and it turned into the White Hors."

I didn't need to be told twice. I floored it. The rear tires sprayed gravel, and we burned a little rubber when the tread caught on the pavement. In a matter of seconds I was braking at the south end of the motel, just in time to see somebody disappear into the end unit. There was a car backed up to the room, and as with most new cars, the headlights had yet to go out. It was a Caddy. Instead of pulling in to the motel lot, I kept heading south.

"What are you doing, man?" Tangles asked.

"I'm not just gonna pull in right behind him. What if he comes back out or is looking out the window?" I turned left at the next side street and turned around.

"It's definitely a Caddy, Shag, and that guy looked pretty big."

"I know."

"It's backed up just like Rudy said it would be. It's gotta be him. What are we gonna do?"

"First, we need to see if it has Georgia plates. I'm gonna pull over just short of the motel, and I want you to run up to the corner of the building and take a look—we'll take it from there."

I did just that, and two minutes later Tangles jumped back in the car and confirmed the Caddy had Georgia plates. I pulled past the motel office on the north end of the property and parked on the first side street.

"What now?" he asked.

I opened the glove box and pulled out the .45-caliber automatic. "What do you *think* we're gonna do? We're gonna go get Holly."

"I figured that. I mean…how? We can't just knock on the door and expect he's gonna let us in."

"Of course not." I pulled back the slide on the gun to double-check there was a round in the chamber.

"Then how? The last time you tried to kick a door in, the only thing you busted was your—"

"Nobody's kicking anything! All right? We're gonna try and get a key."

"*A key?* Just how do you propose we get a key?"

"With this." I pulled Peter Porsche's ATF badge out of my pocket and held it in front of his face.

"Oh, okay. Why didn't you just say so?"

"I just did. Let's go."

After opening the trunk, I handed Tangles the little Glock, and he checked to make sure it was loaded before slipping it in his front pocket. I found the safety on the big Colt, and after tightening my belt, I managed to get it tucked into the small of my back in the four o'clock position. I shut the trunk and said, "You ready?"

"Like Freddy. How's this gonna work?"

"Just follow my lead, as usual."

"Got it." I gave Tangles a fist bump, and we crossed the darkened street toward the marginally lit motel office. I shone my Surefire on my watch and noted it was past midnight. We walked up to the office, and I tried the door, but it was locked. I peered through the window in the door, and nobody was at the desk. There was another door behind the desk that was partially open, and a faint light shone out. I knocked on the door a few times, and when I got no response, I knocked harder. The door behind the desk swung open, and a diminutive Asian man approached the front door. He could barely see over the window, and he wasn't too pleasant.

"We closed. You no see sign? No vacancy. You go now." He waved his hand in a dismissive manner and turned away. I pounded on the door again, and he started letting me have it. "I say you go! We no have—"

I held the ATF badge in the window, and he stopped in midsentence.

"I don't want a room. Open the door. This will only take a minute."

He stepped forward and stood on his tiptoes to get a better look at the badge. "What you want? I do nothing wrong! Why you—?"

"Open the door NOW!" I gave him my best no-nonsense look, and he reluctantly slid back the dead bolt. By the time Tangles followed me inside, the small Asian man was behind the front desk. He was obviously standing on a milk crate or something because we were now eye to eye.

He pointed at Tangles and said, "Who he? He no look like cop. You no look like cop. What kind of cop are you?" I could sense his uneasiness and saw his arm creep toward what I imagined was some sort of weapon hid from view.

"Relax, okay? We're with the ATF." I held the badge out, and he eyed it warily.

"What is ATF? I no know ATF. Why you no have uniforms?"

We were both wearing cargo fishing shorts and T-shirts, not exactly federal agent attire.

"We're working undercover, that's why, for the division of Alcohol, Tobacco, and Firearms. You know what a firearm is, right? You were reaching for one just a second ago."

He looked surprised and started stammering.

"I, I uh, I—"

"Don't lie to me!"

"Yes, yes, okay! I have gun! Neighborhood not so good anymore. I need protect myself."

Tangles slapped his hand on the desk and pointed at him. "You've been drinking alcohol, too, haven't you? I can smell it."

"What?"

"You heard me. You've been in the back room drinking and watching porn."

"No! No, I watch Jimmy Kimmel. He funny man."

"But you've been drinking, right?"

"So I have drink, so I have gun, so what? I no break law."

"That's for us to decide, Mr..."

"Pong. Ping Pong." He handed me a business card out of a cardholder on the desk and sure enough, it read, Ping Phoung, proprietor of the White Horse Motel. I handed it to Tangles.

Mr. Phuong asked, "What this about? Why you ask questions? I do nothing wrong."

I sniffed the air, and asked, "That's not smoke I smell, is it, Mr. Pong?"

"No, I quit ten year ago. Why? What this about? Why you no tell me?"

"I'm glad to hear you quit smoking, Mr. Pong, otherwise we'd have to arrest you."

"Me?! Why?"

"Because you can have alcohol and a firearm, and you can have tobacco and a firearm, but you can't have alcohol, tobacco, *and* a firearm. That's a no-no."

"*What* you say? I no hear that."

"Well, now you have. It's part of the Obamacare law. Three strikes, and you're out."

"Especially if they're Lucky Strikes," added Tangles.

"So, thank your lucky stars," I continued. "You're not in any trouble. But the same can't be said of the person renting the room on the end there." I pointed out the side window at the room on the end.

"Which room you talk about?" He squinted out the window at the poorly lit parking lot.

"The one on the end, with the Cadillac parked in front. We've been following him for weeks. He's wanted for hijacking a semi full of cigarettes, beer, and bazookas."

"*Bazookas?*"

"That's right, and I'm not talking about Bazooka Joe's. So what we need from you is the key to his room. Otherwise, if we have to break the door down and a firefight ensues, well, your motel might end up looking like the Hiroshima Hilton, comprende?"

Mr. Pong looked concerned and started shaking his head. "I knew he trouble. He big like Yeti, but look like Teddy."

"What do you mean, he look like Teddy?"

"His face. His face look friendly, like Teddy Bear, but something no right with him. Here, I give you key." He reached behind the counter and handed me a key that had the number twelve on it.

"Your cooperation will not be forgotten, Mr. Pong. I want you to lock the door behind us and then go back in your office and sit tight until we have Mr. Yeti in handcuffs." Tangles and I headed to the door, and he came out from behind the front desk to usher us out. Just before he shut the door, he said, "Please, no bazookas. I no have insurance—too expensive."

"We'll do our best, Mr. Pong. Just lock yourself in, and don't open the door for anyone but us."

Mr. Phuong did as he was told and locked the door. As he opened the door to his office, he glanced at the keys hanging on the wall and remembered that Mr. Yeti had rented room number eleven as well. He was thinking he should probably give the second room key to the ATF agents, too, but then his eyes wandered to the paused image of the movie he had been watching on his computer; *Yayoi does Hanoi.* He closed the door and settled in front of the computer, thinking, *Nah, how many room key they need?*

Chapter 36

With the realization that the Scarf had turned on him, the Devil's Nephew's plans changed in an instant. There was no way he could waltz the girl into a bank branch in the morning and walk out with a suitcase full of money, not if the Feds were on to him. Leery that they might already be staking out the motel, he parked at a convenience store across the street and watched for a few minutes. Even though he didn't notice any suspicious activity, he debated whether it was worth the risk going back to the room. Then he thought about the possibility the girl had some gold stashed somewhere other than the bank, like the Scarf suggested—*the fucking rat.* The Scarf and the lure of gold were driving his decision making; he didn't want to leave empty-handed, and he didn't want to leave without teaching the Scarf a lesson. He also knew he needed to ditch the Caddy for another ride, and as he eyed the vehicles in the motel lot, he came up with a plan. With his decision made, he knew he had to move fast. If the girl confessed to having some gold stashed somewhere accessible, and he could get his hands on it quickly, great. If not, he would kill her and her douche-bag husband and split. He pulled his phone back out and texted the Scarf the motel address, then added, "Key on tire, let self in, resting."

With his eyes scanning for police or unmarked cars, he pulled out on to US 1 and then turned into the motel lot. He parked the Caddy in front of room number twelve. When he got out, he half expected a SWAT team to appear out of nowhere, and he'd go out in a blaze of glory. He stood there for a second or two and looked around, but the SWAT team was a no-show. He left a room key for the Scarf on top of one of the tires as he said he would and then walked over to a neighboring room that had a light on inside. He looked at the car parked in front of it, a four-door Ford that didn't look too ratty. *That'll do.* He knocked on the door a few times, and as he waited, he heard someone shuffle up to it. He figured whoever was behind the door was checking him out through the peephole.

A man's voice said, "Whatta you want?"

He pointed at the Ford and said, "Is that Ford yours?"

"Yeah, what's it to ya?"

He held up a fifty-dollar bill. "I backed into it and dinged the bumper. This should take care of it."

He heard the guy mumble, "Shit," and then the dead bolt slid back and the guy held the door open a few inches, secured only by a flimsy security chain. The Devil's Nephew started to hand him the bill, and the guy added, "It better only be—"

Wham! The Devil's Nephew slammed his forearm into the door, and it exploded inward as the chain gave way. The door caught the underwear-clad man in the shoulder, and he careened backward toward the bed. A naked black chick opened the bathroom door, and sensing she was about to scream, he pulled out the gun with the silencer and shot her twice in the chest. As she collapsed to the floor, the guy in the underwear tried to bolt past him for the door. He clotheslined him with his left arm and flung him to the bed. With the gun trained on the terrified man's chest, he calmly asked, "Where are your car keys?"

The wide-eyed man had his hands up in a defensive position and pointed to the TV. "On the TV, next to my wallet. You can take that, too. Please don't shoot me, please, please don't shoot."

The Devil's Nephew saw the keys and wallet and shook his head. "Sorry, pal, beggars can't be choosers." He raised the silencer and shot the man between the eyes, scooped the keys off the TV, and shut the door on his way out. He quickly backed the Ford up in front of room number eleven and moments later let himself into the adjacent room. As expected, the lawyer and the girl were right where he'd left them. He crossed the room in three giant strides and ripped the tape off the girl's mouth. She winced, and as she took several deep breaths, he put the gun to her head.

"Where's the gold?"

"The *gold*? What—?"

He slapped her hard across the face and then grabbed her by the throat. As she gasped, he spoke in a low, controlled voice. "I got no time for games. Tell me where it is, or in about two fucking seconds I'm gonna decorate this shit hole with your brains." He let go of her neck, and as she sucked in some air, he added, "So where is it?" Holly could sense something had changed and instinctively knew it was time to play her bargaining chip.

"It's back at the house."

"*What?* Why didn't you tell me when we were there?"

"You didn't ask."

"Bitch!" He backhanded her across the face and added, "*Where* in the house?"

"In my...in my bedroom, in a wall safe...behind a painting." He glanced at his watch. It was after midnight. The Scarf and the Feds were probably on the way. *Shit.* He slapped the tape over Holly's mouth again and hurried into the adjacent room. He ripped the telephone cord from the wall and quickly tied it around the knob of the door leading outside. Then he pulled the shotgun out of his duffel bag and duct-taped it to a chair that he wedged against the air conditioner. He got it pointed where he wanted and had just finished tying the other end of the cord to the trigger when he heard the front door of the adjacent room burst open.

***

Tangles followed me down the sidewalk in front of the motel. Once I got past the end unit with the Caddy parked in front, I cut to the rear of the building and stopped behind a Dumpster. I pulled out my phone and texted, "White Horse Inn DN in room 12 going in."

"What are you doing?" Asked Tangles.

"I'm letting mission control know what we're doing, just in case."

"Just in case *what?*"

"How would I know? That's why I said just in case. If I knew what was gonna happen, I wouldn't say just in case." I saw that mission control had also sent me a text with an attachment whose subject matter read, "DeNutzio images." I opened it and held my phone out so Tangles could see. It showed a grainy pic of a big guy in a parking lot.

"Lotta good that does," commented Tangles. I clicked on the next image from the hotel lobby. It was in color with much better definition.

"He's big, all right," I said. "What color is that hair, reddish blond?"

"Nah, more reddish-brown. It's a hybrid, like a mandarin."

"Why do I bother?" I shook my head.

"Forget his hair, dude, check out that mug. It's like a cross between Howdy Doody and Soupy Sales…like Soupy Doody."

"Great observation. Now remember what that face looks like, and put a few rounds in it first chance you get—let's power the phones down."

Once we had our phones turned off and put away, Tangles asked, "So, how's this gonna work?"

"This guy's a convicted murderer who's also wanted for at least one other murder, not including Peter Porsche. Once we open the door, just shoot anybody who isn't Holly or Dickhead. He's big and bad, so keep firing until you run out of bullets. How's that for a plan?"

"Huh. Can't see what could possibly go wrong with that. Let's do it." We fist-bumped and he followed me around the corner of the building. I looked around the parking lot. It was quiet except for a little traffic on Dixie. I could see through the window blind that there was a light on in the room, and when I pressed my ear against the door, I could hear the TV. I slipped the key into the handle and slowly turned it until I felt the door opening. With trembling knees and a pounding heart, I pulled the big .45 from my waistband and looked at Tangles. He was holding the Glock in two hands up by his head and nodded. I took a deep breath and thought, *Oh, fuck, here we go.* I mouthed three, two, one and burst through the door.

I almost tripped over the legs of Holly's ex who was lying on the floor, tied up and taped to the bed. He rolled over, and I saw he had a shard of glass sticking out the side of his blood encrusted face. I saw Holly bound and gagged with tape around her neck that was wrapped around what was presumably the bathroom doorknob. Her eyes went wide, and she started thrashing her head to the side. I stepped toward her, holding the gun out in front of me, and aimed it at the bathroom door, figuring DeNutzio had to be inside. *Wait a second! How can he be in the bathroom if the doorknob's duct taped around Holly's neck?* I glanced over my shoulder at Tangles, who had a hand on the knob of a second door I hadn't immediately noticed. The door smashed into him as DeNutzio barreled through it. Tangles's gun went airborne, and he flew across the room into the opposite wall and crumpled in a little heap. DeNutzio swung his weapon toward me, but he was too late—his ass was mine. I had the .45 centered on him and squeezed the trigger…but the trigger wouldn't pull. The horrifying realization that I forgot to take the safety off hit me a split second before the bullet did. I felt something akin to a hammer hitting me in the chest about the same time I saw the muzzle flash. I fell backward, and when my head hit the wall, everything went black.

***

Holly looked on in horror as her captor turned his attention to Mark and pointed the gun at him. Tears flooded her eyes, and she screamed, "NO!" But it was muted by the tape covering her mouth. Suddenly, Tangles leaped off the floor and grabbed for the gun while sinking his teeth into DeNutzio's arm. The shot went off target, and DeNutzio howled in pain as he flung Tangles backward against the wall. Tangles's eyes rolled back in his head as he slid down the wall a second time, and DeNutzio pointed the gun at him. Holly cried out as he pulled the trigger, but nothing happened. He cursed as he tried to free the bullet wedged sideways in the chamber, but it was to no avail. *The gun had jammed!*

He tossed the gun on the bed and picked up Kit's gun, which was lying on the floor next to his lifeless body. He wanted to put a bullet in his head and a couple more in the midget and douche-bag lawyer but decided against it, as the sound of gunfire would no doubt have the other motel guests calling 911. He briefly considered slitting their throats, but he was too worried about the Feds barging in at any second. *Time to go for the gold.*

He tucked the .45 in his waistband and pulled the knife out to cut the tape securing Holly to the bathroom door. As he did so, Holly looked at Kit lying face down on the floor, and her sobbing intensified. Wasting no time, DeNutzio manhandled her out the door and into the Ford. Unable to catch her breath with the tape over her mouth, Holly began hyperventilating and promptly passed out.

Chapter 37

As Flingblade drove the old pickup truck north on I-95 past Delray Beach, Rudy pulled out his cell and dialed Tangles again. For the third time since they had left the casino, Tangles's phone went unanswered. Frustrated, Rudy hung up and shook his head.

"How in the hell does that boy expect me to help when he doesn't answer his phone?" He looked at Flingblade and added, "Damn, Bubba, what are we supposed to do? We don't know where they're looking for this guy who snatched Holly, and it doesn't make a lick a sense to search the same motels they already did. Aw hell, why am I asking you? You ain't said spit since Christ was a kid, prob'ly before that, even. Least you're a good driver, I mean, considering you've had a couple. But that's it. No more hooch on my watch, as out of time as it may be." Rudy pointed at the exit sign for Boynton Beach Boulevard and said, "Get off here, Bubba, we may as well swing by Holly's, maybe they came back to regroup, or left a note or something."

Less than ten minutes later they turned off A1A in Ocean Ridge, onto Sabal Island Drive. They looped around to the point, where Holly's house was, and Rudy pointed at the driveway. He was about to tell him to pull in when their headlights swept over several vehicles parked in the circular drive. He held up his hand and said, "Hold on, Bubba," and Flingblade stopped the truck. Rudy recognized Holly's Jeep, but there were two other cars he had never seen before. The landscape lights didn't provide much in the way of illumination, but he could see one was a sports car and the other a four-door sedan. The sedan was backed up to the front door. "Whose cars are those?" He wondered out loud. Realizing Shagball's Beemer wasn't in the drive, his suspicions grew. "Kill the lights, Bubba." Flingblade did as asked, and Rudy added, "Park sideways at the top of the drive, so we're blocking the entrance."

Rudy gave him some hand signals and once Flingblade had the truck blocking the drive, he killed the engine. "I don't know what's going on here, Bubba, but ol' Rudy smells something fishy. The lights are on, but I don't see anybody in the front window. I think we better have us a little look-see, ninja style." Rudy walked the index finger and middle finger of one hand across the dash, and with the other he put a finger up to his lips. "Shhhh...nice and quiet, you catch my drift, Bubba?" When Flingblade nodded, Rudy pointed at his knapsack. "Okay, good. Now, you got anything in there I can use? I'm not sure what's going on inside, maybe nothing, but I don't wanna be empty-handed if the ol' cowpie hits the fan, know what I mean?" Flingblade nodded and rummaged through the knapsack for a few seconds before pulling out a Chinese throwing star. It had seven razor-sharp, arrowhead-like points protruding from the center, and Flingblade smiled as he touched one of the points to his throat.

"What the hell?" asked Rudy. "I don't need a *spur*—we ain't goin' in on horseback."

Flingblade made a throwing motion with the deadly throwing star and pointed at his throat.

"Look, I've seen a kung-fu movie or two in my day, but you can forget it. I can't even throw a Frisbee. What else you got?"

Flingblade put the star away and pulled up a leg of his jeans. It was dark in the cab, and Rudy couldn't see what he was doing, but he heard Velcro ripping, and then Flingblade held up a knife sheath. He pulled a throwing knife out of the sheath, and after switching it with a standard hunting knife he pulled out of the knapsack, handed it to Rudy.

Rudy shook his head and muttered, "Bring a damn knife to a gunfight...shit." He quickly pulled up one of the legs of his own jeans and strapped the knife on. "Oh well, guess it's better than nothin'."

After Flingblade shimmied the knapsack onto his back, Rudy asked, "You ready to go, Bubba?"

Flingblade gave a thumbs-up.

"Okay, if you see me point at somebody that means you got the green light to go all William Tell on 'em. Arrows, hatchets, Ginsu stars, whatever you got in that bag of tricks, feel free to let it fly, only don't be going for the apple on the head, go for the Adam's apple." Rudy pinched his Adam's apple and added, "You with me?"

Flingblade smiled as he nodded, only this time, he added a wink. "Great, I feel so much better now. All right, Kemosabe, let's creepy up to the teepee."

Chapter 38

When Kit and Tangles failed to answer their phones, Stargazer cursed and dialed DICK agent Joe Thomas. It was no time for lightheartedness, so he selected the voice of James Earl Jones on the Oralator. Agent Joe glanced at the speedometer, which was pegged at 110 miles an hour, and took his foot off the gas before answering.

"Hey, boss, I'm getting close, just passed Palm Beach Lakes Boulevard. Where should I get off?"

"Hang on a second." Stargazer looked at the gigantic map of West Palm Beach on the wall in front of him. "You want to get off at Southern Boulevard. The exit's maybe four miles south. Go east until you get to US 1, and then head south about a mile to a motel called the White Horse—room twelve."

"So what's going on?"

"Shagball and Tangles found DeNutzio, but despite instructions to call me before doing anything, they went ahead anyway."

"Shagball and Tangles?"

"The fishing-show guys—the new recruits."

"Oh, right, but if they didn't call you, how do you know what they're up to?"

"Shagball texted me that they were going in, and then they turned off their phones. I'm worried, Joe. They're amateurs. They don't know what they're doing."

"Then how did they manage to find DeNutzio?"

"They...I'm not exactly sure, but it's not important. If they try to barge into to DeNutzio's room, they'll probably get killed."

"Do they know the scoop on DeNutzio? What he's capable of?"

"Yes."

"Then why would they try and force their way into his room? That's suicidal—ballsy, but suicidal."

"What would *you* do if it was *your* wife or significant other who was being held hostage?"

"Good point. If they don't get killed, I might have to buy them a drink."

"That's one thing they definitely *don't* need."

"Wait a second—what are they armed with?"

"They took some weapons from Thomas's Porsche. I think they think it's going to be like the movies."

"They must not have seen the ending to *Butch Cassidy and the Sundance Kid*. But getting back to Thomas, is there anything new?"

"No. I'm sorry, Joe, we need to prepare for the worst."

"I can't believe Thomas might be..." His voice trailed off, and he slapped his thigh. "Damn it! I pray to God I get a crack at—hey, here's the Southern Boulevard exit, I'm getting off. You said head east, right?"

"Yes, then south on US 1. Be careful, Joe."

"Always."

"If the local authorities or anybody else gets called to the scene, use your Homeland Security ID. Try to keep Shagball and Tangles from talking if at all possible."

"Will do." Click.

***

The Scarf was nervous. Actually, the Scarf was nearly always nervous, but having an FBI agent place a transmitter/receiver under his collar made him downright jumpy.

"What if this thing starts beeping or something? I'm a dead man. You guys don't seem to—"

"Relax, Jimmy," said one of the FBI agents in an effort to calm him. "This isn't the eighties anymore. Transmitters don't start smoking and making noise for no reason. That's for the movies. These nanobugs are foolproof."

"Yeah, but are they DeNutzio proof? That's all I care about. This guy has a spidey sense for sniffing shit out."

"Bullshit. You can't smell nothing, and that's what this smells like, nothing. Hell, you wouldn't even know what it was if you were looking straight at it. It looks like a piece of lint."

"I hate lint. Lint is like a cotton maggot. It creeps down your stomach to your belly button and then invites over all its maggot friends. Next thing you know you got a party going on full of mites and bacteria and—"

"Okay, I get it," said the second agent. "You hate lint. Once this is over, I'll buy you an economy pack of lint rollers." Suddenly, the lead agent's radio crackled to life.

"Team one leader, we're in position at the corner of the motel. Medical support has arrived and is also ready. Team two standing by."

"You only got two teams?" asked the Scarf.

"Don't worry, team two is in full SWAT gear. Everything should go smooth as long as you do your job."

"I got a bad feeling about this."

"Let's get it over with quick then, like pulling a tooth. Team two reported that the Caddy's in front of the room, and the TV's on. When DeNutzio is vulnerable, say something like, "You mind if I change the channel?" Or just mention that you're changing the channel. That's when the SWAT team will come in, and we'll be right behind them. Leave the key in the door when you go in. If DeNutzio notices, just act like you forgot. If we see you take it out, don't worry, we'll batter the door down."

"Better plan on it. He notices everything. I think a cab should drop me off in front of the room in case he's peeking out the window."

"If he is, just tell him you got dropped off around the corner so you could scope out the scene."

"Seems like a lot to remember."

"No, it's not. You got dropped off around the corner, leave the key in the door, change the channel—that's it."

"I'm telling you—I got a really bad feeling about this."

"And I got a really bad feeling about my daughter's new boyfriend, but there's nothing I can do about that either. So suck it up, Mouse, it's go time."

"I told you, it's the Scarf now."

"Whatever. Let's get this over with." The agent driving reached across the seat and opened the passenger door. Reluctantly, the Scarf stepped out and walked down the darkened street toward the motel. He hadn't noticed it earlier, but he noticed it now as he walked by—there was a late model convertible red Beemer parked on the street too. *Didn't the girl's boyfriend drive such a car?* The bad feeling had grown, and he whispered into his collar. "There's a red Beemer parked a few cars down."

"So?" Came the FBI agent's reply.

"I'm pretty sure the girl's boyfriend drives a red Beemer. Maybe you should run the plates before I go in. I mean—"

"I know what you mean, you're scared, but don't worry, we got your back."

"Sure you do, until I go in the room."

"Quit talking. Just remember to leave the key in the door, and signal us when DeNutzio's vulnerable."

"What if he's—"

"Just do it!"

"All right, but I'm telling you that might be the boyfriend's car." The FBI special agent in charge turned the car around and had the second agent jot down the Beemer's tag. Then he drove onto Dixie and went to the other side of the motel to join the SWAT team.

The Scarf walked past the motel office, which was closed. The FBI had briefly discussed trying to evacuate the other motel guests, but were too concerned even the slightest bit of commotion would alert DeNutzio and make a bad situation worse. It was hot and muggy, and as the Scarf walked through the parking lot, sweat began forming on his brow. He wiped his forehead with his scarf and thought about how miserably hot it was. He also thought that with a little luck he would soon be in a witness relocation program far, faraway—preferably somewhere not so fucking muggy. Still, the bad feeling he had in the pit of his stomach persisted.

When he got to the Caddy (by far the nicest car in the lot), he reached under the wheel well on top of the left rear tire and pulled out the room key. *So far, so good.* He walked up to room eleven and hesitated for a moment. As he looked around he saw a SWAT guy stick his helmeted head out from the corner of the building and nod at him. He took a deep breath and thought, *Fuck you, you got a gun and a bulletproof vest, alls I got is my fuckin' scarf.*

Even though he had been told to just let himself in, he thought it prudent to knock first. He rapped his knuckles on the door a few times and said, "Hey, Rodge, it's me." When no answer came, he pressed his ear against the door and heard the TV, but nothing else. He exhaled and slipped the key into the door. *Ready or not…*When he turned the knob and pushed the door open, a thunderous boom filled the night air. Splinters of door frame and plaster clattered to the walkway, and as he staggered sideways, he realized his arm had been blown off at the elbow. His legs gave way, and the last thing he saw before passing out was the sight of his bloody hand still clinging to the doorknob as the SWAT team rushed in.

Chapter 39

I felt myself rolling over and a distant voice calling my name. "Shaggy! Shaggy, wake up! Oh my God!" Somebody shook me by the shoulders, and I felt the sting of a slap across my face. As my eyes fluttered open, I looked up at Tangles, who looked scared. He was about to slap me again, but I reached up and grabbed his wrist.

"Why the fuck are you slapping me?"

The expression on his face went from fear and panic to utter shock.

"Dude, you're alive! I can't believe you're alive!"

I put my hands on the carpet and pushed myself up into a sitting position against the wall. I looked down at my chest, and there was a small stream of blood going down my T-shirt from sternum to waist. I suddenly remembered being shot and looked around the room. "Where's Holly? What happened to Holly?"

"I dunno, man, when I came to, she and DeNutzio were gone. Dude, look at your flashlight." Tangles pointed at the Surefire flashlight that I wore around my neck on a lanyard. Most of the tail cap was missing, and the body of the flashlight where it screwed into the tail cap was cracked and dented. The bullet had smashed into it and then deflected into my chest. Fortunately, the velocity of the bullet had been reduced to the point where it was unable to penetrate deep and do serious damage—not that it didn't sting a little. It felt like a hot coal was stuck in my chest, and I could smell burnt flesh. I pressed the tail-cap activation button on the Surefire, which was still attached by a mangled thread of anodized aluminum, and it lit up. "Fuckin' A, it still works," I marveled.

"Dude, that flashlight saved your life. I'm never gonna tease you about it again."

I shone the Surefire on the feet of Holly's ex, which were sticking out past the end of the bed. He thumped them on the floor a couple of times and let out a muffled cry. I nodded toward him and said, "Better check on Dickhead, see if he knows where DeNutzio took Holly."

I ripped open my T-shirt from the tiny hole in the middle and saw the flattened end of the bullet sticking out. I felt around the edges and surmised it to be maybe a half inch deep at the most. Using my hands, I pressed on both sides and the bullet popped out like a lead zit. It hurt—a lot. As blood started to flow out of the hole more earnestly, I heard Tangles ripping the tape off Dickhead. When he pulled the tape off his mouth, he cried, "I've been shot, and my ankles broke! Call an ambulance!"

Tangles was kneeling on the other side of the bed, and his head popped up. "He got winged in the shoulder. He'll be all right."

I struggled to my feet trying to stanch the flow of blood with my torn and bloodied T-shirt. Tangles asked Dickhead, "Where did they go? Do you know where they went?"

"I need an ambulance. I told you, I've been—"

Tangles slapped him hard across the face.

"Ow! Jesus, man, call the—"

"Where did they go?!" I joined in.

"Back to the house. Holly told him she has gold there. Now please call an ambulance, for God's sake."

"Go ahead." I nodded to Tangles. "Call nine one one." Just as Tangles pulled out his cell, somebody knocked on the outside door to the adjacent room and said something. I locked eyes with Tangles and an instant later there was a loud explosion. We both flinched and stood frozen in place for a second or two. That was all it took before the door connecting to the adjacent room burst open again. Dickhead was in the process of trying to get up, and the door caught him flush in the side of his head. As he tumbled across the floor, three guys in SWAT gear charged in with their weapons pointed at us.

"GET DOWN ON THE FLOOR! DOWN ON THE FLOOR!"

Tangles, with his lack of height advantage, hit the floor in an instant. I found myself looking down two shotgun barrels and another automatic pistol of unknown caliber that I wanted to keep that way. I quickly followed suit as the shouting continued. "KEEP YOUR HANDS WHERE WE CAN SEE THEM!" I felt a foot on my back and let out a cry of pain as one of the SWAT guys kicked open the bathroom door.

"Get off my back!" I pleaded. "I've got a hole in my chest. I was shot!"

The guy who kicked open the bathroom door spoke into a microphone attached to his shoulder. "All clear! No sign of subject."

"*Get off my fucking back!*" I yelled as best I could.

Somebody else entered the room and said, "Frisk him."

I felt the foot come off my back, but it was quickly replaced by a knee as one of the SWAT guys frisked me. He found the ATF badge I conned the motel owner with and said, "He's ATF." He handed it off to somebody and continued to pat me down. Finding nothing significant, he said, "He's clean, no weapons."

The guy who told him to frisk me said, "Go ahead, let him up."

He took his knee off my back, and I got up. It was then that I could see the SWAT guys were FBI. There were two guys in suits with bulletproof vests on like the SWAT guys who were still pointing guns at me and Tangles.

"You're *ATF?* What the fuck are *you* doing here?" The FBI guy who appeared to be in charge sounded incredulous.

I was tired, shot, and still a little dazed from hitting the wall. Not sure how to respond and not thinking clearly, my natural instincts took over. "I smelled smoke."

"You *what?* What the fuck are you talking about? Where's DeNutzio? Where's the girl?" The lead agent had an Eddie Munster haircut, and as he holstered his weapon, he pointed at Tangles and Dickhead. "And who the fuck are they?"

One of the SWAT guys was kneeling next to Dickhead. "This guy's out cold. Looks like he's been beaten and shot."

The second suit turned to the door leading to the adjacent room and yelled, "Get those EMTs in here, now!"

The front door to the room flew open, and a pair of EMTs came hustling through, followed by a black guy holding a badge in one hand and a phone up to his ear. Another FBI agent trailed the guy with the badge and said, "I tried to keep him out but—"

"Agent Tom Jonas, Homeland Security," announced the guy with the badge as he put his phone away.

A look of disbelief crossed the face of the FBI agent in charge.

"*Homeland Security? ATF?* You gotta be shittin' me, let me see that thing." He snatched the badge out of his hands and inspected it like he knew what one looked like, which he didn't. "What the fuck…" he muttered as he handed it back.

The Homeland guy looked at me and said, "Shagball?"

"Yeah, that's right. How'd you—?"

"C'mon." He walked over to me. "You're bleeding; let's get you some medical attention." He took me by the arm and started to lead me out of the room, but the FBI agent stepped in front of him.

"Wait just a goddamn second! Where do you think you're going? I need to talk to him." He pointed at Dickhead, who had an oxygen mask over his face and was being put on a stretcher, and then at Tangles, who still had a SWAT guy's foot on his back. "In fact, I need to talk to these guys, too, whoever the fuck they are."

"Sorry." The Homeland guy shrugged. "He works with me, and so does the midget. Let him up." The SWAT guy with his foot on Tangles's back looked at

313

the FBI guy, who was getting more pissed by the second.

"Don't even think about lifting that foot! My informant just had his fucking arm blown off, and nobody's going anywhere till I get some answers!" As if on cue, colored lights started flashing outside, and a siren blared as the ambulance tore out of the parking lot with Dickhead.

"Easy with the foot action," complained Tangles. "You press any harder, I'm gonna drop a deuce."

"Go right ahead," said the agent in charge. He pointed at him and asked, "What's with the midget?"

"He's an informant," replied the Homeland guy.

"*He's* an informant? Oh, that's rich. Didn't know DeNutzio was traveling with the circus. Wait a second, since when does the ATF work with Homeland Security?"

"It's a joint venture."

"Are you fucking kidding me? Well how about cluing in the FBI next time, you asshole! DeNutzio's number eight on the top ten list. It's not like you're the only ones looking for him."

He shrugged. "Sorry, it's a matter of national security."

"National security? *Whose* national security?"

Another guy in a suit with an FBI vest on stuck his head in the door and said, "Frank, the boss is on the line. He wants to talk to you *now*." He held a phone out.

The agent in charge was on the verge of blowing a gasket. "What? How the—? What the *fuck's* going on here?" He stepped outside and said something to the other agent before snatching the phone out of his hand. The Homeland guy whispered in my ear, "You know where DeNutzio went?" When I nodded yes, he said, "Good, don't say a word" then instructed one of the EMTs to tend to me. The EMT quickly tore off my T-shirt, cleaned and plugged the hole in my chest, and then bandaged me up with a gauze wrap that encircled my torso. While he was doing his thing, we heard the agent in charge losing it outside.

"But, sir, DeNutzio gave us the slip! I can't just let 'em waltz out of here without—yes, sorry, of course, I know who's the boss...uh-huh...uh-huh...but *Homeland Security?* Since when do they tell—right. I'm not questioning you, no, sir. It's just that I got an informant who's never gonna be able to grab his ass with both hands 'cause he ain't got one, and I'd like to know what the hell's—yes, there were three in the room. The lawyer must be the third guy, but he's unconscious and on the way to the hospital, which is why I need to—no...no, I heard you...yes, I understand perfectly...No, I don't want to work undercover in Ecuador. Right. We'll stick with him until he comes around and try to get a handle on—yes, uh-huh...I know you have more important things to tend to. I'll keep you posted then... FUCK!"

The agent stormed back in and told the SWAT guy to let Tangles up. Then he looked the Homeland guy square in the eye. "Well, what are you waiting for? Take your midget and get the fuck out of here before I do something I'll regret."

As the Homeland guy escorted me and Tangles out the door, Tangles mumbled, "You mean like pissing off your barber?"

The FBI agent followed us out the door and snarled, "What did you say, you little fucking garden gnome?"

Tangles turned back and smiled. "Nice haircut, Dickmunch. It works for you. Really."

Chapter 40

"Holy shit!" said Tangles. "Did you see the door to the room next to us?"

Actually, I hadn't. The Homeland guy was still leading me by the arm, which I was grateful for because I was feeling a tad woozy. The EMT had given me a shot of something for pain, and while it was working, it wasn't exactly a pick-me-up. I glanced over my shoulder and saw an FBI guy on his knees, snapping pictures of the door. Between the flashes and the crowd of people gathering, I couldn't make out shit.

The lead FBI agent pushed through the crowd and yelled at Tangles, "Hey! You just call me 'Dickmunch'?!"

Tangles flipped him the bird, and we continued walking away.

"What's that guy taking pictures of?" I asked.

"Oh, man, some dude's hand is clinging to the door knob. You don't see that every day."

"It was the FBI informant," said the Homeland agent. "DeNutzio apparently booby-trapped the door with a shotgun." A couple of West Palm Beach police cruisers screeched into the lot, and some uniforms jumped out with guns drawn. Mr. Homeland held up his badge and announced, "Easy guys, I'm with

Homeland Security—the FBI has the scene under control." The cops rushed past, and we stopped next to a black Dodge Viper. Mr. Homeland opened the passenger door and instructed us to get in.

"You drive a Viper?" asked Tangles.

"I sure don't fly it. Pile in."

"Pile in where? It's a two-seater."

He pushed a lever, and the passenger seat fell forward, exposing a very small space behind the front seats.

"You gotta be shitting me," said Tangles.

"Get in already, will you?" I urged. "God knows what's happening to Holly." After Tangles managed to crawl into the back, I slid in the passenger seat, and Mr. Homeland asked, "Which way?" He put a flashing light on the dash and turned it on.

"South on US 1," I replied. "DeNutzio took her back to the house to get his hands on the gold—right, Tangles?"

"That's what Dickhead said before he got knocked out."

As the headlights swept across the chaotic scene in front of us, I saw that the Cadillac was still parked in front of the room.

"Look, the Caddy's still here," I pointed out. "Why would the Caddy still be here?"

"Based on the booby-trapped door, it's obvious he knew the Feds were onto him. He must have switched cars," said Mr. Homeland. As he was about to turn on US 1, I realized how parched I was and remembered the cooler in the back of the Beemer.

"Wait!" I pointed to the north end of the parking lot. "Pull down that side street first; I have some water and antiseptic in the back of my Beemer." I saw no

318

reason to mention the revolver and sawed-off shotgun I also planned on retrieving. He swung the Viper north on Dixie and then took a right down the side street. I pointed out the Beemer, and he pulled alongside it. I winced as I extracted myself from the low-slung seat and seconds later had the Beemer's trunk open. I took the cooler out and placed it on the passenger-side floor of the Viper. After retrieving my Surefire Lawman from the driver's door, I slipped it into the tennis bag and passed it to Tangles in his already cramped quarters.

"What's with the tennis bag?" the Homeland agent asked.

"It's vintage, and it's signed by Agassi. No way I'm leaving it in the Beemer, not in *this* neighborhood. Let's roll!"

***

FBI Agent in Charge Frank Auble watched the Dodge Viper tear down Dixie Highway with a disdainful look on his face. Shaking his head, he turned to his colleague. "You slip a tracking device on that Viper like I asked?"

"Yep, first time I ever tracked a Homeland agent. Sure hope he doesn't find it."

"Yeah? Well, *fuck* that midget-loving—"

"Frank!" Another FBI agent waved at him from the open doorway of a room just down from where the Scarf had his arm blown off. "You better take a look at this." The two agents hurried over, as did a pair of West Palm Beach cops who were talking to some motel guests.

"Whatta you got?" Frank approached the open door.

The agent stepped aside and held his arm out in a welcoming manner.

"Welcome to the Hotel Deadifornia, when you check out like this, you definitely ain't leaving." As soon as Frank and the second FBI agent entered the room, he closed the door behind them, not allowing the local cops to get a look. "Sorry, boys, this is ain't a peep show," he halfheartedly apologized.

"So what's to look at?" asked one of the cops.

"There's two dead bodies inside. They were shot. You wanna be useful, why don't you interview the other guests, see if anybody saw or heard anything."

As the cops walked away, a small Asian man ran up to them while frantically waving his hands. "You say no bazooka! I hear bazooka!"

Chapter 41

I handed Tangles a bottle of water, and we both chugged thirstily as we tore down Dixie. As more sirens wailed behind us, the agent asked, "How far is Holly's house?" I felt the G-force push me back in the seat as he accelerated and saw we were doing eighty-five—on Dixie.

"Assuming we live? At this rate, not very far," I answered. "You're not really Homeland Security, are you?"

"About as much as you're ATF."

"Then who *are* you guys?" asked Tangles from the back.

"When the boss wants you to know, you'll know. Just tell me where to turn."

I gave him a brief rundown of the directions as we blew through light after light. When I finished, I looked over my shoulder at Tangles. "So what happened after I got shot? How come DeNutzio didn't shoot *you?*"

"I dunno. After you went down, he turned the gun on Dickhead. I figured I was next, so I jumped on his arm and chomped down as hard as I could. Dickhead got winged in the shoulder, and he flung me into the wall like a ragdoll. I'm telling you that guy is scary strong. When I came to, he and Holly were gone. That's when I started shaking you."

"You chomped on his arm?"

"Well, yeah. I mean, what else could I do? The guy's a friggin' animal."

"That makes two of you. So why didn't you jump on him when he was shooting at me?"

"Dude, when he barreled through the door, he knocked me silly. You saw what happened. What kind of quest—?"

"Turn left at the second light...on Ocean," I said.

"What the hell did you mean by that, Shag?" Tangles persisted.

"Forget it, it's not like I ever saved *your* life before—oh wait, I did."

"What the hell, man? I saved your life, too. In fact, I saved it today! On the way back from the Bahamas. Remember?"

"Of course I remember, but I saved your life first. Which means by saving your life, I saved my life. It's like I saved myself."

"*What?* Who even thinks like that?"

"Relax, all right? I'm just kidding. Besides, who needs *you* when I have my trusty Surefire to protect me."

Mr. Homeland glanced at the mangled flashlight hanging from my neck as we decelerated past Lantana road. "You are one lucky son of a bitch. Actually, both of you are. DeNutzio's not known for leaving witnesses behind."

"Tell me that after we get Holly back all safe and sound."

322

The Viper continued braking, and we made the left hand turn onto Ocean Avenue in Lantana. I looked at my watch. One thirty. The Old Key Lime House was dark, and the parking lot was empty save for a few cars. I reached in the cooler and popped the top on a cold can of Bud Light. The agent's head swiveled at the sound, and he looked incredulous.

"You can't be drinking beer right now, are you *crazy?*"

"Sorry," I said and handed him a bottle of water. "You're the designated driver."

As we zipped over the new Lantana Bridge, I handed Tangles a beer and told him to take a right at the second light.

"How much farther?" he asked as Tangles popped the top.

"Three or four miles." I took another thirsty pull, and as I felt my stomach rumble, I powered the window down and discreetly belched into the breeze.

The agent looked at me and scowled. "Put that beer away."

"Hey, keep your eyes on the road, Speed Racer," cut in Tangles. His little arm shot out from between the seats, and his finger pointed at the road ahead.

"Christ"—the agent shrugged as we turned south onto A1A—"I knew you guys were gonna be trouble. Hang on."

He floored it, and we were going 110 when I thought I saw the blurry outline of a Manalapan police car zip by. We were going 140 when Tangles and I both started screaming to slow down because of Chillingsworth's curve. We slung around the deadly curve doing seventy-plus miles an hour, and the police lights in the rearview mirror became but a memory as he accelerated again.

"Pretty straight from here?" he asked casually.

"Dude, you just blew the doors off that cop car!" cried Tangles.

"Don't worry about it, just let me know if there's another curve."

"Yes, there is. Just past the inlet it goes right, then left," I responded. We hung on for dear life and seconds later were yelling for him to slow down again. As we flew across the Boynton inlet bridge, we passed a pair of sheriff's cars sitting on the side of A1A. *Super.* We negotiated the curve at the highest possible speed, and I said, "Quarter mile on the right, Sabal Island Drive."

He turned the flashing dash light off, and less than a minute later, we had wound around the circular Sabal Island Drive to the point where it turned back. I pointed out Holly's driveway, and he stopped behind an old pickup that was blocking the end of it. "You know whose truck that is?" he asked. He pulled an HK45 out from under the windbreaker he had on.

Tangles and I agreed we had never seen it before, as he opened the glove box and quickly screwed a silencer onto the end of the gun. "Maybe it's the vehicle DeNutzio's using," he added as he racked the slide. "What's the layout of the house?"

"It's U-shaped with an open courtyard in back. The safe is in the master bedroom, in the southeast corner—back left," I answered.

"Okay, you guys wait here. Whatever happens is gonna happen quick. If I'm not back in five, call the boss."

"Fuck that, man, we're—"

"Look, this guy's as dangerous as they come, and I can't be looking after you two. Just sit tight, okay?" When neither of us responded, he repeated, "I said *okay?*"

"Okay, okay, go already," I urged. When he opened the door, we could hear the sound of sirens racing by on A1A, no doubt looking for a speed fiend in a black Viper.

As Speed Racer disappeared down the dark drive in silence, I said, "Gimme the Mexican antiseptic and the three fifty-seven."

Tangles maneuvered to pull them out of my tennis bag and handed them over. "What are you thinking?" he asked as I spun the cylinder on the meaty Smith & Wesson. *Six bullets, no safety. Good.* Knowing what I was thinking, I uncorked the Padron and took a swallow before chasing it with the rest of my Bud Light. "I was thinking you must be cramped back there."

"Are you kidding? I feel like a claustrophobic sardine. This sucks." I handed him the Padron, and he also took a swig.

"Bet you'd like to stretch those little wheels of yours."

"Hell, yeah. You read my mind, bro."

"Short read." I got out, and Tangles maneuvered out from behind the seat holding the sawed-off shotgun.

"Watch where you point that thing," I quietly warned.

"That's what she said."

"You know what else she said?"

"What?"

"Keep it down." I held up the .357 magnum and added, "You ready to go, GI Bro?"

Tangles nodded, "You know it. Sure wish I had on some camo, though."

"*Camo?* What for? You're so short, you blend into the ground. Besides, it's dark out."

"Thanks, Captain Obvious. Asshole."

"You want obvious? Okay, how 'bout we try not to shoot Speed Racer and vice versa, *especially* the vice versa." I gingerly touched the gauze covering my chest and added, "Trust me, getting shot hurts. Let's go." I took off in a crouch down the driveway with Tangles trailing a half step behind. I stopped behind the big banyan tree for cover. As I surveyed the situation, Tangles whispered, "It's just a flesh wound."

"*What?*"

"I heard the paramedics talking. They said you just have a flesh wound."

"Flesh wound, my ass. The bullet hit me so hard that when I hit the wall, I got knocked out from the force."

"Maybe you just lost your balance."

"Of course I did, you idiot!" I hissed. "You get shot at close range, and *newsflash*, you're gonna lose your yoga pose."

"If you say so, but the flashlight clearly took the brunt of it. The bullet barely penetrated."

"*If you say so?* Are you kidding me?"

"I'm just saying the bullet popped right out, right?"

"It popped right out 'cause it was stuck in my sternum, and I gave it the ultimate Clearasil squeeze. I probably have a broken—" I thought I heard the sound of glass breaking. "Did you hear that?"

"Yes, something broke. I think it came from the back."

"C'mon!"

***

Back in the motel room, Frank's colleague asked, "What do you make of this mess?" There was a guy lying on the bed with a bullet hole between his eyes and a naked chick on the floor with two holes in her in her ample bosom. Frank noted a purse sitting on a chair, seemingly undisturbed, and a wallet on top of the TV. He pulled a pen out of his pocket and used it to open up the wallet. "The wallet's got cash in it."

"So?"

"So it wasn't a robbery." As he put the pen back in his pocket, he noticed scratch marks on top of the TV. He quickly stepped to the window and peered out the ratty curtains. There were half a dozen police cars and sheriff's cruisers with flashing lights parked haphazardly in the center of the lot. It was turning into a proper clusterfuck. Almost all of the motel rooms had cars parked in front of them, which included DeNutzio's rented Caddy—almost, but not all. There was an empty space in front of the room they were in, the one with the dead bodies inside. He pulled out a pair of latex gloves, and as he slipped them on, he said, "Put on your gloves and check the purse for car keys."

"What are you—?"

"Just do it!" As the second agent did as he was told, Frank searched the dead guy's pockets and found nothing.

"No keys in the purse, Frank," announced the agent.

"She have a driver's license?"

"Hang on a sec." He rummaged through the purse some more before adding, "No, no license."

Frank picked up the wallet, pulled the dead guy's license out, and handed it to him. "Find out what kind of vehicle is registered to this guy."

"Why?"

"'Cause that's probably what DeNutzio's driving. He shot 'em dead and took their car."

"How do you figure?"

"The scratch marks on the TV."

"What about 'em?"

"The dead guy dumped his wallet and keys on top of the TV, just like every other schmo that ever stayed here. That's what the scratches are from. Since there's no keys in the room, and no car parked in front, my bet is DeNutzio offed 'em and took the car. He was onto us somehow. Maybe the Scarf was right, maybe he *can* smell a rat blindfolded. Where's the Viper?"

The other agent pulled his phone out and tapped the screen a few times. "The Viper stopped moving. It's about ten miles south of here, in some place called Ocean Ridge. They got there pretty damn quick. That Homeland guy must have hauled ass."

"Of course he did. You know why? 'Cause they're chasing after DeNutzio. Those fuckers knew where he was headed."

"Now we know, too."

"Let's go!"

Chapter 42

Rudy led the way down the small path that ran along the east side of the house. To his left was a chain-link fence marking the property line, hidden by dark and dense foliage. When he saw that the master bedroom light was on, he stopped behind a cluster of palms and whispered over his shoulder. "That's the master bedroom, Bubba. I think there's a slider that leads to the courtyard from it. Maybe one of us should creep around the other side, whatta you think?" He looked back, expecting to see a smiling Flingblade give him a thumbs-up, but there was just darkness. He whispered Flingblade's name a few times before shaking his head and muttering, "Sumbitch went ninja again."

The sound of a door being shut startled him, and he quietly hurried back toward the source at the front of the house. Looking out from the darkness he saw a large man, a complete stranger, hoist a bag into the open trunk of the Ford spotted earlier. *What the hell?* As the man hoisted a second bag, Rudy turned and backtracked in double time. He scampered to the rear of the house and into the courtyard area, then crouched down behind a bush when he heard the screen door slap closed again. His phone started to vibrate in his pocket, and he had to alter his crouched position to get at it. He cussed under his breath as his cell phone ringtone began to play the chorus to the Little River Band's "Lonesome Loser." "Have you—?" He killed the call and held his breath, praying the big stranger hadn't heard it.

***

Holly closed her eyes and tried to push the thought that Kit might be dead out of her mind. It was simply unfathomable. It was even more unfathomable than the thought of still being married to Mark, her lying, cheating, stealing, disbarred, and fresh-out-of-jail ex. The fact that he had also been shot and might be dead didn't faze her at all. She had moved on with her life once, and she would keep moving on whether he was dead or alive. But whether she could move on without Kit was another story. Their life together had been a nonstop adventure since the first day they met, and along the way he captured her heart in a way no man ever had. She knew she had captured his heart, too, or at least occasionally contained it, confident that unlike Mark, his only mistress was the sea. It was a love they both shared unequivocally.

The night prior to leaving for the Bahamas, Kit had been wound up, anticipating the arrival of their secret high-tech fishing boat. She channeled his energy into a robust lovemaking session, and afterward they lay in bed and talked, a rarity. Never one to commit to anything except fishing and happy hour, Kit surprised her when he sprung his latest plan. She recalled their conversation.

"Five years," he had said. "I'll do the show for five more years, assuming this new spy-fishing gig works out. By then we should know what happened to Millie's son, and by then I'll be staring fifty in the face. That's a good time to scale things back; I don't want to be working too hard when I'm fifty."

"*Fifty?* You're not working too hard now," she answered.

"You know what I mean. You'll be looking at forty, and I'll be looking at fifty. That would be a good time to make things official."

"Make *what* official?"

"You know—us, me, you, Mrs. Jansen."

"*Mrs. Jansen?* Are you proposing?"

"It's more like a thought. I'm just throwing it out there, you know, in five years or so."

"*Five years?* Are you serious?"

"What, you think that's too soon?"

"You really think you can go five years without screwing up what we have together?"

"Probably not. That's why I was just throwing it out there."

"Throwing it out there is what you do with a dinner suggestion, you ass, not a marriage proposal."

"Now that you mention it, I *am* a little hungry after that awesome romp...Mrs. Jansen."

"Quit calling me that." Frustrated, she got out of bed and went to the bathroom. When she came back, Kit was stretched out on the bed in his Beer Nuts boxer shorts, his hands clasped behind his head. He was grinning from ear to ear and had a little blue box perched on a nest of graying chest hair. Although it wasn't an engagement ring as she briefly thought it might be, it tugged at her heartstrings nonetheless. It was a simple silver Tiffany's heart; a charm. She promptly added it to the necklace she wore that had a locket with a picture of her and Millie inside—a locket Kit gave her on their Caribbean adventure. The frustration she had felt only moments earlier dissipated in a wave of passion and another robust lovemaking session. Her heart ached now with the thought that it might have been their last.

Suddenly, she heard a brief snippet of a song: "Have you—?" As suddenly as the sound came, it went. Her eyes popped open, and she peered out into the courtyard, where it seemed to have come from. *Was there somebody out there?* She heard the front screen door slapping shut and then the footsteps of the monster who was laying waste to her life. The gravity of the situation came rushing back, and her heartache and despair was replaced with anger and a will to survive. She thought about one of Aunt Millie's sayings: "When the going gets tough, kick the tough in the nuts." With that in mind, she struggled to free herself, determined not to go down without a fight.

Chapter 43

After a few tense moments, Rudy peered through the branches at the sliding doors that led into the master bedroom. Holly, or who he presumed was Holly because of all the duct tape wrapped around her face, was bound and gagged and tied to the foot of the bed. A painting was propped against the far wall, exposing a wall safe, which was open. There were four bags sunken into the bed, and the big stranger stepped into view and grabbed two bags, one in each hand. When he disappeared down the hall, Rudy whispered as loud as he dared, "Flingblade...Flingblade, where the hell are you? I'm going for the girl. If you hear me, cover me."

Rudy rushed to the sliding doors and silently slid them open, signaling for Holly to keep quiet as her eyes grew wide. After he pulled the tape off her mouth, she urged him to hurry.

"Goin' as fast as I can, darlin'. Listen for the front door." He produced the knife Flingblade gave him, and Holly held out her hands. As he sliced through the tape, she took a few deep breaths and listened as if her life depended on it.

***

If there's one thing spending years in solitary confinement improves, it's the sense of hearing. So even as the screen door banged shut, and the sound waves echoed off the great-room tile, DeNutzio detected a snippet of sound that didn't belong. And not just any snippet—it was a snippet of a song that he'd grown to despise while doing time in a juvenile detention center. One of the guards sang it over and over—off-key, of course—while listening to it on a Walkman. It was "The Lonesome Loser" by the Little River Band. They were like the Australian version of the Starland Vocal Band. He'd forgotten how much he hated the song. *Fucking Australians.* Hearing even a snippet of it made him want to kill a kangaroo.

On high alert, he glanced out the French doors at the softly lit courtyard as he walked by. He wasn't positive, but he thought he saw movement in the shrubbery. Walking down the hall to the master bedroom, he quickly devised a plan. As he entered the bedroom he glanced out the sliders to the courtyard, and as he turned to grab two more sacks of gold off the bed, he kept an eye on his back using a mirror on the opposite wall. *Nothing, no movement.* The girl was struggling against her bindings, and it excited him. "Save your energy, toots," he said. "Once I get the gold loaded up, I'm gonna strap you to the bed and do things that'll make you forget all about that idiot boyfriend of yours." He knew he should just take the money and run, but having such a hot blonde at his disposal was too tempting. With a sack of gold in each hand, he headed down the hall, but this time, he ducked into a bathroom. After setting the gold on the counter next to the sink, he pulled out the .45 and disengaged the safety. *What kind of idiot forgets to take the safety off?* He stifled a chuckle and listened with his head cocked toward the bedroom. Moments later he heard the faint swishing sound of the sliders opening and a couple seconds after that heard a slicing/tearing sound.

It was time to make his move, and he quietly stepped into the hall. He heard a soft female voice whisper something inaudible and then a man whisper back, "...listen for the front door." He hesitated and looked over his shoulder down the darkened hall, but all was quiet. There was nobody was there. *Huh.* He quickly figured if they were expecting him to return, then whoever was trying to rescue the girl was likely working alone. *Big mistake.* Holding the .45 out in front of him, he strode into the bedroom.

Holly's hands were free, and Rudy had just started slicing off the leg restraints when it all went wrong. She had just enough time to yell, "Look out!" But the warning came too late.

With one purposeful stride DeNutzio stepped from the hall into the bedroom, and with the next, he stomp-kicked the back of Rudy's head. Rudy dropped the knife as he was driven into the corner of the bed, which shifted from the force.

Holly cried, "No!" as DeNutzio grabbed him by the neck. In no small feat of strength he lifted him six inches off the floor and pinned him against the wall. Holly suddenly realized that when the bed shifted, one of her feet slipped free, and she used it to maneuver Rudy's knife within arm's reach. With DeNutzio's attention on Rudy, she snatched up the knife and hid it in her lap.

"Who the fuck are *you?*" DeNutzio asked Rudy.

Barely able to breathe, Rudy had one thought and one thought only that he wanted to express: "Fling… Flingblade…Fling…blade! Help!"

"What?"

"Let him go!" pleaded Holly. "Just take the gold and—"

"Shut up." DeNutzio pointed the big .45-caliber automatic at her with his other hand. "The only thing I hate more than the Little River Band is a bitch who just won't—*aghhh!*"

Holly saw the blur and felt the whir as one of Flingblade's Chinese throwing stars buried itself deep into DeNutzio's bicep. He dropped the gun, and when he went to pull the star out with his other hand, he let go of Rudy, who scrambled around the bed. The razor-sharp points sliced DeNutzio's fingertips as he tried to yank the star out, and he cursed in pain as another star whizzed through the room and buried itself in his other bicep. Eyeing the gun on the floor, he stumbled forward and dropped to his knees. When he did, something grazed his head and smashed into a lamp on the dresser behind him. Rudy yelled, "Tomahawk him! Tomahawk him!"

With one eye on the darkened hallway where his unseen attacker lurked, DeNutzio reached for the gun, never expecting Holly to roll over and bury a knife into his outstretched hand. He never expected it, but that's exactly what she did, pinning his big hand to the carpet. A brief howl escaped his lips before Holly used her free leg to kick him in the mouth. She grabbed the gun and scooched backward with all her might, managing to drag the corner of the bed with her.

DeNutzio cried "Bitch!" and yanked his hand up a split second before a small arrow slammed into his chest, just below his right shoulder. The combined forces sent him twisting backward, and his hand ripped free from the carpet, sending the bloody knife flying.

Rudy yelled, "Shoot him!" and Holly's hands shook as she struggled to keep the heavy automatic pointed at him. A look of utter disbelief crossed DeNutzio's twisted face as his attacker stepped out of the darkened hallway. He was a little Indian, dressed in black and smiling. There was a bandanna on his head, and he was holding a hatchet by his side. *No fuckin' way.* Anger replaced shock and pain, and he remembered the knife strapped to his ankle. With blood seeping from the arrow wound in his chest, spewing from his hand, and oozing from his biceps, he reached for it. Rudy saw the barrel of a gun glint in the courtyard light and dove behind the bed.

Just as Holly mustered the nerve to pull the trigger, she heard an authoritative voice from the courtyard yell, "*Freeze*, DeNutzio!" DeNutzio turned to see a shadowy figure pointing a gun at him from beyond the sliders. "Put your hands where I can see them!" The voice commanded. On his knees and gasping for breath, he tried to raise his right hand while trying to stanch the flow of blood from the arrow wound with his left. He had seen enough John Wayne movies to know he couldn't yank the arrow out, and pushing it through five or six inches of muscle and tissue was not an option. He spit out a tooth and some blood, courtesy of the kick in the mouth. The same voice instructed Holly to place the gun behind her on the nightstand, which she did. Relieved at the turn of events, she immediately began tearing at the duct tape securing her leg to the bed frame.

DICK agent Joe Thomas stepped through the sliders and swung his gun toward Flingblade, who had the hatchet raised and ready to throw. "Drop it, Geronimo!"

Rudy popped his head up from the other side of the bed and said, "Better do as the man says, Bubba. Gun beats hatchet."

Flingblade dropped the hatchet, and the agent pointed the gun at Rudy. "Who the hell are *you* guys?"

Still on his knees, Rudy instinctively raised his arms. "I was about to ask you the same question, Bubba, but the important thing is we're on the same side." He pointed at DeNutzio and added, "Point that thing at him, not me. Don't let the face fool you, he may look like one of Jerry's kids, but trust me, he's an animal!" Knowing that it was possibly the most accurate statement ever made in the history of the world, Joe Thomas swung the gun toward DeNutzio, who sneered. Feeling that he had the situation under control, Agent Thomas uncharacteristically relaxed his guard *just* a fraction.

"You all right, ma'am?" he asked Holly.

"Yes, I'm fine. I just need to get this tape—" Then she looked past him toward the courtyard. Her eyes grew wide, and her jaw dropped like she'd seen a ghost. Alarmed, he turned to see what she was looking at. That's when the Devil's Nephew made his move.

Chapter 44

After hearing something get smashed to pieces, I started to take off for the corner of the house, but Tangles grabbed me by the arm. He whispered, "Wait! We should check out the trunk." I stopped and turned to see that he was pointing at the open trunk of the car backed up to the front door.

"Forget the trunk. Let's go," I quietly urged.

"Dude, Holly could be in there."

"Shit, of course, right. Okay, c'mon." As we ran over to the car, Tangles whispered, "You should listen to me more often."

"And you should shut up more often." I shone my mangled Surefire into the trunk and was semirelieved that Holly wasn't inside. Instead, there were two burlap sacks that we both recognized as being part of Holly's gold cache. Tangles jabbed the side of one using the butt of the sawed-off shotgun, and we heard the coins clink in confirmation. "He's swiping Holly's gold," he commented. "What should we do?"

"I don't care about the gold, I care about Holly. Hide in the bushes, and if he comes out the front door, blast the shit out of him." I ran for the corner of the house, and Tangles started to say something, but I didn't hear what it was. I was only thinking about Holly. I heard voices as I hurried down the dark path and stopped by her bedroom window to listen. I heard someone cry out in pain, but fortunately, it wasn't a woman. I started to creep around the rear of the house, but froze when I heard Speed Racer yell, "Drop it, Geronimo!"

Geronimo? I thought. *Was there some sorta code word he forgot to tell me about?* I continued to creep around the back of the house and stopped under another window to listen. I couldn't believe it, but I thought I heard Rudy's voice. Now I was really confused. *Rudy? What the fuck?*

With both hands on the .357, I peeked around the corner into the courtyard. I could immediately tell two things: the sliding door to the bedroom was open, and it was definitely Rudy's voice. Then I heard Speed Racer and...*Holly?* Was that *Holly's* voice? I stepped into the courtyard in plain view of the bedroom and lowered my gun when I saw that DeNutzio was on his knees, and Speed Racer had him at gunpoint. Holly stopped talking in midsentence and looked at me like I was from Mars. Speed Racer turned to see what she was looking at, and that's when the shit hit the fan.

Although it happened in the blink of an eye, it seemed to play out in slow motion. It was like watching a football game when the linebacker blitzes from the blindside, and the quarterback never sees him. It makes you cringe, no matter which team you're rooting for. The only difference was, instead of a linebacker, it was the Devil's Nephew. He launched himself up and across the room with the ferocity of a giant hellhound unleashed from the fiery gates of Hades and stuck his head squarely in Speed Racer's back. One of his meaty paws grabbed Speed Racer's gun hand by the wrist, and as they tumbled through the open slider, the silencer on the HK45 spit fire as the weapon discharged. Rudy flinched as a picture on the wall next to his head shattered, and I yelled for Holly to stay down as I sidestepped the struggle in front of me.

"Shoot him!" cried Rudy. I wanted to, but I couldn't get a clear shot as they tumbled across the dimly lit patio. DeNutzio managed to pry Speed Racer's gun loose, and as it clattered across the patio, Speed Racer also yelled, "Shoot him!"

"I'm trying to!" I yelled back, wondering if anybody but me realized the potential consequences of firing a .357 at two guys wrestling, hoping to hit the right one.

Holly yelled, "Don't shoot Kit!" *What?!* Confused, I turned to see what she was talking about, and Tangles stepped out from the bedroom with the sawed-off shotgun pointed in front of him.

Suddenly, a god-awful shriek erupted behind me, and I spun around to face the source—DeNutzio. He had been on top of Speed Racer doing a proper job of strangling the shit out of him, and then Speed Racer reached up and drove the arrow in his chest an inch or two deeper. DeNutzio literally howled at the moon with his head thrown back. His surgically altered face was a mask of rage and pain. The shriek abruptly halted as he swatted Speed Racer's arms away with one hand and landed a vicious overhand right with the other. In the pale moonlight I got a good look at him for the first time and realized he had an arrow sticking

341

out of his torn up Hawaiian style shirt. Not only that, but he had something stuck in each blood-covered arm that glinted in the moonlight. *What the hell?*

I yelled, "Stop!" but not before he hit Speed Racer again. I could tell by the sound his head made when it cracked against the stone patio that he was likely out cold, and he was. I was about to follow up with "Stop, or I'll shoot!" or something like that, but Tangles announced his arrival by racking the slide on the sawed-off shotgun. DeNutzio froze.

"That's right, asshole!" He said, as he stepped next to me with the shotgun trained on DeNutzio. "Put your hands in the air, or say your prayers."

"It's you two again? I shoulda slit your throats when I had the chance."

From the bedroom, Rudy yelled, "Shoot him, son! Don't give that big son of a bitch another chance! He's not right!"

Tangles was as surprised as I was to find Rudy on the scene, and he turned at the sound of his voice. *"Dad?* What the hell are *you* doing here?"

"If you ever answered your damn phone, you'd know."

Like Tangles, I was momentarily distracted and took my eye off the ball. In my peripheral vision I sensed movement, but I was too late. DeNutzio had pulled the unconscious Speed Racer up with one hand and with the other had produced a big knife. Using Speed Racer as a human shield, he held the knife to his neck as he slowly lifted him off the ground.

"Drop the guns, or Superfly gets it!" he warned as he backpedaled into the yard.

"I can take him," whispered Tangles.

"Sure you can...and you'll take out Speed Racer, too," I shot back.

"Then shoot him. Shoot him in the head."

"This isn't the movies, you idiot."

"I said drop the guns!" repeated DeNutzio.

"Hey," I offered, thinking negotiating might be the way to go. "How about *we* drop the guns, and *you* drop the knife, and we just call it a draw. No need to wake the neighbors. We'll try to kill each other again sometime. What do you say?"

He dragged Speed Racer deeper into the yard and replied, "You first."

Tangles said, "He got you there."

"Shut up." I saw a shadow dart between the palm trees behind DeNutzio. *Or did I?* I couldn't believe how fast he was dragging Speed Racer with him, despite his injuries. He *was* crazy strong.

"C'mon, man," I urged. "Set him down, and you can walk away. Besides, there's nowhere for you to go. It's all water back there."

"Not if you have a boat." He used a palm tree to lean up against to catch his breath.

"Not the Robalo," whispered Tangles.

"You think you're getting the keys to the boat, you're crazier than I thought," I answered loud enough for him to hear. Then I turned to Tangles and whispered, "That's why you don't leave the keys in the boat." When Tangles didn't say anything, I added, "Right?"

"Shit."

From the tone of his voice I knew he'd fucked up. It was a tone I heard a lot.

"Are you serious?" I asked, knowing that indeed he was.

"I swear, I never, *ever* leave the keys—"

"I was wondering who was stupid enough to leave the keys in the boat when I scoped it out earlier," said DeNutzio. "Figures. Short midget, short brain."

For once, Tangles didn't defend his stature. Instead he said, "Okay, I'm putting the gun down." I looked on in amazement as he laid the shotgun at his feet.

"What the fuck are you doing?" I hissed.

"Hey, it was your idea, unlike the Robalo, which is mine. Remember? You gave it to me."

"Now you're thinking right, Shorty," said DeNutzio. "Step away from the gun, and tell your pal to do the same with his."

"I was bluffing," I whispered to Tangles.

"About giving me the boat?"

"No, you moron, about laying down our guns."

"Easy for you to say. You don't *have* a boat. But if you did, like I do, you wouldn't want some psychopath bleeding all over it, especially the teak." Tangles took a step back.

"*What?!*"

"You heard me, it's not like it's all fiberglass, and you can just wash it off."

Suddenly, Speed Racer started coming to and began struggling with DeNutzio, who had a big arm wrapped around his neck.

"Put the gun down and step back, or I'm going ear to ear on him!"

"Okay, okay. Don't forget about the neighbors," I repeated. As I laid my gun on the lawn, I took a quick look around. I was expecting to see some houselights flick on as the neighbors across the water awoke to the commotion, but none did. I let out a deep breath and took one hesitant step back, making sure the guns were still well within reach.

"Don't!" cried Speed Racer, as DeNutzio shoved him forward toward the guns.

"Let him go!" I urged. "It's a tie, we'll call it a tie."

"A tie is like kissing your cell mate. But if you want one, I'll give you one. It's called a Sicilian neck tie, and it looks like this." He yanked Speed Racer's head back and stuck the point of the big knife under an ear. I was convinced he was about to slit his throat when a shadowy figure stepped out from a palm tree behind him. The figure raised an arm and something reflected in the moonlight a split second before DeNutzio's head parted like the Red Sea. It made a sickening sound like a cross between punching a pig and chopping wood, and although I was a good ten feet away, something slimy hit me in the face. *Nice.* DeNutzio dropped like a sack of wet potatoes, and Speed Racer stumbled forward and fell to the ground. To my amazement, the smallish person who stepped into the moonlight was dressed in black, like a ninja.

"Wow, that was gross," said Tangles as he wiped some cerebral cortex out of his hair. "Who's the ninja?"

"I see you met my friend Flingblade," answered Rudy as he stepped out of the shadows.

"*Flingblade?* You *know* him?"

"Know him? Hell, I hired him. Sorry about the mess. He works better when he's not on the sauce."

Chapter 45

"Kit!" I wiped the cranial splatter from my face and turned to see Holly rushing toward me. She had her arms extended and was coming in for a power hug, seemingly oblivious to the fact that my entire torso was wrapped in gauze. I was so glad to see her that I took her in my arms and squeezed her until it hurt, which was immediately. When I winced in pain and let out a grunt, she released me, exasperated. "Oh my God, I forgot you were shot. I *saw* you get shot. I thought you were dead. How did you—?"

"He's fine," said Tangles. "It's just a flesh wound."

"Don't listen to him. I *did* get shot. Right here." I clicked on the mangled Surefire dangling from my neck and shone it on my chest. "Right there, right where that little spot is…is that blood? Am I bleeding again? Shit, I'm tired. I need a beer." Holly gently touched the spot on my chest and kissed me on the lips.

"Whatever," added Tangles. "The paramedics said it was just a flesh wound."

"Shut up." I shone the light on Speed Racer and helped him to his feet. "You all right?" I asked.

"I think so." He rubbed his neck behind his ear. When he held his hand out, I could see it had some blood on it. I could also see he had something funky on the back of his neck.

"Dude, you might wanna wipe your neck."

He took off his windbreaker and wiped himself off as he looked at DeNutzio, who lay half in and half out of the shadows. "I thought he was gonna cut my head off. Jesus, that was close. What happened?"

"He got tomahawked," said Rudy. "Thank God Flingblade finally sobered up. He was downright wild with that first arrow."

I told Holly to look away and shone the Surefire on DeNutzio. There were about forty coquina pavers that formed a walkway from the courtyard to the dock, and his butterflied head came to rest on one of them. It was split perfectly in half by the hatchet buried in his skull and a trail of ants had already started nourishing themselves on its gooey contents. After noting the arrow in his chest had been driven all the way through his back as a result of the fall, I clicked the light off.

"Is he dead?" Holly asked.

"Very."

"I take it Geronimo saved my ass," said Speed Racer.

"Among other things, yes."

"Who's this Geronimo?" Holly asked.

"He's some ninja Rudy hired. Don't ask me how or why. Wait a second, where'd he go?" I shone the light around, but he was nowhere to be seen. Speed Racer took his phone out of his pocket, and a few flashes went off as he snapped some pictures depicting how DeNutzio met his maker. *With the mother of all Excedrin headaches,* I imagined. "Where the hell did he go?" I repeated as I scanned the surroundings.

"Where does the wind go, Bubba?" Rudy said. "Figure *that* out, and maybe you'll find him. Good luck though, 'cause he's some sorta Ninjun. And his name's not Geronimo; it's Flingblade."

"They sure got that one right," quipped Tangles.

"Amen to that. Flingblade? C'mon out now. You still got work to do. Flingblade?!"

"Keep it down, will you? You're gonna wake the neighbors," I warned. "In fact, let's go inside and figure out what we should do. Besides, I'm tired, and I need a beer."

"Me, too," seconded Tangles.

"Good idea," agreed Speed Racer. "I need to call the boss, pronto."

"Then let's go." Holly and I turned to head back to the house, and the Ninjun called Flingblade was standing right there. He startled both of us. Holly gasped as she covered her heart with her hand.

"Will you quit doing that?" Rudy said. "Sorry about that, Miss Holly." He looked at Flingblade and shook his head. "C'mon, Flingblade, let's figure out how to get that big bastard in the back of your truck."

Flingblade didn't move. He just held up a hand and rubbed his index finger and thumb together.

"Oh, right." Rudy reached in his pocket and handed him a wad of bills. "That'll put a few more quills in your quiver."

"What's going on here?" Speed Racer inquired.

"Why isn't he talking?" Tangles asked.

"He's mute, son. He can't talk."

"Is it contagious?"

"Not so far."

It was late, going on three o'clock in the morning. The landscape lights in the front circle and the courtyard lights in back had switched off by timer. I could see through the middle of the house, and a pair of headlights swept across the top of the drive before coming to a stop.

"Shit," I commented.

"What, you thought it was contagious, too?" said Tangles.

"No, idiot. There's a car stopped at the top of the drive. It's probably an Ocean Ridge cop. You're not supposed to park in the street." I looked at Speed Racer. "You're the one with all the badges, better move the Viper and work your magic, right? We'll stash DeNutzio. Who's got the keys to the pickup?"

As Speed Racer took off around the corner of the house, Flingblade pulled a set of keys out of his pocket and jingled them.

"Better let me move the truck," said Rudy. "Toss 'em here." Flingblade tossed Rudy the keys.

I looked at Tangles. "Drag DeNutzio back by the dock. Try to keep him hidden. Chop-chop."

"He's big. I could use some help."

"Flingblade, help Tangles drag the body," said Rudy. "Like the man said, chop-chop." Rudy made a chopping motion with his hand before disappearing around the corner of the house. Tangles and Flingblade each grabbed one of DeNutzio's legs.

"C'mon, Kit," said Holly. "I want to see how bad you're hurt. Let's go inside."

As we reached the courtyard, Tangles's voice carried on the strengthening wind. "It's just a flesh wound."

Chapter 46

DICK agent Joe Thomas (aka Speed Racer), didn't have time to lick his wounds, literally *or* figuratively. The knot on his head, the shiner above his left eye, the cut on his neck, the bruised ego—all would have to wait for attention and further introspection. As he reached the top of the driveway, he noted that Shagball's instincts were correct. There was an Ocean Ridge police cruiser pulled to the side of the dimly lit road and a cop standing behind the Viper. The cop was shining a flashlight on the license plate while talking into the radio mic on his shoulder. *Shit.* He decided to go with the best-defense-is-a-good-offense approach, hoping to offset the beat-up-black-guy-in-a-rich-white-neighborhood look that he had going on. In other words, he whipped out his Homeland Security badge.

"Agent Tom Jonas, Homeland Security," he announced, trying to sound in control.

The cop finished talking into the mic and shone the flashlight on him.

"Homeland Security?" the cop repeated, sounding skeptical as he took the badge and gave it a quick once-over. When he handed it back, he shone enough light on the agent's face to see he had a swollen eye and a little blood on his neck.

"What happened? What's going on?"

"Oh, nothing much. There was a minor incident, but it's been resolved."

"Looks like it got resolved on your face. You *sure* everything's all right?"

"I'm fine. Everything's fine."

"Sure it is. It was just a minor incident, a couple of bumps and bruises. I should see the other guy, right? Is that what you're saying?"

"No...but uh, yeah, right. Look, officer, why don't I—"

"Huh, that's funny. A little while ago we had a minor incident, too, but it *hasn't* been resolved. Yet. Somebody in a Viper with lights on the dash blew through Manalapan and into Ocean Ridge at an extremely high rate of speed, nearly hitting a couple sheriff's deputies parked by the inlet bridge. That wouldn't be you, would it?"

"Nobody nearly got hit, not even close."

The cop shone the flashlight on the old pickup parked half in the street across the top of the driveway.

"You know whose pickup that is?"

Rudy's voice preceded him as he stepped out of the shadows around the front of the pickup.

"That would be mine, officer. No need for any tickets, I'll just—"

"*Rudy?*" The officer sounded incredulous. "Is that *you?*" He shone the flashlight on him as he stepped closer. "Son of a bitch, it *is* you! What the hell are *you* doing here?"

"Uh, what uh, how do I—"

"It's me, Bruce. I ride my Harley to the chikee bar at the Old Key Lime House every Sunday. You've been taking care of me for a couple years now."

As they shook hands, Rudy recognized him as a customer. *Crap.*

"Of course, now I remember, rum and coke, right?"

"Bingo. You gotta love the cuba libre."

"Sorry about that, Bubba, you caught me off guard. You never told me you were, uh...an officer of the law."

"Regulations. I do a little undercover work now and then. I'd appreciate it if you kept that on the down low. So what's going on here?"

"Here? Nothing. Just, uh, just came over for supper."

"It's almost three in the morning."

"It was a late supper."

"I'll say." He pointed at the house, which still had lights on inside. "I didn't realize you ran in the same circles as Holly Lutes."

"I don't. My son's partner is her boyfriend, and we were just—"

"Whoa, whoa, whoa, *what?* I didn't know you had a son."

"Neither did I."

"Huh?"

"It's a long story. How 'bout we catch up at the chikee bar on—"

"Wait a second. Your son's partner is her boyfriend? There's been a rumor going around the department that he's the fishing-show guy from Lantana."

"That's right, he goes by Shagball."

"Shagball? No shit. But if he's your son's partner, that's kind of a *Three's Company* situation, except heavy on the sausage, right? I mean really, who's shagging who?"

"Watch it now, Bubba. It's not like *that*."

The officer laughed and gave Rudy a playful punch in the arm. "Oh, c'mon, Rudy, I'm just kidding. I know who Shagball is. Hell, everybody around here does. He made the national news yesterday when he claimed to find flight nineteen over in the Bahamas. Turns out it wasn't, but he sure got a lot of publicity. The show's hilarious. Especially the midget Tangles. What a little ballbuster *he* is. He's amazing; it's like he's almost human."

"That would be my son."

"*He's* your son?! Oh, shit, I—I'm sorry if I—"

"No offense taken, Bubba, but like you said, it's getting late. How 'bout we just—"

"Sure, whatever you want, Rudy. Just one more thing, though." He shone his flashlight on Speed Racer and then back to Rudy, checking out their suspicious looking poker faces. "Were you involved in this so-called 'minor incident' this gentleman from Homeland Security was telling me about?"

Rudy looked at Speed Racer and answered in the form of a question. "Homeland Security?"

"Yes, he was involved," Speed Racer said quickly. "He's with me." He held his breath and prayed Rudy would be smart enough to play along, so they could rid themselves of the pesky cop.

"Are you kidding?" The cop shone the light at Speed Racer then back at Rudy. "He's kidding, right? No way you're with Homeland Security."

Rudy started to stammer, "I, uh, I—"

"He's an informant," said Speed Racer. "He does some undercover work, just like you."

"No fucking way. Is that true, Rudy?"

"Which part?"

Suddenly, the officer's shoulder-mounted radio crackled to life. *"One ocean twelve, you there?"*

The officer held up his hand and asked them to stay put. "This is one ocean twelve." As he spoke he saw the garage door to the Lutes house open.

"One ocean twelve, what's your twenty?"

"The south end of Sabal Island."

"Seems the sheriff's department and the Manalapan police have a couple of FBI agents pulled over at the Ocean Inlet Park, and there is some kind of confrontation going on. Check it out and report back." As he listened, he watched the car that was backed up to the front door of the house get pulled into the garage. It was dark, and he was too far away to determine the make.

"Roger that, one ocean twelve on the way." He looked at the Homeland Security guy and then at his unlikely accomplice, Rudy.

"First it's Homeland Security, and now the FBI? What the hell's going on around here?" He hurried around to the driver's side of his cruiser and added, "Get those vehicles out of the road, will you? And try not to wake the neighbors."

"God forbid," said Rudy as the driver's door slammed shut. The officer powered down the passenger window and leaned across as he started the engine. "What was that?"

"Got it, I said. Got it. Hey, Meeting of the Minds plays Saturday night at the Key Lime. Try to make it. They're great."

"Sounds good. I'll be back as soon as I find out what's happening at the inlet. If you're still here, I'll be glad to give you an escort home, if you haven't been drinking, that is."

"Not in years," Rudy lied. "Every time I do, I get in all kinds of trouble."

"Smart man." The window powered up and the officer took off down the road.

Rudy exhaled. "I didn't think old Cuba Libre was ever gonna leave, Bubba, especially when he started doing that Colombo thing. Did you catch that?" Rudy turned around.

The Homeland Security agent had his cell phone out. "No, I was too focused on the one-ocean-twelve thing. He was really into it. Problem is he's nosy, and he'll be back. That's not good. Let's pull the cars in the drive. I need to make a call."

Rudy could sense his unease and asked, "So what if he comes back? *You're* Homeland Security, and the Homeland's a little safer now that the big psycho got the ax, right?"

"No, not really."

"What do you mean? You don't think it's safer?"

"No, I mean, I'm not Homeland Security."

"Oh, *shit*. Are you *kidding* me? Tell me you're kidding, Bubba."

"I'm afraid not, but those FBI agents that Cuba Libre went to see are the real deal, and my guess is they'll be here soon."

"So who the hell *are* you?"

"It's complicated." He pressed the speed dial on his cell and put the phone to his ear.

"No, it's not. Complicated is how one phone call from my son can take me from a molten-hot craps table at the Miccosiouxkee Resort to this mess I'm in now. This is like a bad Quentin Tarantino movie. Just remember, that Ninjun I hired saved your ass back there, Bubba."

"Trust me, I won't. I'm gonna thank him as soon as he rematerializes. Park the truck in the drive so it's facing out. We gotta move."

As Rudy slid behind the wheel of Flingblade's pickup, he heard the fake Homeland Security agent talk into his phone. "Boss, you're not gonna believe this…"

Rudy started the engine and muttered, "*You're* not gonna believe this? I don't believe this, and I'm in it." *Every time I drink*, he thought. *Every time I drink.*

Chapter 47

True to my word, the first stop was the refrigerator for a beer. I popped the top on a Negra Modelo and handed Holly the bottle of water she asked for. A few moments of silence ensued as we chugged away.

Then Holly said, "Kit, we should call the police, right? We have to call the police. There's a dead guy in my yard."

"Actually, I think they dragged him out back by the dock. That sucks that he bled all over the coquina pavers."

"I don't care about that! *You* almost got killed. *I* almost got killed. *Everybody* almost got killed."

Tangles came strolling in and said, "I hate to tell you this, but it looks like Peter Porsche *did* get killed. We're pretty sure he got dumped in the Lake Worth spillway."

"You see? We *have* to call the police."

"I think they're already here," I said. "Speed Racer's probably talking to them right now. Let's wait and see what happens, see what he says."

"Who is this Speed Racer guy?"

"He's our savior. Don't look a gift horse."

"Don't *what?*"

Tangles opened the fridge and helped himself to one of my Negra Modelos, as he was prone to do.

"Help yourself," I said.

"Don't mind if I do. These things are *tasty*." I shook my head at his apparent inability to recognize sarcasm. As Holly headed off to the master bathroom to retrieve a first-aid kit, I said, "Where's what's-his-name? The Ninjun."

Tangles smacked his lips after downing half the bottle and responded, "I showed him where the hose was. I think he's cleaning up his cutlery. He's got his shit spread out on top of the dock box. Hatchets, knives, you name it. He even had a crossbow and a hacksaw in his knapsack. Old Flingblade was armed to the teeth, that's for sure. I can't believe Rudy. How did he even know to come here?"

"I don't know, but thank God he did. What about DeNutzio?"

"I found a tarp in the dock box and put it over him. He's behind the hedge."

"Good."

Holly came back with the first-aid kit, and I asked Tangles to move the gold from the front bushes back to Holly's bedroom. As he left the kitchen, Holly opened up the first-aid kit on the counter and said, "You're bleeding."

I looked down, and there was a little dot of blood that had leaked through the gauze. Knowing that it wasn't serious, my natural instincts took over. "Baby, it takes a lot more than a bullet in the chest to stop me from saving you."

Holly was taking another swig of water, and she spit some out through her nose. It wasn't exactly the reaction I was hoping for, and I added, "I'm serious, Holl, I was worried sick about you."

She wiped her nose and laughed before stepping up and kissing me full on the lips. "I knew you would come for me," she whispered in my ear.

Unbelievable as it may seem, I didn't respond, "That's what she said." The moment was too perfect. Even though I had been up for nearly twenty-four hours straight and was coming down from an adrenaline high, the crush of her breast, combined with the kiss and breathy double entendre, had me harder than Chinese checkers. "I'll always come for you," I grunted back.

As we kissed, she rubbed me before pulling away.

"I know." She smiled. "But not right now. Right now I'm going to redo your bandage."

"I think I should move that Ford that's backed up to the front door first."

"Why?"

"I have a feeling some people are looking for it. We should put it in the garage."

Holly insisted on moving the Ford herself, concerned that I might hurt myself more, so I went in the garage and pressed the automatic door button. I hurried to the side wall, and as the door lumbered open, I slipped out into the darkness. It was hot and humid, and I noticed the wind had picked up like a squall was getting ready to blow through. While Holly maneuvered the car into the garage I surveyed the top of the drive. A car was stopped on the road but the headlights were still on. I could faintly see the silhouettes of three men and a flashlight that went on and off a couple times. *It had to be a cop.*

Back in the kitchen, as Holly recleaned and bandaged the hole in my chest, I worried that Speed Racer and Rudy were having a problem with the police.

Tangles came walking back in and said, "The gold's on the bed. Man, is that shit heavy. Rudy and Speed Racer are still talking to the cop."

"You sure it's a cop?" I asked.

"Yeah, I crept up to get a look. It's an Ocean Ridge cop."

"There must be a problem. Shit."

"What the hell are we supposed to do with DeNutzio?"

"Didn't I hear Rudy say something about throwing him in the back of the truck? Sounds like a good idea to me."

"You're right, he did say that."

"That's crazy," Holly said. "Let's get the police in here and tell them what happened...tell them everything." She finished rewinding the gauze around my torso and added, "There you go. I can't believe you're not more seriously hurt. You're the luckiest man in the world. That silly flashlight saved your life."

"I told you it was just a flesh wound," Tangles said.

"I can't wait for *you* to get shot," I said. "Then we'll see—"

"Don't even say that!" Holly said. "It's a miracle we're all okay."

"Except for Peter Porsche."

"You know what I mean."

"Sorry. You're right, baby. I'm all tuckered out. Did I tell you that on the way back from the Bahamas we met Johnnie Depp?"

"Yeah, right. You *are* tired…and delirious, too, I might add."

"True story," Tangles said. "He was with Debby Gibson. The lucky bastard's bangin' her like a windup monkey."

"Oh, c'mon!" Holly pushed Tangles's shoulder, and he spilled some beer.

"Interesting way to put it. Classy, as usual," I said, "but it's true, they were—"

We all heard the front door slam shut and Rudy call out, "Tangles? Holly?"

"In the kitchen!" I answered.

Rudy and Speed Racer hurried into the kitchen.

Speed Racer said, "Look, we have to move quickly. The FBI could show up any minute, and I really don't want to try to explain this."

"Where's Flingblade?" Asked Rudy.

"Back on the dock," answered Tangles. "Watching over you-know-who, probably combing some arrow feathers."

Rudy looked at Speed Racer, who nodded, indicating his approval to explain the plan.

"Okay," said Rudy. "My deal with Flingblade includes disposal. That means taking old split-head back to the Everglades. So let's drag that big sumbitch to the pickup and get Flingblade going before these FBI guys or Ocean Ridge's finest show up."

"Seriously?" said Holly.

"Yes," answered Speed Racer. "Under the circumstances, yes. I've been in touch with headquarters and have the green light."

"C'mon!" said Rudy, waving me and Tangles toward the back door. "I need some help." Rudy and Tangles

365

were already out the back door, and I was a step behind when Holly said, "Kit, wait!"

"What?" I stopped in the doorway for a second.

"What do you mean, what? This is crazy!"

"Please," said Speed Racer. "I need you to straighten up the bedroom and put the gold away. I'll help you, but we need to hurry. We should kill the lights, too."

Holly shook her head in disbelief, and I said, "Baby, just do what the man says."

Holly looked at Speed Racer. "Exactly who is 'the man'? Who *are* you?"

"He works with Peter Porsche; he was his friend. He was sent to help us."

"Oh, I'm sorry. I'm so sorry about what happened."

"Thanks," acknowledged Speed Racer.

"Honey, this is no time for condolences, we gotta *move*. If we screw this up, the new boat goes kapoof."

"Of course," I heard as I headed out the door. "It's all about the boat."

I hurried down the path, and as I neared the dock, I heard Tangles say, "Holy shit!"

I quickly shone my Surefire behind the hedge, expecting to see him standing over DeNutzio's tarp-covered body, but there was nothing there. As I passed the hedge I could see Tangles and Rudy standing next to the dock box and Flingblade hosing off the concrete pad in front of the fish-cleaning table.

"What's going on? Where's DeNutzio?" I whispered. I shone the light at Flingblade's bare feet, and there was blood—a *lot* of blood. On the edge of the lawn were five big bags of garbage and one smaller one. "Whose garbage is that?"

"That's ours, Bubba," said Rudy. "It seems there was a little, uh, miscommunication… and ol' Flingblade done chopped him up."

"WHAT?!"

"Quiet," whispered Tangles. "The neighbors, remember?"

"A *little* miscommunication? Are you kidding me?" I hissed.

"Hey, Bubba, don't look at me, it was your fault."

"*My* fault? How is it my fault? You hired him."

"When you told him and Tangles to hide the body, you said 'chop-chop.'"

"I meant to hurry. That's what that means, chop-chop."

"Not to a mutant Ninjun it doesn't," quipped Tangles.

"Shut up. And he's a mute, not a mutant. There's a diff—"

Suddenly, a spritz of water hit me on the side of the face. Flingblade had turned the hose on me. I looked at him wearing my what-the-fuck-was-that-for expression. He pointed the spray nozzle to the side and made a chopping motion across his arm before smiling and giving me a big thumbs-up.

Rudy said, "Look at the bright side, Bubba. He'll be a lot easier to carry this way."

"Oh my God."

Chapter 48

Knowing that DeNutzio was a wanted killer and that Speed Racer was on the scene to deal with the FBI and the local cops, I hadn't been overly concerned about the situation. I figured the worst thing that could happen would be if the man of a million voices rescinded his offer to me, Holly, and Tangles—no big deal. Thanks to Aunt Millie, Holly was a very wealthy woman, and my own bank account wasn't doing too badly either, thank you very much. I would still get a new boat, and after patching things up with Jamie, the show would go on. The only difference was it wouldn't be the most pimped-out fishing vessel ever to cruise the high seas, and Uncle Sam wouldn't be paying for it. *Shit.* But now that DeNutzio got the Hefty treatment, things weren't so clear-cut, so to speak. Being caught with garbage bags full of body parts doesn't lend itself well to claims of innocence.

I nervously looked across the canal at the other waterfront homes to see if any of the neighbors appeared to be roused by our activity on the dock. Fortunately, everything appeared calm and quiet, and the lone fisherman we had seen earlier in the night was long gone. The wind was a steady fifteen knots coming out of the southeast, and the palms fronds were swaying. Flingblade finished hosing the blood off the dock and hung the hose on the side of the fish-cleaning table. I used a hand to wipe the water off my face and pointed at the dock box.

"You didn't use any of my fillet knives, did you?"

He shook his head and made the chopping motion across his arm again.

"Yeah, yeah, I see you chopped him up. You ever decide to get out of the people-chopping business, I could probably hook you up at Benihana." I looked at Rudy and added, "Where the hell did you get this guy? Wait, I don't even wanna know. You heard Speed Racer—the FBI could show up any minute."

"Flingblade made the trash, and Flingblade's gonna dump the trash. We just need to get it in the truck, and he'll be gone like a Seminole wind."

"What does *that* mean?" Tangles asked.

"It means since Flingblade cut him up, Flingblade—"

"Not that, the wind, the—"

"Forget about the Seminole wind!" I interrupted. "We need to go *now.*"

I picked up the smallest garbage bag, and Rudy said, "That's his clothes and shoes and such."

"Great." I put the bag down and did a quick calculation. DeNutzio weighed two fifty (give or take), which, if evenly distributed among the other five garbage bags, would amount to fifty pounds a bag. It was a big if, though. Something told me that proper weight distribution wasn't Flingblade's top priority. I grabbed a bag in each hand and lifted them to see what we'd be dealing with. One bag wasn't too bad, maybe forty pounds, but the other was sixty plus, and stuff was shifting around. It was awkward, and I was afraid something might poke through the bag. I set them down.

Rudy hoisted one and exclaimed, "Damn, Bubba, they're kinda heavy. Let's drag 'em."

As Tangles started to drag one, I said, "Stop, just leave 'em. If a bag rips, it'll leave a trail of blood and God knows what else. I'm gonna get the dock cart out of the shed. We might be able to do this in one trip. I'll be right back. Make sure Flingblade didn't miss anything."

I took off across the lawn and around the side of the house to where the shed was. I opened the doors and was about to click on my Surefire when something flashed in my peripheral vision. A police car with its flashers on pulled into the drive, followed by another car with a flasher on the dash, like something an FBI agent might use. *Oh, crap.* I ran around the back of the house to Holly's bedroom and ducked my head inside the open slider doors.

"The cops are here! I think the FBI is, too."

Holly was on her knees picking up some broken glass, and Speed Racer was setting the lamp back on the nightstand. The gold was safely put away. Holly looked up, and Speed Racer said, "I can handle them, but what about DeNutzio?"

"We didn't have time to put him in Flingblade's truck."

"Shit, let me think—"

"We'll get rid of him, don't worry."

"You sure?"

"I'm sure he's not staying here. At least most of him isn't."

"This is serious, Kit," said Holly.

"More than you know. I'll be back as soon as I can, just do what he tells you."

"What does *that* mean?"

"It means listen to Speed Racer. I gotta go!" I ducked out and ran for the dock, knowing full well the innuendo would drive her crazy, but not as crazy as finding out DeNutzio got the Flingblade special on her dock.

"Kit!" she cried out in frustration. I disappeared down the path. There was no turning back...on a number of levels.

***

FBI Agent in Charge Frank Auble followed the Ocean Ridge cop as he turned onto Sabal Island Drive and complained to his partner again. "I can't believe those fucking local yokels pulled us over."

"How were they supposed to know, Frank? You didn't have the flashers on."

"I forgot! You should have noticed."

"I noticed you're making some questionable decisions, like slapping a tracer on a Homeland agent. That was a bad idea. We shouldn't even be here."

"DeNutzio's on the top ten list, do you have any idea what this'll do for our careers if we get credited with taking him down?"

"No, but I know what'll happen if the boss finds out we disobeyed orders. We'll be sent to South America—the jungle, Frank. I'm talking about the jungle. They got leopards and snakes and shit."

"Don't worry about it. When we nail him, the boss will love it."

"I dunno, Frank, you ever been to Guyana? I heard it's just like Ecuador. They got these Stone Age-looking pygmies down there with blowguns and poison darts. I think they're cannibals. I saw it on a National Geo—"

"Will you shut up!?"

They pulled into the circular driveway to the right. Parked on the left, facing out, were an old pickup and the Viper with the tracer on it. Holly's Jeep was parked off to the side along with a Porsche, and Frank said, "I don't see a Ford. Maybe DeNutzio dumped it for the pickup."

"With a hostage to deal with? I dunno, Frank. It doesn't feel right."

"You know what else doesn't feel right? Listening to you second-guess every call I make. So shut up, and let me do the talking." The Ocean Ridge cop parked in front of them, and they met him at the walkway that led to the front door. The house lights, which were blazing only minutes earlier, were now dark.

"Like I told you at the inlet, this is a waste of time," said the cop as the FBI agents approached. "The Homeland Security agent said—"

"But you didn't talk to the girl, right? You didn't check the house," said Frank.

"Well, no, but—"

"She was kidnapped."

"*Kidnapped?* Kidnapped and taken to her own *house?*"

"It's complicated."

"Look, I know you guys are FBI and everything, but it just doesn't feel right, you know what I mean?"

"I told you, Frank," said Frank's partner.

"Shut up."

"Trust me, if Holly Lutes was kidnapped, I'd know about it. Ocean Ridge looks after its own."

"Yeah? Let's see about that. Let's see what happens when we knock on the door." Frank pulled his weapon out and headed toward the door, motioning for his partner to go to the side.

"Whoa! Hang on a second, partner." The cop grabbed Frank by the elbow and stopped him.

"What."

"That's not the way we do things in Ocean Ridge. You're gonna scare the residents like that. I'll do the talking." The cop pushed past him and knocked on the door, and the FBI agents flanked him out of sight.

***

"Change of plans," I announced. I grabbed the bag with DeNutzio's clothes and jumped on the boat. "The cops and the FBI are here. Looks like we're gonna have to do a burial at sea. Start handing me those bags—hurry."

"Not on *my* boat," said Tangles.

I fired up the engines and said, "Good idea leaving the keys in the ignition. Very convenient, thanks."

"That's the last time that will ever happen, guaranteed."

"Sure it is."

Rudy handed me a bag and said, "What about Flingblade?"

"He's not blocked in, so tell him to sneak out and skedaddle. If anybody can do it, it's him."

Flingblade handed me a bag of body parts, and Rudy said, "You heard him, Flingblade, you're good to go."

Flingblade held his hand up and rubbed his index finger and thumb together. Rudy said, "Don't I get a tribal discount since you don't have to—"

"Rudy, c'mon, we don't have time for this."

"All right, all right." He shoved another wad of bills in Flingblade's hand. "Don't spend it all on Schlitz and Mad Dog." Flingblade smiled and shot a thumbs-up.

Tangles handed me a bag and said, "This is fucked up, Shag. Are you sure this is a good idea?"

"*Good idea?* It's not even an average idea, but unless you feel like explaining to the authorities how DeNutzio ended up Cuisinart ready, it's the only one I got. We'll dump him offshore, and then I'll drop you and Rudy off at the Lantana ramps. You can hole up at your apartment." Rudy handed me another bag, and I added, "Make sure Flingblade doesn't leave any of his, uh, stuff behind."

"You heard him," replied Rudy as he turned around. "Make sure you got—Flingblade? Flingblade, where are you?"

I scanned the dock, but Flingblade had vanished. "He's gone," I said. I started untying the stern line.

"Like a Seminole wind," Tangles replied.

"No, he's just gone," Rudy corrected him.

"Oh, c'mon! What the hell does that mean, then?"

"Grab that last bag and untie the bowline. Let's go," I urged. Tangles handed me a bag as Rudy untied the line, and then they both jumped in the boat. We shoved off and putt-putted around the point toward the Intracoastal—minus the running lights. Tangles managed to fit three bags in the forward fish box and the other three lay on either side of the small cockpit in the twenty-foot Robalo. When we reached the main channel of the Intracoastal, I flicked the lights on and warily throttled up. In the dark it's never a good idea to go any faster than idle speed, but the extenuating circumstances had me violating protocol.

"What about the marine patrol and the sheriff? Aren't they stationed at the inlet?" Rudy asked.

"Thanks for reminding me. I wasn't nervous enough."

"Shag, I think the wind switched around," said Tangles. "It's coming straight out of the east now."

Back at the dock I thought it was out of the southeast, but it had either switched, or I was wrong. It was definitely coming out of the east. It would make going out of the inlet harder, especially if the tide was going out. *The tide.* "Did you happen to notice what the tide was doing?"

"It just turned. It's going out. I could see the crabs on the seawall. I don't know, Shag, it's gotta be pretty snotty on the outside. I don't like it. Forgetting about how bad the inlet is, whatever doesn't sink is gonna end up on the beach."

I throttled down as we reached the inlet cut. I could see white foam as waves crashed into the north jetty. To make matters worse, there was a sheriff's cruiser on the inlet bridge with its flashers on.

"There's a cop on the bridge, Bubba," Rudy pointed out.

"Shit. Let me think."

"What's plan B?" Tangles asked.

"This *is* plan B. Christ, what a mess."

"I know a place we could dump him," Rudy volunteered. "They'll never find a trace of him. Guaranteed. I've been thinking about it a lot lately."

"That's, uh, that's kinda creepy, Dad," said Tangles. "Where?"

"Up by the Lantana Bridge."

"Where by the bridge?" I asked.

"Just go before somebody catches us with this goomba gumbo, will you, Bubba?"

I didn't need to be told twice. Rudy was convincing, and I was more than anxious to be rid of our cargo. Once again I throttled the boat too fast, in complete violation of night-boating protocol. With Tangles up in the bow watching for hazardous obstacles like immovable channel markers, we raced up to the Lantana Bridge, less than three miles to the north. I slowed the boat down when we passed the last channel marker before the bridge and asked Rudy, "Where's this spot you're talking about?"

If I hadn't been so brain-drained and body tired, I would have asked him earlier. I knew the area like the back of my hand and couldn't fathom a place to dump DeNutzio where he'd never be found. It was a fairly wide but shallow part of the Intracoastal. It's not like we had the ability to weigh the bags down, even if there was some kind of secret hole Rudy knew about.

"Go over there, to the left." Rudy pointed.

"By the *boat ramps?*" Tangles asked. "What are you thinking?"

I turned the boat toward the ramps, puzzled. "Yeah, what's your plan, Rudy?" I inquired.

"Go past the ramps."

"Past the ramps? Where? By the drift boat?"

"Past the drift boat."

"That's the Old Key Lime House."

"I know. That's the spot."

"WHAT?!" Tangles and I cried in unison.

"Are you nuts?" I added.

"In the basin on the inside of the docks, between the chikee bar and the outside dining-room seating."

"You *are* crazy," said Tangles. "This is the kind of thing that could get you fired."

"Listen, this is Florida's oldest waterfront restaurant and bar. For the last hundred and thirty years, people have been dumping food scraps into the water. I know you've both seen the way those catfish devour anything that gets tossed in. If you got enough food, it's a feeding frenzy every time."

"True, but it's French fries and sandwich scraps, not—"

"They're catfish. They'll eat anything. You know that," interrupted Tangles.

"But we're not talking about bite-size scraps here!"

"It used to be, if a feeding frenzy lasted long enough, if there was something big," countered Rudy, "the bigger fish that hang out by the drift boat would home in on the action, and that would be it, no big deal. But now, with the new bridge, and the added docks and fishing pier, there's more fish than ever around here—big fish. Real big fish. I've seen it."

"Yeah, but when you're talking about something big, you're not talking about legs and arms and—"

"No, but hear me out, Bubba. A couple redneck shark fishermen were drinking here late one night, maybe six weeks ago. Their boat was tied up on the

378

end of the dock, with the stern sticking into the basin. They were the last ones to leave. I was cleaning up the bar, and I heard a loud splash. At first I thought one of them had fallen in trying to get on the boat, but when I walked over to check it out, they sped away, laughing. I looked in the water and realized they had dumped the carcass of a wild boar, a *big* one. I went back to cleaning the bar, and within a minute or two I heard a ruckus like you wouldn't believe. I returned to see what was going on, and those catfish were feeding like nobody's business. Within five minutes some bigger fish started showing up. I don't know if they were barracudas, or jacks, or what, but they went nuts. Five minutes after that, the first bull shark came, and the rest of the fish scattered. The next day before my shift started, I walked around the dock to see if I could see anything, but there was nothing there—like it never happened."

"Jesus," said Tangles.

"What about the bones?" I asked.

"Even though it's only six or seven feet deep at high tide, there's a hundred and thirty years of bio-muck on the bottom. There must be ten feet of that—minimum. Anything heavy that doesn't get eaten probably sinks to the bottom of the muck after the crabs have their way."

"You're serious."

"Damn straight, Bubba, unless you got a better idea. Pretty soon the early birds are gonna be rising. We gotta do *something*." I pulled up to the dock and decided to nose the bow into the basin because of the receding tide. When I killed the engines, it was spooky quiet, even with the wind.

379

"I can't believe I'm doing this," I whispered. "This is like my own backyard. Layne's a buddy of mine."

"And he's my boss," reminded Rudy.

"If this goes wrong, he won't be for long, and I'll be banned from my favorite watering hole. I'll have to move."

"It's *already* gone wrong, Bubba."

"He's got a point," Tangles agreed.

"No kidding, so let's do this and get the hell out of here."

Chapter 49

Holly's mind was reeling. Things were out of control and happening way too fast. Bad decisions were being made left and right, she was sure of it. Kit told her to do whatever the man standing in front of her said to do, and she couldn't believe her ears. "You want me to tell them the dead psycho in my yard just drove away? Are you *serious?*"

"Yes," said Speed Racer. "Tell them you paid off your ex-husband's debt, and he left. Don't say that you were kidnapped; don't even use that word. Just say it was a misunderstanding."

"A *misunderstanding?* He killed Peter Porsche. He tried to kill Kit and Tangles, and he was going to kill me. Heck, he almost killed *you!*"

"Look, you want to tell them the truth, go ahead. Just realize that you and your friends will be front-page news and will be facing serious scrutiny as to how you became involved with someone like Marzio Giancarlo DeNutzio, aka the Devil's Nephew."

"The Devil's Nephew?"

"That's what they named him in prison."

"This keeps getting better. He should have stayed there."

"Agreed, but once the connection is made that his uncle was killed just a few miles away in front of a storage unit owned by the C-Love Marina—which happens to be owned by you, well, there's no telling—"

"You know about what happened with the marina deal?"

"Of course."

"Oh my God."

"And it goes without saying that if we can't keep this quiet, I'll probably be out of a job, and you guys will never get to start yours. It's too bad, too. I heard the sport-fishing yacht that the boss built for you is about ready, and it is one *incredible* vessel."

"Really?"

"Yep. I heard the surveillance capabilities, security features, and computer systems are real next-generation, Star Trek kinda stuff."

"You didn't happen to hear *what kind* of computer—"

There was a knock on the door.

"It's your call, Miss Lutes," Speed Racer said. "What do you want to do?"

"What do I *want* to do, or what am I *going* to do? Believe me, they're two different things." Holly headed toward the front door, with Speed Racer a step behind. As she turned some lights on along the way, she added, "You just had to mention the boat, didn't you?"

"Just doing my job. I'll be around the corner listening if you get in a pinch."

"A *pinch?* You call this being in a *pinch?*" she whispered.

Another set of knocks ensued just as Holly reached the front door. She looked out the peephole to see one of the local cops rapping away.

"Hang on," she said, as she flicked on the porch light and opened the door.

"Holly Lutes?" asked Bruce the cop, aka Cuba Libre. He had heard from some the guys on the force that she was a real looker and was 99 percent sure it was her, as evidenced by the rockin' hot way she filled out a pair of shorts and a tank top. *My, my, my.* He had seen in her in traffic and caught glimpses here and there, but he never got a good, full-on look. *The guys were right.*

"Yes, that's me," she answered.

"Miss Lutes, I'm sorry to bother you at this time of night, but I ran into a Homeland Security agent at the top of your drive a little while ago, and I see his car is still here. Is everything all right?"

"Yes, I'm fine. Everything's fine. Thanks for checking."

"This is gonna sound a little strange, but you weren't by any chance kidnapped, were you?"

Holly forced a laugh and replied, "Kidnapped? No, there was just a little, uh…misunderstanding is all. Besides, what kind of kidnapper takes you to your own house?"

"That's what I said," snorted the cop. "Oh well, glad—"

"Misunderstanding!?" said Agent Frank Auble, as he stepped from the side of the house. "My informant had his arm blown off, and there are two dead bodies back at the motel. Where's DeNutzio?" He held his badge out in one hand and his gun in the other. "Frank Auble, FBI."

"What dead bodies?" Holly asked.

"Yeah, what dead bodies?" the cop echoed. "You didn't say anything about dead bodies. Put the gun away, will you?"

As Frank put his badge away and lowered his gun, he gave his partner a quick nod, directing him to go around the back of the house. Then he looked at Holly. "The dead bodies at the White Horse Motel, three doors down from where you were being held. We figure DeNutzio killed them and took their car. We think it's a Ford. Did he bring you here in a Ford, or did he dump it for the pickup?"

Holly squinted as she looked out at the dark driveway. "What pickup?"

"That old beater right—" He turned to point at the pickup parked at the end of the driveway, but it was gone. *What?* "Where did that pickup go?" He looked at the cop, who appeared equally confused, and said, "I don't know, I didn't hear it go. Wait a second, that's—" He almost blurted out "Rudy's" but didn't want to blow his cover. "Someone working with Homeland Security was driving the pickup."

Confused, the FBI agent looked at Holly. "Did your boyfriend just leave in that pickup? Where's the midget?"

"No he's..." Holly tilted her head slightly as she heard the faint but unmistakable rumble of the Robalo's twin Evinrude 88s pass by. "They went fishing."

"*What*? You're trying to tell me the guy that got shot in the chest, the guy wrapped up in five miles of gauze, he decided to go *fishing*?"

"It was just a flesh wound."

"Are you kidding me?"

"He's with Tangles. The snapper are biting."

"I heard about the snapper bite," said the cop. "Plus, you know, they do have a fishing show."

"Bullshit."

"No, it's true. The show's great. It's hilarious."

"I know about the show, you idiot! I'm talking about her story."

"Nothing, Frank," said Frank's partner as he came walking around the side of the house. "Nothing in back. I heard a boat, though; don't know if it means anything."

Frank turned to Holly, looking pissed. "So where's DeNutzio?"

"He's gone."

"What do you mean he's gone? What happened?"

Holly ignored him and looked at the officer. "Officer, it's late, and I'm tired. There's really nothing to be worried about. My ex-husband showed up with this man that he owed some money. I paid him what he was owed, and he left. That's pretty much it. It was a misunderstanding. I don't know anything about any dead bodies. That's crazy talk."

"Then you won't mind us taking a look inside then, right?" Frank asked. "I mean, since you don't know anything about anything, right?"

"Just stay right there," said Speed Racer, as he emerged from the inside hallway, where he had been eavesdropping. As he stepped past Holly, he shook the cop's hand and then turned to the FBI agent. "Weren't you told to back off? You heard what she said, DeNutzio's gone. He was gone when we got here."

"Then what's the harm of taking a look inside? Hey, what happened to your face?"

"You're one to talk." Speed Racer's phone vibrated, indicating he had a text. He pulled it out and quickly read, *Tracking device on Viper/right rear bumper.* "What!?"

"What is it?" the cop asked.

"Can I use your flashlight for a second?"

"Sure." He handed him his flashlight, and Speed Racer glared at the FBI agent as he clicked it on.

"I was wondering what made you show up here, Frank. I mean, really, who kidnaps someone and takes them to their own home? How could you possibly think that?" Speed Racer shone the flashlight on the rear of the Viper and walked toward it as everybody watched.

"What are you talking about?" Frank asked nervously. "What are you—what are you doing there?"

Speed Racer crouched down and felt around under the bumper for a few seconds before pulling something out. "Got it!"

"Got what?" the cop asked.

"Oh, shit," Frank's partner said.

"Frank's partner knows what it is," replied Speed Racer as he walked back to the lighted porch.

The cop turned to Frank's partner and asked, "What is it?"

"It's a fucking one-way ticket to Guyana." He turned to Holly and added, "Pardon my French, ma'am."

"It's a tracking device, Officer," said Speed Racer as he handed him the small silver disk that looked like a watch battery. "These fine FBI agents took it upon themselves to plant a tracking device on another federal law enforcement officer's vehicle." He looked at Frank and added, "Somehow I don't think this is what your boss had in mind when he told you not to interfere with my investigation."

"Fuck."

"Hey, watch the language, pal, there's a lady present," said the cop as he puffed out his chest.

"Sorry about that."

"It's okay, I just want to call it a night," Holly said. "I'm really tired."

"You're not alone," said Frank's partner.

"Shut up."

"It's up to you, Frank," said Speed Racer. "You want your boss to find out what you did, or do you want to be on your way, and we'll just forget about this?" He took the tracer from the cop's hand and handed it to him.

"I'm not going to Pygmieville, Frank," his partner said. "End of story. Let's go." He grabbed Frank's arm in an effort to lead him away, but Frank shrugged free. "Wait a second, but—"

"No buts, Frank. DeNutzio's not here, and there's an APB out on the Ford—we'll find him."

Finally accepting that DeNutzio was more than likely long gone, Frank decided to swallow his pride, despite all the questions he had. Plus, like his partner, he really hated snakes. He extended his hand out to Speed Racer, and as they shook, he said, "Sorry about the, uh...*misunderstanding*."

"It happens. Good luck finding DeNutzio."

As the two FBI agents drove off, the cop turned to Holly. "I can have an officer posted at the top of your drive if you'd like, if it would—"

"No, no, I'll be fine. But thank you, Officer. Thanks for checking on me."

"Please call me Bruce." He smiled and shifted from one foot to the other, on the verge of being smitten. Speed Racer coughed to break the awkward moment, and Holly feigned a yawn, even though she was truly tired.

"Sure, Bruce. Wow, is it late. I really need to get to bed."

Officer Bruce handed her his card and said, "If you have any problems, I'm a phone call away, twenty-four seven. Ocean Ridge looks after its own."

"Thanks, Bruce." She smiled. "Good night."

He started to walk away but then thought of something and turned around.

"There is *one* more thing, Miss Lutes, if I may?"

"Please call me Holly. What is it?"

"The FBI agent said that Shagball was shot in the chest. Is that right? He got shot during this... *misunderstanding?*"

Holly thought she was home free, and he caught her off guard. "Shot?" she repeated.

"Yeah, shot. That's what he said, right?" By asking her to confirm what was said, he expressed a miniscule degree of uncertainty, which was all she needed.

"Oh, you thought he said, 'shot'?" She laughed. "No, no. He was shocked in the chest. 'Shocked,' that's what he said." She looked at Speed Racer and added, "Right?"

"That's what *I* thought he said."

"Really? That's not what it sounded like to me. How did he get shocked in the chest? How does *anybody* get shocked in the chest?"

"It was a fishing accident. A freak fishing accident."

"How so?"

"He got shocked putting line on an electric reel."

"*What?*"

"It happened in the Bahamas while they were filming a deep-drop segment. He just got back."

"I saw that on the news yesterday! They thought they pulled up a piece of flight nineteen. Everybody did for a while."

"It happened right after. That's why he came back."

"So, he's okay, then?"

"He wouldn't be fishing right now if he wasn't. Like I said, it's just a flesh wound…a little burnt flesh. He's fine, really, no need to worry."

"Classic Shagball," he laughed as he shook his head. "Can't wait to see the show."

"He's classic, all right." Holly feigned another yawn, and he took the hint by shaking Speed Racer's hand and nodding to Holly. "Glad everybody's okay. If anything comes up, just give me a call."

As he drove off, Holly looked at Speed Racer and exhaled deeply. "Holy cow, was *that* nerve-racking," she said.

"Are you kidding? That was impressive. Really. *I* even started to believe you. How did you come up with that shock story? That was great."

"Kit's producer didn't tell him they were going to the Bahamas to deep drop until they got there. When he called, he mentioned how much he hated it and hated using electric reels. I decided to try and talk to the officer the same way Kit would—you know, right out of my tush. I can't believe it actually worked."

As they shared a laugh, she held up one of her hands. "Look, my hand's still shaking. I need a drink. C'mon." Speed Racer followed her into the kitchen and gladly accepted a beer. She poured herself a glass of pinot grigio. Holly clinked her glass against his beer bottle and toasted, "Here's to not being dead. Long live life."

"Amen to that." After they both had a taste, he added, "I saw you tilt your head when you heard that boat go by. That was them, right?" He walked over to the French doors and looked out toward the dock, seeing nothing but the silhouette of some palm fronds swaying in night breeze.

"Yes, that was definitely the Robalo."

"So where do you think they went to dump—"

"La, la, la, la, la, I'm not *listening* to you." Holly had her fingers in her ears, not wanting to talk about where her boyfriend might be dumping a dead body.

"Oh, right, got it." He looked at the palm fronds again and realized the wind had picked up. "How big is the boat?" he asked.

"About twenty feet, why?"

"It's blowing pretty good out there. If they went offshore, it's gotta be rough."

Concerned now, she said, "Let me put on the Weather Channel." As she reached for the remote control, she noticed the open FedEx envelope next to the phone. There was another open envelope sitting on top of it with her name handwritten across it. *Wait*

390

a second. She remembered opening the FedEx envelope but didn't recall pulling out the other envelope. *What the hell?* She checked inside the FedEx envelope to see that it was empty and saw the return address was from St. Maarten. *St. Maarten?*

It had been an emotional roller coaster of a night, but despite her waning adrenaline rush, her heart skipped a beat. She pulled the letter out of the envelope and began reading the frail handwriting across the page. In a matter of moments she realized the roller coaster had a special car waiting for her, and the ride wasn't over, not by a long shot.

Chapter 50

Rudy put his hand on Tangles's shoulder and asked if he had any snacks.

"Really? This is making you hungry? I'm starting to worry about you."

"No, not for me. To chum up the fish. I think that'd be best."

"Oh, yeah, I probably got something." I stepped aside as Tangles opened the small access doors under the helm and pulled out an old bag of pretzels.

"Perfect," Rudy said. He took the bag up to the bow, dropped it on the deck, and stomped on it a few times. Tangles and I watched as he tore it open and flung some pretzel crumbs into the basin between the chikee bar and the dining area. At the sight of the pretzels my stomach rumbled. It seemed like forever since I last ate. I found myself fantasizing about a large helping of oxtail with all the trimmings from my favorite Caribbean style restaurant, Top Taste, only a few blocks away.

After about a minute of silence, I asked, "Where's the fish?"

Rudy looked at Tangles. "Were those salted or unsalted?"

"*What?* What diff—?" Suddenly, there was a small splash as the first catfish sucked down some pretzel. Then there was another, and another. Rudy threw out more pretzel crumbs, and as the catfish picked up their slurp-happy pace, Rudy said, "Okay, hand me a knife."

Tangles handed him one of the knives hanging on the side of the center console and asked, "How should we do this?"

"You got another garbage bag? A clean one?"

"In the console…Shag?" I opened the access doors, and with the aid of my mangled but lifesaving flashlight, I found a garbage bag. I stepped up to the bow, where Rudy was, and handed him the bag.

"How's your chest?" he asked.

"Tired, like the rest of me. Why?"

"Well, since you're the biggest, I was gonna have you hold the bags over the side while I slit the bottoms."

"Don't you mean biggest *and strongest*? It's not just big. It's big *and* strong."

"I see somebody must have mentioned something about that paunch you got working there. Is that about right, Bubba?"

"Bingo," Tangles said.

"Shut up. Here, gimme that." I noticed the catfish bite seemed to be fading so I took the pretzel bag from Rudy and flung out the rest of the remnants. A swarm of hungry tentacled mouths appeared at the surface, and the feeding intensified. I grabbed one of the body bags off the deck and held it over the side. Rudy felt around for a good spot to stick the knife in, and did. He slit open the bag, and random pieces of DeNutzio went kerplop in the warm, murky water. I looked the other way. Rudy instructed Tangles to put the bag with the clothes into the clean garbage and to do the same with the other bags once they were emptied. I handed the first empty bag to Tangles and hoisted another bag off the deck. On our third bag, Rudy commented, "You guys are doing good. Just like a conveyor belt, keep it going."

"This is your, uh…first time doing this, right, Dad?" said Tangles.

"Are they eating?" I asked. I didn't wanna look at what was going on and didn't hear a lot of activity.

"Don't worry about it. They'll eat, just keep 'em coming."

As I reached in the fish box to get the last two bags, I questioned Rudy's strategy. "I don't know, Rudy, seems like a stretch going from pretzel crumbs to chunks of hairy man ass." Suddenly, there was a large splash on the port side of the boat, under the dock, followed by an equally large splash on the starboard side

"Did you see that? What was that?" asked Tangles. I handed him another empty bag.

Rudy answered, "I told you bigger fish would come."

"I bet it was a jack crevalle. Well, well, well."

"That's not how the saying goes," I corrected him.

"Maybe it's a new saying."

"Maybe not."

By the time I held the last bag over the side, the basin was a splashing and thrashing mess. Rudy made the final slit, and something hit the water that made a different sound from the rest. I couldn't help it and shone my Surefire on the water just as DeNutzio's head popped up to the surface. It was neatly split in two, held together only by the top of his severed spinal chord. As Tangles grabbed the bag from my hand, he saw it, too, and said, "Oh, nice. That's totally—"

In the blink of an eye, DeNutzio's head disappeared with a loud sucking slurp as the fat lips of a large jewfish engulfed it. Just like that, it was gone.

"Jesus H. Christ! Did you see that?" I asked a little too loudly.

Rudy was looking the other way and whispered, "See what? I see we better get the hell outta here, Bubba, that's what I see. Let's go."

Tangles said, "Holy crap, that was big. What was that?"

"Well, well, well, it was no jack crevalle. It was a jewfish. A goliath grouper. I can't believe there's a jewfish lurking around here."

"You thinking what I'm thinking?" said Tangles.

"What?"

"We could do a show here."

"You ain't gonna *have* a show if we don't get the hell outta here," Rudy quietly urged.

I was in total agreement, so I fired up the engines and running lights and idled around the Old Key Lime House tiki boat. At the boat ramps I let Rudy and Tangles off. It was only a short walk across the parking lot to Tangles's apartment above the sushi restaurant. The plan was for them to ditch the garbage bag stuffed full of DeNutzio's clothes and DNA in the dumpster on the way.

As I motored off into the darkness, Tangles called out, "Don't ding my boat."

Less than fifteen minutes later, I wearily tied off back at Holly's dock. It was four in the morning. The house was dark except for Holly's bedroom, and as I trudged across the back yard I stepped on something squishy. I paused long enough to wipe my foot on the grass and when I reached the courtyard, Holly came rushing out of the bedroom. She threw her arms around me, and I winced when she squeezed me tight and kissed me.

"Oh, baby, I forgot you're hurt. I'm sorry."

I kissed her back and replied, "I'll be fine, I'm just whupped. Thank God you're all right." We went in the bedroom, and I sat on the bed and kicked off my boat shoes.

"Did everything go all right?" she asked as she sat next to me.

"I think so...I hope so. We'll know soon enough. What happened here after we left? Where's Speed Racer?"

"I gave him an ice pack for his face and told him he could stay in the guest room. I'm pretty sure he's asleep. I heard snoring."

"What about the cops and the FBI?"

"They weren't here long. I gave them a song and dance show that would have made you proud. I told them I paid off DeNutzio, and he left. They think he's in the Ford."

"That could be problematic seeing as how it's in the garage."

"Before Speed Racer turned in, he said he had a truck coming big enough to carry the Ford and the Porsche inside. It's supposed to be here later this morning."

"Well, that's good, the sooner the better. Lord, am I tired." I stretched out and laid my head on the glorious pillow.

"What happened to Mark?"

"They took him away in an ambulance, but he'll be okay. It's not like he had his arm blown off."

"What?"

"Don't worry about Dickhead, all right? He's fine. Better than I am. I'm the one who got shot in the chest."

"He said he'd give me the divorce. He'll sign whatever I want."

"I'll believe it when I see it. He's still a dick."

"Just forget about him, okay? Oh my God, I almost forgot to tell you. I got a FedEx. You're not going to believe this, but Millie had twins! She didn't just have a baby boy, she had—"

"A baby girl. I know, I read it, too. What a day. What a night."

"Since when did you start reading my mail?"

"Oh, I don't know, since it was already open, and I thought it might have something to do with you being kidnapped...Geez."

"Oh, right, of course." She stretched out beside me and tenderly kissed me on my forehead as I closed my eyes. "You were my knight in shining armor. You and Tangles, as much as I hate to admit it."

"Don't forget Rudy and Flingblade...and Speed Racer, too."

"Of course I'm not forgetting them, but you led the way. Kit, I thought I'd lost you." When she kissed me on the cheek, she smelled like lilacs, and a tress of her damp hair brushed my face. *Damp hair?*

"Did you take a shower? I asked. "You smell nice."
You smell nice. In other words, I felt my balls rumble.

"Ugh, yes, I had to. I didn't want any trace of that horrible man on me for any longer than necessary."

"He *touched* you? What did he do to you?" My eyes were open now.

"Not like that. Well, not really. I mean, he grabbed me and groped me and left a couple of bruises, but it could have been so much worse. I don't even—"

"Me neither. I don't want to think about it either. Just tell me you're okay."

"Yes, I'm fine. But Kit, I thought you were—"

"No more thinking. C'mere." I snaked a hand behind her head and pulled her into a passionate kiss. She ended up straddling me and whispered, "I thought you were tired," as she reached a hand down my shorts.

While it was true I was exhausted, nature was dictating my next move, and my nature was horny. "My eyes are tired, but Mr. Johnson won't let me sleep."

She nibbled on my ear as she stroked me. "That's not nice of Mr. Johnson." Her breasts were in my face, and I reached my hands up under her tank top.

"No, it's not."

"I bet you'd like me to discipline him."

I grunted my confirmation as she held me firmly in her hand.

"What was that?" she asked before proceeding to lick my ear.

"Yes, discipline him by all means. Beat the shit out of him."

She laughed and sat up, maintaining a firm grip on my unit. "I'd love to, sweetie, but you've been shot, and I don't want to hurt you, remember?" She lightly touched a finger to my gauze-wrapped chest and smiled. The she-devil.

"Oh, that?" I smiled back, both of us knowing the inevitable was about to become evitable. "Don't worry. It's just a flesh wound."

Chapter 51

Speed Racer successfully coordinated the loading of the vehicles into a cargo truck the next morning and left in the Viper after promising to be in touch. Then it was back to bed. It was time for recovery and relaxation. A little R and R, if you will. That was the order in the days to follow, and that was what we did. Well, that and a lot of pressure washing DeNutzio's DNA off the coquina pavers and dock, not to mention Holly's bedroom. Peter Porsche's body was found a few days later, and the paper reported that he'd worked for the EPA and had committed suicide. *Right.*

Despite what happened, Tangles, Holly, and I were excited when the man of a million voices called to say his offer still stood. Our new boat would be ready for a shakedown cruise in a couple weeks. In preparation, I quit my long-time job with a Palm Beach real estate investment group. This came to no one's surprise, because the fishing show had been taking up more and more of my time.

When Holly asked me if I would miss anybody, I told her only my secretary, Jan. She was a supremely efficient dynamo, excellent with computers, and so trustworthy she couldn't even take a hint. Long story short, when I mentioned that Jan told me she wanted to quit, too, Holly ended up hiring her. She had been concerned about keeping tabs on the marina business while we were away and wanted a fresh set of eyes and ears around. "Not that I don't trust my staff," she assured both Jan and me. "It just seems prudent." It was another one of those times I could see the influence her aunt Millie had on her. She was nobody's fool.

The Saturday after Labor Day, Rudy chartered the Old Key Lime House's tiki boat, for Marie's birthday. Although the party barge was permitted for thirty-five plus the captain, Marie wanted to keep it more intimate, and about half as many were invited. The plan was for the tiki boat to leave at four o'clock, and everyone was to meet at the OKLH chikee bar beforehand. Holly and I arrived about three fifteen, and the bar was in full swing. Tangles invited an off-duty hostess, and he was chatting her up next to Ferby, who was captaining the tiki boat. Rudy and Marie were all smiles as they talked to a couple of Marie's close friends who came up from Key Largo. Dani and Michelle happened to be working the chikee bar, and as Dani was handing me a couple of drinks, I heard Tangles say, "Hollywood! Hey, man, what's going on?"

I turned to look, and there was Hollywood, looking all Hollywood as usual, with his pretty wife in tow. I handed Holly her pinot grigio, and she asked, "Who's Hollywood?"

"He's an old buddy of mine. He fishes out of Palm Beach."

"Yummy."

"*What?*"

"Tummy…my tummy feels better now. This pinot is good." She grinned at me and winked. *The minx.*

I quickly whispered, "*He's* married, and *you're* spoken for."

She playfully punched me in the shoulder and replied, "I was kidding, you goof."

"Shaggy! How's it going, bro?" Hollywood slapped me on the back, and introductions were made all around. Once everyone was acquainted, Hollywood asked the girls if he could have a minute with me and Tangles.

We walked out on the finger dock, and Hollywood jumped down into the cockpit of his thirty-three-foot Strike. I crouched and looked back toward the restaurant, half expecting to see a foot, or hand, or a decomposing fleshy something or other, washed up on the rocks below the decking. Fortunately, there was nothing. Hollywood grabbed a couple of envelopes from a compartment on the dash and climbed back on the dock.

"Here you go, boys." He handed us each an envelope.

'What's this?" Tangles asked.

"Johnnie Depp's gratitude—what else?"

I stuffed the envelope in my cargo shorts with a "Thanks, bro," and Tangles let out a whistle as he opened his and saw it stuffed full of hundreds.

"Holy shit! There's gotta be—"

"Five grand, just like he promised. For an actor, he's all right, you know?"

"Hell, yeah! Wooo!" Tangles made a fist pump. "This is awesome, thanks, man. How did you know we'd be here?"

As we walked back to the bar, Hollywood explained. "I called Shag this morning to say I had the loot, and he told me you guys would be here. He said you were going on a party cruise."

"It's for my mom's birthday. Hey, why don't you join us? We'll be back by seven."

"Oh, I don't know, man. We were just gonna grab a bite and—"

"We got food, we got booze, we got music—"

"And we got caaaash," I added. "We're *thick* with cash. C'mon, dude, let's whoop it up."

"You sure? I don't know."

"I'll clear it with my mom," answered Tangles. "It'll be no prob."

"Then I'll check with Kerri. If she's game, we're in."

"Great."

As soon as we got back to the bar, Rudy ushered everybody out to the tiki boat, and we boarded. Late arrivals were Hambone and his wife, Mo, who, unbeknown to me, had become friends with Marie. Robo the dockmaster also showed up, along with his wife, Judy; Robo was an old friend of Rudy's. Everybody was getting situated when Hambone nudged me in the side and pointed at the parking lot. "Check it out, Shag." I turned to see a white stretch Hummer creep through the packed parking lot and stop at the edge of the seawall.

"Who the heck has a Hummer limo?" asked Holly.

"Hellifino," I answered, wondering the same thing. I didn't have to wonder long. The driver got out wearing a prototypical driver's outfit, complete with the funny-looking cap. He was big, though, real big. He opened the rear door and out stepped a friggin' honest-to-goodness Indian chief. Or at least that's what he looked like. He wore a full headdress, suede leggings and moccasins, beads, the whole nine yards. *Incredible.* The driver went around to the trunk and hoisted a case of something up on his shoulder as Rudy called out, "Willie! Glad you could make it!" Willie waved and stood to the side as a pair of gorgeous legs swung out of the limo. The legs carried the body of a stunning young woman in a suede miniskirt and thigh-high suede boots. She had on a tight white V-neck T-shirt with jade necklaces galore and some type of Indian tiara on her head. She looked like Hiawatha in *Moulin Rouge.* I felt a jab in my side, and Holly whispered, "You wanna take a picture?"

"Ho-lee crap," said Hambone, who was treated to a jab from Mo.

I looked at Hollywood who had his sunglasses tilted down and was eying her the way a wolf eyes a crippled rabbit. His wife pushed his glasses back up and admonished him. "Behave yourself for once, please."

The driver handed the case off to Ferby, who set it behind the bar and fired up the engines. With the chief and his girl safely on board, the boat left the dock, and Rudy introduced them.

"Everybody, this is Chief Willie, chief of the Miccosiouxkee."

The chief raised his hand and nodded, "How...is everybody doing?"

The way he stretched out the "how" drew laughs and broke the ice.

"Did he just say 'how'?" I heard Robo whisper to Judy, who whispered back, "Yes, quiet. That's what you get for buying a hearing aid at Harbor Freight."

"And this is?" Rudy lifted the hand of the smoking-hot Indian girl and kissed it, as the chief replied, "Dancing Deer."

"There you go," said Rudy. "It's my old friend Chief Willie and his, uh, his—"

The chief put his hand up to his mouth and whispered, "Squaw. She's my squaw. You should know that."

"Right, of course." Rudy nodded. "And this is his squaw, Dancing Deer. First stop is the sandbar by Beer Can Island. Let's have some fun."

"I *bet* she dances," mumbled one of Marie's friends, as Ferby increased the throttle. Tangles was talking to Hollywood on the other side of the boat, and I heard him call "Shag!" He pointed at the chief and made a chopping motion across his arm. I had been thinking the same thing: so *that's* how Rudy found Flingblade.

"So," said Holly. "Are you going to tell me what Hollywood gave you and Tangles back at the dock?"

"You were watching?" I raised an eyebrow.

"I was trying to get a look at his boat and saw him hand you guys something. Tangles looked pretty happy about it. Still does." She pointed at him. He was dancing with the Key Lime hostess. "Maybe it's that envelope sticking out of your shorts?"

"I swear you're part eagle." I pulled out the envelope and handed it to her. "Keep it down, don't show everybody." She quickly peeked inside and gasped.

"Oh, my God, it's stuffed with hundreds."

"Shhh."

She quickly shoved it back in my pocket, seemingly worried. "What's it for? Oh, crap. Don't tell me you smuggled something back from the Bahamas. Please don't tell me you're that stupid."

"Of course not, it's a tip, more or less."

"More or less? A tip? Right. How much is in there?"

"Five grand. Tangles got the same. Hollywood got ten."

"Puh-leez. And what exactly did you guys have to do to earn this supposed tip?"

"Not much, really, other than rescue the biggest movie star in the world from a hijacker and then give him a ride to Freeport with his pop-star girlfriend. Did I mention the hijacker was McGirt? You remember him, right? He was—"

"Oh, c'mon!"

"I swear! Ask Tangles. Hell, ask Hollywood."

"You're trying to tell me you rescued Robert Downy Jr.?"

"No, Johnnie Depp. I thought I told you. I mentioned it the night you got...*you know.*"

"I thought you were joking."

Tangles danced his way across the boat, and Holly apologized to his date when she pulled him to the side.

"What's going on?" Tangles asked.

"Why did Hollywood just give you that envelope?"

Tangles looked at me questioningly, and I said, "Go ahead, tell her."

"You really wanna know?" he asked.

"Yes, the truth, please."

"I'm a high-priced gigolo, and Hollywood's my pimp. Wanna take a ride on my merry-go-round?" He reached around like he was going to grab her butt, and she slapped his hand away.

"Only in your dreams, little man."

"Only in my dreams? Hey, that's a Debby Gibson song. We should play some Debby Gibson."

"Did I hear someone say Debby Gibson?" asked Hollywood as he walked up with his wife. "That was one hell of a day on the water. Johnnie Depp is something else, not the least of which is generous. I'll give him and the Giblet a lift anytime." Me and the guys laughed at the mention of "the Giblet."

"Wait a second," said Holly. "You're really serious?"

"About what?"

"About this Johnnie Depp thing, what else?"

Hollywood looked at me funny and said, "You didn't tell her?"

I suddenly felt Holly's eyes shooting laserlike daggers my way. "No, he didn't."

"I did tell you, you just didn't believe it."

"It was epic," said Tangles. "Debby Gibson is the bombadero."

"Check it out, Holly." Hollywood struck a pose. "Johnnie Depp thinks I look like Christian Bale."

"Wait a second!" I protested. "*I'm* the one who said you looked like him. I said it years ago. That's why I nicknamed you Hollywood."

"I thought it was because of my stellar screen presence when I took you out on the Strike for one of your early shows, remember?"

"Yeah, I do. I think we got skunked."

"The hell we did, we caught—"

"Will somebody *please* tell me the whole story?" Holly interrupted.

Ferby turned the music down, and all the guests listened as we recounted our trip back from the Bahamas and the extraordinary encounter with Johnnie Depp and the Giblet. Of course, I neglected to mention the full extent to which we were acquainted with the sleazeball McGirt.

As soon as Ferby dropped anchor at the sandbar next to Beer Can Island, Rudy got everybody's attention. "First off, I'd like to thank y'all for coming. As most everybody knows, tomorrow is Marie's birthday. I'm not gonna say which one, but it has a zero on the end."

"Watch it, honey," said Marie at his side.

There was predictable chuckling, and Rudy smiled. "But today is an even bigger day. The reason being is the love of my life and mother to my fine son, Tangles, has agreed to be my wife. We're getting married, people!"

This incited a lot of clapping, backslapping, and other congratulatory responses.

Tangles proudly announced, "I'd like to make a toast." Everybody quieted down, and he continued. "Here's to the best damn bartender and father anybody could ever have: Rudy!" He bumped his plastic Solo cup against Rudy's bottle of water, and as we joined in with a chorus of hear, hear, I heard Rudy whisper to Tangles, "Thanks for the justice, Bubba."

"Justice served," replied Tangles with a fist bump and a smile. "So I guess this makes me in charge of the bachelor party?"

"Sure thing, son, but you better make it quick."

"Why's that?"

"'Cause we're getting married right here, right now."

"WHAT?!"

Although Rudy's announcement didn't come as a huge surprise to most of us, it seemed nobody expected to be witnessing a ceremony. As the shock wore off, the women voiced concern they didn't have proper gifts.

"Don't worry," Rudy assured them. "No gifts required. We're *way* ahead of the game. The owner of the Old Key Lime House, Layne, God bless his horny soul, surprised me by comping the tiki barge, and Chief Willie brought a case of Dom Perignon. We'll get into that as soon as he marries us." A robust round of applause was followed by a toast to Layne and Chief Willie. Then Rudy took Marie by the hand and said, "What do you say darlin'? Ready to become Mrs. Travis K. Rainbow?"

"That's really your legal name?"

"It's the one that gets me the VIP treatment at all the casinos. Once we tie the knot, same applies to you."

"Tribal law," added Chief Willie. "I make new ones all the time. Just like Obama."

"Well," said Marie before kissing Rudy on the cheek, "what girl doesn't like rainbows, especially when there's a lovable pot of gold at the end like my Rudy Booty?"

All the girls giggled, and the guys went, "Ugggh."

Rudy was beaming. "All righty then, Chief. Let's get this show on the road."

"I need to powder my nose first, honey," said Marie. "Just give me a minute or two."

As Marie went to use the bathroom, a pelican swooped over the boat, causing a few women to duck. Everybody watched as it rose up about a hundred feet in the air and hovered for a couple seconds before tucking its wings under and going into a dive. "Look at that," said one of Marie's friends. The pelican streaked toward the water like a bullet, bill first. It had homed in on a shiny fish and was going in for the kill. With a splash it crashed head first into the water less than fifty feet from the boat—but something went horribly wrong. Instead of disappearing under the water and emerging with a fish in its bill, as was the norm, its bill and head buried into the sandbar. Unfortunately, it was only two feet deep where it torpedoed into the water.

Was its vision impaired, or could it just not resist the shiny fish? I wondered. It looked like a good-size pelican, and I concluded it probably wouldn't have made it to adulthood with bad eyes. Regardless, the poor pelican's butt and legs were sticking out of the water, and its legs kicked furiously as it tried to free itself. Mercifully, a guy from a nearby boat waded over and pulled the pelican out of the sand. The good news was he undoubtedly saved the pelican's life. The bad news was the pelican's bill was bent at a forty-five-degree angle, and it would probably die of starvation without medical attention.

"In case anybody decides to take a dip," I said, "better use the ladder."

"Wow, that's crazy," said Hambone. "You ever see that before?"

"Never."

As the injured pelican paddled over to Beer Can Island, Ferby led Rudy over to the bar. "You sure you want to do this?" he quietly asked him. "I mean, you're a sixty-something-year-old bachelor, you know? Marriage is serious business."

"I'm one hundred and fifty percent ready to take the plunge."

"You should be two hundred percent. Take it from a man who's been there. It's a plunge all right. It ain't like sticking your toe in the kiddie pool. It's more like Mexican cliff diving. It's a drop, a deep drop. You need a woman who has some depth to her, someone who can pick you up when you fall and right you when you stumble. 'Cause if your woman's shallow, she's gonna take all your sardines, and you'll end up just like that pelican."

"Is this your idea of a pep talk, Bubba?"

"I'm just saying that's the way it is. *I know.*"

"Well, don't worry, 'cause my Marie is sweeter than cherry pie and deeper than space—especially the space around my heart."

"Not really sure what that means, but I can see you got a fork in you. Good luck, brother. Marie's a fine woman. Good luck keeping your head out of the sand."

Ferby bumped his plastic cup against Rudy's water bottle.

"Thanks, Bubba. I plan on staying in the deep end."

Marie came out of the bathroom, and Rudy escorted her to the bow, where Chief Willie was enjoying the company of Dancing Deer. Actually, all the men were enjoying the company of Dancing Deer. Sometimes words are overrated, and the visual is enough. As Rudy and Marie held hands, and the chief began his spiel, I maneuvered Holly so we were in the stern, behind everybody. Then I put my arm around her and kissed her on the forehead.

"That was nice," she whispered.

"Hey, I'm a nice guy," I whispered back. I noticed another pelican hovering over the channel between Beer Can Island and the sandbar and said, "Check it out." I pointed my finger just as the pelican went into a dive, and we watched it submarine into the channel with a splash. A second or two later, it popped up to the surface with a sardine in its bill and unceremoniously gulped it down. *Sweet.*

"That's me and you, baby," I whispered.

She looked at me funny. "Which one of us is the fish?"

"Neither. The fish is life. We're gonna gulp it down together. We're the pelican."

"We are?"

"Yes, especially with the new boat on the way. This Uncle Sam gig should be interesting. If we can keep our head out of the sand we might even find your long lost cousins."

"That shouldn't be a problem. You know I like it deep." She pinched my ass, and I hopped forward a little, almost bumping into Dancing Deer's incredible caboose. She must have felt or heard my foot on the deck because she looked over her shoulder. I mouthed, "Sorry," and she smiled with a wink. I heard Rudy and Marie say their I-dos, and when I watched them seal it with a kiss, I got it. Or at least I thought I did. Don't go head first for that shiny fish unless you know what's underneath—words to live by. *Maybe there's an Aesop's fable in there somewhere,* I mused. I gave Holly a squeeze and counted my blessings, and she wiped a tear from the corner of her eye. Some things are worth the wait.

THE END

Note to Readers: If you are wondering about some of the spelling please read the disclaimer at the front of the book.

COMING in 2015: The next Shagball and Tangles's adventure: The DICK Files.

For more information go to: www.acbrooks. net

46499373R00239

Made in the USA
Lexington, KY
05 November 2015